The Alderwild Wood

by:

Zena Bernstein

In remembrance of my
Mom and Dad and sister Ro

Foreword

Some of you who are about to read The Alderwild Wood will already know of Zena Bernstein. You may have seen her drawings in one of the dozen story books that she has illustrated, books such as *Mrs. Frisby and the Rats of Nimh*. You might have visited The Studio on Horse Thief Bay and viewed, or even purchased, some of her wonderful art. Or you might have stopped at one of the summer art shows along The Thousand Islands Parkway where Zena and her husband Ian often had their own booth.

However, The Alderwild Wood is Zena's first venture as a writer and here's what she has to stay about her Journal:

On the following pages I shall try to describe and give insight into the culture and traditions of the different fairy groups, gnomes, dwarves, and trolls living here in Horse Thief Bay. Horse Thief Bay lies in The Thousand Islands region of the St. Lawrence River.

Most of the fairies living here in the Bay, islands, and land immediately adjacent to the River are indigenous. They have been living here since the beginning of time, long before the arrival of the gnomes, dwarves and trolls.

The fairies, gnomes, and dwarves learned to live in harmony with the natural elements of the land and the animals which inhabited it. They were, and still are, at one with Nature and respect Her. They do not destroy Her. They are not alien to Nature like trolls and other related fiends.

The lands of the fairies here on the St. Lawrence and elsewhere are being laid waste and the waters polluted by trolls and their kind. The plight of the fairies and wildlife must be addressed now while they are still with us before they become extinct. Many are already on the endangered species list. The gnome and dwarf populations are also decreasing in many areas, even though they are much hardier than the fairies.

Woods, forests, small groups of trees, fields, even gardens must be set aside to accommodate them. The rivers, lakes and streams made clean again. Only we can fix these problems."

The Alderwild Wood is a wonderful tale. It is full of magical beings such as Natterjack the dwarf, going about their "ordinary" lives in an environment under siege from our so called modernization. While the story is full of fantasy, the environmental threat is a deadly serious topic for Zena. A few years ago Zena was asked for a synopsis of her book with an emphasis on her relationship with the characters in the Journal. Here's what she had me write:

I do not imagine the characters in this Journal or see them....I live them. I become each character. I fit into their skins and live their lives. I see each character from within each character. I take on their thoughts, their thinking. The inhabitants of The Alderwild Wood and the Bay are parts of my persona.

In some ways, this Journal is a sort of autobiography of my thinking and doing. It hurts me when I see a wooded area being cut down and the land turned to grass for manicured lawns. Where are the animals and birds to go? The natural habitat that the animals and birds once dwelled in has been taken over and altered by thoughtless, unthinking, and often, uncaring individuals, who only see their little space of land to care for and don't see the wider picture. Groups of humans see only their own small plot of land and the cutting down of a few trees. Then another family group who move in next door think that if they cut down just a few trees too, it won't matter. Soon what we have is the diminution of land with trees, plants, and animals shrinking rapidly.'

The Alderwild Wood is a book, a journal that is suitable for all ages. It will grow with your children as they grow. It is stuffed full of art with over 150 pieces from Zena and Ian - some serving as illustrations and others as adornment, but all found in Nature within Horse Thief Bay and The Alderwild Wood. Enjoy, and as Zena would say: *"Tomorrow is another day. You may see Natterjack and friends when you go on your next walk."*

Don Taylor - editor, but mostly a friend.
Horse Thief Bay, August 2018

A Very Busy Time

September 1

Crickets are singing and summer's bloom and greenness is fading. The level of the river has dropped considerably. Some types of water weeds have already died. Snails have become stranded on the newly formed sand bar connecting the mainland to the island.

I sat outside on the front steps of the cottage. The air was chill, the sky a deep azure blue. The first sliver of the new moon was resting in the west. I heard a splash, which came from the farther edge of the island. A Great Blue Heron has claimed a rock there. He comes every morning and evening and has caught many fish over the years.

September 2

Another day of rain! The rain drops cause dimples on the water's surface. Rings form, spreading out, overlapping, intersecting other rings, there is constant motion.

Today the Heron stands on the mainland dock. The water there is much more shallow, and fish and frogs are more easily caught. I walked across the sandbar to the mainland. I spotted many very small footprints. They were not the usual animal footprints. They were coming and going in all directions. I followed one set of prints, which looked like those of a human's, but they were extremely small. They led to the tangle of Purple Loosestrife roots along the shore.

Standing on one of the roots was a fairy. Another fairy had begun to climb a Loosestrife stalk. These fairies seemed not to have wings or pointed ears as many writers and artists of fairy tales make them out to have. The Elven folk living here in Horse Thief Bay and the Alderwild Wood, Ian and I know of, because we have met some of them before. They do not wear pointed shoes, nor do they have pointed ears.

I do not know to which race these fairies belong. They carry baskets, perhaps for collecting the stranded snails. Their fingers and toes, what little I could see of them, seemed very long. I did not have my magnifying glass with me.

September 10

Ian's plane arrived on time. He had been home visiting his family for a few weeks. We ate supper at the Classic Diner in Watertown near the airport and did not arrive at the island until 8:30 P.M. We needed flashlights to see our way through the tangle of weeds and brush along the shore. It is good to see Ian again. I do miss him greatly when he is gone. There was so much to talk about, the sighting of the fairies in particular.

September 11

After lunch we walked across the sandbar to the mainland. There were no fairies to be seen anywhere. We then walked up to the top of the hill, and surveyed the Wood for a suitable site to build our new home. We found an area at the high end of the Wood from which the river and the island could be seen. The site we chose for the house was on the lee side of the hill where it will be protected from the north winds of winter by a high wall of Precambrian Granite.

Northwest of the site flows a brook we have named "The Alderwild", along which clumps of Alder and Maple trees grow. The head of the brook arises in a hollow of Hickory, Birch, and Maple trees. Its banks are high but as the brook meanders down towards the river, it slowly falls away to the lowlands where there is a large stand of Alders. The brook continues on through the marsh carpeted with Sensitive Ferns, Horsetail, and Marsh Marigolds in the spring.

A magnificent old Oak tree grows on the site's southwest side. To the east of the Oak tree we shall cut down some of the dead and smaller trees.

We spent the whole afternoon cutting down the dead trees and digging up some of the small saplings by hand. We were both very sore by the time we stopped.

September 12

We were still sore this morning but managed to work at the site from 10:00 A.M. to 5:00 P.M. and accomplished much work. It was still light when we walked back to the island.

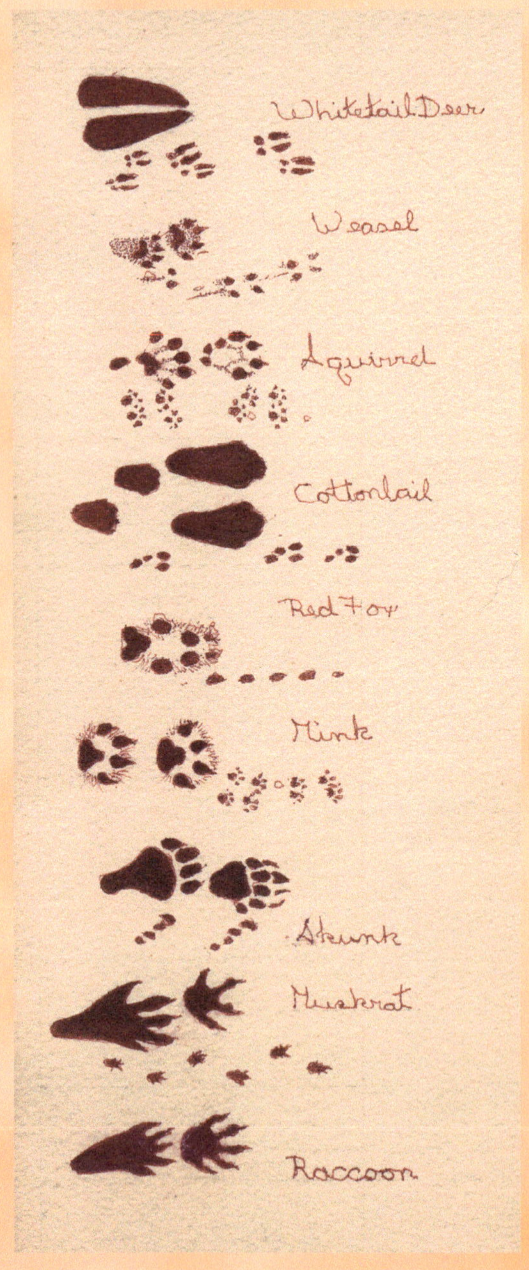

Some Maple and Basswood leaves had loosened themselves from their moorings and floated to the ground. They lay like a quilt of many colors: red, orange, and yellow. We gathered some of them to spread out on the studio floor. Leaves will keep their color when brought indoors from the elements. They smell lovely and create a great atmosphere for drawing.

A greater expanse of the sandbar was now visible. Many footprints leading in all directions came into view as we gathered the leaves. We could hardly contain ourselves upon seeing the foot prints of elves. This would be Ian's first time at sighting these particular fairies.

There were many sizes of footprints, Chipmunk, Whitetail Deer, Weasel, Grey Squirrel, Red Fox, Mink, Muskrat, Raccoon, and others. The Great Blue Heron prints were there as well.

As we scanned the area some of the Maple leaves were moving on their own, without the help of the wind. I picked up one of these leaves. To my great surprise, there crouching in my hand was a fairy. It was different from the fairies I had seen earlier. This fairy had wings which were similar to those of the Mayfly.

The fairy was only three inches high and light as a feather. I was speechless. I realized that I had better set him down quickly, as every movement I made frightened him.

Many leaves and clutches of weeds were moving about in this manner, all without the aid of the wind. My hunch was that under these leaves, more of these beings would be found. It was getting late and darkness was beginning to close in on us. There will be another day to see elves.

September 13

We arose with the sun and arrived at the site by 9:00 A.M. The air was crisp and clear, with the chatter of birds preparing to migrate south.

We met two of our neighbours who were also our friends. They were Dwarves, the father Natterjack and his son Bracken. Three Gnomes accompanied them, the father Larix with his sons Newt and Lich whom we had met before but did not know well.

Natterjack and Larix sported great beards, but neither had pointed ears. Of the sons only Bracken had some growth on his chin. We hoped they would help us to design

our new abode to be built in the same manner as theirs but with some alterations.

Natterjack said that was their plan. We were overjoyed and speechless. What great fortune! Their timing on the scene could not have been more welcomed.

By nightfall yesterday, we were beginning to have second thoughts. We must have been out of our minds to think we could build the house ourselves. I had been thinking of Thoreau's cabin on Walden Pond. He built it himself. We have built bridges, docks, and stairs before but not an entire house.

After a brief silence Natterjack spoke, "We will help build a house for you in the style of ours". We were intrigued and desperate. He appeared to be very much in earnest, so we believed him. He said, "It will be strong, weather proof, and warm. I will allow room for Ian's height 5'8". No problem. My crew and I have built many homes before and it will be finished before the cold weather sets in and the ground freezes."

What more could we ask for! Natterjack asked us to stand aside. I handed him a paper with some of our ideas as to what was needed and important to us. Ian and I stood and watched silently while Natterjack drew a design for the house in the sand, using a stick to draw a few lines for the shape and design of the foundation.

Curved lines replaced our straight ones. Our rectangular floor plan was disappearing quickly. A great change was in the making. Ian was becoming anxious. I thought it best to return to the island and allow Natterjack and company to do their thing.

Although Ian and I had just had our first real visit and conversation with our new friends, we felt great trust in them.

September 15

This morning Natterjack walked over to the island and presented his plans for the house. The drawings showed the shape, size, and placement of the windows and rooms. The house is to have several levels with quiet spaces where either of us could be alone to read or observe the woods while still being near one another in case I fell.

We each have a large work area. Ian's is on the second floor with three skylights and windows on the side facing the river and one large patio door with a deck. My room is on the main floor. Our new home looked like something imagined in a fantasy tale but one that was made real. The design of the house has an extempore feeling. The three of us walked to the mainland and up to the site.

The night's moist air still hung on the bronzing bracken. The water level of the river has dropped even more. The canoe will have to be pulled up high onto the shore and turned over for the winter.

When we reached the top of the hill, Bracken and Larix were there to meet us. We all walked to the site. We were amazed to see the foundation mostly finished. We could hardly believe our eyes. It looked wonderful. Ian and I could not have designed it so well and creatively. Our creativity lies in other areas.

We did not stay at the site today but decided to look for more fairies on the ever expanding sandbar. There were many more coloured leaves, snails, and fairy shrimp lying on the sand. We looked around for moving leaves but there were not so many. For a short while I thought the fairies had become frightened and had hidden themselves. I had hoped that I might find the same elf, which I had held in

· 8 ·

my hand the other day. No such luck! However, we did come upon a small clump of dried Crisp Pondweed moving towards a stand of Alder on the mainland shore. We followed it and saw several more of them just ahead. They were moving in single file, hugging the riverbank. Some clumps looked to be larger and higher above the sand than others.

I knelt down slowly and laid my finger in the path of one clump. It stopped and so did the others behind it. At first I saw only two pairs of legs then several arms stretching upwards, holding the matted water weeds. With one big push the weeds were thrown aside. Unlike the other Fairies carrying the Maple leaves, these had no wings and they were taller.

The Fairy in front seemed annoyed with me. The one behind him smiled. They seemed not to be frightened of us. I spoke to them and smiled. I also used hand gestures and laid my finger

on the ground. I nodded and apologized and pointed to myself and then to the island. I pointed to him and then to the Purple Loosestrife. He understood, shook his head no, and pointed up the hill to the woods, and then nodded yes. The Fairy standing next to him pointed to the building site and then to us. We realized they must have been watching everything that was going on in the Alderwild Wood.

It suddenly occurred to me that the Wood was not really ours but theirs. We should have asked their consent. They seemed to approve however.

Just then three crows landed in one of the tall White Pines on the island. I looked up and realized the day was far spent and evening fast approaching. We waved goodbye.

September 21
The Building of Our Home Begins

We have been helping Natterjack and company the last several days. He has had a crew of nine working with him. The house has been completely framed in. Ian has been helping, holding the uprights in place, and horizontals level while a gnome or dwarf stands on his shoulders, holding the joints together. I passed boards, nails, and whatever else the workers needed. There were times when my help was not needed and I was able to sit down on a rock and sketch. I did some drawings of the house and the men working on it. I soon found I had company. Sitting on some of the rocks surrounding me were elves of different races.

These elves were small, very, very small. Some had wings while others had none. Most looked impish. Some of them were clad in greenish grey and others were in several shades of brown and sienna. Their skin was light coloured,

hair wiry, eyes bluish-green, and ears pointed. I was wrong
in thinking that elves did not have pointed ears. My
mistake!

These imps kept throwing acorns at me, just to get my
attention. When I turned to face them, they had big grins
on their faces. It was not long before they began to climb
onto my shoulders. Then, they were on my head, using
my hair to pull themselves up. They seemed to rummage
around for the longest time. One crawled into my left ear
and another tweaked my nose. I had to be very careful not
to brush these fairies away. One could fall, break a wing, or
even be killed. I was even afraid to open my mouth in case
one climbed in and was inhaled. I began to make all kinds
of sounds, some low and some high pitched. They must also
have noticed a look of panic on my face. They soon climbed
down from my head and ears onto my shoulders and
drawing pad.

September 22

Because it rained today Ian and I didn't go out for a
walk, but rather spent the day in our studios on the island.

Linden Leaves

Ian worked on a paper-
mâché mask of a leaf fairy.
I elaborated on some of my
sketches, those of the impish
folk. Earlier this evening,
we pulled our beds into the
living room by the wood
stove. We shall sleep here
until the house is finished
enough to move in.

September 23

Still raining. Another day spent indoors. Tomorrow, Natterjack and several Gnomes plan to come here and help Ian carry wood to the site.

Ian and I collected this wood over the past several summers. We found the boards in the mud at the bottom of the Bay. Wood of all shapes and sizes, new and old, tree limbs, beams, and boards that loosed themselves from old docks and fallen trees. They have all floated down river and some have drifted into our Bay. In time, they sink and become covered with mud. Within a few years, the water and mud wear the boards smooth, leaving the grain of the wood raised. Bottles too, of all shapes and colors, blue, green, brown, and clear have become part of this floating maze of debris found in our Bay.

September 24

This morning, our troupe of friends arrived at 8:30 A.M. We were ready, wearing long johns under our work clothes. As we stepped outside, we could hear the chatter of the Black-Capped Chickadees and White and Red Breasted Nuthatches. They were flitting from branch to branch in the Pitch and White Pine trees. The birds become much tamer this time of year. Except for the Red-breasted Nuthatches, the others will stay the winter.

There were eight of us to carry the wood and bottles across the sandbar and up the hill. Three of the impish

fairies had come along for the fun of it. They sat on some of the long boards that Bracken carried. When each load of boards were dropped off at the site, the imps would jump off and climb onto someone else's shoulder for the trip back to the island. I carried just one board but Ian was able to carry many.

While the fellows were getting stacks of cedar shakes, two-by-fours, two-by-sixes, and flooring to the site, I went off on my own. I walked back to the open area of the Alderwild Wood, where the sun's rays still bring warmth in full measure to the soil. When I reached that area, a wondrous thing occurred before my eyes. I was witness to the birth of a Wood Sprite. I did not say a word but let my eyes see and my mind absorb all that was unfolding before me.

The Sprite had been developing in a Ground Cherry Lantern under the decaying leaves. I suddenly realized that I was not the only observer of this happening. The mother Wood Sprite was standing on the leafy ground, bent over to watch for the appearance of the young Wood Sprite infant. She was there, ready to help lift the child up into her arms. When I looked up, I saw other Wood Sprite mothers doing the same thing, anxiously waiting with their ears to the ground to hear the cries of their child being born. It was a lovely sight to behold. Each babe was quickly wrapped in Milkweed down or Sphagnum Moss before the infant became chilled. There are just a few races of elves who have their children born outside of the womb.

Most mothers of the Elven races carry their unborn children in their wombs, thus they have a limited number of births at one time. Those Elven mothers who have their children born outside of the womb in a protective natural casings, are most likely to have multiple births. However the mortality rate of these offspring is greater. The newborn are much more vulnerable to the spraying of insecticides, fertilizers, and also weed killers. All of these different chemicals are used by the humans.

We had brought a lunch with us today. A large flock of Canada Geese flew overhead in their V formation, followed by two smaller groups heading south. A magnificent sight!

Ian and the others walked back and forth to the island, carrying wood some six or more times. The wood and bottles will be used last, in the decor of one of the outside walls and window. The new house, for it is beginning to look like a great work of art, will certainly not be a conventional home. Its construction is so artistic, creative, and extemporaneous. Much the same approach I take when painting. I find It is much more exciting and fluid. It adds to the suspense.

September 25

Another sunny day! Just what we needed! More rocks were required, so Azulla, one of Natterjack's sons, and I gathered many small ones from along the shore. Larger rocks were procured from the broken face of the great wall of Precambrian Granite, standing to the north of the house. Fraxin, his son Perch, and other strong dwarves, helped Ian with the larger ones.

September 26

The colouration of the leaves on Hill, Club, and Watch Islands is so beautiful now. The scarlet and yellow leaves of the Maple, the yellow leaves of the Birch, and their white

Portrait of Natterjack

trunks are in such contrast against the dark green boughs of Hemlock, Cedar, and White Pine. The trees with all their splendour retrace themselves on the smooth surface of the river.

Today was a day of rest for everyone. It gave Ian and me a chance to visit with Natterjack and Azulla. The four of us sat down on a fallen tree trunk and a couple of rocks on the mainland shore.

Natterjack has thick greying hair with some wave to it. He has such a wonderfully long moustache, with streaks of white and orange running through it, which he has braided

on either side. His arms are short, belly robust, legs thin.
I would guess his age to be late forties or early fifties. He
seems to possess a heart unencumbered with great worry.

Azulla is a handsome lad with reddish hair, which he
has allowed to grow longer than his father's. He is slender
but not skinny.

We had a wonderful conversation with the fellows and learned so much.

We tried to encourage Natterjack to do most of the talking. He spoke of nature and autumn. It was like listening to poetry without rhyme. It seemed to flow on a slow and measured beat, a song to Nature. It is the soul song of the inhabitants of Horse Thief Bay.

September 29 - Birth of a Fairy

I have been working on a drawing of the newborn Wood
Sprite. It is coming along well. I seem to have let go of all
my inhibitions and begun to explore. I have found a deep
trust in myself.

The drawing describes the Sprite child lying inside
a Ground Cherry Lantern just about to be extruded onto
a bed of autumn coloured leaves on which the lantern is
resting. The leaves surrounding the lantern are in layers
which provide warmth to the growing foetus. The colors,
shapes, and veins of the leaves are seen through the layers
above it. The shapes and colors, which are emerging from

the overlapping of the leaves are fantastic. There is so much movement in it. I am excited.

There is another species of Fairy living among the leaves of the Basswood tree. The wings of the Basswood Sprites are in the shape of the Basswood leaves. However, rather than carrying the zygote, the fertilized egg in her womb, she carries the eggs in small roundish cases on her wings. They remain in their cases for approximately a week and a half at which time they hatch into larva.

The newly born larvae eat aphids which both parents collect for them. Within a very short time the larvae transform into pupae from which emerge the sprites who are identical to the adults but much smaller. It takes the full summer before they are full size adults.

Gathering Acorns

Autumn, The Time of Floating Leaves

September 30

Autumn is the time of the year Er, (Earth) prepares for Her long winter's sleep. It is a time when Er replenishes herself. She takes nourishment from the leaves, which have fallen, the sticks, which have dried, and the seeds, which have ripened. The rain and snow to come will quench Her thirst and cause the seeds to grow. Most of the water dwelling animals and fairies will hibernate in the mud at the bottom of the Bay or in small caves under the island.

Puncum, (Wetland fairies), Alderling (Woodland fairies), Gnomes, and Dwarves do not hibernate but spend the winter indoors working on numerous projects.

Trolls, Traugs, Norgs, and other nasties batten down their habitats for the time of the Cold Winds, Rain, and Snow.

Many birds fly south. Those birds that remain here find shelter in the Cedars, Hemlocks, and White Pine. The birds depend on Na, (Nature), daughter of Er, to provide them with seeds and small open areas in the river's ice for water. If Na cannot provide enough food for the birds and squirrels, the Dwarves and Gnomes must help gather food.

October 1

The main structure of the house has been framed in. The interior walls are up and the roof finished. Natterjack has used some of the same materials in building our home as are found in their homes. However, I did ask him to put 12 inches of fibreglass insulation in the roof and 8 inches in the outside walls. He agreed to go along with my request.

Gnome and Dwarf homes are insulated differently. To cover the outside walls and roof, he used a tar paper type insulating material before laying hand cut cedar shingles on the roof and some areas of wall. Stones and boards were also used on the walls.

The house is beginning to look enchanted, magical, more like something found in a children's book of fantasy. We are both very excited and can hardly wait to take occupancy. The evening star shone brightly as we headed for the island.

October 3

Ian and I left the island late this morning. As we walked across the sandbar, I noticed that there were no more drifting Maple leaves. There was only one clump of water-weeds with legs headed towards the shore and the Purple Loosestrife.

Natterjack told us that most of the fairies living by or in the water are in hibernation or nearly so.

Leaves crunch under our feet. Their aroma mingles with the odours arising from the soil. Intoxicating! The sound of the leaves crunching, the birds chattering, the Canada Geese overhead honking, and the splashing wavelets upon the shore brings to my soul an inner peace and tranquillity, which is music to my ears.

It is Na's music. It reminds me that I must always protect and revere Her music that it may continue in the years to come.

Our spirits were high. Everything has been moving along well with the house construction. We shall be moving in shortly, in a matter of a few days.

When we reached the mainland we decided to take a different path to the building site. There was no particular reason for the change in direction. As we entered the wood we realized the trees were very dark, almost black, the leaves hanging limp on their branches. These once mighty Oaks appeared not to have a breath of life left in them. The wild grasses about their feet were also smitten with a black stain. All things in that place looked drear and melancholy.

Death of The Alderling Child

Deep ebony crows were perched on a number of the Oak branches while some circled overhead. The air was becoming oppressive. Crows were caw, caw cawing. The cawing still rings in my ears. The stench was terrible. My heart pounded loudly in my chest.

Just ten feet ahead something lay on the ground. It was wrapped in an aura of light. Our pace quickened. We saw that it was a young child, a fairy, a boy. His arms were too small for me to feel a pulse. His entire body was only a few inches long. I lifted one arm. It was limp. The fairy was dead. The glow which radiated from this child was one of innocence and purity of heart, a heart untouched and unfettered by evil. His outer body had repaired itself. The wounds inside were too serious. Trolls, like humans, are mortal. The Mortals, the humans, made the wounds. His soul had taken wing.

There was no odour arising from his body. We looked about us. From where was the stench emanating?

As Ian and I searched the ground we found disemboweled squirrels, chipmunks, and toads. They lay in piles here and there. The smell was not from these bodies either.

Ian walked further and soon called. I went to him. He found the putrefied bodies of what I thought must be some race of Trolls, Norgs, or Traugs of whom Natterjack had spoken.

These fiends must have killed one another fighting over the food the dead Alderling or the animals would have provided them.

We did not stay long. We felt ill and were overcome by such a horrible sight as well as the rotting, decaying smell.

We left and looked for Natterjack, Bracken, or anyone else from the site.

We found Natterjack and Bracken together. They were collecting Bracket Fungus from the trunk of a White Birch Tree. I think I shall relate the remainder of today's events tomorrow. It has been an exhausting day and I have a splitting headache.

I awoke early. It was still dark. The night was just beginning to steal away and the stars, one by one, went out. I laid another couple of logs on the fading embers of the fire. The horizon grew lighter. The trees were silhouetted against it. The birds were just waking. The river was calm and smooth like a mirror.

I have had little sleep. I was continually thinking of yesterday's carnage. When I am with Na, my mind is at peace. There is harmony between the natural elements and the animals, Fairies, Gnomes, and Dwarves who inhabit the Wood. Na calms me, yet at the same time challenges my mind. She holds many truths. The events of yesterday have shaken these feelings in me.

Yesterday, when we reached Natterjack, he saw that we were in great distress. We sat down and told him all we had just seen and most sadly the sight of the dead fairy child. Natterjack and Bracken were both visibly shaken by the news. Tears came to their eyes as they did to ours. It was then that we learned the child was an Alderling. Bracken left us to call to arms a group of Alderlings, Gnomes, and Dwarves. Natterjack went to summon the Suund, the Healer. She lived near the roots of two very old Maple trees standing side by side. The trees had originated from one seed.

Bracken returned with a group of strong, young fellows neither Ian nor I had met before. The Alderlings were very small compared to Bracken or Larix. However, they were taller than the imps who were pestering me a few days ago.

It was difficult to comprehend how they expected to defeat the Trolls or other fiends who might still be lurking

in the stand of Cattails and brush nearby. These monsters
were very large. It would be like David killing Goliath. The
group of Alderlings had only small shields and spears.
Some had no armour. However, they did have small bags
hanging form their waists. Some Alderlings also had
stones and slings tucked in their pockets. They came
prepared to do battle and yet they did not expect any such
confrontation.

It was daylight. I wondered if that had anything to do
with it. I had heard that Trolls do not walk about during the
day, or else they turn to stone.

Soon Natterjack appeared with the Suund. She looked
like a toad but walked upright. I thought my eyes were
playing tricks but this was not so. I was not mistaken. She
was a toad, a female, Bufo Americanus to be exact.

We all walked down the path to the area of the slaughter.
As we drew nearer, the stench from the rotting and bloated
carcasses grew stronger. Natterjack, Bracken, Azulla, and
the Alderlings kept a close eye on the trees and shrubs
around us, making sure there were no fiends lurking about.

Ian and I both tied handkerchiefs over our noses. The
sight of the corpses was gruesome.

The Gnomes brought shallow woven baskets made from
the reeds found near the shore. These were used to carry the
smaller animals. The Dwarves pulled litters behind them
to carry many of the larger animals back to the Alderwild
Wood for burial.

The Suund went to the Alderling child still lying in a
glow of light. She passed her hands over the child, chanting
softly in a tongue I was not familiar with. Then from under
her shawl, she drew two small bags. From one bag she took a

small amount of white powder, which she spread lightly over the body. A yellow powder taken from a second bag followed this. The particles of both powders remained suspended just an inch or so above the body.

The White powder came together to form clouds, the yellow as stars. Chanting more loudly, she passed both hands over the body and then back to her face. She repeated this several times and then stepped back.

The Alderlings stepped forward pulling a golden litter. It was lined with white feathery Milkweed down. They laid the child upon the litter and then left with it. There was no confrontation with Trolls.

The remaining inhabitants of the Wood left with heavy hearts. These animals had been their friends.

Bracken and Natterjack stayed behind. They dragged the carcass of each fiend to an open area near the water's edge. Here sunlight would reach the bodies. Light and fresh air are most feared by these demons of the Night and Twilight.

Trolls turn to stone if they are caught by the light of day. Other fiends' bodies shrivel with the arrival of the sun but still live on. Their eyes blinded, they forever walk the earth never able to stop and rest. Their souls will be in ever lasting pain and torment.

After the bodies were carried away, the Suund brought forth a much larger bag containing a courser powder. She walked back and forth over all the ground, casting the powder where the fiends had tread and fallen. She was purifying the land in that place. The foul smell dissipated. The Trolls and their kind would not walk there again, at least not for some time. However, demons were still entrenched in the nearby lands.

October 7 At Work Again

We began working on the house again today. I felt very numb in spirit. An air of sadness hung over everyone at the site. No sound of laughter or clever repartee was heard. Silence prevailed except for hammer against nail and saw through wood. Even the birds seemed not to speak.

The roof is completely finished except for some caulking at the base of the chimney and bathroom vent where they meet the roof. The outer walls, which are being built using rocks, are nearly complete. Those walls having Cedar shingles were finished.

Those boards from the river bottom are still soaking in water until the crew is ready to use them. It prevents the wood from splitting while driving a nail through it.

The house looks great. It will not be long, just a few more days and we shall take occupancy. We left the site early and returned to the island by 5:00 P.M.

I feel that now I am better able to further describe the events of yesterday.

One week ago, we only knew a small group of inhabitants of the Alderwild Wood, mainly those working on the house. Many of the inhabitants of the Wood, both animal and elves, are either preparing for hibernation or are tucked in their warm homes like most of the Alderling and Puncum are.

However, in just two days we have become deeply involved in the lives of these fellow beings. We have become acquainted with their grief. We have witnessed a great tragedy of the fairies. Animals of all kinds sat with us as well.

When all the animals, which were killed, were buried, the Suund stood by the site chanting. She summoned their souls to take wing and fly to the Land Beyond The Horizon.

The child was then brought forth on its golden litter. The thrumming of harps and the tingling of bells could be heard. A procession of Fairies, Gnomes, and Dwarves was formed. In single file, hand in hand, they wound their way around trees and over rocks, holding torches and singing. It was the most beautiful sight and experience, and saddest event in my life.

The Fairies told us that death is another part of living. In death the spirit, the soul continues on in a different form. The soul becomes one of the stars above. The body becomes part of the living, growing world of flowers and ferns. Sadness fell over the inhabitants of the Alderwild Wood.

The Alderlings carried the prone child, which was now placed upon an Oak leaf, down through the Valley of Horse Tails. Upon reaching the brook, The leaf was placed upon its pellucid waters where it would float to the open river and The Land Beyond The Horizon. The inhabitants of the Wood stood all along the banks of the Alderwild.

October 9 - Moving In

We now have running water, electricity, and the inside walls are up. Even the wood stove is in place.

Today, boiled linseed oil was applied to the exterior wood siding. We will be using a two-burner hot plate for our stove until the kitchen is complete. The refrigerator arrived this morning. Tomorrow morning, we shall move in.

Most of the trees in the Alderwild Wood except for the Beech and Oak have shed their leaves. The Witch Hazel have little yellow spidery tufts growing from the nodules on each branch. Under the tufts, there are pods, which are now mature. The pod shells have burst open and have each spit out two black seeds.

October 10

It has been raining all day. We spent the time getting the cottage ready to close for the winter. It is a big job. I have folded all our summer clothes and towels and stored them in trunks and old suitcases. We have a real problem with mice. We washed the floors, covered the chair cushions, and emptied and cleaned the refrigerator. Ian drained the pipes and water heater. Tomorrow the windows will be boarded. It has been an exhausting day.

October 11

We awoke early this morning. Natterjack, Bracken, and Azulla came first thing, right after breakfast. They helped Ian to board the windows and began carrying clothes, cots, a dresser, two rocking chairs, and both of our drawing tables as well as one chair and several stools.

Then they carried the remaining boxes of books, radio/Cd and tape player, more books, microscope, and a bioscope. Most of the food had been taken to the house two days ago. Just the remaining breakfast food had to be packed. Everything had to be carried across the sandbar and up the hill. This went on for a good part of the day.

While the men carried on with their work, I cleaned the new house. Plaster, wood, and sawdust had to be swept up. Windows and floors, needed to be washed, and the woodwork dusted.

As the fellows brought in the furniture, I had them put most of our good furniture for the living and dining rooms, kitchen, and bedrooms, which were in storage against the living and dining room walls. Our cots were set near the wood stove. Books, boards, and bricks were taken to my studio for the time being.

Nothing is put in its rightful place yet. The walls in all the rooms still need to be painted. Hopefully, tomorrow we will begin painting the two studios and bathroom. For our own sanity, it is important that we get our studios finished

and completely in order first, one place where we will both be able to do our artwork free of chaos. We have already bought most of the paint.

The fellows left by 4:00 P.M. Natterjack said they will be back tomorrow. A half hour later, Natterjack returned with a hot supper, which we welcomed. His wife, Draka, had prepared it. We sat down by the fire and used boxes as tables and thoroughly enjoyed the hot meal. Overcome by exhaustion, we did no further work.

October 12

Natterjack, Bracken, and Azulla arrived mid-morning. We were up and had already eaten breakfast. We thought they had come to visit, but no, they had come to help us paint the walls. We had planned to do them ourselves but we did not complain. In fact we were overjoyed! We could hardly wait to get started!

Ian and I chose the paint colour "Fresh Pineapple Yellow" for our studios. The ceiling will be "Eggshell White". We plan to buy a tan coloured carpet for both rooms and possibly the rest of the house.

Ian walked to the island to get a stepladder from under the cottage. When he returned, he began painting the ceiling in my studio first. While we waited for it to dry, Ian painted the ceiling in his studio. By the time he had finished painting his ceiling, the ceiling in my studio was dry enough for a second coat. Then Natterjack and Bracken began painting the walls, one used a short handled roller and the other a long handled one. Azulla and I opened the cans of paint and stirred them well. The work was moving along quickly. We stopped at 1 o'clock in the afternoon for lunch. Draka had prepared a lovely meal for us. Dandelion and potato soup with slices of bread made from cattail flour; stewed Mandrake fruit with Wild Ginger syrup, Stag horn Sumac Tea, and dried wild apple slices made up the entire meal.

After lunch, we moved into my studio while the walls in Ian's studio dried before giving them a

second coat. We did not finish painting my room until late afternoon. At 5:00 P.M., we decided to quit for the day to get a fresh start in the morning.

October 13

The fellows were here by 9:30 A.M. We began the second coat in my studio. Everyone liked the color. It was bright and sunny, but not too yellow. While Natterjack and crew continued painting, Ian and I drove into town to buy carpeting for the two studios, upstairs hallway, and bathroom. The color we finally chose was a rich medium brown with flecks of "Burnt Sienna". It is lovely. The rolls of carpet were too long to fit into our own car and so the store delivered them this afternoon.

When we arrived home, my studio had its second coat. The fellows were about ready to give Ian's room the last coat. They were finished by 3:00P.M. They had time to give the upstairs hallway its first coat "French Vanilla". The ceiling is finished. It was given two coats. We thought it best to give all of the ceilings throughout the house two coats.

October 14

By this evening the carpet for both studios was laid and the woodwork varnished. The rooms were ready to be furnished. The walls and ceiling were done. The bathroom ceiling was finished and the walls were given their first coat of "Pastel Lime Green". We liked the colour so much that we decided to paint the walls of the two bedrooms the same color as well. It is such a warm colour, like a gentle breeze, if air had a colour.

October 16

The upstairs rooms are finished. The carpeting for the bedrooms and bathroom is laid, the colour: "Silver Moss". Quite beautiful! My studio downstairs Is finished. The living and dining rooms and kitchen we will paint and carpet later. We are much further along with finishing the interior of the house than we thought possible.

However, I am having difficulty living in such a state of chaos. I need some sense of order before we move on with painting the remaining rooms. Before settling down, we realized we needed to finish painting the ceilings and walls of the living room, dining room, and kitchen as well as choosing the carpet colour for those remaining rooms and arrange the furniture before we could host a party.

For the colour of the living and dining room walls, we decided to paint them soft "Desert Sand" and for the kitchen we chose a "Pineapple Yellow". We decided that we would quickly paint those rooms ourselves. The carpeting in the living and dining rooms will be "Dusty Rose". For the kitchen we thought it best to put down linoleum flooring with a small beige organic pattern.

Working together we painted the three rooms and finished painting them in four hours. Laying the carpet and linoleum, we asked Natterjack if he and a few of the fellows would help Ian lay it. He nodded, saying", Of course, no problem at all."

We had all of the remaining furniture, which was in storage, brought to the house this morning. It seemed as though every physically capable Dwarf and Gnome from the Alderwild Wood was here to help. They carried all of the furniture to each room where it belonged. They even set up our beds, complete with mattresses, sheets, pillow cases, and blankets.

Ian's drawing table, books, boards, and bricks, art supplies, clutter, and more things with and without names and one red dinosaur candle were put on one side of his studio. He wants a little more time to think about where everything should be placed. I did the same with my studio. The remaining furniture was set aside in the living room.

I cannot believe how much stuff, things, odds, and ends we possess. I wondered what all of these things were for. At the time I acquired them, I must have had some good idea. As I thought and considered each thing, my mind was jogged; some of my original creative thoughts came back to me. I then began to have serious doubts as to whether I shall get them done in this lifetime.

For those things, which I had no idea about, I thought I might think of something. The more I thought about my creative ideas; it occurred to me, perhaps if I hurry, I might use them before I die. I then placed each thing, both certain and uncertain, into the box, basket, or pail from which it came.

October 17

Today we took life more easily than we have these last few weeks. We both needed thinking time, each relaxing in our own studio, looking over our books, paints, and other art supplies. Also, we needed to build our bookshelves with bricks and boards while listening to music or one of our audio books. We put a few posters on our walls to create a friendly environment. Ian and I spend most of our lives in our studios, the woods, and the island.

I like to have some of the things I've found outside: dried weeds, wasp's nests, wood, bones, and even some of my old toys from childhood around me. These objects interest, stimulate, and inspire me. I found my Betz microscope, and the bioscope and set them up on a low table. Along with these two instruments and my 8x and 10x loops, I will be able to study the living food, the one-celled animals, and diatoms, which the Water Sprites, and Puncum eat.

By this evening both, Ian and I had erected our bookshelves and arranged our books in categories. We filled the drawers with paints of every kind, and containers of all sizes for our brushes, pens, and pencils.

Floristane, my dog and Stripe, Ian's cat are uncomfortable with staying in their new home. Too many boxes on the floor, and the furniture is out of place. The couch Floristane likes to sleep on is filled with everything from pots and pans, blankets and towels, to books. I think they will accompany us to our bedrooms tonight.

October 18

When we awoke this morning, the bracken was crisp with frost. As the day warmed and the sun rose higher, the white ice crystals began to melt. Breakfast was relaxed unlike other mornings. There was no need to rush. The house was warm. The island cottage is closed. The holding tank emptied. We have enough wood for the fire to last the winter.

We went into town for a large order of food. A party for everyone who helped us in so many ways was in order. The get together will be a chance to meet those residents of the Alderwild Wood who we have not yet met.

Turkey, ham, roast beef, green salad, potato salad, stuffed mushrooms, cranberry sauce, white wine, and much more. It will be great to celebrate the near completion of our new home. I suddenly realized the Fairies and Elves in our Wood would have a different diet of foods from the types that we like to eat. When speaking to Natterjack about the party, I discussed with him their diet. His response was, he would handle that matter.

October 20

The party went well and was enjoyed by everyone. We met many of the fairies and elves of the Alderwild Wood who came. Very little food was left over to be put away.

November-1 Meeting Hatch and Pody

Much has happened since last I wrote. During the closing days of October Ian and I met Hatch and Pody. They are from the Alderling community. Natterjack and Bracken introduced us to them at the party.

They came again to our home today. It was warm and

so we sat outside on our veranda. We stacked two boxes for our guests to sit on. It raised them to the height of my shoulder. Otherwise it would have been difficult to speak or to hear them. It was still a struggle to understand what they were saying. They are only a foot high. Their mouths are so small and voices so soft and lilting. The language Hatch and Pody spoke was also different than ours. I would have been able to understand them better if I could have read their lips. Their lips were so small I could barely see them.

Natterjack came to my rescue. He repeated the words and translated the ones I could not understand. I asked Hatch why we had seen so little of him and his kindred during the month of October. His reply was that by mid-October, when the cold weather sets in, the Alderlings return from their summer homes on the banks of the Alderwild Brook, to their dwellings underground for much of the winter. They do not hibernate but do take more naps. They like to keep warm and snug, while participating in many activities. Only occasionally do they venture out into the cold for more twigs and bracket fungus for their fires.

By mid-October the Alderlings have already collected

enough wood and food to last until the end of April. Much of the food such as fish, snails, Fairy Shrimp, Dandelion greens, and Chicory roots are dried. When the weather remains warm for longer hours, they return to their summer cottages.

The Alderlings are a family-oriented society. During the long winter months, the mother often sits at her loom, weaving the silk like threads gathered from spider webs during the summer by her children. As the threads are collected, the eldest daughter wraps each strand around a wooden spool immediately, before it becomes tangled. Some plants, Stinging Nettle and the stalks from the Milkweed plant also provide the Alderlings with thread to weave into strong material for clothing and sails for their boats and those of the Puncum. The children too are kept busy stuffing pillow casings with Milkweed and Coltsfoot down.

The father makes musical instruments and toys for his children and also for trade with Fairies in other communities on the mainland and islands.

Hatch and Pody had much more to tell us. They were here for three hours. That is a very long time for Alderlings to be talking. Their lungs are so small. They were very pleased that Ian and I have taken such an interest in learning about them and will return again another day. Evening has come. The days are becoming shorter and shorter. The trees are without leaf except for the Beech. Its leaves hang on until spring. All other trees stand bare against the cold blue of the evening sky. The sickle moon is already waning as I look out our window.

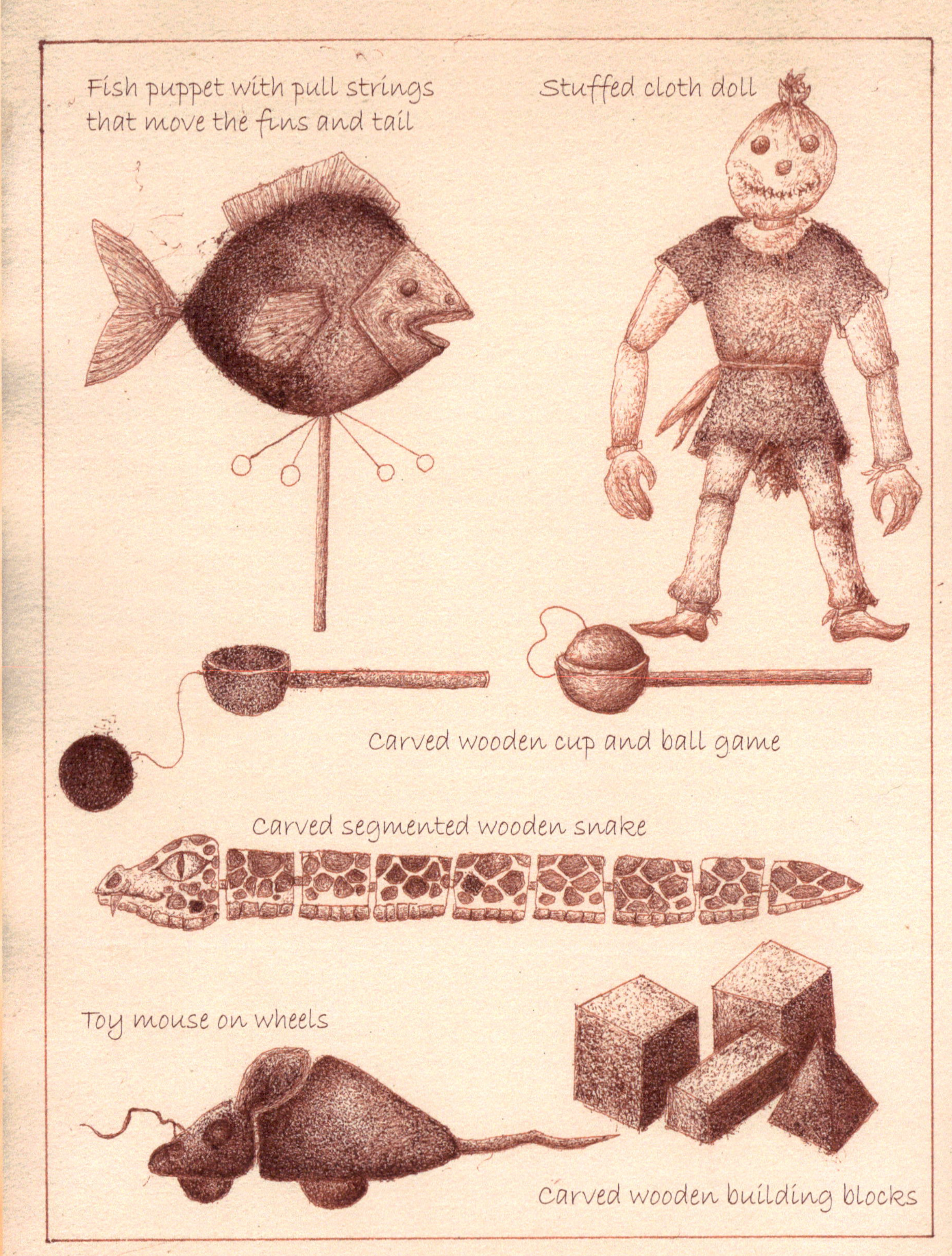

Fish puppet with pull strings
that move the fins and tail
Stuffed cloth doll
Carved wooden cup and ball game
Carved segmented wooden snake
Toy mouse on wheels
Carved wooden building blocks

November 2

Our dog Floristane awakened me early, just as dawn was conquering the morning. The fire in our stove was nearly out, and only a few embers remained. I quickly added a couple of logs. The wood was very dry. In a matter of minutes, flames were licking the logs' rough bark. I placed my chair just a few feet away. Floristane lay on the floor by my side. As I sat, a few birds began to chirp as the edge of the sun came up very slowly over the horizon. Clouds of mist rose from the river.

The water is warmer than the air. It was ethereal, dreamlike, and very moving: a magical time of day.

When Ian awoke, we had breakfast and then decided to take a walk through the Alderwild Wood and visit with some of our neighbours. The leaves and twigs crackled under our feet. The air was cool and the sun shone brightly.

We first met up with Natterjack and Bracken. They were doing some small repairs on a few of the houses before the snow flies. Azulla and some of the other fellows were cutting up branches which lay on the ground from the heavy rain and wind storms this past spring and summer.

Some Gnomes were sitting on the bridge over the brook, playing their flutes. We visited with them for a short while but soon realized that the day was passing quickly and we still wanted to get over to the island to see how things were doing there. We walked down the hill to the edge of the water.

There were some large footprints in the sand, but they were not of someone with bare feet. When we reached the island, much had changed. There was more wildlife about. There were three deer grazing, a Red Squirrel, and numerous White and Red- breasted Nuthatches, Black-

Capped Chickadees, Purple and Yellow finches. They will all stay for the winter except for the Red-breasted Nuthatch.

We were surprised and pleased to find the Gnomes, Lich, Newt, and Salus. They stopped what they were doing and we exchanged greetings. They spoke with a thick accent. Their words had hard edges, Nordic perhaps or maybe Germanic ancestry. They had a basket. We asked them what were they collecting. They showed us. There were quite a number of:

Ram's Horn Snail
Giant Pond snail
River Snail

Zebra Mussels
Fresh Water Clam
Crayfish

Evening was approaching. We left the troop to continue their gathering of foodstuffs. It is of the utmost importance for them to collect as much food as possible before the ground freezes and the snow blankets the Bay.

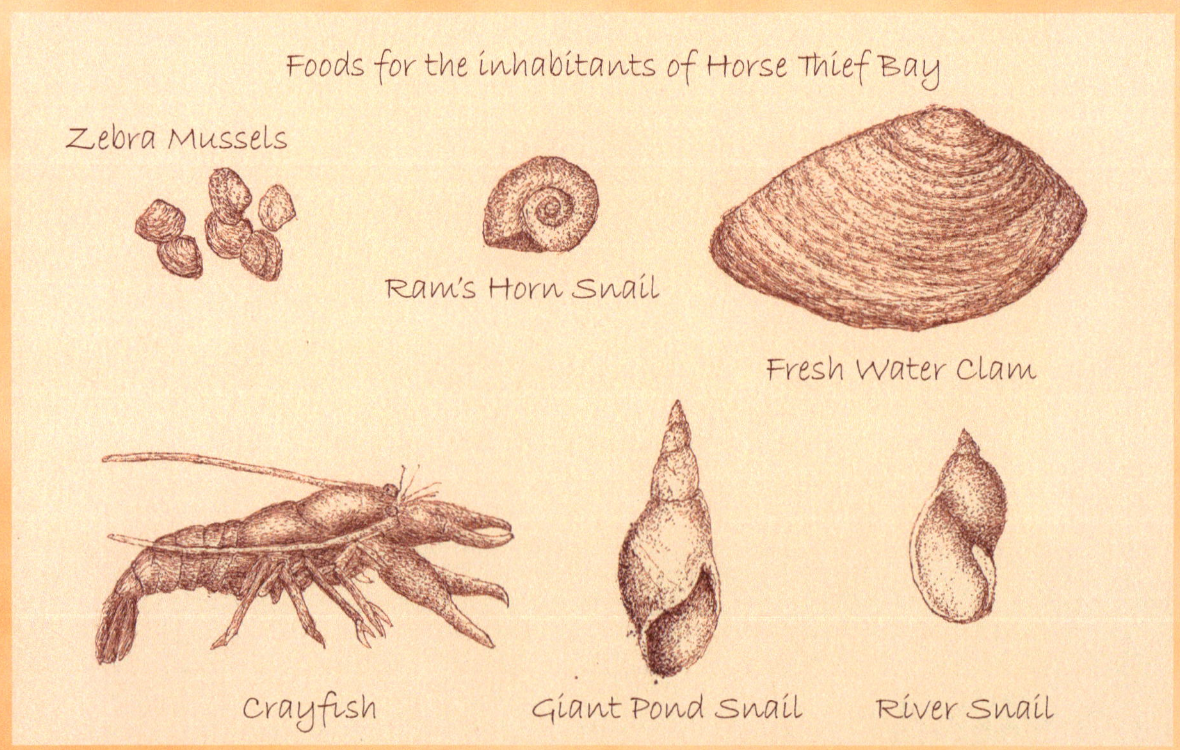

November 3

It feels like winter. Ice is forming quickly in the Bay. The ice will help insulate the inhabitants living below it when the temperature above falls below freezing. Fish and all other aquatic life either move to deeper water or find shelter under the blanket of fallen leaves, sticks, and decaying plant life covering the mud bottom.

November 5

Natterjack visited us yesterday and again this morning. We learn something new each time he comes. He is like a walking encyclopedia. This morning he spoke to us about Water Sprites. We will not see them until summer.

Water Sprites

Water Sprites are beings living in the shallow water between the island and the stand of cattails along the mainland shore and caves under the island. Water Sprites are one of the races of Elves who hibernate. They winter over inside the Cattail seed heads. By late September the burnt umber heads are soft and fluffy inside and very warm. The male Sprite drills a small hole in the side of the cattail. Only the female and her daughters enter the head. The male spends the winter apart from the family. It is not certain the reason for this. Perhaps there is just not enough room for him. The daughters will assist the mother in the delivery of the newborn in the spring.

Sprites usually give birth to four or five offspring in March. This gives the infants time to nurse and be weaned by the end of May. The young must fledge by then because the seed head in which they are living will fall apart from the ravages of winter. Only a few of the silk threads still remaining hold the Cattail seed heads together. Not all cattail heads have hibernating Sprites within them.

By late winter one can usually identify the heads, which contain the Sprites. The heads with a great deal of fluff remaining are the ones which were occupied by Sprites.

When the young Sprite emerges, its wings are beige with irregular burnt sienna spots outlined with burnt umber. These colors camouflage the young Sprite so that Red-wing Blackbirds and Marsh Wrens will not mistake them for insects and eat them.

There is also the Troll Witch who lives near the cattails whom the Sprites must be wary of.

November 6

When we awoke this morning grey clouds lay one against another. The Alderwild Wood seemed dark and pensive. Hummocks of amber grasses and Sensitive Ferns stood in pools of ice- coated water. I wondered if Hatch and Pody would come today. It looked menacing outside. It was a day to stay Indoors.

Ian and I had a simple breakfast. We both wanted to get an early start on our work. Ian has been occupied with his paper-mâché masks. I have been working on my studies of some of the inhabitants of the Alderwild Wood.

I am also trying to work out a method by which I may organize my findings. Data is something I shall collect on the different races inhabiting our Wood, Gnomes, Dwarves, Sprites of many races, and of course the many animals.

My goal is to compare one race to another simply and completely. Not only do I wish to study the physical differences but also their culture, habits, beliefs, laws, and diet. I also think it very important for me to include in this study the physical and psychological effects the changing environment is having upon them.

There is the encroachment upon their lands by both well-meaning people and Trolls. The polluting of their river and the diminution

of their habitat and food sources by all of us is a serious concern for all of the inhabitants of Horse Thief Bay and the peoples of the Wetlands of the river. Even our Bay has been threatened and that is not yet the end of our problems here. The woodland around us is being cut down. The wetland is being tampered with.

November 7

Hatch and Natterjack came today. Pody was not feeling well. He is of a more frail constitution than Hatch. It is almost the middle of November when all of the Alderlings are keeping warm in their underground lodgings.

I gave Hatch some small pieces of woollen material to cloak himself for the walk home. I asked Hatch what they do when a member of his community becomes ill or is injured. He said they have their herbal remedies, which are in most cases quite sufficient. However, if the illness or injury is more serious, they send for the Suund.

Hatch and Natterjack stayed for two hours. I gained a great deal of information concerning their culture, holidays, and the language of the Alderlings.

Dark clouds began to gather as Hatch spoke. Soon white flakes appeared, turning the dark trees into ghostlike beings stranded in the Wood. Both men soon left. Natterjack tucked Hatch under his coat. I look forward to spring when we can meet more of the Alderlings and Sprites.

In order to simplify and clarify all that I have learned from Hatch, I have decided to use an outline format.

The Alderling: A Race of Elves Living in the Alderwild Wood of Horse Thief Bay.

I. Physical Attributes
1. Average height: 12"
2. Skin color: fair
3. Build: men are small boned, strong biceps and triceps, long fingers and toes, once used when climbing trees
4. Facial features: fine, angular
5. Build: women plump, big bosomed, a good head of hair
6. Hair: light brown and wavy.
7. Nose: men's are pointed; women's are rounded
8. Eyes: Blue predominantly, however sometimes brown occurs meaning the parents have intermarried with a Puncum (Wetland Fairy) whose eyes are brown. Intermarriage is becoming more common.
9. Wings: just nubbies. At one time their ancestors lived in treetops and needed wings to fly from treetop to

treetop. Their long fingers and toes were needed to climb down the trees to collect nuts and berries which had fallen to the ground. Finding enough food and safe places to live and to hide from animals and other wild creatures, a group of these elves never returned to the treetops. The places where they once hid became their dwellings. Since the need for wings no longer existed, over hundreds of years, these appendages have all but disappeared. They have become nubs or nubbies.

II. Clothing
1. Oak and Maple leaves are most often used during the late spring and summer months, sometimes with a shirt made from the threads of the Stinging Nettle plant.
   a. The leaves are made supple with the oil extracted from eels.
2. The skins of eel, carp, and other fish are stretched and softened for use in making clothes and also as a waterproof material on the roofs of their summer homes.
   a. Threads are taken from the Milkweed stalks and woven into material. Its uses are many; clothes, sails, and Tria nets.

III. Jewelry
1. Only a carved wooden toad pendent hangs from the neck. The Toad is a symbol of life and wisdom.
   a. Jewelry is only worn during festivals
2. Hairpieces made from fish bones and certain pieces of wood are used to hold their long hair in a knot in the back or top of their heads.

IV. Diet
1. The Alderling have a large variety of edible plants
   which they obtain almost year round
   a. All of these plants are found in the Alderwild
       Wood, Valley of the Horsetails, Fern Marsh, and in
       the shallow waters of Horse Thief Bay.
2. They also eat Fairy Shrimp, snails, and minnows. Other
   fish include Yellow Perch, Rock Bass, and larger fish
   given to them by the Gnomes or Dwarves. Later in the
   summer, when the water is warmer, they put on swim
   trunks and collect Dragonfly and Damselfly larvae.
   Sometimes they are even able to catch a Johnny Darter.

Plants

Acorns	Shagbark Nuts	Wild Grape Tea
Mandrake fruit	Hickory Nuts	Berry Spikenard
Wild Ginger	Spring Beauty	Elderberry
Beechnuts	Rock Tripe	Plantain Wild
Lettuce Saxifrage	Fiddleheads	Blackberry
Wild Apple	Partridge Berry	Dandelion Dock
Ground nuts	Brake-Bracken	Ground Cherry

Meats and Other Fine Food

White-lipped Land Snail eggs	Pine Sawyer eggs
Grubs	Minnows
Sawfly larvae	Caddis Fly larvae
Damselfly larvae	Worms
Cave Snail eggs	Mushrooms
Slugs and their eggs	Dragonfly larvae
Sow Bugs	Tent Caterpillars
Wood Roach egg packets	Mayfly Larvae
Aphids	

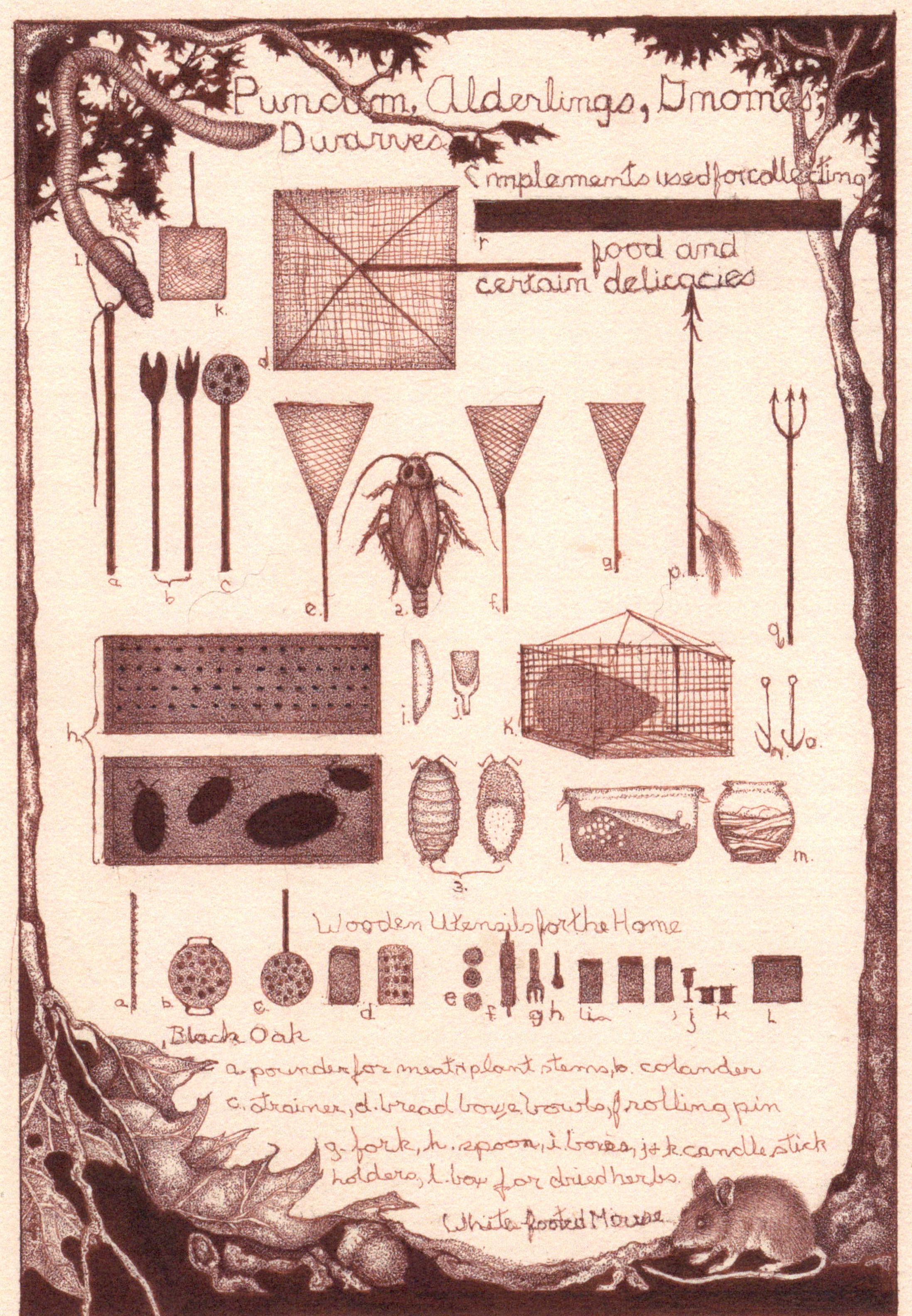

Puncum, Alderlings, Gnomes, Dwarves
Implements used for collecting
food and certain delicacies
Wooden Utensils for the Home
Black Oak
a pounder for meat & plant stems, b. colander
c. strainer, d. bread box & bowls, f. rolling pin
g. fork, h. spoon, i. boxes, j & k candle stick
holders, l. box for dried herbs.
White footed Mouse

V. Hunting and Fishing (see drawing on p. 49)
1. They do not hunt or kill animals
2. They do catch fish
3. They do hunt all of the above insect larvae and slugs
   (See the drawing on p. 49 for hunting & fishing tools)
   a. Noose for catching worms
   b. Tools for digging
   c. Strainer for lifting water plants
   d. Net for catching a group of minnows
   e. Large Tria net for catching fish and crayfish
   f. Medium sized Tria net
   g. Small Tria net for catching Johnny Darters
   h. Box for keeping Sow Bugs alive
   i. Scraper for scaling fish
   j. Scooper
   k. Large net for trapping Crayfish and water
       animals to keep alive
   l. Glass container for raising slugs and slug eggs
       for eating
   m. Glass container with damp bark for raising Sow
       Bugs
   n. Fishing hook
   o. Fishing hook
   p. Spear for fishing
   q. Spear for fishing

VI. Tools
Very few tools are required for catching and collecting
food. The most difficult foods to catch are the Wood
Roach and Earth Worm.
   a. Both move very fast.

    b. A net is needed to catch the Wood Roach.
    c. A slip-noose attached to the end of a short stick is used to catch the Earthworm

1. The worm is slippery, slimy, and wiggles and turns, pulling itself back into its hole. The aim is to quickly slip the noose over its head and around its neck and pull it tight.
2. The roach often carries its egg packet attached to its rear. A net is popped over the roach while another Alderling detaches the packet.
3. Other Tools Used:
    a. Many tools are made from fish and animal bones.

VII. Wooden Utensils for the Home
(See the previous drawing on p. 49 - bottom half)

VIII. Transportation
1. There is little need for transportation as they rarely leave the Alderwild Wood except for fishing in the shallow water of the Bay. They are able to find most of the food to sustain themselves in the Wood.
2. Food not found here, they trade for with other communities and other races living in the Wood and Horse Thief Bay. Occasionally they trade with several communities on Hill Island.
3. They do make litters for carrying the dead, sick, and the aged, as well as very young children.
4. Sledges are made for carrying rocks, twigs, etc.
    a. Neither the litter nor sledge has wheels. They have runners like those of a sleigh, which are curved in the front and back which allows them to glide over tree roots and other irregularities on the ground.

5. They build two types of boats for use on the Alderwild
and the river.
   a. A canoe made from Birch Bark, which is used in
       early spring when the snow melts and the brook is
       full and fast flowing.
   b. A raft constructed from Black Willow branchlets
       is used when the winter run off has ended. The
       brook has become tame and meanders around
       tussocks of Sensitive and Royal Ferns dotted with
       Marsh Marigolds. The raft is also used in the Bay.

IX. Housing and Means of Travel
1. In winter Alderlings live in dwellings approximately
   two feet underground, sometimes deeper.
   a. Their apartments are connected to each other,
       forming a circle. Within the circle is the
       Community Room.
   b. The community room serves as a dining room and
       the Learning room. There are small recesses within
       the room, which serve as a library and there are
       several quiet spaces where the elderly play chess,
       read, and some elderly women like to get together
       and quilt, knit, or crochet and have tea. There is
       also a space within the circle to house several looms
       for those who like the company of others when
       weaving.
   c. There is a lower level just below this floor, which
       has a very large communal room, and is used
       on occasion by all of the inhabitants in times
       of severe cold. (Across is a drawing for the Lower
       Level.)

The Lower Level

During extreme cold spells the Alderling move to the lower level. There are no apartments for individual families. Mattresses for sleeping are laid on the large area of floor.

Ram's Horn snail

The tiled floor is based loosely on design of the snail shell.

Sphagnum moss

Cattail seedhead used as insulation between inner and outer walls.

Lower Level Floor Plan

1. Woodstove
2. Bathtubs
3. Sink
4. Toilets
5. Shelf for Lime
6. Toilets
7. "

8. Bedding, sheets, blankets, pillows
9. Countertop
10. Room for drying Herbs
11. Insulation
12. Faucet
13. Sink
14. Cover
15. Funnel for rain water
16. Cistern
17. Outer tile wall
18. Cold Storage
19. Dividing wall
20. Ice Room
21. Storage - mattresses

d. Just off this room is the larder, where apples, duck
   potatoes, wild grapes, Elder berry juices, wines and
   Mandrake apples are kept cool.

e. A second room is used for drying and storage
   of Dandelion leaves, Dock, Lettuce Saxifrage,
   Hickory and Beechnuts, Cattail roots, Chufa, etc.
   Clay storage jars hold many of these nuts and
   tubers once they have been ground. Dried fish also
   hang from the ceiling.

f. This lower level also contains a cistern, which
   holds the community's water supply. (See next
   page) Rainwater is collected in a funnel shaped
   vessel made from clay, which has been glazed and
   fired twice. It narrows and becomes a tube filled
   with sand and a layer of charcoal. This removes
   the impurities and bacteria in the water. The tube
   extends downward for thirty inches before it
   connects to the cistern. There is a fine mesh screen
   at the bottom of the tube to keep the sand and
   charcoal from entering the cistern.

2. The Apartments:
   A clay wall separates each family dwelling.

   a. The façade of each apartment looks onto the
      Community Room, also known as the Learning
      Room.

   b. The front of each home is constructed using tree
      branches sliced in half and smooth and shaped
      to look like the trees of the Alderwild Wood. No
      two facades are the same. Behind the facade,
      handmade paper is stretched, forming a wall.
      Some of the negative spaces between the upper

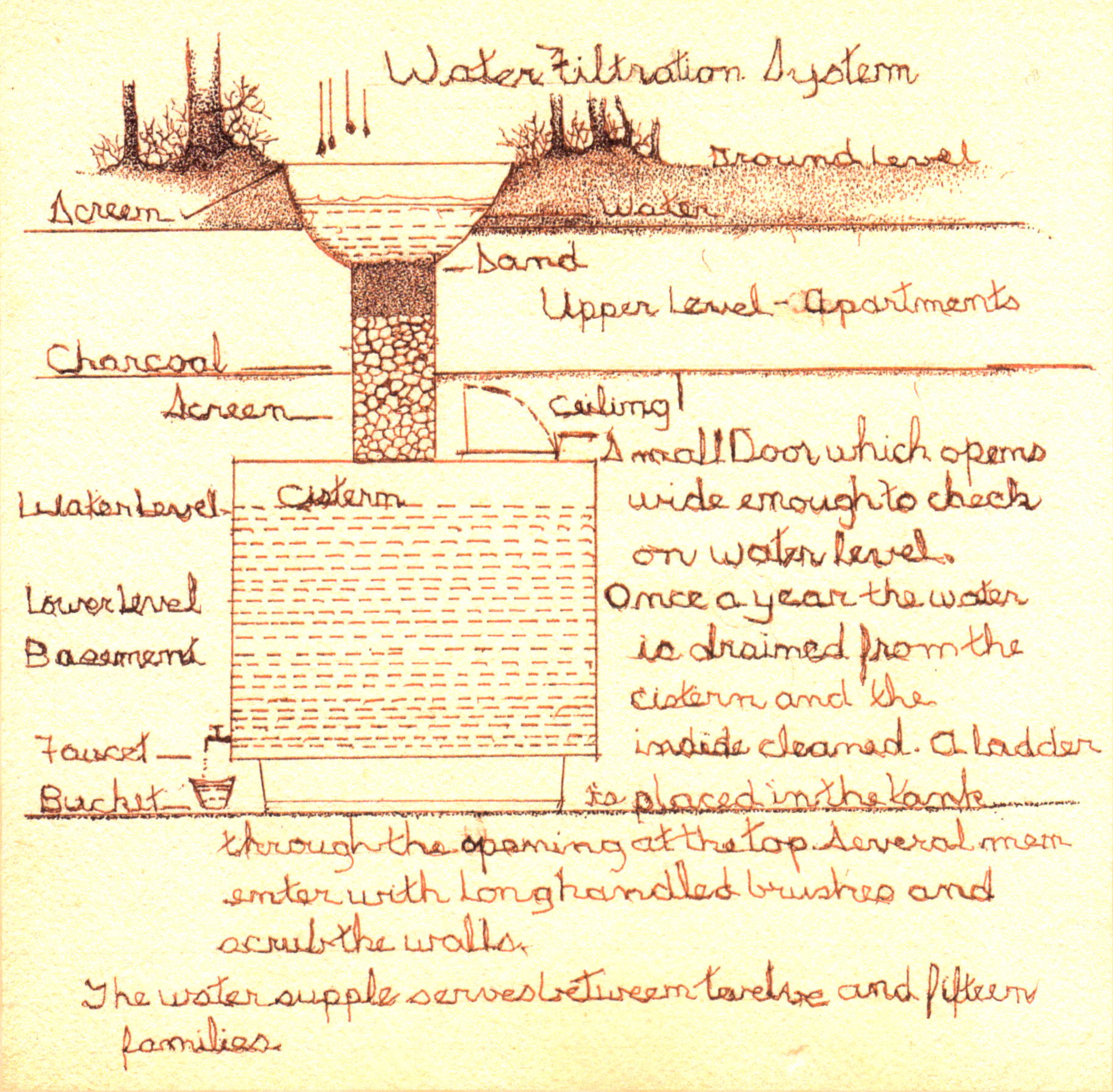

branches are cut out to allow heat and air to circulate throughout the community.

c. The size of each living space varies, depending the size of the family. Exceptions are made for wood carvers, musicians, artists, writers, and poets. Alderlings love the arts and support and encourage the young who are of that mind set. Most of these individuals need privacy and quiet and so are given apartments with studios or music rooms and the like.

The Facades of Six Dwellings

d. Some rooms are designed for singles still looking for partners (2 on the drawing above), a widow or a widower with child (3 and 4 on the drawing), elderly couples; the extended family; grandparents; parents; couples with four to six children (1 and 6), and artists (5).

e. Each dwelling has a wood stove, which backs onto the stove in the next apartment so that the two stoves share one chimney. Wood stoves, along with a series of vents between rooms and dwellings are able to distribute heat evenly throughout the compound.

f. The very young children are called Linglings and play in the Community Room. Older children weave baskets, extract thread from Milkweed and Stinging Nettle stems, and learn the craft of the potter.

   i. The boys learn the craft of canoe and raft making by building miniatures of these boats.

   ii. There is an area of the room for children who are learning to read and write.

g. In the evening, beginning with supper, all members of each family come together as a community. It is truly a room where the intellectual and emotional growth of each and every child develops.

i. Strong family and community bonds are made. Individual achievements are encouraged too. This allows the child to find his or her identity and a means to express him or herself.

ii. Songs and stories of the Ancient Ones are told. It is also explained in stories about the Beginning, When the World Was Young and From Where Did The Alderlings Come.

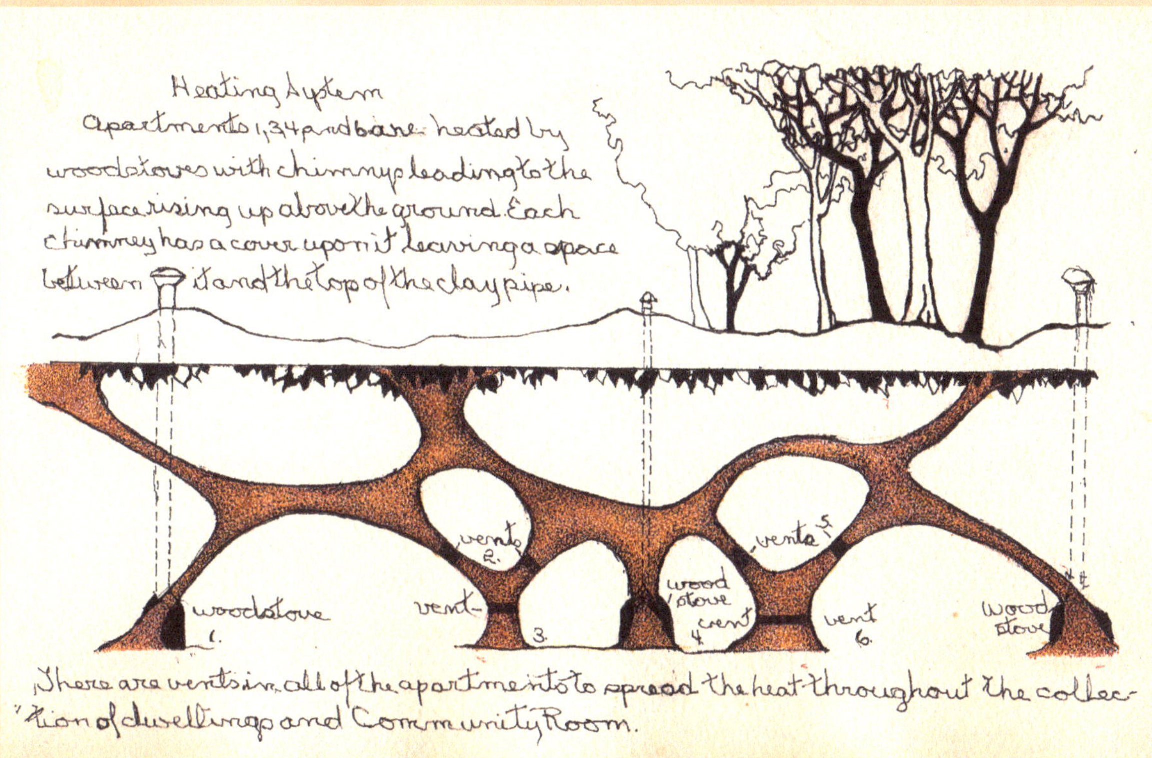

3. Spring - Summer Homes

i. In mid to late April the Alderlings move to their spring- summer homes on the banks of the Alderwild Brook. Some of the young, the more adventurous couples etc. build their homes on stilts among the tussocks of ferns and Marsh Marigolds.

    ii. Those houses built on the banks of the Alderwild Brook are built of clay, wood, grasses, Bracken, and Sensitive Ferns.

    iii. Those built on stilts are not built of such sturdy materials.

X. Festivals and Holidays.

1. They are celebrated by all of the communities of Horse Thief Bay, I shall describe later.

XI. Death

1. When an elder of the Alderling tribe dies the body is laid on a raft of aged cattail stalks tied together. On a separate raft, the paddles he used during his lifetime along with fish, snails, and other edibles are laid to comfort him on his Journey to the Land Beyond the Horizon.

2. The two rafts are then carried in a procession of Alderlings, Gnomes, Dwarves, and other Fairies to the banks of the Alderwild. Lanterns are held high to light the way. The two rafts with their precious cargo are laid on the still water to be gently carried to the Great River and the Land Beyond the Horizon where the Ancients dwell. The Earth will be nourished. The Alderlings will become part of the Great Story. The story will be told and retold and remembered by the children and their children. No one is forgotten.

Death Raft

November 15

The amber twilight of evening ushered in a long, cold night. The days have grown shorter, and the nights are now longer. The enchanting voices of the early night, the Whip-poor-will, the Peepers, the croaking of the Bullfrog, the Great Blue Heron, and the crickets have long ceased. Most of the Herons have flown south, along with the Whip-poor-will. The frogs, peepers, and crickets have gone into hibernation. There is neither moon nor twinkling stars tonight to light the dark.

Early yesterday evening a strong wind began to blow in the Alderwild Wood. Voices were speaking in the leaves. They were accompanied by very unusual and strange sounds. The trees creaked and moaned. Loud rustling of dry leaves came from several directions. There were also heavy thudding sounds against something hard, as an axe to a tree. Then there was wrenching and tearing, and crashing of heavy branches to the ground. We were afraid. Mournful sounds lifted and were carried by the wind through the Wood.

The trees knew what was happening. They knew that one of their kin was being attacked. It was their mournful cries we heard. The animals fell silent and became afraid. All creatures and the Elves felt besieged and stayed hidden. There was nothing they could do. It was very dark. The Trolls were out. There were so many. They were so large and they were very strong. Too many and too strong! The Dwarves, Gnomes, and Alderlings were no match for them. They could perhaps subdue one or two Trolls but not eight or nine. The night seemed never ending. The Trolls held dominion over night, and the Alderwild Wood.

Trolls long ago came out of the day light and into Darkness. The night protects and allows them safe passage through the woods. Night fires their spirits. Night is their master. They may never return to the light of Day again. They stopped caring for the trees, the wildflowers, the water, and the creatures that swim in the river and roam the woods and fields.

Instead they turned their backs on Na and began to lay waste all that was beautiful. They were banished by Nature (Na). They had lost their souls. However, many escaped and still walk the land.

If Trolls are caught entering the light of day, they are turned to stone. For some Trolls their eyes are burned and made blind, never to see again. They are very stooped from the weight of the trees growing on their backs which they planted there as camouflage to hide themselves from the good folks of the Alderwild Wood. However they never took into consideration that saplings will grow and grow into large trees with many roots, some very large ones which wrap around them reaching to the ground holding them as prisoners. I have heard stories about Trolls but never expected to be witness to something like this.

The Morning Star appeared. Dawn would soon follow and shed Her light on any remaining Trolls gloating over their night's destruction. We heard the Trolls screaming as the light struck their feet, and then their legs. They were trapped, rooted to the earth. No amount of twisting and turning freed them. Soon they were completely enveloped by the light. Their bodies were so contorted in the struggle; they remained in that configuration in stone, never to move again.

With the full light of morning all of the Fairies, Gnomes, Dwarves, and animals of the Bay slowly came forth. The women, children, and elderly were asked to remain in their dwellings until all danger had passed.

Ian and I went out to see what had happened. It was terrible. I had all I could do to throttle down my emotions. The big Oak tree by the side of our house had been brutally and savagely attacked. Limbs were hewn and torn off. Other branches were just hanging by slim bands of bark. There were huge gashes in the trunk, mortal and deep. The tree is not expected to live.

A great band of bark had been torn asunder by the Troll's axe and the teeth of a Traug or Norg, fiends related to trolls. The vessels carrying nutrients and water to the buds, leaves, and roots, found in the inner most layer of bark, had been severed. Not even the unguents of the Suund could save this tree. It would die a slow death.

Ian and I felt very guilty. If only we had turned on the outside lights to our house, perhaps the Trolls, Traugs, and other fiends would have turned to stone or fled. They would never hurt or maim any of the inhabitants of Horse Thief Bay.

Natterjack saw us sitting on our doorstep; both of us were in tears. It was a great old tree. It had given shade to the wildflowers, shelter to the birds and squirrels. Under its roots lived a small group of Alderlings, a family of White footed mice, a Star-nosed Mole, and a young couple of Short-tailed Shrew.

I felt queasy and had to lie down for a while. By afternoon, I was somewhat better. I walked to Natterjack and Draka's home near Bern Ridge. I had never been to their home before. Draka came to the door and invited me in. Natterjack too had been resting .The three of us sat down in the kitchen by their wood stove. It was comfortably warm. Draka put some water on for tea. The coziness of their home and the warmth of their personalities was just what I needed.

Ian and I had a difficult time trying to deal with such an outrage to both the land and its inhabitants. The death of the Alderling child and the animals in October was our first encounter with the devastation left by Trolls and their kind. This time, however, we were in the very midst of it all. We heard it happening and we did nothing.

Natterjack and I had been talking for three hours. There was still so much I wanted to learn about these creatures. However, it would have to wait for another day. Emotionally I felt a little better. Although the sky was still quite light, I still had to wicker up my emotions for the short walk home. Natterjack offered to walk with me. I told him that I would be fine.

The Wood, nearly bare of leaf except for the Beech, loomed on either side of me. I thought not only of the Trolls but also of the Norgs and Traugs who wander the Wood in twilight. Shadows danced and grew longer.

November 18

Neither Ian nor I have slept very well these past three nights. Any bit of noise awakens us. We kept thinking the Trolls have returned. We arose at first light. It had been a windless night. I looked out the window and hoped that no more evil had taken place while we were asleep. All sounds put my senses on alert. I hope Natterjack will come today.

Natterjack came by at 1:00 P.M. He brought with him some very old looking papers, a book, its pages crumbling at the edges, and an ancient scroll wrapped in soft leather. He was prepared to talk about the Trolls. The papers contained two stories about Trolls going back six to eight hundred years in time.

Ian stopped his work and pulled a chair up to the table. I reached for a couple of lined notepads. I wanted to write down as much as I could, word for word, as he translated the stories from the ancient languages of the Gnomes and Dwarves who first dwelled here.

Trolls

There are three main groups of Trolls from whom all other Trolls are descended. These are the Troloxica, Atrolpia, and the Trolconitum.

Troloxica:

Troloxica, which means Troll with poisonous skin, are the worst of the Trolls. These Trolls become poisonous from ingesting Poison Ivy. Everyone Fairy, Gnome, or Dwarf, is strongly affected by close contact with this race of Trolls. One may develop inflammation of the skin, ruptured sores, and terrible itching. If the poison spreads to the eyes, it may cause temporary blindness, or for some Elves, the loss of sight has been permanent. Also one can become infected just by brushing up against a blade of grass or dead leaf which the Troll may have laid upon or stepped on.

The Troloxica live in packs of five or six, sometimes gathering in larger groups. They are deceitful, malicious beings, bad tempered, of low intelligence, and having no skills except those of destruction. They are dirty and foul smelling, having never washed. Their skin looks hideous, having many open draining sores. They are oblivious to the fact that they were at one time human. They do not hide their appearance.

The eyes of many Troloxica still retain some of the blue color from their childhood and teens. Their skin is rough and leathery. Their teeth are sharp. Drool hangs from their mouths and mucus drips from their noses. Their bodies have become more hairy as they became more trollish. They have lost touch with humanity.

They have not yet become serious predators but prefer carrion: dead animals, rodents, birds, and road kill.

Carrion has a stronger flavour. For a quick snack, they eat Earthworms and grubs. If for some reason, carrion is not available and they have been without food for some time, they will kill Elves and, in rare instances, Gnomes or Dwarves.

On one such occasion, in the year 830 A.D., February 13, a Friday, a Dwarf walking in the snow covered woods of Dark Point was killed and eaten by a group of five Troloxica.

This information was found in the book Natterjack brought, "The History of Horse Thief Bay," written in 958 A.D. by a Dwarf named Amselgrund Dampfboot. He was the Community Historian at the time. The winter of 830 A.D. happened to be a very hard one. It had begun snowing early in November, just a little each day, occasionally snowing heavily the entire day. There had been no January Thaw. Gnomes And Dwarves had to dig tunnels leading from one dwelling to another. The temperature for many days remained at minus 26 degrees F.

The Dwarves still had a good store of food. However, they were at the end of their supply of wood. It was necessary for a few of them to climb up to the surface of the snow. It had an icy crust, hard enough to hold the weight of the Dwarves. They could walk on top of the snow without falling into it deeply. The snow would be over their heads if they did. It was nearly eight feet deep. The Dwarves' average height was only four feet high.

Numerous dead branches lay on top of the snow. Wind and ice had caused them to break and fall. The Dwarves began collecting the wood and had already gathered a large quantity of branches and had piled them near their snow tunnel. Just as they were about to return to the hole, one of the Dwarves had lost his balance and fell, sliding down the hill to its foot.

As he tried to stand up, he broke through the icy surface, sinking into the snow up to his chin. It was late afternoon. The sun was retreating behind the trees. It was twenty minutes before the Dwarves returned from the hole with some rope. They tried over and over again to throw the rope far enough for the buried Dwarf to reach. There was much calling back and forth between the Dwarves. Their loud voices aroused five sleeping Troloxica, who were famished and hadn't eaten in five days.

The Dwarf was caught, stuck in the snow and was killed and dragged away. There was nothing the other two Dwarves could do to help. They looked on with revulsion. All they could do was to save themselves.

A stone was inscribed with ancient writing. It was placed on the site where the Dwarf was killed. It still stands today, covered with moss. Natterjack once showed it to me but I had never learned the story behind it.

The Troloxica now live in rock caves just west of High Pines Point. They have destroyed many of the trees and wildflowers, which once graced that small paradise. During the summer and early autumn, they remain in that area. However, during the winter, when food becomes scarce, and there are no road kills, they become nomadic.

It was the Troloxica who entered the Alderwild Wood on the night of November 15 and killed the Great Oak.

I still have hopes that, in time, the old Oak Tree will still show some signs of life and the Suund, with Her powers of healing, can save the tree.

The moon looks cold as it rides across the sky. The inhabitants of the Alderwild Wood say that a tortoise named Anwa carries the Moon on his back each night. They say that Anwa is one of the Ancients. He is as old as time. The Moon is very heavy and can roll off his back. Thus he wears a saddle like harness to hold the moon in place and that is why he moves so slowly.

Most everything I now see is through the eyes of Hatch and Natterjack. I use the Alderling names, which they had given Earth Er and Nature, Na. These names have given me a greater intimacy with Nature.

When I walk through the Alderwild Wood, I am truly not alone. The Wood is an on-going spiritual experience. I find peace with myself, and harmony with Nature.

Although Nature is always changing from hour to hour, day to day, month to month, and season to season, She is still a constant. Every day has its morning and afternoon, its darkness and its light; and its dawn and its evening. No matter how much each hour changes from the one before, there will always be the next hour and then there is tomorrow. There is a basic structure, which holds all life together. Words cannot truly describe what is seen by the eye and felt by the soul. It is different for each person.

A New Addition to the Alderwild Wood

A group of Canada Geese looks as if they decided to spend the winter in our Bay. They did not fly south to the Gulf of Mexico with the others in October. They are sitting on the ice, which now extends about ten feet past the island.

We have another addition to the inhabitants of Horse Thief Bay. Since early October, we have had wild Turkeys walking through our Wood. They come every day, sometimes twice. At first there were only five. It remained that number for several weeks. One became so brave it hopped onto our porch and pressed its beak against the window. When Floristane moved, it was not frightened. It remained for some time. We had been feeding them cracked corn for several weeks when they were joined by ten more. Most days all of them come, sometimes just the original five. Ian has also taken cracked corn to the Canada Geese near the water.

Tomorrow is Novaricum, an important holiday for the Alderlings, Gnomes, and Dwarves.

Novaricum: A Time of Reflection and Meditation, Joy, and Thankfulness.

Novaricum is in some ways similar to our Thanksgiving. However, it is taken more seriously. All of the families living in the Alderwild Wood who are not in hibernation gather together in the Great Hall. A community breakfast is held. After all have eaten all they can to fill their appetites to capacity, even their big toes, both Gnome and Dwarf males split up into groups of two and three. Strapped to their backs are knapsacks filled with foods of all kinds: smoked fish, wine, drinking water, flour, dried fruits, and vegetables.

Carried in a hand held case is a small saw, hammer, and nails; twine and rope, and a sealant for leaks of one sort or another. Well loaded, the teams head for each and every settlement in the Bay. One team even climbs to the top of High Pines Point. There are a few humans living there as well as a small community of Elves and Gnomes.

The Dwarves, Fraxim, Perch, and Azulla headed for the stand of cattails at the foot of Dark Point. The Puncum and Water Sprites live there.

By early September Puncum families have moved to their winter quarters near the rear of the stand of cattails where it borders Fern Marsh. Here they have built one or two large lodges to house the entire population of thirty to forty individuals. It is much easier to insulate the lodges and keep them heated with clay stoves they have built.

The walls and floors are covered with carpets woven by the Alderlings. The roofs are first covered with a layer of cattail stalks, and then Oak leaves for weather proofing and then finally thick moss.

This will most likely be the Dwarves final visit until spring unless an emergency arises, illness occurs, or an injury happens to someone.

They leave the Puncum with extra pillows and comforters made by the Alderling. Food, drinking water, Elderberry wine, and some baked goods are left with anything else they may need. The Puncum sleep a great deal during the winter. They do not actually hibernate. Their metabolism slows. They do have periods of wakefulness when they have need for food.

The Dwarves next check on the dwellings of the pregnant Water Sprites. They are now encased and sleeping in the cattail seed heads with one or two daughters born last March to help in the delivery of the babies. Each seed head houses one mother.

The father, after sealing the mother in with silken threads, leaves with his sons to live in a compound in the rear of the stand of Cattails, where it borders Fern Marsh. There are two lodges which hold the elderly, the in-firmed, the children, and all of the male Water Sprites.

The job for the Dwarves is to make sure the thread holding the seed head is tight. If the casing looks weak, Azulla or Fraxim will use twine to reinforce it. Each and every head is checked. The work is difficult. They could slip and fall through the ice.

The Alderling community is quite well prepared for winter. Because of its design and layout, all dwellings are interconnected, radiating from a hub, which is the Community Room.

The elderly and infirm are easily looked after in this type of setting. They are very much a part of the family fold. Children consider them all as grandparents and treat them with great affection.

The Gnome and Dwarf families live in their own separate dwellings. They are not connected to any central hub. Their dwellings are like row houses. Paths and bridges connect the homes on the outside. Since Gnomes and Dwarves often live far beyond their hundredth birthdays, the elders are given special attention. They are not as mobile as they once were, especially in winter.

Unlike the Alderling elders who enjoy and relish community living and are very social, Gnome and Dwarf elders like their independence; and they enjoy and treasure their own space.

One elderly Gnome gentleman is working on the History of Horse Thief Bay. Another is a violin and cello maker and also likes composing music in his spare time. There are two husband and wife teams, one Gnome, the other a Dwarf, researching the genealogy of the two races. In the spring and summer they get together and compare notes.

Those young adult males who are still in their twenties in both Gnome and Dwarf communities are given the responsibilities to check on these families and several very reclusive bachelors once a day. They see to it that they have food and firewood. The bottles in their wine cellars are turned. The fresh water cistern in each cellar is checked for leaks. They change the charcoal in the drinking water filters. Any extra needs of the elders are tended to at the same time.

Although the elders and infirm are looked after every day during the year, they are still given extra supplies of food, water, and firewood during Novaricum.

Occasionally, during the winter, there will be several days of heavy snow, which prevents the residents of the Alderwild Wood from leaving their dwellings. It is of the utmost importance that the elderly, infirm, and sick have an extra amount of everything, such as food, wine, water, and wood, for their comfort and survival.

Even the cord to the bell system is checked. This is to make sure the cord leading from one elder's dwelling to the neighbour's adjoining apartment is not frayed but is still strong. All the elder has to do if help is needed is to pull the cord. The cord has been threaded through a small hole in the abutting wall. After all work is done, the families of both communities get together again and partake in a feast held in the Great Hall.

The Great Hall

In the middle of the Alderwild Wood is a flat area. There are no large trees growing on it, only saplings, just a few in number. The larger trees grow along its outermost edge. It is shaded, dry, and with only a few major roots traversing it.

The Gnomes and Dwarves have excavated a large underground room in this area. They call it the Great Hall. Weddings, Socials, games, and holiday festivities are held here during the cold months or when the weather is inclement.

Underground tunnels are gradually being dug to join the hall to both the Gnome and Dwarf communities. The tunnels, when they are completed, will be very long and need considerable bracing to prevent the ceiling and walls from collapsing. There are also many trees and boulders to skirt. In time it will be done.

At present a tunnel connecting the Alderling settlements to the Great Hall is the only one completed. Their winter settlement is not far from the Hall. The tunnel was just finished two months ago.

The tunnel has given the Alderlings access to the Gnome and Dwarf families during the autumn and winter

months. Up until this time they were cut off from all the
other inhabitants of the Alderwild Wood. The Alderlings
being only twelve inches high, and their dwellings not
much higher, made it impossible for Gnomes and Dwarves
to visit them.

The Hall is one of great beauty. It has a vaulted ceiling
and walls covered with a plaster-like substance between
areas of wood panelling. The floor is made of oak. Some
of the walls have woven tapestries of Gnome and Dwarf
folklore. They depict life in the old world, Northern Europe,
where their ancestors once lived. There are also old tapestries
woven by the first settlers in Horse Thief Bay. Others are
more recent from the 1800's, showing scenes of steamboats
owned by some of the summer residents taking a cruise on
a sunny afternoon. There is even a tapestry with a scene
showing the stolen horses being brought to the rivers edge
in Horse Thief Bay where
they swam across the
river, first to Hill Island,
then Wellesley Island,
and then to the U.S.
mainland. For a long time
there was quite a trade
going on in stolen horses.

Today, tables twelve
feet long with wooden
chairs and benches were
set along both sides of
the tables in the main
hall. Then plates, glasses, and utensils for sixty people
were arranged on the tables. The families seated themselves

before bowls of boiled Duck Potatoes, Dandelion greens, and platters of roast wild Turkey, Ruff Grouse, and broiled Great Northern Pike were brought out.

Ian and I were delighted to be invited to the feast. However, we were a bit concerned about how Ian was to enter the hall. The door was only four and a half feet high. He had to crawl on hands and knees. Once inside he was able to stand up since the ceiling of the Great Hall was high. He was faced with yet another problem, the tables being very low and the chairs small. He was given a wider bench to sit on and he ate with his plate on his lap. I had no problem with them because everything was just right for me.

We thoroughly enjoyed ourselves. We had never eaten wild turkey or grouse before. The taste was stronger than farm raised turkeys, but it was delicious. It was served with gravy; its ingredients were secret. I hope someday to obtain the recipe. Elderberries were served with it instead of cranberry sauce, and Elderberry wine. For those wishing a white wine with their meal the Dwarves had made a very nice not-too-dry Dandelion wine. The children drank Elderberry juice. The dessert was baked apple, garnished with candied Wild Ginger and Ginger syrup.

When the meal was over and the dishes cleared, the tables were folded and placed against one wall. The chairs were then arranged to form a semi-circle. Some folks brought cushions and sat on the floor, as did Ian.

Stories were told, interspersed with some light music. The stories were of a reflective nature but light hearted. For the most part, they described incidents, which happened during the summer while swimming and boating took place, the big fish that got away, the boat that leaked and sunk with two men in it, and their rescue from the leaky boat.

There were poems eulogizing the sun, the rain, and the bounteous gathering of mushrooms, rose hips, seeds, and the catching of many fish. There were even songs about the Spring Peepers and Bullfrogs. The adults and children joined in the singing. One young Gnome named Acura played a sonata for the cello written by the resident composer, violin, and cello maker. His name was Mustafa.

Fraxim and Nitella's son and daughter, Bursa, and Capsella sang a duet. It was all so beautiful. Natterjack gave thanks for all of the wonderful food and the good health the community was enjoying. His stories and music were still flowing when we left the hall at 9:00 P.M.

November 28

Ian and I did not take time out to celebrate our Thanksgiving, feeling that we had just joined in the festival of Novaricum, which is similar to our holiday. We feel so very thankful for our good fortune in living in the Alderwild Wood. All of the many inhabitants of the Wood have been wonderful neighbours and fine friends. Each have their own unique personality and we have become very fond of all of them.

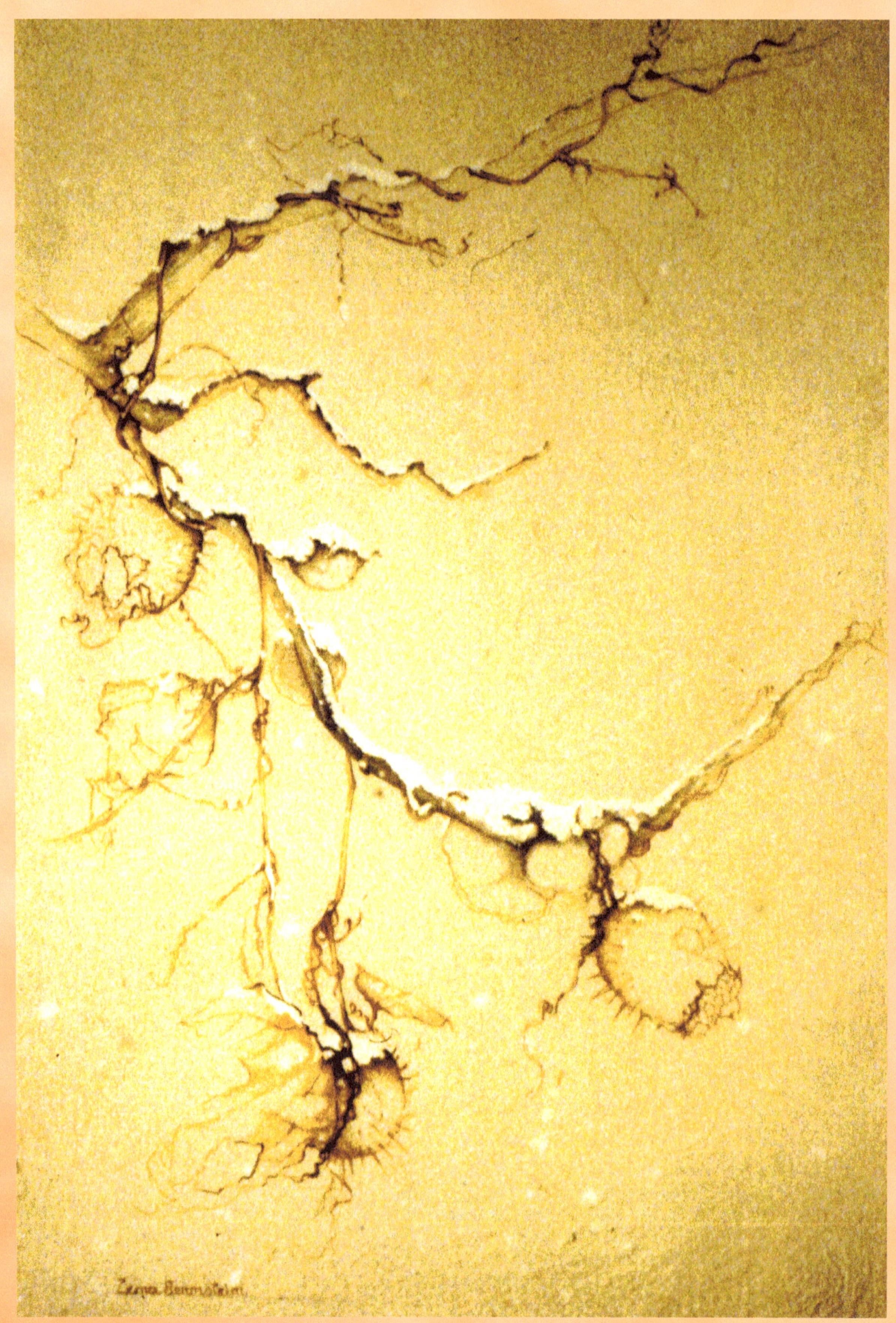
Zeeva Bernstein

The Time of Cold Winds,
Rain, and Snow

December 1

December's cold breath is biting and penetrates to the bone. The Beech leaves still keep their grip on their branches. Oak leaves dance in the air. Snow has lightly shrouded the Wood and all is temporarily silent. The white raiment exquisitely traces each branch and twig.

December 5

The weatherman has predicted snow for late tonight and tomorrow. That sounds great. I do love it when it snows. I become like a child. I run to the window with ooh's and ah's. When the snow is thick and blowing and I can barely see the trees, I am ecstatic and can barely contain myself. I look forward to tonight.

Snow is gentle and quietly floats as it falls to earth. Each flake is a perfect crystal.

December 6

Yes, it did snow last night, and it is still snowing. It has snowed all day, at times a near white out. The Hemlocks on the far side of Fern Marsh, about midway up High Pines Point are scarcely visible. The composition is one of varying shades of grey verticals; each one is a different thickness. My heart feels light, effervescent, my head too, no pain today.

All is still under the deepening coverlet of snow. The Leopard Frog and the Common Toad, so active in the spring and summer, lie buried deep in the frozen soil. All life lying beneath this snow blanket is held suspended.

It is quite some time since we last saw Hatch and Pody and longer still before we shall see them again in the spring. We did see them briefly at the Novaricum festivities.

December 8

What joy! Totally unexpected! Natterjack stopped by with an Alderling child's Primer, which Hatch had given him just before the snowstorm. He came prepared to stay and explain the language to me.

The spoken language of the Alderling has some similarities to our own. Most of the time, they use just the endings of our words. For example; ock=rock, mander=salamander. Sometimes this rule is broken and the beginning syllable is used as in Wa= water. I was curious as to how and from whom the Alderlings saw our language, which they most certainly have had to. Their alphabet also has twenty-six letters. However, the letters look very different, and only a few of these letters of the Alderling alphabet closely resemble ours.

The Twenty- six Letter Alderling Alphabet
The St. Lawrence River

The following exercise is taken from the Alderling child's primer. I shall write it first in English.

"The river is long and wide. There are many islands in the river. Some islands are just rocks while other islands have many trees on them. The birds sit in the trees. Deer, Muskrats, chipmunks, squirrels, and raccoons along with some people live on the islands. Gnomes and Dwarves also inhabit a few of them. Fairies, Elves, Nymphs, and Sprites live on all of the islands. Trolls and other evil beings are becoming more common on all of the islands of the river."

ABCDEFGHIJKLMN
OPQRSTUVWXYZ

B= Beetle =
D= Hill =
F= Fish =
G= Great Rams Horn Snail = G
H= Cattails with frond =
I= Dimple Cattail =
J= the Path for a journey
M= Mouse =
N= Nut Hickery =
T= Singe =
W= Wave =
Y= Water Witching Wand = Y
P= Pear =
Q= Clam =
R= River
S= Stream =
U= Acorn =
V= Valley =
X= Two sticks Crossed =
Z= Lightning =

Translation: Uh Wrence Ver

Uh ver s ong d ide. Ere re any ands nn uh ver. Ome fun ands re ust ocks, ile erz ands ave any reez on en. Uh birds it nn uh reez er, krats, munks, irrels, coons, ong it ome eple ive on uh ands. Omz d Warves so abit a ew fen. Airez, Vez, ive on lf uh ands fuh ver.

The Alderlings use only uppercase letters when using their own letters and language. The following is the story as The Alderling would write it.

The Alderling seem to interchange the plural "s" with a "z". I do not understand why this is done. I do find their writing very pleasing to the eye. Their paper is handmade by the Puncum. It is a work of art in itself.

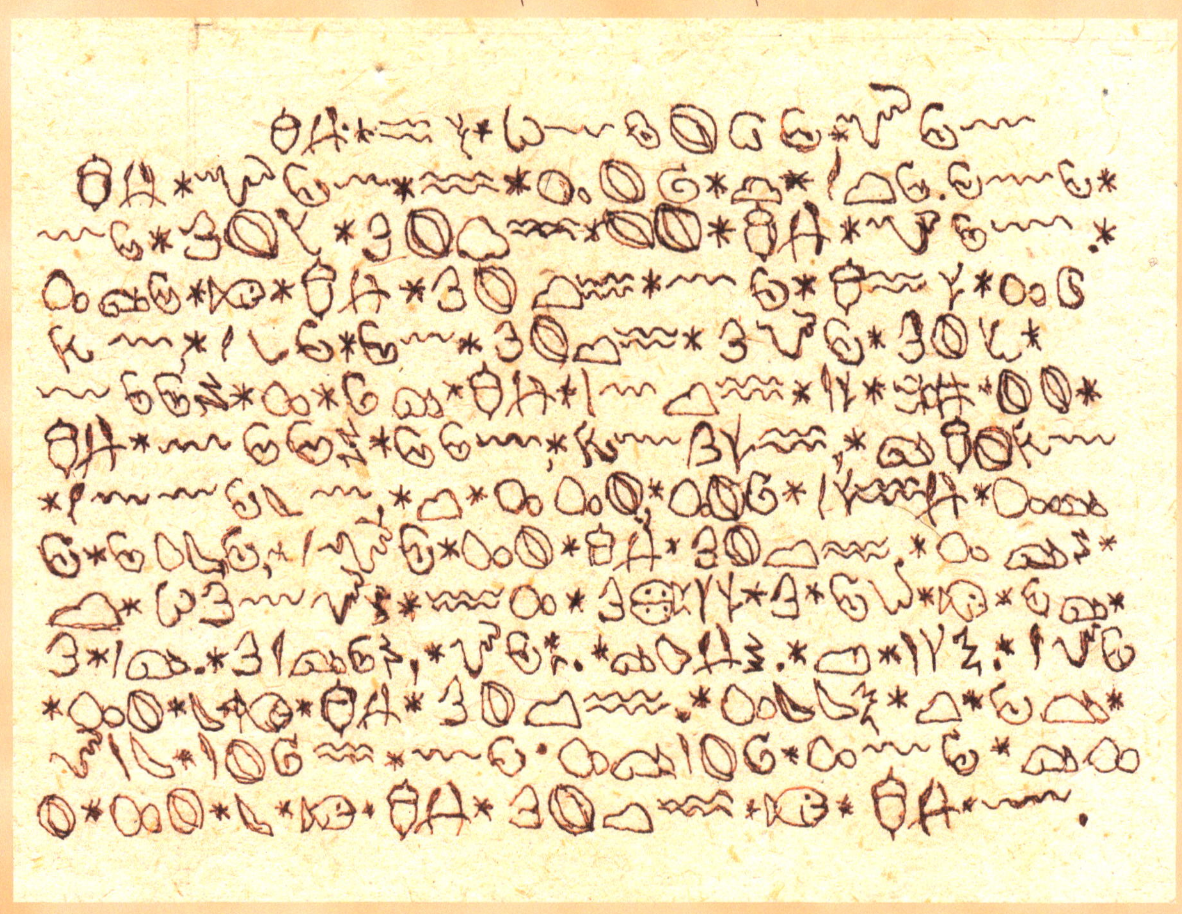

December 12

This evening has been serene and still, clear, and cloudless. The stars are like burning coals flickering in the vast darkness of the universe. Sometimes I feel so much a part of this all encompassing blackness, studded with its thousands and thousands of twinkling points of light. I like to stand on our porch and marvel at its wondrous beauty. Then there are those times when I feel so much alone and afraid that I shall be swallowed by the dark, and so wish then to sit by the wood stove reading and writing up my notes.

I have been studying the Alderling child's primer. The story reminds me of my early Latin lessons which I had to translate. I am really getting the hang of it. I have decided to translate some of the stories from a few of my own children's books into the Alderling language. It has been fun.

December 14

Ian came in this morning with a vacated hornet's nest. He found it on the outskirts of our Wood. It is in perfect condition, grey with streaks of white throughout. All of its occupants died with the first frost.

At summer's end the male hornet fertilizes the Queen before she leaves the nest to take up residence in a rotted tree or log. Sometimes, she will find a protective niche under decaying leaves and twigs. The male dies. In late spring or early summer she will start a new colony and a new nest will be built.

Christmas will soon be here and Hanukah too. We have been so busy we have hardly had a moment to stop and think of anything else besides our work

December 18

Roger came today and helped Ian get our Christmas tree set into the tree stand and erected. It is a lovely tree, a spruce that has been allowed to grow wild. The branches have not been pruned every year. It looks very natural, an old fashioned tree about ten and a half feet high.

Ian and I spent the day decorating the tree. Each ornament hung on a branch brings to mind how my mother and I, and now how Ian and I acquired it, from whom or from where, the name, the store, the town or city, and when. Each ornament has its own story. Some balls date back a hundred years and more. They have been passed from one generation to the next generation. My grandmother passed it onto my mother, then to me. The tree with its decorations and toys and books underneath it tells a family story.

Under the tree is Teddy Stumpf; my mother's Teddy bear from 1908. There is the autograph book, which was my Uncle John's from the 1890's. A toy sled my Uncle George made for my mother in 1914. There are also toys and books from my childhood. Such memories, such fun! I like to share them with our friends. We did not finish trimming the tree and house until midnight.

Come to our Christmas Party

When: Dec. 24th
at 7:00 P.M.
For: Dessert
Where: Ian & Zena's
Bring your families.

December 19

We slept late this morning. We ate breakfast, and then put the empty boxes and papers away and Ian vacuumed the floor. The tree looked wonderful. We sat for a while, admiring it and looked through some of my old children's books.

December 20

It snowed last night - another six inches. The green boughs of the Hemlock were laden with a mantle of white. Ian and I have decided to host a Christmas party and so spent the rest of the day writing out invitations, and Ian delivered them. It will be held on the evening of December 24th at 7:00 P.M. for dessert.

Invitation List

Dwarves	Gnomes
Natterjack + wife, Draka	Lich and wife, Petra
Son - Azulla	Son - Caddis
Son - Bracken + Cymbella	Son - Salus
Bursa + wife, Capsella	Newt + wife, Osmunda
Daughter - Nitella	Larix + wife, Coloma
Son - Fraxim	Daughter - Acura
Thapsa + wife, Berga	Son - Sala
Daughter - Celesta	Silvas
Daughter - Onoclea	
Son - Perch	and to all the fairies not confined to their homes

I spoke to Natterjack to see if there was any possible way to bring some of the Alderlings. He will see what he can do. By 5:00 P.M. Ian had delivered all of the invitations, and all have accepted. We will bake cookies tomorrow and the next two days and lastly, noodle pudding on the morning of December 23rd.

December 21

Ian and I arose early. We had a long day of baking ahead of us. We ate quickly. We got the card tables out, pulled out our rolling pin, measuring spoons and cups, food processor, bowls, butter, eggs, sugar, flour, spices, citron, walnuts, almonds, chocolate, and cherries.

The dough for the Butter Cookies, Lebchuken, and Springerly has to be prepared the day before and refrigerated overnight, which we did. We made double the amount of dough for all three kinds. Chocolate Chip and Walnut, Pecan Sandies with cherries, Shortbread, and Strawberry Fakes were made today. It is now 1:30 A.M. and time to go to sleep.

December 22

We baked fourteen batches of cookies and two batches of Strawberry Fakes. We finished cleaning up this afternoon. Fortunately, the house has been cleaned and everything is in order. We are ready for our guests.

December 23

Most of the morning was spent making the Fruited Noodle Pudding. We then wrapped our presents for each other and placed them under the tree.

It was cold outside but the sun was out and the sky was very blue. We decided to dress warmly. Ian pulled out a couple of chairs, and we sat on the porch. The Blue Jays were calling and the Black-Capped Chickadees and the White-

Breasted Nuthatches were chattering. There were several Goldfinches and Purple Finches at the thistle feeder too.

The river is not altogether frozen across to Hill Island. The last few nights have been very cold. The bright afternoon sun melted the snow just a little but enough to give the surface a coating of ice. It glistens in the sunlight.

December 25

Our party was a success. Everyone seemed to enjoy themselves. Natterjack and Draka introduced us to several Gnomes and Dwarves whom we had not yet met.

We had asked Natterjack to invite everyone in both communities to come. I do not think anyone stayed behind. There were many handshakes.

When Natterjack and Bracken arrived, they were carrying a large rectangular basket between them. It was three feet long by two feet wide, by two feet high. It was made from grape vines and saplings. It seemed to be lined with a soft material. It was brought into the kitchen. When

the cover was lifted, out climbed twenty-two Alderlings, Hatch and Pody included, and a small number of Wood Sprites, those who were still awake. Ian and I were amazed to say the least. A full house!

Some folks brought musical instruments. They played them and sang songs. Early on in the party, the music and songs were soft, slow, and lilting. However, by late night, feet were stamping, hands were clapping, and couples dancing.

Some of the guests brought homemade Elderberry wine. It was excellent. I think it was the wine, which added to the high spirits. Stories were told about amusing events in their lives. Everyone enjoyed the noodle pudding and our tree. Some of the folks were reminded of the ornaments, which had been on their Christmas tree when they were young or were on their grandparent's tree.

When Gnomes migrated to North America, they brought the tradition of decorating an evergreen tree with them. It was not done in celebration of Christmas but to welcome winter and the snow it brought.

The white mantle of snow covered the land and gave the plants and animals protection from the drying cold winds and freezing temperatures.

The snow, as it melts, fills the rivers, lakes, and streams with water. It brings moisture to the soil for the plants and trees so they may grow.

Some people, when they tired of dancing, sat down on the floor by the tree and played with some of the toys and read some of the books. They became children again.

It was quite an experience to see people, very small ones, sitting on top of the English clock, the desk, on the back of the couch, under the tree, riding stuffed dogs, and sitting in the arms of the bears. Some Fairies were sitting on some of the stronger branches of the Christmas tree. Some Alderlings had wrapped themselves with tinsel. Others sat looking at their reflections in the balls. No ornaments were broken; they took extra care not to.

I heard someone call my name. It sounded far away. It was Pody, standing on the top of the tree, holding onto the top ornament. He waved!

As each of our guests left, we handed them a package of cookies as presents. We had also baked very small cookies for Natterjack to give to the Alderlings; those who were able to come to the party and those who were not. We made up new packages of cookies for the extra gnomes and dwarves we did not know were coming. The party was over by 11:30 P.M.

December 26

The next day, the tree looked beautiful. It sparkled with its many coloured lights, reflectors, and ornaments. After supper we sat and listened to some Christmas carols and ate some of our cookies with a small glass of wine. We turned off the lights in the room except for those on the tree and clicked the outside lights on to watch the snow falling.

December 27

Another sunny day! We watched a Bald Eagle family standing on the ice about twenty feet from the Island. They were picking and tearing at something very large. We could not tell whether it was a fish or animal. The large male Eagle tried to fly off with it, but it was too heavy. The female and three immature Eagles looked on. We had never seen Bald Eagles before. It was awe inspiring, such strength and majesty.

December 28

As I looked out the window this morning, a Red Fox was crossing the ice between the Island and High Pines Point. He had spotted the remains of the carcass left by the eagles.

December 31

New Year's Eve, It has been a good year. I have Ian's friendship, companionship, and his love. My life is richer and better for it.

We have met many fine folk here who are good and sincere. They and their ancestor's stewardship of Na's trees, the Alderwild Wood, the Valley of Horsetails, Fern Marsh, and the Alderwild Brook has been one of caring, protecting, and great concern. They have done well. Ian and I hope to continue to be good caretakers.

January 5

Snowdrifts of soft curves, lights, and shadows cover our world. The trees of the Alderwild Wood are caught in a river of white waves. A mantle of grey clouds hangs upon us as the snow continues to fall. The crystalline flakes are small and gentle in spirit as they lay one upon another in slumber on the ground. No sun today, nor moon tonight. All things, plants and animals, are wrapped in Na's white protective shroud, like a comforter on one's bed. Na appears dormant and quiescent.

January 8

The Alderlings and Puncum, like all other Elves, Fairies, and animals of Horse Thief Bay and the Thousand Islands are aboriginals. They have been here since the beginning of time. They are indigenous to this land. Over thousands of years the Alderlings, Puncum, and others have developed their own culture, one that is more closely tied and in sync with Na than ours.

Festival of Geladas

We have been invited to the Alderling Festival of Geladas. It means the Time of the White Cover and Grey Trees. The other inhabitants of the Bay now observe this holiday too. It will be held in the Great Hall tomorrow.

The Time of the White Cover and Grey Trees is the season of the year when the Earth becomes frozen, and the air is keen. The water of the Great River, St. Lawrence and Horse Thief Bay becomes hard. The time when the snow falls fast and the wind howls in the Wood. Only the Alderwild Brook and Willow have open trick-lets of water. The snow is welcomed for it protects the inhabitants of the Wood and Wetland from the freezing winds of Wi (winter). The snow brings water to the river, the Alderwild Brook, and Willow. The seedlings and mature plants of Spri (spring) will begin to grow again when the great luminary of Er (Earth) rides westward and higher across the sky on the toad's back, and the days grow longer. The snow melts.

January 9

We went to the Great Hall today to partake in the festival. Ian had a bit of a problem entering the hall this time. Ian is slender but somehow his rear got stuck in the doorway. He was most embarrassed. Natterjack, Bracken, and Azulla tried to push him forward but no luck. Then we realized the problem was Ian's backside. It was too high even though he was on his hands and knees.

Natterjack climbed up onto his back. Bracken and Azulla each took a leg. When Natterjack jumped onto Ian's rear, the other two pulled on his legs. He was suddenly flat

on his stomach and was able to crawl in.

The Great Hall was decorated with all sizes of snowflakes cut from white paper by the children. They were hung from the ceiling at different levels.

Soon after we arrived, the play began. The Lingling's, as the Alderlings called their little ones, had been dressed to look like snowflakes. They entered the stage very slowly. Then an older Alderling child appeared as the Sun. Soon there were numerous other children, all sizes, dressed to look like trees.

The Snowflake children danced, weaving rhythmically in and out between the trees. As the tempo quickened, more children entered as smaller snowflakes. The dance became a frenzy of snowflakes. Suddenly, all of the flakes collapsed onto the floor.

A child dressed in green entered. She was dressed like a seedling. She crouched down, her movements were slow. Her arms were covered with green material to look like young leaves. First one arm was extended as she slowly straightened her body. Then the second arm unfurled and she removed the green mantle covering her hair. A yellow flower appeared, a Dandelion, one of the first flowers of Spring, Spri. The dance ended. The play was very well done. Wonderful! Everyone in the hall stood up and clapped.

This was the first time the Alderlings, Gnomes, and Dwarves held the festival together in the Great Hall.

Soon the long wooden folding tables were taken from their places against the wall and set up in rows. Ian and I sat down in the company of Natterjack, Draka, Bracken, and family. I had wanted to sit near the Alderlings and get to know them better. However, when I saw what they were about to eat, I changed my mind.

Their first course:
Marinated Slug Eggs.

Second course:
Toasted Sow Bugs with Beechnut Muffins, Boiled
Shagbark Hickory nuts with preserved Fiddleheads, served
with Roasted Snake and Worm in a Mushroom Sauce.

Third Course:
Dessert: Baked Wild Apple with Candied Ginger and Syrup

Drinks:
adults: Elderberry Wine
Children – Lemony Tasting Sumac Tea

We thoroughly enjoyed ourselves and met many more
people. Ian got into a conversation with Fraxim, another
artist. He is a weaver of tapestries depicting Dwarf lore. Ian
invited him to come to our home to see his masks. Fraxin
then asked Ian to come to his parents' home, # 4 Overlook
Lane, Mac Mountains.

January 10

As I looked out my studio window a squirrel of mixed
parentage was at our bird feeder. It was absolutely gorgeous.
Its back was grey with a brownish tinge, while the chest was
white with black and burnt sienna stripes on either side. It
looked as though it was a mixture of red, black, and grey
squirrels, all of them live here. I have never seen one like it
before.

January 11

Today I heard the lone call of a Robin. It called a number of times but there was no answer. I do not know why it arrived here so early. The ground is thickly covered with snow, not a bare spot to be seen. The temperature dropped to minus 27F last night. It is only 11 degrees F now. There are no worms to eat. I hope it will eat some of the thistle and sunflower seeds that Natterjack, Bracken, and Ian have put out for the other birds, squirrels, and raccoons. There is also an ample supply of cracked corn for the deer.

January 12

Natterjack, Bracken, Azulla, along with Lich, Caddis, and Newt, were out in the Bay today, cutting blocks of ice.

Once cut, the blocks are lifted and placed on sledges. Then the blocks of ice are strapped tightly for the long and difficult haul up Dark Point Hill, also known as Troll Hill. It is the same hill where we found the dead Alderling child.

The Trolls live there periodically but they do not come out during the daylight hours. When the Trolls become too numerous and threatening, both Gnomes and Dwarves go into the area in early evening with torches and route them out. They do not kill them unless they themselves are attacked. The Trolls are usually so frightened by the fiery torches, they panic and run. Then the Suund is asked to come and purify the land again.

The path leading up Troll Hill is not at all dangerous during the hours between mid morning and mid afternoon. Natterjack and company use this path because it has the least amount of brush and fallen branches in which the sledges could become entangled.

Lich and Caddis pulled some of the blocks of ice to Hemlock Ridge, where they are stored in an underground community burrow. All of the Gnome settlement's perishable food is stored there.

The Dwarf community keeps its ice in a rock cave in the Mac Mountains.

January 17

Men from Hemlock Ridge and Mac Mountains are out on the ice in the Bay again today. They have cut large holes in the ice and are fishing. This is a very enjoyable sport for all. They will catch Great Northern Pike and Yellow Perch.

The Pike is a large fish and will feed many mouths. The Yellow Perch is small and so several will be given to the Alderlings. However, since the Alderlings too are small, one Perch will feed a goodly number.

January 19

It snowed all night and did not stop until noon today. The sun came out for a short while. As I was looking out our window I saw something small trudging waist deep through the newly fallen snow. It was coming from the direction of Hemlock Ridge. I reached for my binoculars and saw that it was Hatch. He had a bundle of twigs strapped to his back and looked to be heading for Humpy Hill under which the Alderlings live.

We have had quite a long cold spell. The Alderlings must be running low with their firewood. One of the Gnomes or Dwarves would have brought the wood for them if they had asked. The Alderlings are a very independent folk.

January 26 - January Thaw

The main channel of the river has opened. Ice flows drift with the current. A pair of Bald Eagles were standing alone on one of the islands of ice. Bright sun, snow, and ice all glistened. The channel will freeze over again tonight when the temperature drops.

I heard the Robin call again. There was no reply. I feel for it.

January 28

The White- breasted Nuthatches chat. Black-capped-chickadees flit from branch to branch. Male and female Downy Woodpeckers climb the trunk of the White Pine just outside our window. They peck at the bark seeking hidden insects or grubs. They also take food from our feeder.

January 30

Snow again! It shrouds the marsh and wood. The trees appear as ghosts with arms outstretched. Fairies sleep within Goldenrod Galls and Milkweed Pods.

High above in the treetops the Wood Sprites sleep in the vacated squirrels' nests. The chipmunks sleep in their dens underground. The red, black, and grey squirrels are still very active. They do not hibernate.

The black and grey squirrels have already mated and will have two to five young sometime in March. The young will be very small, blind, hairless, and helpless when born.

February 5

More snow! Our world is encased in downy white fluff. The air is cold and dry. With every breath of wind, crystals of snow glitter like a profusion of diamonds thrown into the air.

We have not seen Natterjack, Bracken, or any of the Gnomes since January 17, when they were ice fishing and brought a pike and two Yellow Perch. They have not been out there since; I think it has been too cold for them.

February 7

Today was lovely. The sun's warmth was penetrating. Ian shovelled through the snow as far as the main road. The snow was up to my waist. It restricted me to keeping on the path only.

As we walked we noticed a few dark areas on the snow. Upon closer examination we realized the dark areas consisted of hundreds of black dots, which jumped when disturbed. Ian ran into the house for some plastic vials. We caught a few dots and brought them inside to examine with an 8x power loop. To our great surprise we discovered the spots were Snow Fleas. They often spend warm winter days on top of the snow. Otherwise they wait for the sun massed together under damp leaves.

February 10

It snowed all night again. When we awoke this morning, White Pine and Hemlock branches were heavily laden with a white blanket.

Every branch of tree and shrub, each weed and blade of grass was traced in cotton wool and diamonds. The browns and ochre's of yesterday are gone. It was a land of fantasy and reality mixed. Puncum and Wood Sprites sleep.

Alderlings sit by their stoves reading, weaving, and playing chess in the quiet room. Some of the older men sit carving wooden toys. Children learn their letters, the painter and musician are busy working at their crafts. No one is idle.

Gnomes in winter are late sleepers. They enjoy a big breakfast. A thick slice of bread made from cattail pollen tops and ground rose hips is toasted and spread with Elderberry jam. Either Sumac tea with a sprig of mint or a cup of Chicory, a coffee substitute followed by a short nap serves as a warm sweet herbal beverage when mixed with a bit of honey.

By noon the men folk are out of doors spreading cracked corn for the deer, squirrels, and turkeys. Thistle and sunflower seeds are set out for the birds. Dried fish fillets are laid out for the Red Fox.

The women are soaking dried Milkweed and Stinging Nettle stems they collected in the fall. When they are supple, the long fibres will be pulled from the fleshy matter and spun into thread. They are then woven into materials for clothes, sails, and even roofing for some of the Puncum homes.

The Dwarves have taken to their shovels, digging tunnels to both Gnome and Dwarf communities. Once again, neighbours meet, chat, and say their good mornings.

We sit at our breakfast table and marvel at such a wondrous sight and are invigorated. I take a mental picture; a camera will not do. Only my mind can see and absorb this beauty. I need not say anything for it to be felt and understood. I feel both calm and excited at the same time. It is a good day for a painting.

Nature gives stability to my life. It is always present, whatever its outward appearance. It creates moods. It may affect me differently than it does Ian. He may see snow as a slight bother at times, while I receive it as a pleasure.

Each tree now stands alone as well as being one of many. I am now able to distinguish the Witch Hazel more easily with its open pods. No leaf hangs beyond its branch. The Beech, on the other hand, still holds tenaciously onto its leaves, not letting go until spring. In May as the new buds swell in their axels, they push away last year's leaves.

Icicles melt and form as the sun arcs across the sky. In between the snow capped rocks and boulders, in deep ravines, lie snow covered doors to Gnome and Dwarf dwellings. Some elderly folk live within. The younger members of the community have come to their rescue, uncovering their doors and digging paths.

A Gnome with a long grey beard and cane stepped forth arm and arm with Natterjack and Bracken on each side. They walked cautiously down the rocky slope of Hemlock Ridge. Natterjack then took over and carried him on his shoulders to the Great Hall. All of the elderly Gnomes and

Dwarves were being taken where they could more easily be looked after.

When I saw the old Gnome, it occurred to me that he might know much of the history of Horse Thief Bay and some of the nearby islands. He may even have witnessed the illegal trade of horses back in the 1800's. Gnomes live to be very old. I must ask Natterjack to introduce me to him.

February 14

I heard the Robin again. It is so early; so much snow still lies on the ground. I hope the Robin will survive another month or two of winter. Perhaps he eats some of the seeds we have put out for the other birds. I hope he eats more than just worms. There is still a long while before the snow melts and the ground thaws.

February 16

A happy day for me! I spoke to Natterjack for a moment yesterday. I asked him if he could arrange a meeting with the elderly Gnome. Natterjack and Lich came this morning, bringing the old man with them. It was quite a sight. Natterjack was once again carrying the Gnome on his back. A good thing too! The snow was waist high.

They addressed the old gentleman as S. Oakenbaum. He was a funny looking Gnome. He had a very long beard. His arms and legs were thick with a round roly-poly belly in between. His face too was round with a dimple in each cheek. He smoked a pipe and wore a red pointed hat. He stood on the floor while Lich helped him takeoff several layers of warm clothing. When finished he sat in the stuffed chair by our wood stove.

.The smoke from his pipe smelled lemony, not like regular tobacco. He said it was a special blend of Lemon Balm, Wild Bergamot, and mint. Each herb can be used as a tea. Ian's ears perked up so to speak, when he discovered that these herbs could be used as teas. In fact this gave him the idea to put the kettle on. He reached for some cups, and got the tin of Raspberry Tea.

We visited for a while and then S. Oakenbaum pulled out some very old papers from a leather folder. Lich had been carrying it. My excitement grew as he spread the papers out on the table. I became my most patient self. It is something I have learned to be from my friendship with Ian.

Yes, these were papers describing the migration of the Gnomes from Northern Europe and Scandinavia to Horse Thief Bay. And, yes, he was prepared to tell the story and history of the Gnomes as well as that of the Dwarves. What joy!

February 17

Much was accomplished yesterday. I took notes. We settled on a format to be used for both Gnomes and Dwarves. There should first be an introduction to describe their physique, mental prowess, and characteristics of their nature.

Gnomes and Dwarves

Both Gnomes and Dwarves are very intelligent, strong in character, self-reliant, determined, skilled in many activities and tasks, and physically and mentally strong. They have great stamina and prowess. They never shirk from their responsibilities. They are good-natured and always find the humour in life. Even though they are quick to laugh, they are very serious when the need arises.

Weight for both is an issue due to the fact that they both love to eat. They do enjoy good food, which their wives cook plenty of. Life is to be enjoyed. The Suund has warned them on several occasions to lose weight. Having roly-poly stomachs is not good for the heart. They need to diet, lower their food intake, and exercise more.

They have good night vision, and their senses of smell and touch are extraordinary.

Gnomes average two feet high, more or less. Dwarves are taller, between three and four feet high. Both races live in close proximity to one another in the Bay. They often work and socialize together. Many of their holidays and festivals are the same. This was not always the case before settling together in Horse Thief Bay. In fact when their ancestors were still living in Northern Europe, there were some bloody battles between them in which neither side was victorious. Both sides lost many good people, a waste of many lives. It is a period in their history no one likes to remember. The memories of those old battles are a lot of old baggage to carry with them and would thwart the making of new friendships outside their own race.

Gnomes tend to have a fairer complexion and either light brown or blond hair, sometimes wavy, sometimes straight, sometimes long, and sometimes short. They usually have either blue or hazel eyes.

Dwarves tend to have darker skin and medium brown hair, most often straight, occasionally wavy. Eyes are usually brown unless they are of mixed parentage. Their languages are very similar in both spelling and sound.

Both groups are artistic. The Gnomes tend to engage themselves in the crafts of pottery, woodcarving, and weaving. The Dwarves find their creativity in painting, print making, and batik.

Gnomes and Dwarves are quite adept and most original in the building of their homes. They sometimes have friendly competitions with one another to see who can build the most outrageous but still practical homes. This leads to some of the most innovative and interesting of structures. Our home is one of them.

The two groups feel good about themselves. They have well developed egos but they are not at all pompous. They know their strengths and weaknesses, their capabilities, and what they can achieve. They are positive thinkers; curious, willing to take risks, explore new fields, and new avenues of knowledge. No matter how old, they remain interested in life and all it has to offer.

February 19

There was another meeting with S. Oakenbaum, again accompanied by Natterjack and Lich.

Today he delved into the first Gnome migration from Northern Europe and Scandinavia. S. Oakenbaum brought another leather pouch made from Reindeer hide. It contained pieces of rib bones, which were inscribed with glyphs and pictographs. He also took out some broken shards of pottery and round and rectangular clay tablets, all of which bore glyphs. There were even pieces of hide which had writing on them. He laid this collection of artifacts on the table and we moved his chair next to mine.

Silvas Oakenbaum and the Story of the Migration of the Gnomes to Horse Thief Bay from Northern Europe

Gnomes have always been a peace loving people, living simple lives, tilling their fields, which skirted their villages of sod and wood dwellings. They tended a few sheep, some chickens, along with hunting and fishing to sustain them. They avoided any confrontation with the roving bands of marauding Trolls. They built stone walls and watchtowers around their villages, hoping for protection from these beings. Never the less the walls were breached.

By the second century of the Common Era, the Gnomes as well as the Dwarves were finding themselves under constant siege by Trolls.

Gnomes and Dwarves living in settlements in Southern Europe, in Italy known then as Italia, had to flee the savagery of the Roman legions as the ever expanding Roman Empire spread northward through Italia.

The Gnomes in these areas wished only to tend to their olive groves, vineyards, and farms. They were no match for the highly trained and armoured soldiers, especially the Trolls who followed along just behind them. The Trolls burned the villages, killed the livestock, and scorched the fields of grain as well as the vineyards and the olive groves. They took the land for themselves. The Gnomes who did not flee in time were taken to be used as slaves or they were killed.

Gnomes who were able to flee the onslaught left with only their clothes, farm implements, seeds, and cuttings from their grape vines and fruit trees. Their oxen drawn carts headed north with some livestock and the elders walking behind.

The Dwarves stayed longer in the south. They felt they could fend off the advancing Trolls, but this was not to be. The battles were too bloody, and too many lives were lost. They too left their homes, taking only their flocks of sheep with them. Following in the footsteps of the Gnomes, they made their way over the Alps into the province of Germania. Many lost their lives climbing the Alps, as had happened with the Gnomes. They were not prepared for such cold weather and the high altitudes. There were also avalanches and wild animals to contend with.

Once the Gnomes and Dwarves reached Germania, they settled into small communities. The land was heavily treed and the weather much colder. They built sod and wood houses and cleared small patches of land. They began to farm. They planted their seeds and the cuttings from their fruit trees and vineyards. They tended their sheep and acquired some goats and a few cows. They set down roots and began to feel safe and secure.

They hunted and fished, living an agrarian life. For nearly two hundred years, they lived peacefully and prospered. Then they began to feel squeezed and were terrified.

Bands of marauding barbarians were descending in force upon both Gnome and Dwarf villages, ransacking their farms and crops, scorching the land, and stealing their livestock; and more Gnomes and Dwarves, while defending their farms and themselves, were killed. Some Dwarves were taken to become slaves. Families were separated. Whole villages were thrown into measureless panic.

In the year 310 of the Common Era, at the Battle of Norgrun, the Viking, Sharp Tooth and his warriors decimated the Gnomes and Dwarves who had banded together with pitchforks and knives in hand to defend themselves. A very large group of Trolls were on the move, pushing westward from Asia. The land was defiled and ravaged; terror reigned absolute over the minds and hearts of the villagers.

The remnants of Gnome and Dwarf villagers packed as much of their belongings into wagons and headed north. One group, after a year of wandering and hardship, reached a small settlement of Gnomes living on the Baltic Sea.

Another mixed group settled further west on the coast of Poland and the Baltic Sea. Still others constructed villages on the coast of Germany and The Netherlands. The Dwarves migrated no further north than the coast of Northern Europe. Both Gnomes and Dwarves established permanent villages. The villages grew and again the people prospered. The men of both races became shipwrights, carpenters, and fishermen.

They built wonderful boats to ply the rough coastal waters off the countries now called Estonia, Latvia, Lithuania, Poland, Germany, and the Netherlands.

They also explored the creeks, bays, and fjords of Finland, Sweden, and Norway.

The Gnomes joined the Dwarves in their exploration of the coast of Sweden and Norway, and the islands off Denmark. The land looked interesting to the Gnomes. It was well forested besides having large tracts of open land. Small settlements of Gnomes already dotted the coastlines of these counties. However, the interior lands when investigated looked to be fairly unpopulated.

When the Gnomes returned home to their villages, they

discussed with their families, what they had seen. The elders were not yet ready to move again. There was still a good measure of peace and tranquillity in their villages and surrounding lands. They felt no threat from Trolls or marauding barbarians. However, many younger Gnomes felt the urge to explore and settle in the new lands they had seen and investigated while fishing on the Great Sea, but there were not enough young yet to form a large enough community needed for safety reasons.

It was two years later before a group of forty Gnomes left to look for new lands suitable to build new communities.

Before leaving, the Gnomes had to build boats large enough to carry themselves, cows, sheep, goats, and geese. They also needed to make clothes and blankets, and food had to be collected, dried, and stored. They needed enough provisions to last a year. It would take time to build homes and clear enough land for their vegetable gardens, plant the seeds, and time enough for them to grow and be harvested.

The Gnomes dried fish, mushrooms, fruits, and berries. They made reed baskets and clay jars for the storage of grains, wheat, oats, and barley. They picked and dried wild rose hips. They also needed clay vessels to store their wines.

The boats were made from oak. The boards were one inch thick, cleaved from tree trunks, which were naturally curved or bowed intentionally by the Gnomes. They had several methods of achieving this.

1. Boards were cut from naturally curved tree branches and trunks. Often rot set into the trunk and the branches broke off before they were thick enough in diameter to take boards from.

2. In time it was found that by tying a rope around the top of a fifteen to twenty foot high oak sapling and gently bowing the tree in stages, finer quality boards could be had. Here and there, throughout the forest, oaks could be seen in different stages of bowing.

    Oaks are slow growing. Thus it could take more than one generation of Gnomes living to the ripe old age of one hundred or more before the diameter of the tree trunk was great enough for it to be cut.

3. As the tree grows taller the top of the tree is drawn closer to the ground by shortening the length of the rope. Also the lower branches were removed in order for the nutrients absorbed by the roots of the tree to grow mainly into enlarging the diameter and length of the tree trunk.

    Enough of the upper branches of the tree must be left in order for its leaves during the spring and summer months to draw the energy from the sun which will bring about growth.

     The depth of the curve can be manipulated as well just by altering the distance between the base of the tree and the stake securing the end of the rope to the ground.

     By the end of the second year the boats were finished. They were shallow drafted. The bow and stern were built nearly the same. Thus the boats would not have to be turned around in order for them to head in a different direction or to go back.

In building the hull the boards were overlapping which made the boat more flexible in the high seas. The sail was square, made from woven sheep's wool. The sheep had two types of wool; an outer layer and an inner layer, which were very strong and impenetrable, and making it waterproof.

Along each side of the hull were round openings for the oars to be inserted when needed.

During these two years while the men worked on the boats, the women spun thread from the stems of Stinging Nettle plants. Then they wove the thread into material for small sails for their boats, for clothing, blankets, and ropes of all thicknesses and lengths. Thread made from Milkweed stalks was used for making ropes as well but not for clothes.

The Gnomes were at last ready for their long voyage. More and more Gnomes and Dwarves were fleeing north from central Europe. The earth was scorched, villages set ablaze, and animals slaughtered. Coastal villages were now becoming over-crowded. Over the next ten years waves of Gnomes migrated to Finland, Sweden, and Norway.

Crossing The Baltic Sea

The Gnomes set sail in July when there was less chance of stormy weather and fog. There were rounds of farewells and many folk to wave them good-bye.

They sailed along the coast of Poland, battling the mountainous waves of the Baltic Sea. By the time they reached the coast of Germany the weather had calmed. Then heading north they passed some of the islands off Denmark. The ships stopped at a few of these islands and explored them. While at one island a small group of Gnomes decided to stay. There were already a few Gnome families living there. All of their possessions and some livestock were taken ashore to establish a village and a port of call.

The ship sailed on through some of the narrow passages between the islands. Upon reaching the coast of Sweden the Gnomes explored each and every cove, bay, and inlet, finally dropping anchor on the northwest coast of the country near what is called Stromstad today. They settled along the coast, for they liked living the rugged lives of fishermen, the salt air, and the pounding surf on the rocky shoreline.

It was not long before another boat set sail from a port on the coast of Germany headed for Sweden. However, the boat ran aground off the coast of one of the islands they were passing. The passengers saved what they could of their belongings and livestock and swam ashore. Three Gnomes drowned. People already living on the island helped save the Gnomes. Without their help many more Gnomes and their animals would have perished. The food was lost. There would be hard times ahead, but they would survive.

Some months later, having repaired their boat, they arrived on the coast of Sweden just south of Stromstad. They trekked inland where they found great forests covering the mountain sides and lush valleys carpeted in green. There were waterfalls and fast flowing streams. They built homes of wood and sod. They dug the soil for their vegetable gardens, ploughed the land, sowed their fields of wheat and barley, and milked their cows.

In time many boatloads of Gnomes and even a few Dwarves landed on the shores of both Norway and Sweden. Thriving communities grew along the coast as well as inland.

All the migrating Gnomes took on the habit of the Gnomes who were indigenous to these countries. All of the males, females, and children wore red pointed hats, which stood out against the whiteness of the snow in winter and the greens and browns of spring, summer, and fall. No one ever seemed to get lost.

In time Norwegians and Swedes appreciated the Gnomes. They considered them as bearers of good fortune, since Gnomes tended to their sick and injured animals.

Many Swedish and Norwegian families set a chair or two by their hearth for the unexpected but welcomed Gnome caught in a snowstorm. Some families even set a place and an empty chair at their dinner table for the Gnome who may be just passing by. People often joked, respectfully that is, about the number of Gnomes there were in the countryside. They would say they were like rabbits, always multiplying. There were so many Gnomes. They could be seen at any time of day, running back and forth across open fields, sitting on roadside walls and fences, in trees, and barns. They milked the cows, tilled the land, tended sheep, and were even smithies. The Gnomes were thoroughly comfortable and at home in their new lands.

Gnome families were growing larger, having more children, more immigrants, thus more hamlets. Sod and wooden homes were popping up everywhere. They forgot about such creatures as Trolls and Dragons. Wave upon wave of Gnomes were leaving mainland Europe. They now came from the Netherlands and France, even from as far away as Spain. The word was spreading, that Norway, Sweden, and Finland were safe havens for Gnomes.

Dwarves were now moving in greater numbers northward. They were taking over some of the settlements vacated by the Gnomes. There still remained some Gnome villages on the coast but not nearly so many as before.

Gnomes from Spain, France, and the Netherlands made their way north using the village of Harlingen on the Northern coast of the Netherlands as their point of departure for the Scandinavian countries. Norway, Sweden, and Finland were becoming quite populated with Gnomes. Not only were the Indigenous Gnomes of these growing in number, but the number of early Italian, German, and Polish Gnomes grew as well. Now there were Spanish, Dutch, French, and Flemish speaking Gnomes.

Some of the early Gnome immigrants, those of German and Polish descent, were becoming restless as more and more Gnomes entered their countries. They felt they needed more elbow room, so to speak. They began to complain to one another and became short tempered, curt, and unpleasant. Before the land became crowded, they had been paragons of courtesy and humility.

Thoughts of travel, sailing ships, and new lands slowly began to enter their minds. The elders did not entertain such ideas. It was in the younger Gnomes, the second and third generations, which these ideas began to take hold. Words and phrases such as exploration, new lands, large ships, and provisions were heard in most of the conversations of the young, especially the men and boys. Gnomes of other villages began to discuss these same ideas.

Soon these ideas were set forth in a plan. Four ships were to be built, each holding fifty passengers, livestock, and provisions to last a year, perhaps longer. There would be need for Gnomes of all backgrounds and professions: Shipwrights, men who knew how to navigate the seas, oarsmen, men to raise the sail, and all other sundry chores in managing a ship. Fishermen, cooks, carpenters, smithies, and those who could heal both men and animals were also needed. It was four

years before the boats were finished and food and all other provisions enough for two hundred people and livestock were ready. They had no idea whether more provisions could be procured on the way.

In May of the fourth year, four boats left the southwest coast of Norway. The waters of the North Sea and North Atlantic were treacherous. The waves crashed over the bows, but the ships were strong and stood up against such pounding. The conditions were perilous and some Gnomes died.

Orkney, Shetland, and Faeroe Islands

Upon leaving Norway, the four ships headed due west, having learned that a group of many sparsely inhabited islands lay in that direction. This information turned out to be true. After many days at sea the islands came into view. Today they are called the Orkneys and lie off the coast of northern Scotland.

The ships anchored in deep water off shore. They launched several sealskin boats of five men each to explore some of the larger islands. Three of the islands were quite flat, having extensive moors inland. There were also a number of lakes, which meant that there would be a good supply of fresh water. On the principal island they found a great stand of hardwoods. Other islands were treed as well. There were occasional marshes where wildfowl were seen. The scouts found safe harbours for the boats.

The men were gone for five days. The criteria by which the scouts would determine whether the land was suitable for establishing settlements was decided by the Gnomes before they left Norway.

The Gnomes in the four ships were to establish a network of permanent settlements on the newly found lands. Eventually these communities would become a trade route connecting to the Scandinavian mainland and the northern coast of Europe. It would also be a route for transporting Gnomes fleeing Europe's turmoil.

The scouting Gnomes returned with enough positive information to fulfill the criteria required.

Criteria

1. The land must be arable, suitable for ploughing and cultivation.
2. The soil must be fertile for growing crops.
3. There must be enough grazing land for sheep and cattle.
4. Enough wildfowl for hunting to supplement their diet of fish and crustaceans, mussels, and mollusks.
5. A source of fresh water, a stream, lake, or river would be needed.
6. If there are already inhabitants on such lands, will they be friend or foe.

The Gnome scouts did meet up with some of the inhabitants of these islands. There were both Gnomes and Dwarves living side by side and they seemed to be very old and not many of them. The scouts wondered how long the Gnomes and Dwarves had been living on these islands and where was their place of origin.

There was a third group of inhabitants, numbering more than the other two races combined. They were not as tall as Dwarves or as short as Gnomes. They seemed to have some of the characteristics of both groups. The scouts thought these individuals came about through the union of Dwarves and Gnomes. This occurred so long ago that their offspring had grown and had children, and their children had children until most children born became a third race. The scouts referred to them as Betweenies or Midlings.

The population of the main island was not large. They seemed to be friendly in nature but were somewhat afraid. They probably thought these newcomers to be foe but hoped they were friendly. Several of the scouts were invited into an older Gnome's home, a home, which housed more than one family, mother, father, children, and both sets of grandparents. They spoke a different language, which did not sound Germanic in origin.

The visiting Gnomes were able to communicate well enough with the inhabitants to let them know that they were friendly. They too wished to settle down and live on some of the less inhabited islands.

At first the inhabitants were a bit dubious about this request, especially when they saw four ships anchored offshore with many people aboard. The scouts reassured them, telling them that not all of the passengers would be coming ashore. In fact there would only be fifteen. Another fifteen would be settling on a nearby island. There would be another ship arriving from Europe soon with more Gnome immigrants. They would settle on some of the other islands.

A spokesman for the Midlings told the Gnomes that there was another group of islands to the north, which were even less inhabited.

Upon leaving these islands, the Gnomes taking their advice sailed north. The first ship was away, having left fifteen Gnomes behind on the island. The other three ships followed shortly after. The wind blew hard, catching the white crest of every wave and carried the spray of each for great distances, drenching the Gnomes. It was a few days before the Gnomes encountered the group of islands, now known as the Shetlands.

The Shetlands were a rocky archipelago of many islands with very irregular coastlines. The coasts on the western side of many of the islands were steep and rocky. There were great areas of desolate stony land. The southern coast of the main island had sandy beaches and dunes. Scouts reported the interiors of some of the islands were covered with great expanses of moor where sheep and cattle could graze. They found no evidence of Gnome, Dwarf, or man residing on the two islands they explored.

These islands were much more rugged than the two islands they had visited in the Orkneys. They still seemed suitable for establishing a small settlement of hardy folk. A group of twenty was left with their possessions, food, drink, one cow, one bull, and two sheep. Fish, mussels, and wildfowl were abundant. Two small boats were left behind.

One ship, being emptied, returned to Norway for more Gnomes while the remaining three ships sailed further north. They came upon the Faeroe Islands. These islands were heavily influenced by the Gulf Stream, which tempered the cold on the western most islands. The hills were barren; there were no trees. There was a plateau on top of basalt cliffs, some towering two thousand feet above the restless sea. Great waves broke upon the rocks with explosive force, bursting into clouds of spray and surf. There was evidence that some of these islands were inhabited.

At first the party of six scouts saw a few abandoned houses. This led them to think that the conditions on the island were too bleak and desolate and so the inhabitants left. Upon further exploration of the island they found a few homes, which were occupied. They knocked on the door. A Dwarf came, his face looked ravaged by the ceaseless winds, which blew across the islands. His face belied the gentleness of his voice and manner when he invited them in.

The scouts learned from him, that there were no Gnomes living on the island. Nor did he think that there were any

living on the others. The scouts were the first Gnomes he had
ever seen.

The Dwarf's language was very difficult to understand.
However, between gestures and facial expressions, the
Gnomes were able to convey all they had hoped to learn
about the islands:

1. The houses were half sunk in the ground. The roofs
   were sod and a stone wall surrounded each dwelling to
   protect it from the wind and ocean spray.
2. Wildlife, birds, wildfowl, otters, and seals were in
   abundance. Sheep grazed at will, and some cows and
   horses could be seen.
3. Fish, mainly Cod were caught. The inhabitants also
   dried Cod for trading.
   There were no beaches and so in stormy weather the
   waves of the Atlantic crashed directly and violently
   on the rocky cliffs, slowly wearing them away. Many
   of the slopes and plateaus were grass covered and
   treeless.
4. The scouts asked the elderly Dwarf if he and the other
   inhabitants of the island would mind having a group of
   twenty or twenty-five Gnomes settling on their island.

That evening a council of Dwarf elders and the scouts
was held to consider the request. The scouts explained their
needs and desires. They said they came as friends. They had
no desire to disrupt or infringe upon their way of living.
They wished only to live in peace with their neighbours.

Nearly all of the Dwarves consented and welcomed
the Gnomes. Only a few disgruntled Dwarves voiced
opposition. The idea of another race living on their island
was repugnant to them.

Upon returning to the ships, the scouts described all that they had seen and heard - the land, the moors for their grazing animals, wildlife, food sources, fresh water, and the type of dwellings they had seen. Then the scouts told them that there were no Gnomes living on the island, just Dwarves. These people looked favourably on the Gnomes as neighbours. A group of twenty volunteered to settle there.

If after a year, the settlers found living on the island was too rugged and isolating, they could leave, either to look further on or sail back to Norway on a returning ship. Provisions, cattle, sheep, food, their possessions, and two small boats were left for the Gnomes.

The three remaining ships sailed northwest until land was sighted, and so the ships dropped anchor. The land was broad with numerous mountains. The ships rested far from shore, for they saw a mountain spewing fire and liquid, thick, red, and black was pouring down the sides of it. Trees were being covered with it. A great swelling column of deep grey smoke was rising higher and higher in the sky. The Gnomes were afraid. They had never seen fire and smoke come out of a mountaintop. They spotted a few villages on the coast and could not understand how people could live there when a mountain was on fire. Were there other mountains that did the same? Were they the dwellings of fire breathing dragons? Was it true that dragons really did exist? Fearful thoughts ran through their minds.

They saw men in fishing boats and people on the shore. Scouts were dispatched. They rowed their boat across to one of the fishing boats and spoke to them using some manner of speech and sign. The fishermen invited the Gnomes to come ashore, and they did.

The outcome of these conversations was that the island was quite safe to live on and establish a settlement along the coast. Birch trees covered some of the lower mountain slopes. There were hot springs to bathe in. The growing season was short but long enough for some crops to mature. The fishing was good, the winters mild due to the North Atlantic drift of the Gulf Stream.

There were many volcanoes, not all of them active. There were lava fields, glaciers, and geysers. The coastline was highly irregular. There were fjords and navigable bays. The rivers were not navigable because they were frozen. A thick carpet of moss covers the land. Where there is no snow, there are large areas of grassland.

There is little wildlife: the Arctic Fox, Eider Ducks, seabirds, and seals.

The islanders had brought with them, many years before, a small number of domestic animals, which had increased substantially. The inhabitants, who looked like the Midlings of the Orkney Islands, were very encouraging and sincerely hoped the Gnomes would settle there.

They asked the scouts to bring the captain of each ship and group leaders back to the islands to talk. Winter would be setting in soon. The Gnomes should not leave Iceland until spring. Their ships would get stuck in the pack ice and the hulls would get smashed. The Gnomes would die of cold and starvation.

The islanders made such a persuasive case, the Gnomes decided to stay. However, the Gnomes wondered how it could be managed when there were one hundred and thirty of them.

The Midlings developed a plan. They and the Gnomes would erect six wooden framed circular tent-like structures with sealskin stretched over them. These homes were similar to yurts. There would be an opening at the top for the smoke from their heating and cook fire to escape. With a team effort they could be built quickly. The shelters would be constructed near a hot spring for warmth. Each dwelling would hold between twenty and twenty-five people.

The island's residents billeted those Gnomes who had young children, women who were pregnant, and those that were sick or elderly. Tolerance would be the key word in thought and act for the Gnomes if they were to survive emotionally and physically. They had done very well while living on the ships, where squabbles, disagreements, and arguments had been handled civilly.

Before any yurts were constructed, there would be feasting. The Gnomes were exhausted, hungry, and emotionally drained. Food and warm baths in the hot springs would be most welcome.

An assortment of foods, fresh fish, and drinks were laid before them. They ate until they were fully sated. They had not eaten so well since before leaving Norway. They were not to worry about any volcanic eruptions. They were safe. When the meal was over, they walked back to their ships, crawled into their hammocks, and fell asleep. During the following week the round yurts were erected and the sealskins were stretched over the frames. The three ships were totally emptied of food, bedding, and livestock, and then were drawn up onto the shore for the winter.

The Next Leg of the Journey

In May of the following spring, a second ship left, heading back to Norway. Eighty immigrants chose to remain in Iceland.

Over the winter the Gnomes got to know the Midlings and met some of their grandparents, who were Gnomes and others Dwarves, who had not intermarried. The elders were in remarkably good health, the oldest being one hundred and fifty-two. It was believed their longevity was due to their diet, the hot springs, and the care given them by the community. The Gnomes were impressed by the friendliness and warmth of these people.

Those folks who chose to sail further on had begun to take their possessions, livestock, food, grains, fresh water, wine, dried fish, and fowl back onto the remaining two ships. The islanders urged the Gnomes to leave quickly, not to tarry, get sailing to Greenland. They should stay there just a short while to pick up more provisions, and then be off before the heavy fog arrives.

However, if the fog sets in, the Gnomes were advised to remain on the southwest coast of Greenland in temporary shelters. It was the only habitable land on that island. They would find fish and Arctic Hare. It was inhabited. There were a few Dwarf settlements on the coast. No Gnomes had ever been seen there by the Icelanders, but that did not necessarily mean there were none.

Upon leaving Greenland the Gnomes were to sail southwest. There is a land of great size and beauty. There are many forests and a long river, which leads into the belly of the land. The senior of the Icelanders told the Gnomes, "We

The Gnome Migration Route Map

have not seen this land but we have heard stories of it. All of the stories we have heard were from different individuals, but they were all very much alike, so we believed them to be true.

They were told that the further southwest they traveled along the Great River, the winters would be less harsh, and the climate would be milder. There is a time for cold winds and snow, and the greening time, when new life pushes up through the dark soil and animal babies are born. Then there will be time for the growing and ripening of crops and fruit, when insects sing, and birds chatter, and painted leaves float to the earth and animals sleep.

This land is beyond that edge, beyond those clouds. It is a real land. We have heard of it. The Stories tell the truth. Go there for us. Do not fear."

The Gnomes waved their goodbyes and set out on their long journey to Greenland. They encountered stormy weather. Great waves crashed over the bows and tossed the ships about, as if they were toys. The sail on one of the ships received a large tear. It looked dubious as to whether it would hold up until landfall. Both ships eventually made it to the southern coast of Greenland. They looked for an area of coast, which would afford them protection. They found this on the southwestern side of the island. There was a thick fog.

Temporary dwellings were set up. The Icelanders had given them three circular yurts. They had no idea how long the fog would last, days, weeks, or even months. Each day the Gnomes scouted the coast. They fished and hunted wildfowl. They ate mollusks and berries and drank fresh water. There were many mouths to feed. They did not know how long they would be there or how far it would be until they reached land again.

There were Dwarves living on the island. They looked wild and woolly and were not very friendly. However the Gnomes did manage to glean some information from them, and after three months of waiting, the Gnomes set sail.

The Dwarves told the Gnomes to "Sail due west until a large area of land was sighted on the starboard side. Follow the coastline southwest." They would soon see land on their port side as well. They would be entering a wide expanse of water now known as the Gulf of St. Lawrence. Continue to follow the coast on their starboard side, for how far and for how long the Greenlanders did not know. They had never been there but had heard the stories. The stories, though from different individuals, were the same. They believed them to be true.

The Gnomes were also told that many animals of different sizes and kinds roamed the forests. The Dwarves also told them not to wear their red pointed hats. They should wear either green or brown according to the seasons. This way, animals would not see them so readily. Do not be too conspicuous. Blend in with the foliage. See what the animals are like, friend or foe.

The St. Lawrence and The Land of Many Trees

The Gnomes chose not to settle on the coast of Greenland. The land was too stark and harsh. Perhaps others would settle there in the future.

The two ships reached the coast of Labrador by mid-August. The Dwarves had told them that the further up river they sailed, the more temperate the climate, thus the Gnomes sailed on. They were weary of the near constant cold. They yearned to see spring and enjoy its warmth, and the summer when crops grew and ripened.

The Gnomes still had a good supply of food, wine, and fresh water. They decided to sail, as far up river as possible while the weather was still warm. The further they sailed, the more varied the trees became. They saw hillsides of Black Spruce, interspersed with Maple, Oak, and Birch.

There were large animals with broad, flat horns that looked like tree branches. They also had beards. They were Moose. Black and Brown Bears roamed the hillsides. Along the river the Gnomes saw beavers, muskrats, skunks, and porcupines. Squirrels ran up and down trees and rabbits scampered over the ground. Deer grazed along the shore.

Wildfowl of many species were seen. The Gnomes were awestruck. After four days of sailing they found a safe haven for their ships and set anchor. Approximately twenty male Gnomes left the ships to erect temporary tents on the banks of the river and collect wood for their campfires.

When the tents were set up most of the passengers disembarked to stretch their legs and walk along the shore. They wished to take in the beauty of it all. Others remained on board, a little nervous. They relaxed, just sitting on the deck, soaking up the sun. Those on shore thought it best to stay in small groups. No one was to go off exploring on their own or wander very far from the river bank.

Many of the Gnomes did not realize how very tired they were. They did not remember how good the soft grass would feel under their soft feet, how the sweet aroma of the soil rising to their nostrils would relax their little grey cells. The nearly silent measured lapping of the waves against the shore was subduing their thoughts. Nature was wooing their spirits into a deep and dreamless sleep. All fell asleep where they lay. The sun was still high. They could rest for now.

Some Gnomes managed to stay awake. They picked blackberries; others collected bright green algae from rocks in the shallow water near shore. They boiled it and dipped a few of their red hats into it. The hats did not turn green as they had hoped but a muddy brown. It would do.

Evening campfires dotted the riverbank. The Gnomes who had fallen asleep during the afternoon were well rested and would keep watch that night. The night was warm but not humid. The stars shined upon their faces. Many animal voices were heard but they did not threaten the sleep of the Gnomes. Those who lay awake turned their thoughts to the dragonflies they had seen flitting about in the sedges in the shallow water near shore. The turtles basking in the late sun on partially submerged logs. Leopard Frogs jumped as the Gnomes walked along the shore. Words could not describe all that they had seen and felt.

Night passed uneventfully. With the first light of dawn birds began to chatter and Gnomes awoke and stretched, anxious to explore the local terrain. As they breakfasted some began to think this might be a good location to establish another settlement. Although they had only a quick glance of the land the day before, it looked promising.

By noon several groups of male Gnomes had investigated the surrounding land. They had found a swift flowing stream, berry bushes, and arable land suitable for growing crops. There was a sparsely treed area where the trees could be felled and brush cleared for growing barley, rye, and oat seeds they had brought with them. There was enough land for their cows, sheep, and goats to graze.

The timber from the felled trees would be used in building their homes. There were enough branches scattered throughout the wood for cooking and heating their homes, they need not cut new wood for that. There were fish to catch and wildfowl to hunt. All the criteria for building a community was there before them. Even the climate seemed just right.

While walking through the woods the Gnomes did encounter some wildlife. First they met a few White-tailed Deer, then numerous grey and red squirrels. There were no big animals such as bear or moose just yet.

There seemed to be no human life such as Gnomes or Dwarves about. They decided to establish a community here. There were enough wild edibles nearby which could supplement their provisions.

Rock Tripe	Arrowhead tuber	Spring Beauty
Blackberries	Cattails	Rose Hips
Wintergreen	Blueberries	Ground Nut
Wild Grapes	Dandelions	Elderberry

A small group of Gnomes brought their possessions and one tent ashore. If they set to work immediately, they could build permanent wood and sod homes for each family by late September. Among the Gnomes who stayed at this site were several who, while exploring, saw something other than an animal or insect. There were a number of these creatures. Some had wings, and some did not. There was one with wings who was sitting on a branch. The Gnomes were mystified by it. These were living creatures looking very much like humans but in miniature and they could fly. They flew from branch to branch, from blade of grass to rock, from one Gnome's shoulder to another. They tweaked a nose, pinched an ear, and flew circles around the heads of the scouts. They seemed to be very happy and carefree.

The exploring Gnomes told no one else about seeing these creatures.

The ships lay anchored for a week. One ship was emptied of its passengers, their possessions, its remaining livestock, and provisions, leaving only enough food and drink for its captain and crew for their return trip to Norway.

The last of the four ships took on provisions of wild edibles while those Gnomes who were staying behind were helped to get situated in their temporary shelter. Large Branches were stacked in a circle to contain two cows and two sheep.

Time was passing. Crickets were singing loudly, crows cawing, and birds were flocking. It was time to move on. There was a change in the air. Summer's bloom and greenness was passing and the Bracken bronzing.

The ship pulled away at the break of day. The Gnomes knew neither how far up river, nor how long it would be before they would find a suitable site for another settlement.

The river's current was becoming stronger. The water grew rough and ahead was white water, which the Gnomes were not expecting. The river had been idyllic in temperament compared to what they had appeared to be sailing into.

The question uppermost in the Gnomes' thinking was should they continue on and try to shoot the rapids? Would the ship hold up against the pounding rocks against the hull? Do they dare? They decided to row the ship into a small protective bay and drop anchor. The immigrants had sailed the wild and dangerous North Sea and had crossed the

North Atlantic Ocean, which was no easy task, and they survived both. They had an excellent captain, navigator, and crew to sail the ship but even that perhaps was not enough for what lay ahead.

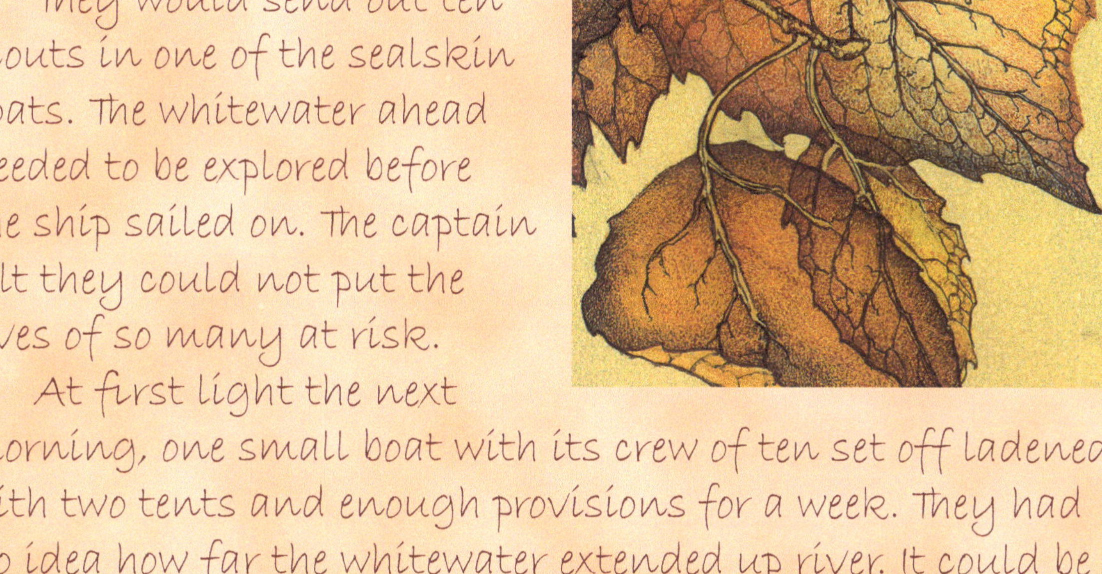

They would send out ten scouts in one of the sealskin boats. The whitewater ahead needed to be explored before the ship sailed on. The captain felt they could not put the lives of so many at risk.

At first light the next morning, one small boat with its crew of ten set off ladened with two tents and enough provisions for a week. They had no idea how far the whitewater extended up river. It could be just a few miles, or many. They would also be driving their boat against the current which would slow them down.

After rowing just a short while, the Gnomes came upon the main body of rapids. They were overwhelmed. Rocks and boulders shot up through the white-capped waves. Within minutes they realized they were facing an impossible situation. They turned around in retreat and were soon back to where they had left the others. They pulled their boat to shore and tied it in a safe place.

This was quite a setback but no matter, they would find an alternative solution.

The ship and sealskin boats would have to be transported overland. The ship was unloaded and the Gnomes' possessions and provisions were packed into the three remaining sealskin boats. A tarpaulin woven from the fibrous stems of the Stinging Nettle plant was used to cover each boat.

Several trees were felled and their branches were removed and the trunks cut into ten foot lengths, and then laid them on the ground. The logs were to be used as rollers. Each boat was set upon three logs, which were spread apart so that one was under the bow, one in the middle, and the last log under the stern. Ropes were tied to the bow of each boat. A ramp was built to pull the ship on shore and it too was set on rollers.

When pulled, each boat would roll forward, leaving the log at the stern end free. That log would then be carried forward and placed under the bow again. Each boat and the ship would be moved forward in this manner thousands of times before they would pass the whitewater. It was also necessary to clear a path through the brush for the boats to pass.

There were three groups of Gnomes. One group to clear away brush and fallen branches. The second group to pull the boats and ship, and a third group to quickly move the logs that were freed at the stern end and place them under the bow as each boat moved ahead.

It took the Gnomes eight days to pull the boats forty-four miles, just a little over five miles a day. The skin on their hands was worn raw by the rope, even though they had wrapped torn strips of clothing around their hands to try to protect them.

The Gnomes' faces and arms were cut and scratched by Blackberry brambles and Buckthorn branches. The sharp rocks tore their soft leathery shoes.

By the time the migrants reached a place where they could launch the ship and an area of forest suitable for a camp sight, all were exhausted and some were discouraged. The long trek had been difficult, nerves stretched, tempers at knife-edge, and their morale was fluctuating. However, the journey was not fraught with fear. They met many animals of different species along the way. At first they were afraid of a few of the larger ones, the Brown Bears in particular. The bears were so large and they growled, but the bears and other animals seemed to sense that the Gnomes would not hurt them and were not a threat to their lives.

The Gnomes were a peace loving, gentle, and caring people. They, like some of their kindred at the last camp sight, saw small human like creatures flitting about. One moment the creatures would be sitting on tree branches or under ferns, the next moment on the heads of the Gnomes. Some were winged, but others were not. They were impish beings, often playing pranks on the Gnomes.

Even with all of their mischievousness these human like creatures, or fairies, were helpful to the Gnomes. They could not communicate in language, but by sign they were able to direct the Gnomes to berries and other wild edibles.

Even more perplexing were mysterious looking beings which at times appeared to be solid and at other times translucent. They were seen just now and again and spoke a language unknown to the Gnomes. Yet at the same time

the meanings of the words were understandable. They
spoke very slowly and softly with a lilting meter as in
poetry. They spoke words to fill the soul and ease the heart.
These creatures were imbued with the wisdom gained from
many centuries of experience while they were alive. They
were spirits who lived in the world between life and death.
Gnomes called these creatures Wood Knars. They had come
from the trees felled by the winds of Na and at one time
were nourished by Her. Now as the trees lay on the ground
they returned those life-sustaining nutrients to the soil.

Those parts of the tree where the branches met the trunk
and where centuries before they had been shoots for new
branches, now after death, became living spirits wandering
the wood, shepherding and guiding those who walked there.

Another New Settlement

The tents were set up quickly, fires started, and food
unpacked. Duck Potatoes were roasted and fish grilled.
Dandelion greens were picked from along the riverbank and
boiled; they were bitter but they did help to staunch their
hunger.

The Gnomes were drained physically as well as in
spirit, and laid their heads down for sleep soon after eating.
The fires were stoked throughout the night. There was a
growing chill, and the days were shortening. The Maple and
Birch leaves were beginning to turn color and drifted to
the ground, some landing on the surface of the water and
floating downriver with the current.

The Gnomes had lost a great deal of time carrying the
boats overland. They would need to do some serious thinking
after they had rested.

It was afternoon of the following day, after much hard thinking and discussion, before a decision was reached. A majority of the Gnomes felt it was best to remain the winter at this site. The year was waning and already into the third week of September. They had no knowledge of what lay ahead. There might still be more "Whitewater", and difficult terrain. The ground too would soon freeze. Those wishing to explore the river and land, and perhaps establish a settlement further up the river could do so in the spring.

The ship and the three sealskin boats had not been launched yet. Logs were buttressed against both sides of the ship's hull to keep it from tipping to one side or the other. It would be used for temporary housing.

The three sealskin covered boats were emptied and turned over. They were raised up to use as roofs for more housing.

Birds gathered and flew south. Many had already gone. Great flocks of Canada Geese were heard and seen flying over head in their long V formations. Crows were still about, cawing loudly. Chipmunks were preparing their dens for hibernation. Squirrels were madly gathering Hickory nuts and then burying them to be collected later. The leaves of the Birch, Maple, and Willow were nearly off. Those of the Oak and Beech still remained. The coyote with its plaintive cry could be heard each night.

The tempestuous winds of the northwest began to blow and cold air began to settle about the Gnomes. The trees creaked and moaned. Dark clouds hurried across the sky

and soon snow began to fall. The Gnomes were settled in.
They had enough time to make their temporary shelters warm.
If they were careful, there was enough food to last the winter.

Spring Melt

Each day the sun rose earlier and arced higher in the sky.
The ice melted and the birds rejoiced. Many colors and shades
of brown and burgundy began to appear as the snow slowly
receded. Rivulets of water began flowing over the moss covered
granite. Rock Tripe became soft and rubbery. Poly Pode ferns
unfurled their fronds. Green was appearing on the riverbank.

Ice still remained at river's edge, but where the water was
deep, the ice was gone. Scooters and Red Crested Mergansers
swam along the edge of the ice as life returned to the river.
The pink and blue flowers of the Blunt-lobed Hepatica, one
of the earliest spring wild flowers to bloom, opened with the
morning sun and closed at twilight. The white flowers of
the Dutchman's breeches followed shortly after. They grew
in mass, filling every nook and cranny of every wall and
outcropping of rocks.

The Spring Peepers sang out with all the energy they
could muster. With the ever quickening tempo of spring
chipmunks woke from their long winter's sleep. They
scampered over the rocks and fallen leaves looking for food.

The Gnomes too began to stir. Many were anxious
to get on with building more permanent dwellings and
establishing a settlement. Their provisions were running low
and wild edibles were needed.

There were not very many edible plants so early in the
year. There were Hickory and Beechnuts, and the red berries
from the Wintergreen plant, and Rose hips to be found and

eaten. The Rock Tripe clinging to the large boulders could be boiled and eaten in an emergency. The inner bark of the Hemlock, a conifer, could also be boiled or eaten raw. It would provide strength and nourishment for the Gnomes. Then there was a large stand of Cattails growing near the riverbank. Although the seed heads and stalks were dead, the roots were still edible and very nutritious when cooked. The Gnomes would not die from starvation.

Not all the Gnomes wanted to settle down just yet. Some wished to explore the land further up river. Where did this vast and long body of water lead? What lay at it's beginning? There was just a small group of Gnomes left, the last of the immigrants from the four ships, which left from Norway so very long ago.

The Land of Hope and Promise

After spending several days digging up Cattail roots and collecting nuts, the small group of Gnomes set out in their ship, also taking two sealskin boats.

It was a quiet morning. The sun rose warm and the river was calm. There was not enough wind to fill the sail. The men had to row but they did not have a strong current to battle. They rowed many leagues before stopping for the night. They had passed several islands, and there looked to be more ahead. The ship was anchored in a small cove where the Gnomes spent an uneventful night and awoke to another warm and glorious day. No one wished to remain here and settle down yet but wanted to continue on. They were curious to see more islands.

On their starboard side lay the mainland where the great forest of White Pine and Maple and massive Oaks interspersed with Beech and Shagbark Hickory and stands of Hemlock reached the riverbank as far as the eye could see. Not a tree had been felled. Elk and White-tailed Deer could be seen grazing in some of the more open areas of shoreline. A long unbroken stretch of land

lay in the distance on their port side. The river was wide and deep in that area. They continued to hug the shore of the mainland. More islands of different sizes came into view. They had entered the Archipelago of many islands, now known as the Thousand Islands of the St. Lawrence. Some consisted of one or two large smooth rocks with only one tree and a few blades of wild grass. Other islands were just a little larger, having just a few pine trees. A few very long islands had many trees and looked quite habitable. The shores of all of the islands were rocky, some rising twenty feet or more.

They saw smoke rising above the trees and became nervous. They wondered if the campfires were those made by Trolls or Humans. The Gnomes sailed on, keeping a more watchful eye.

Several hours of full daylight remained. The river was becoming shallower and its bottom sandy. The Gnomes kept a careful and constant watch to keep the ship from going aground. On both sides the land was closing in. There was a

large island on the port side. Cattails hugged the mainland shore. The river bottom could be clearly seen.

As they continued, the distance between the mainland and the island widened. When they reached the western end of the island there lay a great body of water ahead. Since the river was still calm, the Gnomes steered the ship straight across it to a large promontory of land. They were looking for a less exposed, more sheltered bay.

The river deepened as the land along the ship's starboard side rose sharply, which then dipped into a low green hollow studded with White Birch. The Gnomes were awestruck. There was so much for the mind to take in.

The shoreline had become much more irregular than what the Gnomes had seen thus far. As the ship turned towards a flattened point of land, there would be another small cove or bay. They continued on but the sun was lowering and they needed to find a bay soon and drop anchor.

Rather unexpectedly the Gnomes came upon a bay in which a small island rested. To the right and rear of the island, the distance to shore was at most fifty feet. To the left of it the bay widened and was deep. Five scouts got into one of the sealskin boats and rowed to the island first. They found wild blueberries, Juniper bushes, a few saplings, and grasses, as well as a number of White Pine and a few Pitch Pines. Then they paddled to the mainland, which gradually sloped upward. At the top of the hill the land flattened in a wood of mixed trees. At its western edge the trees dropped off steeply into a dell where a small brook flowed gently into a valley of Horsetails and a marsh of Alder trees and Sensitive ferns before it entered the river.

Bordering and protecting the Bay and woodland stood a

ridge of steep rock worn smooth by the elements and time. It blocked the cold winds of the north and west.

The Bay and surrounding land met all the requirements for establishing a settlement as set forth by the immigrants before they left the coast of Norway.

It had even more. A good climate for growing vegetables, fresh water, trees, a safe harbour for their boats, and even a shallow area with a sandy bottom for their children to swim. Many wild edibles and flowers grew there; it was beautiful.

More To Come

In the coming years more waves of Gnomes would cross the North Atlantic, using the same route and expanding the first settlements and building new ones. The three ships, which had returned to Norway, would set out again several times over. Other ships would be built, bringing Gnomes directly from the coast of Spain, the Netherlands, France, Germany, Poland, Lithuania, Latvia, Estonia, and even as far away as Finland. At the time of these migrations, the countries mentioned were not separate and were not yet called by these names.

A hundred and thirty-eight years after the first wave of Gnomes left Europe, the Dwarves set out, following the same route. North America was a great uncharted continent.

Stories documenting the causes and events leading up to the first migration of Gnomes from continental Europe to Norway were written on clay tablets, reindeer hide, sealskin, birch bark, and bone. The ancestors of Silvas Oakenbaum and the other Gnomes living in the Alderwild Wood brought many of these artifacts to Horse Thief Bay.

Over the years, Silvas collected many artifacts, some dating as far back as seven hundred years and earlier. He has over seventy five tablets, numerous pieces of bone, many reindeer ribs and hides and sealskins with inscriptions on them, and some jewelry. He also has several scrolls and manuscripts written while the Gnomes were still in Europe, and others written after they arrived in North America. Silvas even has several very early maps, which had been sent back to Norway for future crossings not long after the Gnomes first crossed the Atlantic. He also has several maps drawn of the early settlements along the St. Lawrence River.

Among his papers there are accounts written up like census reports. They detail the size of the population in each settlement along the route, beginning with Norway and including the Orkney, Shetland, and Faeroe Islands, Iceland, Greenland, and each of the settlements along the river. These accounts also included the deaths in each settlement and their causes, whether it was malnutrition, accident, murder, starvation, or old age.

There are also detailed notes on climate, soil conditions, agriculture, the growing period, and type of crops grown. Facts about hunting and fishing are listed. A census including these and other facts was taken every two and a half years. It was necessary. This information was needed in case there were any problems in any of these areas; they could be looked into and improved upon if necessary.

In several instances the population of a settlement was transported to a different island. The lack of enough arable land and harsh conditions made living on some of the islands nearly impossible. Gnomes were starving, and newborns were dying shortly after birth. These facts were important to Gnomes wanting to immigrate from Northern Europe and Scandinavia. Based on this information, they could make better decisions as to where they wanted to live.

February 28

I never expected to find such a wealth of information concerning the Gnome migration from all across southern and central Europe. I am sure there are pockets of Gnomes left in some of the more remote areas of Europe, in the mountains, forests, woodlands, and fields.

Seeing the collection of artifacts Silvas has, the glyphs, pictographs, and early writings in script, first hand are amazing. I feel truly privileged. He has explained the writing and symbols on each tablet and skin to me. He has taken such meticulous care of them. He wears gloves when he handles them. By doing so, the oil on his hands will not stain them. The maps and manuscripts are so beautifully presented. They were like works of art.

Silvas has given me so much of his time for the last nine days. His translations of the manuscripts, scrolls, and tablets and his collection of artifacts will be his legacy to all of the inhabitants of Horse Thief Bay and to the Gnomes especially.

Silvas has also written of the Dwarves journey to the Bay, and has given a lot of his time to researching all of those inhabitants who were here in the Bay long before the arrival of the Gnomes. They include the Water Nymphs and Sprites, the Wood Nymphs and Sprites, the Wood Knars, the Puncum, and the Alderling.

Silvas will tell me the stories of all bit by bit as he is able. He is 135 and is slowing down. He needs to take a nap each afternoon. He has asked me if I could help him with his ongoing research of these early inhabitants. He knows that I am very keen on finding out all I can about them too.

March 1 - Signs of Spring

I heard crows cawing this afternoon. They have returned early. I like to hear them. It usually means spring is on its way. Ian put out more cracked corn today. We are nearly out of it. Between turkeys, other birds, deer, and squirrels, it does not take long to finish a twenty-five pound bag of feed.

The Downy and Hairy Woodpeckers have been working very hard drilling for Bark Beetle larvae. The Woodpeckers find our house of interest too. There are already several large holes, which must be covered.

Yesterday our pair of Pileated Woodpeckers were causing chips to fly on our neighbour's tree. They are a rather solitary bird. We rarely see them.

March 2

Each day the sun climbs higher in the sky. The days grow longer. The ice melts on the river. The deepest part of the channel, where the current is strongest, is the first to open. The ice in the Bay is the last to leave. Icicles form in the afternoon and their measured drips stop as the sun flushes behind the trees. Evening ushers in the night. Stars twinkle as the moon rides across the sky.

March 3

This evening the wind blew with biting breath through the snow covered Alderwild Wood, our home. The image of every tree, rock, fern, and wildflower has been etched on my mind. They have become so much a part of me. The Alderwild Wood is necessary for my emotional survival as well as the animals and Fairies living in it. The staccato tapping of tree branches, one against another, their trunks moaning and creaking with the cold, Beech leaves fluttering, the night sky with its moon, and glinting stars all have a profound effect on my psyche.

Tomorrow Silvas is coming shortly after breakfast, staying for lunch, and leaving just after 1:00 P.M.

March 4 - Fleeing Dwarves

Silvas arrived with more skins and manuscripts this morning. He came prepared to discuss the Dwarf migration to North America.

The Dwarves closely traced the route traveled by the Gnomes one hundred and thirty-eight years earlier. They were a stubborn people. They thought that they were strong enough to hold back the onslaught of the invading

Barbarians and Trolls and still come out of the fray as victors, but that was not the case. They were too few and ill equipped. In truth they were no match to fight anyone. They did not have the heart needed for killing people.

In the battles where the Dwarves did take up arms, they were cut down so badly only a few walked away alive. At the battle of Trachtprugel in central Germany and again at the battle of Tot, they were decimated.

The Dwarves, like the Gnomes, could not live in a constant state of fear of death and destruction. They were always having to move or face being slaughtered. Dwarves from all over Europe and western Russia were being pushed out of their homes and villages. They trekked to the northern coast of Europe and for a while remained in the villages left by the Gnomes. After some years there, they began to feel the need to move on. They built ships larger than those of the Gnomes in order to transport more people and livestock. Over a period of four years the Dwarves built six ships and many smaller sealskin boats.

They decided to bypass Norway and the Faeroe islands, but they planned to stop briefly at the Orkney Islands to unload some needed provisions for the Gnomes living there. Then the Dwarves sailed on to Iceland to drop off more provisions. Although it was not planned, a large group of Dwarves, fifty in number, upon meeting and talking with the Gnomes, Dwarves, and Middling's of Iceland, decided to stay and build a settlement there. All their possessions and livestock were taken ashore. One ship returned to the German coast while the others continued on.

The Dwarves would not stop at Greenland unless the fog was too dense. They would sail through the Straight of Belle

Isle, located between Newfoundland and Labrador on the mainland of North America.

All five ships did reach the Straight in fairly good condition. Of the three hundred and seventy passengers remaining on board after leaving Iceland, five died of dysentery, two fell overboard and drowned, one was stabbed, and there were three births, two boys and one girl all healthy. They proceeded to sail along the coast of New Brunswick.

Up River

After resting and taking on provisions at the first of the Gnome settlements, on the coast of New Brunswick, the five ships left to sail further up river. Upon reaching the area now known as Montreal, they stopped and explored the land. It was already September. The air was growing chill. The leaves on the trees were turning color and drifting to the ground.

The land was well treed. Although the river was wide there, the Dwarves found a suitable harbour to pull their ships out of the water to dry land for the winter. It was decided that all should stay there for the time being. The voyage across the Atlantic had been long and difficult. Those Dwarves wishing to go further could do so in the spring when the Redwings returned to the Cattails along the riverbank.

With the arrival of warmer days and melting snow, the Dwarves who wished to move on began to pack their possessions and gather provisions. It had been decided over the winter that a large group of Dwarves would stay behind and establish a permanent settlement. Gnomes were already living there and doing well.

The land could support more people without damaging the environment, if they took care to protect it and the wildlife. The native people, the Indians, had shown the Gnomes already living there how to live in harmony with nature, both plant and animal. Some trees could be cut, some fish caught, and some animals hunted if needed. However, there needed to be a balance. No one should take more than necessary, just what was needed. They must not disrupt the balance of Nature and Her inhabitants. Eighty Dwarves remained.

Two ships emptied their passengers and returned to Europe. The three remaining ships continued on their quest. They took the same route up the St. Lawrence as the Gnomes had traveled. They found areas to build their communities as well as settling down next to Gnomes settlements.

When they reached the White Water Rapids, they found the Gnomes had dug a canal bypassing the turbulent waters. It was now indicated on all the Gnome maps of the St. Lawrence River. All the settlements listing the population of each, as well as bays, shoals, weed beds, depth of water and good fishing spots were indicated on a map.

The canal made the St. Lawrence navigable in that area. Since boats no longer had to be pulled ashore and set on rollers as the first Gnomes had to do, it cut short the journey up river by eight days.

As the ships sailed on, small groups of Dwarves disembarked at each port along the way. Two more ships returned to Europe. One ship remained, carrying the last twenty immigrants. After two more days of sailing, in the cool of the evening, as the sun began to sink westward behind the trees of High Pines Point, the ship edged its way into Horse Thief Bay. They were the ancestors of Natterjack, Bracken, and the other Dwarves now living in Horse Thief Bay. The first stars of evening glinted in the sky.

March 5 - The Last of Winter

A biting wind blew through the snow covered wood this evening. The trees groaned and sighed. Beech leaves fluttered. Tree trunks creaked. Although the moon shone brightly, the night sky seemed dark and cold. The stars twinkled but did not cheer the spirit. I am glad to be indoors.

I still have bad memories of that horrible night last autumn when the Trolls attacked our Oak tree with such savagery.

I can see candlelight in the windows of the Gnomes and kerosene lamps in the Dwarf community. I wonder if they too fear that something is afoot with the Trolls tonight.

I do not think so. Natterjack once told me that Trolls, Traugs, and Norgs seldom come out of their lairs when it is snowing, or when the snow that has already fallen is deep. They tend to sleep a great deal in winter.

Tomorrow I shall undertake a study of present day Gnomes and Dwarves and their relationship to the Alderling and Puncum.

March 7

Natterjack stopped by this morning. He seemed restless, a bit out of sorts, grumpy, and bored. He is becoming weary of the snow and would like spring to come soon, as we all wish.

The snow is still deep. Every few days there is a fresh layer of snow, not a great deal but enough so that the level of snow never seems to diminish. Everyone in the community must still walk through snow tunnels they carved out for themselves earlier in the winter.

The tunnels not only lead from one home to another but also to the different feeding posts set up for the birds, squirrels, turkeys, and deer.

The Gnomes and Dwarves while doing these chores also check on the health and well being of all the creatures they feed. They even put out fish fillets for the Red Fox. He is a frequent visitor. Just yesterday I saw a Red Fox walking on the ice near shore. There was a flock of Purple Finches and Goldfinches at our feeder this morning.

Natterjack told me the Gnomes and Dwarves cannot ice fish every day. The temperature in late winter fluctuates so much that the ice is not always safe to walk on. I asked him what other things do they do when they cannot ice fish. He replied," the men repair their tools and sharpen their axes. In the evening we make household utensils, toys, flutes, and fifes. We also tell stories, remembering old friends and relatives and retracing their ancestry as far back in time as possible".

"Much of our history has been oral but this practice is changing. One member of each clan is now put in charge of recording the stories and bits of information gleaned from these communal gatherings. The member chosen to do the recording is called the "Keeper of the Books" or the Historian. As the stories are being told, he jots down on paper made by the Puncum any scrap of history, new names, births, deaths, marriages, honours, professions, settlements, and legends discussed. He makes a note of whatever comes to mind and may be of some consequence, then he researches it."

The Historian pulls out the old books and interviews the elders, some of whose minds are quite clear, others not so much. Some family members glorify and embellish the facts. Some are negative beyond reason. It is up to the "Keeper of the Books" to sort out fact from fiction.

There are times when debating and arguing take place. For every question asked there may be more than one answer.

March 8

Puddles form on the ice by day and then freezes at night as the temperature drops. Soon the entire surface of the ice will be watery. Cracks develop, the wind blows, and the ice shifts. Large ice flows float slowly down the river. Some come into the Bay. Sheets of ice collide, stacking one on top of another. They groan and moan, ever in motion, bumping, separating, and melting.

The sun arcs higher in the sky, its rays more potent. Icicles melt, but as the evening nears and the day grows colder, they lengthen again.

March 9

Last evening Bracken stopped by and asked us if we would both like to come see some of the projects he and the other Dwarves were involved in. Of course we accepted the invite. He came for us early this morning. It was our first visit to their workshop.

I do not venture out of doors much when there is ice and snow on the ground. I tend to fall easily, often hitting my head. With Ian and Bracken on either side of me, I made it safely to their workshop.

We thoroughly enjoyed ourselves and were fascinated by their work. They were designing shields and masks. Their masks were fearsome looking. The shields were both round and ovate.

The masks were representations of Trolls, Traugs, and Norgs, destroyers of Na. The round shields had stylized designs representing the destruction of the environment. The oval shields had stylized representations of the peace, tranquillity, and beauty of Na. The colours and designs were striking.

The women had been busy in Bracken's workshop cutting out tunics and painting designs on them for the festival. The Festival of the Grata usually occurs each year on April 5th, the first day of the New Year for all of the inhabitants of Horse Thief Bay. The Festival lasts for seven days and usually coincides with the Spring planting of seeds, which are mostly started indoors.

In actual fact, the Festival is a time for the inhabitants of the Bay to vent their frustrations, fears, and anger towards the Trolls and their kind, hence the reason for the mock battles.

Normally the Dwarves, Gnomes, and Fairies cannot physically fight the Trolls in a true battle and expect to win, but with some help from the humans, they may hope to stop the abuse of the land, trees, various wildflowers, the river, and even the rock formations, which have been here for as long as time itself.

Many humans tend to look at but do not really see or feel the same outrage and disgust towards the violation of Na by the Trolls and their kind.

Unlike the Dwarves, Gnomes, Fairies, and other races of the Bay, Humans tend to not care quite so much about the abuse of Na inflicted by the Trolls. In fact, there seems to be much apathy among humankind.

Grata is not just a time for pent up anger to be released

and relieve the souls of such bitterness. It is also a time when the spirit is replenished with new life and hope, just as the Spring brings new life again to Na.

The festival is also a time when men repair their sledges and tools and make some new ones if needed. On occasion they will build a boat for use on the Alderwild and River. Their homes too often need repairing, especially if the winter has been a really brutal one.

Young Dwarves and Gnomes, carrying baskets, walk along the outer edge of the Alderwild Wood near the road where the humans drive their cars. While out walking on the humans' roads, the young Dwarves and Gnomes pick up any empty soda cans, beer bottles, trash paper, and other garbage that humans often toss out their car windows.

On the night of the 5th day of Grata, all of the regular labour in the Bay ceases and preparations for the festival get under way.

Women bring out clay jars filled with Chufa and dried Cattail flour. Smaller jars and bowls, which contain candied Wild Ginger Root, Mandrake Jam, and Elderberry preserves are also brought out. Elderberry and Dandelion wines and several kinds of juices are served in pitchers. Chufa meal and Cattail flour are mixed with dried Dandelion leaves and flowers to be baked into round buns. Muffins made from Ground Nuts and Cattail flour are laid out in long low baskets. Rock Tripe, a sort of flat fungus, is boiled, then sautéed in Bullhead oil. Boiled Arrowhead tubers, and Shagbark Hickory nuts, dried and then roasted are placed in large bowls and are brought to the table. The men bring smoked Yellow Perch, fresh Great Northern Pike, and marinated Water Snake.

When all is ready, the food prepared, and everyone is gathered around and seated, the feasting begins. Stories are shared. The meal is not hurried. Time is taken to savour each course. When everyone is finished, the tables are cleared and the elders light up their pipes. The aroma of Lemon Balm fills the air.

The stories told are cheerful. It is a joyous time. There is music and singing, line dancing, and jigs. Fifes, flutes, harps, and other stringed instruments can be heard at one time or another during the activities.

Presents are given. There are toys made for the children - boats, and fifes, flutes and dolls, and rattles for the very young. Gay, brightly coloured costumes are worn. Elderberry Cordial is sipped.

The celebrating continues long into the night. The children have already fallen asleep on their mothers' or fathers' laps. By 2:00 A.M. the partying is over. Everyone must rest up for the next day's activities.

The families tend to sleep until 8:30 in the morning. The adults do not eat breakfast but fast for the entire day until late evening when they have a light meal and retire early.

The children do not take part in the fasting until they are thirteen years old, when they are considered to be young adults.

The men gather their masks, swords, spears, and shields and don their tunics.

The Dwarves, wearing the masks, which are very fearsome, play the part of the Trolls. They emit terrible cries, roars, and grunts.

The Gnomes take the part of the defenders and protectors of Na from those who would despoil Her. They do not wear

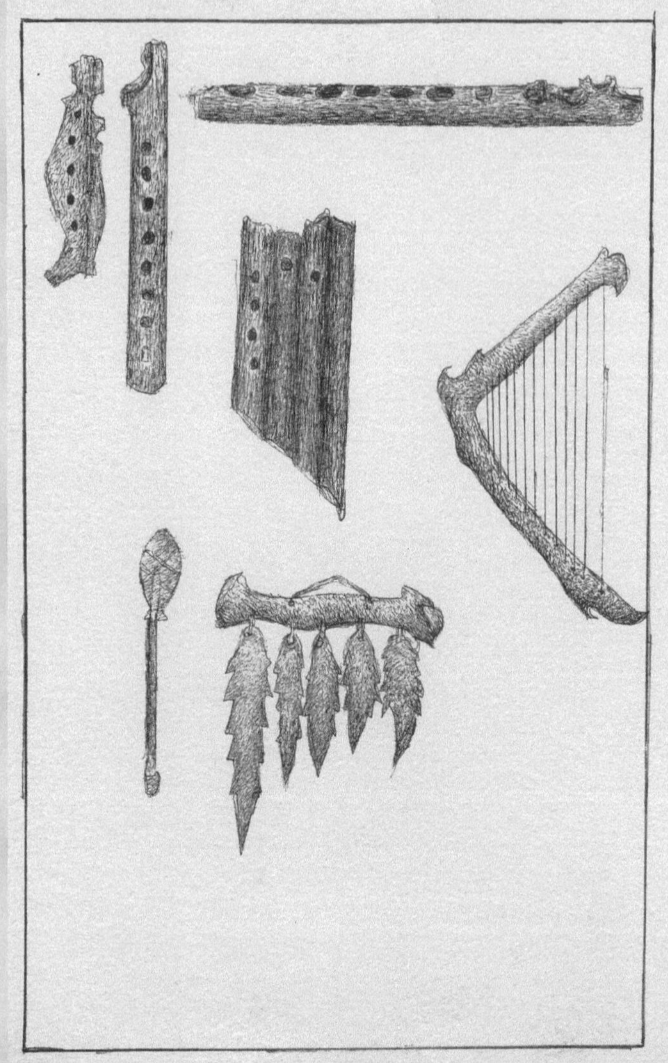

any masks for they play themselves, true protectors. They take up their swords, spears, and shields and prepare themselves for the mock battle to ensue.

There are no real winners. Neither side can claim victory. The Gnomes hold their ground but not much more. The Trolls gain more than they lose.

I asked Bracken if the masks and shields were used in battles with other settlements or just used in defence against the Trolls. Bracken said that they were just used in mock battles during the Festival of Grata. The clothing, masks, shields, wooden swords, spears, bows, and arrows will be seen later as part of the festival.

March 14

I have written of the upcoming Festival of Grata in narrative form, as it was told to me by Silvas Oakenbaum over the past five days.

Silvas is a master storyteller. For many, many years he has been telling the story of the Creation, the Puncum, the

First ones, the ongoing siege of Na by the Trolls and their kind; and the Coded Laws Na gave to the Puncum in the Beginning when the Earth was Young.

Silvas is still going strong. I do not think that he has ever tired of telling the story each year, to each new generation. It is a mission. He sees the impact it has on the young and even on those who have heard the story year after year. He knows that the message expressed in these stories must continually be kept in the forefront of everyones mind.

He sees that the stories are still important to all by the tears that are shed and by the cries and shouts that are heard. We all need to be reminded, and to take action.

Ian and I have been invited to take part and share in the festivities of Grata in April. We are looking forward to it.

March 16

I saw a Bald Eagle today. They are so majestic. It gives me a thrill to know that we have them coming here to the Bay. I feel so fortunate. We also have three White-tailed Deer feeding in front of the house this morning.

Ian is working on another paper-mâché mask of one of the Alderling he met last autumn in the Valley of the Horsetails. It looks very good. Another masterpiece!

March 17

A flock of geese flew in their V formation over the house this morning. They are very early. They usually do not arrive until the middle of April. One year, it seemed as though all of the geese forgot that they were supposed to fly north and suddenly it dawned on them. On May 1st thousands of geese flew over the island. The entire sky, from horizon to horizon was filled with honking geese flying in formation with long trailing sides. All day and into the night I could hear them. I have never seen anything like it before or since.

March 18

Although we have not known Silvas for very long, our friendship with him has grown quite close. We have a great respect and admiration for him. I very much want to ask him about the herbalist. Natterjack, Bracken, and Hatch have avoided telling me anything substantial about Her whenever I have brought the subject up. There is a mystique, an almost mythological aura that surrounds Her. All who speak Her name say it with the great reverence reserved for someone very special.

We have seen her just the once and at a distance at the Alderling funeral. She looked like an elderly toad but stood erect on her legs, not all fours. She seemed to be a creature of great wisdom and mystery. I sent Silvas a note by way of Natterjack, asking him to come for tea when the weather cleared. I asked him if he would tell me about this lady, who looked like a toad and was held in the highest esteem.

March 19

Another day of heavy wet snow! The black and grey female squirrels should have given birth to two to five young each by now. They are born blind, hairless, helpless, and needing their mother's milk for five weeks. The adults have suddenly become very active in our garden, digging up the acorns and Hickory nuts they had buried last autumn. I would have a hard time finding anything with the snow still on the ground.

There are also half grown squirrels, both black and red, running up and down the trees. They must be from last year's second litter born in late summer.

March 20

The first day of Spring or Spri as the Gnomes and Dwarves call it. The Greening Time.

Spring brings warmth from the sun and zephyr winds. It is a time of rebirth and renewal. The earth greens, and old plants send up new shoots from their old roots and tubers. New seedlings push their heads through the soil from last year's ripened fruit.

March 24

The rushing waters of early March have begun to flow down the Alderwild Brook and the Willow more slowly now. The two brooks have become more tranquil to sit by. They meet and spread out into the flood plain of Fern Marsh. Only hillocks and tussocks of wild grasses, Sensitive Ferns spore cases, and the matted roots and dead leaves of the Marsh Marigold stand high enough not to be submerged.

Natterjack stopped by with a note from Silvas this morning. He will come tomorrow, weather permitting. Silvas asked if Ian would make some of his Bee Balm tea and Elderberry muffins, which would be most delightful. Candied Wild Ginger root would be a very nice touch as well.

Ian was flattered and most willing to share his tea and Ginger root. He would bake a batch of muffins too.

March 25

Silvas Oakenbaum arrived at 1:00 P.M. on the shoulders of Natterjack. It was very muddy outside. Silvas was well bundled, wearing his woolly red pointed hat pulled down over his ears. There was a scarf, heavy sweater, pants, and boots. Natterjack helped him remove his outerwear and boots. He then set him into one of our stuffed chairs by the wood stove. He also handed him his cane, which had a sleeping rabbit carved on the handle.

He did not bring a single paper or artifact with him. I was a little surprised. Ian offered him a cup of tea. He declined," Not just yet, a little later". With hands and feet warmed, he cleared his throat and began to speak. He told us that there are written records on deerskin, Birch bark, clay tablets, and paper made by the Puncum. There are also rock paintings describing the story. He would take us to see the paintings this summer. These records go back thousands of years describing and depicting individuals like the Healer. She is a constant figure in the stories told by the Puncum, Alderling, Gnomes, and Dwarves.

In the retelling of these stories from one generation to the next, and one race to another, some changes have occurred. However the basic tale has not changed. Over the centuries in the recounting of these stories, the different narrators and scribes have added their own embellishments to the facts. The facts, however, are easily uncovered. The different races and cultures have the Healer referred to by other names, a name in their own tongue. She was even known to the First Puncum, The Ancients, from the time the Earth was young.

I asked Silvas if She was some sort of apparition. She looked to be of a physical substance, a living, breathing creature, but She looked like a Toad. Was she a creature who never dies for her to last so many thousands of years? Was She ever born? How did She come about?

Silvas told me to wait. I was getting too far ahead of myself. He said that She was not an apparition but a living, breathing creature of toad origin, a Bufo Americanus.

However, every now and again, the genetic make up of the toad's fertilized egg is altered by some act of Na. The reason for the change is unknown, only that it does happen. As a result an extraordinary being is produced. In her outward appearance, She looks like a toad except that She stands on Her hind legs and Her limbs move and function like those of a human. The great difference between Her and a normal Bufo Americanus is the make up of her brain cells. They are radically changed.

She has great intuitive powers comprehending truths beyond our immediate understanding. She is aware of and most fervently against the assault on Na by the Trolls and their kind.

Silvas told us his thoughts why this phenomenon, this mutation of nature occurs. There has always been in every race and culture a need for a being that is incorruptible.

She is a being who has gathered the wisdom of all the ages past, to impart this knowledge to all of Na's family, Her inhabitants.

She has been and will be there to pass on the lessons for caring for the wounded, both physical and emotional. Her lessons include the preparation of unguents and tinctures from herbs and wild flowers found in the Wood. She speaks the words to heal the wounds of sorrow. She provides the knowledge and wisdom to tend to and protect Na's resources, her trees, her birds, the fish, and all of the creatures of the land and water. She teaches the principals of cohabitation.

She herself cannot save Na but can only imbue Her knowledge to those who will listen to Her and are willing to take up the challenge and responsibility of Na's care. There are those who do not heed her words. They are the ones without souls, the creatures of the Dark World, the Norgs, Traugs, Atrolpia, Troloxica, and Trolconitum. They, when first born and later as children, had the potential to have souls. Perhaps they did have souls when young but at some point in their lives they turned dark. There are also many humans who ignore the needs of the environment and do nothing to protect what is good. They are careless and selfish.

Silvas ended his account of the Healer or Suund as the inhabitants of the Bay call her by saying that the altered fertilized egg of the toad is not a mistake or a malfunction of the zygote but a deliberate act by Na. It is an act with the sole purpose of creating a being that would be the conscience and teacher to the Puncum, Alderling, Gnomes, Dwarves, and humans throughout the ages.

Why did Na bestow such a responsibility on a toad? The Toad is common looking, unassuming, and humble. The Toad was there in the beginning. She carried the sun across the sky from east to west. She carried the Light, which illumined the Dark Places of the World. She illuminates the mind, the conscience of all of those who will allow Her light to shine upon them and Her wisdom to guide them.

Silvas stopped and sat back, taking his glasses off. I could see that he was emotionally and physically drained. It is difficult to tell a story with so much emotion connected to it. He felt every word of it, as did we.

Ian brought out muffins and tea, and they were welcomed. In the future when Silvas comes to tell us a story, I shall be more careful. I must watch to see that he does not become so tired. If the story is long, it should be told over a period of several days. It was 5:00 P.M. when he left. It was a long afternoon of talking for someone his age. He told us that he would return again with more stories.

March 26

I cannot believe it. It snowed again yesterday but did not begin to stick until late afternoon. By this morning the ground was thickly covered again, no more brown patches showing.

I heard a Robin call. This time there was another to answer it. Our pair of Pileated Woodpecker friends came and were drilling feverishly on a couple of our trees whose tops halves had broken off in the ice storm a few years ago. I had left the trees standing with the hope the pair would like them.

March 28

It was a bright sunny day and warm. The sky was bright blue with not a cloud to be seen. The river was a deep blue with bright white ice flows. They moved slowly down river. Large patches of earth, leaves, and bright green moss are beginning to appear. A welcomed sight! Even a few Snow Drops that Ian planted in the Wood are showing their heads.

I have not yet seen any chipmunks. They should be awakening soon from their long winter's sleep. The Crows were cawing and six deer were nibbling on some of the grasses where the ground was bare.

The ice in the shallow areas of the Bay is now quite spongy and porous. There are no Black Scooters, Red-crested or Hooded Mergansers, or Buffleheads swimming along the edge of the ice yet. They are usually here in February. It seems strange not to see them.

March 30

Snow again, about an inch. I am really anxious for spring weather to come and stay. I look forward to the greening of the wild plants and then their flowers. It is a wondrous sight to see hundreds of Dutchman's Breeches, Spring Beauty, and White Trillium. They will be appearing in mid and late April.

Every time I look out over the river, the Bay, the Alderwild Wood, our Alderwild Brook, Valley of Horsetails, and Fern Marsh, I know how fortunate I am to live here. I am truly glad the Sprites and Nymphs, the Puncum and Alderling, Gnomes, and Dwarves all dwell here too. They have cared for Na well and have taught us much.

April 1

It may be April on the calendar but the weather is not. Grey clouds hurry in quick succession. The air is cold and raw. A few drops of rain have hit the window. I doubt that we shall see anyone for tea today.

The rain to come hemmed and hawed, a few drops now and again all morning and part of the afternoon. At 3:00 P.M. there was a deluge. Great torrents of water raced down the Alderwild and Willow. Some Alder trees were uprooted, docks torn from their moorings, and even some of the summer homes of the Alderlings and Gnomes were swept away. These homes were thought to have been built high enough on the banks of the brooks to be safe.

Splintered boards, wood shingles, and even beds and chairs were seen floating in Fern Marsh.

We could not see the destruction taking place from our home. We learned of it from Natterjack, when he came running to the house for rope. He and a few of the other Dwarves and Gnomes hoped to save a few of the remaining docks by tying them to several trees. Nylon fishing line was also needed to tie to the furniture and summer homes of the Alderlings. It was rather doubtful whether any of their possessions could be saved. Their homes and furniture are so small and fragile.

Ian went with Natterjack to help. They were able to save several chairs, two tables, and a four-poster bed, belonging to the Alderlings.

Ian returned after an hour and a half. He was saturated. Hatch and Pody were told to stay in their underground dwellings with their families. They could be swept away by the fast flowing water.

There will be need of much repair and rebuilding. Some of the Alderling homes were totally washed away. All of the residents of the Alderwild Wood community will help those who lost their homes or those whose dwellings needed to be repaired before they are safe to live in again.

A couple of Alder trees were uprooted and now lay across the main passage to the Alderwild Brook. Tomorrow they will have to be removed, cut into smaller pieces, and put to one side. If not they could cause even more extensive flooding during the next heavy rain.

My one great worry is, how are the Puncum? Has anyone checked on them?

April 2

The Puncum are safe and well, no injuries. Natterjack, Bracken, and Azulla checked on them yesterday. Their winter quarters and a few of their spring- summer homes sustained some damage but nothing which could not be repaired easily. Their homes were high enough. For a while it was nip and tuck.

April 3

The next day the weather continued to be raw, with a coldness to the bone. No rain, just a grey overcast sky and occasional blustering winds. Everything that can be done at this time to secure the remaining docks and homes has been done.

We heard today that a few of the Gnomes residing on the banks of the Willow had some damage done to their homes and docks. However they had a more serious situation to deal with. Two very young Gnome children had escaped their mother's attention and stepped out of doors to see the raging water. They fell in and were caught up in the strong current. Fortunately they had the good sense to hang on to a passing board. It carried them into Fern Marsh where they were found clutching onto a clump of Alder trees.

Nature does not pamper us but gives depth to our soul and strengthens our will. Each day is a challenge, ever changing, never the same. We are surrounded by such diversified life. Every day presents itself anew.

April 4

When I awoke this morning I suddenly realized that tomorrow is the first day of the Festival of Grata. It is the beginning of the New Year for the inhabitants of Horse Thief Bay. It lasts for seven days.

With so much attention focused on the storm and its aftermath, I nearly forgot about the festival. I am wondering if it will be postponed a few days.

2:00 P.M. Ian walked to Natterjack's home to find out what is happening with the preparations for tomorrow. He also went to see if there was anything more we could do to help.

He did not return until 5:30 P.M. The celebration is on. A few of the activities will be changed but all of that will be addressed tomorrow at the communal breakfast set for 8:30.

I wonder if any animals will come. Silvas briefly mentioned that there are animals in the Alderwild Wood who speak. It is a kind of broken English dialect. Silvas also seemed to imply that there are certain plants that converse with plants of their kind. This is something I must look into. What a find if this is true!

April 5

When we awoke this morning three White-tailed Deer were grazing just outside our window. We bundled up with warm clothes. It was quite chilly but the sun with its bright yellow face was just coming up over the horizon. The prospect for a clear day looked promising.

Ian and I set out for the large clearing under the trees near the east bank of the Alderwild, at its head. The brooks have tamed considerably since the storm.

On our way we met up with many Dwarves and Gnomes. A number of them were coming from High Pines Point, the Plain of Wal, Hemlock Ridge, the Bern Hills, and East of the Mac Mountains.

Many of the Puncum, Alderlings, Rocklings, Leaflings, Wood Sprites, and Nymphs had already arrived and seated themselves. The Water Sprites and Nymphs had not yet wakened from hibernation. It was still too cold, not for another month at the earliest. A few Gnomes and Dwarves had come last night with their sleeping bags, bedrolls, and tents.

A cacophony of sounds in many tongues and accents, which I did not know, rose from the gathering. Fairies from one race mixed with those of another. There were some there who must have been deaf for they communicated with one another in sign.

I did not see any anthropomorphic animals, nor did I see the Suund. They may have been there but there were just so many individuals.

There were Fairies sitting in the trees. From a distance they looked like a flock of small birds perched on the branches. There was a Gnome on crutches. He had injured his foot. Another had his arm bandaged in a sling. I wondered if these injuries were incurred during the flood.

To our great joy there were Fairies flying about. We had not yet seen any flying before. We could hardly believe our eyes. It was unbelievable!! We have never experienced such intense delight. There they were, right before our eyes!

Ian was not just happy, he was enthralled, enraptured. He was speechless! I think we both wished we had wings too and could join them. Some Fairies were flying upside down, and turning over and over like stunt pilots in an air show. Ian and I were buzzed a few times. Such fun!

There were some Fairies who take a straight vertical shot upwards, turn quickly, and then swoop down, pulling out just before they hit the ground. Ian was so caught up in watching these antics, he was not aware of his body bending, twisting, and turning. I asked Azulla, who was sitting next to me, what type of Fairies were they? He said the Fairies, which were green and looked like Maple leaves but smaller were Leaflings. Those fairies with tan and ochre coloured wings the shape of Basswood leaves were Leaflings as well but from another race. Wood Nymphs had wings with the contours of Birch leaves.

Suddenly we heard a loud bell ring and someone, I think it was Natterjack, called everyone to attention. "Please! Everyone! Breakfast is about to commence, buffet style. Just come in and help yourselves. There is plenty of food for all. Signs have been placed on each of the tables displaying the names of the foods. Alderlings, Wood Sprites, and other Fairies have different diets and so we have tried to accommodate all of your needs"

"Afterwards, please stay in your seats. An important meeting will be held. Because of the storm and subsequent flooding, our normal activities performed during the first days of Grata will be suspended. We must now focus our attention on repairing and rebuilding the homes and docks damaged or destroyed entirely along the Willow and Alderwild Brooks. There may also be need of buttressing of the supports holding up some of the Puncum homes. This will be at the confluence of the two brooks in the delta. Now tuck in and enjoy. We have a hard day's work ahead of us". Everyone moved into the Great Hall where it was warm.

I was somewhat surprised. There seemed to be no bitterness or anger towards Na by those in attendance. I spoke to several of the Gnomes and Dwarves. Each responded to my questions concerning the flood with nearly the same answers. Nature like humans has many moods. These moods may fluctuate from day to day or hour to hour.

The negative aspects of Life and Na must not be allowed to control or dominate one's thinking. Adaptation is the key word to living successfully with Na. Negative situations may be physically and emotionally handled much better with a positive attitude. However, the damage done to the environment by Trolls is another matter.

By 10:00 A.M. all had finished eating breakfast, introduced themselves to any newcomers and were ready for the task ahead of them. The women took care of the cleaning up.

The men began by collecting all of the debris from the damaged and destroyed homes. They hoped to use some of the wood, especially the beams again in the framing of the rebuilt homes.

The room dividers, which were made from Common Rush and Cattail fronds and stalks, would have to be replaced. Women wove mats made for roofs while the men framed the houses, laid the floors, put up outside walls, and thatched the roofs.

Some of the dwellings belonging to the Puncum were damaged but nothing they could not handle themselves. A few of the main supports needed shoring up as well as two or three roofs were in need of repair.

The men worked very hard, stopping briefly for lunch. They worked until dusk, when they could no longer see their hands.

The women too worked long hours, weaving mats for roofs and walls, for the Puncum and Alderling summer homes.

Another group of women spent the day preparing the food to feed so many individuals. There were not just those living in the Alderwild Wood to feed but also those who came from High Pines Point and beyond the Mac Mountains to the east.

Soon after everyone had eaten a late supper, all retired to their homes, tents, and sleeping bags.

The Alderlings had invited all of those folks, Puncum, Nymphs, Sprites, and anyone who was less than twelve inches high and left homeless by the flood, which included animals as well, to take shelter in the Alderling Common Room. Gnomes and Dwarves were given lodging in other Gnome and Dwarf homes and ours too. We also took in an entire raccoon family. A great number of beds were also set up in the Great Hall.

The Common Room was a large room in the basement just below the Alderling apartments. The Alderlings use it in times of severe cold weather. The floor around the outer edge of the room had been covered with sweet Yellow Clover and some dried grasses collected last year. All who accepted the invite found accommodations most welcome. The foot thick layer of clover and grasses was very comfortable and sweet smelling. Infants were laid on the sweet smelling grasses lined with the fluff of Coltsfoot and Milkweed.

The Suund was asked to look in on some of the elders and children. The flooding had not only caused much material damage to the homes and docks but also many injuries. Fortunately most of the injuries were not serious. They ranged from minor cuts and bruises to strained backs, a broken arm, and one broken leg.

Some of the very young and elderly have experienced emotional distress, acute anxiety, nightmares, and palpitations of the heart. For these individuals the Suund prepared a tea using the extracted oil collected from the fresh leaves of the Lemon Balm plant picked last summer. This, in conjunction with the aroma from the burning oil, would have a calming effect for most.

For those who suffered cuts and bruises, the Suund applied a decoction of Self Heal to the wounds. It is mild and does not sting.

One elderly woman was having difficulty with an irregular heartbeat. She was given a small dose of powdered Bloodroot in water to stimulate the heart and produce a more even beat. Bloodroot is poisonous so the Suund is very careful in its use.

Some of the children had coughs and sore throats. The Suund gave them a gargle of Self Heal.

It was not until 11:00 or 11:30 P.M. before the Suund finished caring for the injured. As she was about to leave the Alderling compound an elder came to her with a message. She was needed at once at one of the Gnome dwellings.

A young Gnome wife was in labour two weeks prematurely. It was her first pregnancy and she was to have twins. The Suund felt that it must have been the excitement and turmoil, the confusion, and heartbreak caused by the flood, which brought on the labour so early. Concern was etched on the Suund's face as she hurried to the Gnome's dwelling. On her way she stopped at her own home first to pick up a vial of powdered Blue Cohosh root.

Upon her arrival at the young woman's home, the Suund asked the husband to boil water for tea as well as for the delivery. Into a cup of hot water she added a small amount of the powdered Blue Cohosh root. This would ease the pain of birthing.

At 3:00 A.M. twins were born, a boy and a girl, both healthy. The Suund remained at the bedside of the mother and infants until the stars abated and Dawn arose from her long night's sleep. The birds began to chatter and soon

the Suund left for home, knowing that all was well with the
newborns and their mother.

    The Suund's dwelling and apothecary is under the roots of
the twin Maples born from one seed. She too could sleep now.
Others would look after Her patients in the Common Room as
well as the new mother. She would look in on them later.

Again today everyone got back to work cleaning up and rebuilding. Ian too pitched in as he did yesterday.

As for myself, I thought it best to continue on with the journal, taking down notes of my observations of the festival and the new emergency. Just as important is the manner in which the residents of the Bay and the Alderwild Wood, our friends, their friends and neighbours from East of the Mac Mountains and those from the West, from High Pines Point, have rallied and come together to help those in need.

What is also important to me is how they are coping psychologically. They have not panicked. Everything is being handled in a calm and orderly fashion. They have been through difficult times with Na before. Na has many moods. They are a part of Her being. One must accept Her by adapting and being mentally and physically prepared.

Most everyone in the Bay and the Alderwild Wood belong to a team. Each team has certain duties to perform when a disaster of one kind or another strikes.

Other mothers in the Bay are also giving birth to young. The Red Squirrel has given birth to six blind and helpless babies without hair. They will not open their eyes for another twenty-seven days. It is an anxious time for the mother. She will nurse them for more than a month. By the end of May they will be out running here and there and up and down trees, learning all the skills needed to become independent. They will remain with their mother all summer.

Gnome and Dwarf infants, unlike many small animals, are not born blind. They are helpless at birth and for many years thereafter. However, they do have a head of light brown hair on arrival. By the time they are a year old, they are able to walk quite well on their own. There is a great deal for them to learn, both practical and emotional.

Lessons to Learn

1. How and what to take from Na, just what is needed and no more.
2. How to live in harmony with Na. Cohabitation.
3. Do not fell trees unnecessarily.
4. Plant new and young trees where those have been cut down or died.
5. Do not waste Na's natural resources.
6. Limit the number of fish caught or animals hunted.

Young Gnomes and Dwarves, Alderling and Puncum are taught the R words: Respect and Responsibility for Na and All Living Things: Plant, Animal, Tree, and Rock, Water and Air.

1. Give generously of oneself.
2. Let the Mind be open to all ideas.
3. Seek the Truth.
4. Have Patience.
5. Be Humble and Do Justly.
6. Enjoy the small things of everyday life. If one waits for something big to bring them happiness, a lifetime of many small pleasures will be missed.
7. Be willing to compromise, to get along with, and relate to others.

With so much to learn, Gnome and Dwarf children do not leave the family setting until they are nearly twenty-one years old. Fairy children do not stay with the family quite so long, late teens.

Gnomes as well as Dwarves are bonded together for life. There are no divorces in Gnome, Dwarf, or Fairy society. The willingness to discuss, listen, compromise, to care in the tenderness and sensitivity of their mate keeps their vows first made at the time of their marriage strong and lasting. This is a belief they have all learned from earliest childhood how to live with one another. They are taught how to communicate and relate to one another, family, friends, neighbours, and strangers.

All of the inhabitants of the Bay, including the young learn about cooperation and sharing. This is an ongoing process lasting all of their lives.

Many animals, the Grey and Black Squirrels, Flying and Red Squirrels, White- footed Mice, Moles, Voles, Shrews, Rats, Rabbits, Muskrats, and Deer all give birth to their young between mid March and May.

It is that time of year when Su warms Er, insect eggs laid last fall hatch, worms move about in the soil, and plants sprout new tender shoots.

Toads, Frogs, and Salamanders wake and soon lay their eggs in the shallow pools of water lying between the tussocks of dead grasses, which are just beginning to send up new green shoots. Sensitive Ferns, Fiddleheads, are just emerging through the thick brown coverlet of damp leaves.

April 7

There were a number of Robins hopping about this morning. It is good to see them digging in the moist soil and pulling up worms.

Several flocks of Canada Geese flew over the house this morning too. I even heard a Red-winged Blackbird calling from the stand of dead Cattails in the Bay. They have come to claim their nesting sites. The females will arrive later.

April 8

A few Snow Drops and Crocuses are in bloom this morning and Spring Peepers are trilling. Ian was off again at 8:00 A.M. to join Natterjack and the rest of the men with the rebuilding of the Alderling summer homes. The work is coming along well. There was just so much to do. Ian leaves the house at 8:00 and does not return until 4:00. He has been helping out every day since the time of the flood. He is becoming a master builder as well as a fine artist.

The Sun has finally shown its face, the clouds are gone, and the bright blue sky reigns. The Alderwild is quite tame now. A Lion turned into a Lamb. There are still a few patches of snow in the deep recesses of the Wood but the snow is melting fast. A few Coltsfoots are in bloom too. It has a single yellow flower resembling that of a Dandelion. However its stem is scaly, not smooth and it blooms earlier.

To my great delight and joy of joys, She was there, the Suund. Silvas Oakenbaum told me that She speaks

and understands
many tongues,
English being
one of them. I was
seated on a log
about twenty feet
from Her. I stood
up very slowly
and walked over to
Her. I was nervous
and hoped that She
would not be afraid
of me. She saw
me approaching
Her but remained
picking the leafy
scales of the
Coltsfoot's stem.

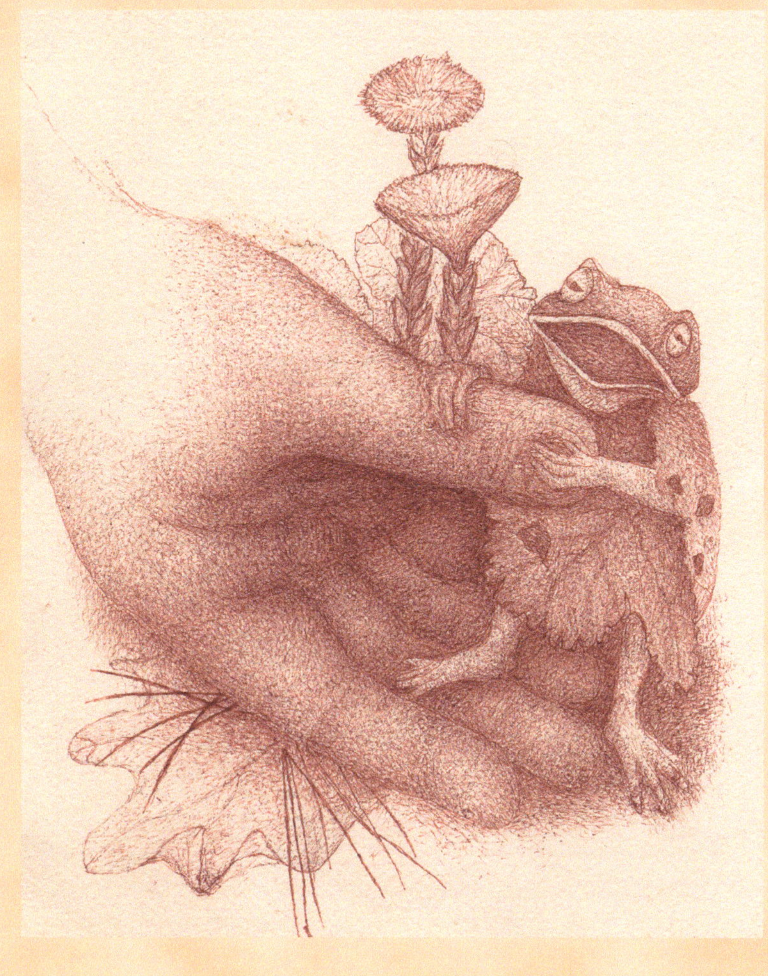

    Upon reaching the Suund, I sat down on the path near Her and the flower. As is my habit, I automatically put out my hand to shake Hers. I then realized the situation was an awkward one. She immediately took charge of the situation and stepped onto the index finger of my left hand while holding onto my thumb for balance. She took one more step up with Her left foot and sat in the palm of my hand. She was not at all nervous.

    I said, "Hello" and smiled. I wondered if a toad could smile if she wished to. How could Her mouth form words or show expression when it is made of hard bone? Our lips are made of soft pliable flesh. She did respond with "Hello" but Her mouth did not appear to move. Her tongue must have formed the word, I think. Something like a ventriloquist. I cannot explain it.

I asked Her what exactly she was doing. She understood me immediately and showed me. As She picked each leaf scale from the stem of the Coltsfoot She placed it gently into a small basket, which She carried on Her right arm. She then motioned to me to take Her to a warm sunny spot in the clearing where I was to sit down.

Taking a leaf from Her basket She began to scrape the hairs off the underside of each leaf into a clay bowl, which she had earlier placed on a rock in the sun. This done, the hairs were left to dry thoroughly before placing them in a vial. The hairs would later be boiled in water, then cooled and used as an emetic for certain kinds of poisons accidentally ingested by an animal, Dwarf, Gnome, or Fairy.

The leaves too would be used. She laid them out to dry and later they would be placed on a small fire of Bracket Fungus. The smoke from it would be inhaled by a few of the elders who were not well and were staying in the Common Room and Great Hall. It helped relieve their - difficulties in breathing, chest congestion, and bronchitis. The remaining fresh leaves would be boiled with a little sweet nectar taken from the Honeysuckle flowers last spring to give to the children as a gargle for their sore throats and coughs, but not to drink. The white fluff of the Coltsfoot seed head would be used later for filling comforters and pillows and also spread out on the soil from which new plants would grow.

It was a very strange feeling speaking to a toad. Stranger still was to hear Her reply.

It is late and time for bed. The repairs and rebuilding of homes and docks is completed. By tomorrow most everyone who took refuge with the Alderlings and Gnomes will be able to return to their homes. The wounded emotions will take a little longer to heal.

April 9

All work on the houses has been finished. By 5:00 P.M., everyone retired to their homes, bathed, and rested. At 7:00 P.M. All returned to the Great Hall where they feasted and made merry. Ian and I joined in the celebrating. The meal was kept simple but hearty. The big day for feasting will be on the 12th. Tonight was just a time for relaxing, singing, and dancing after so much hard work.

A group of Gnomes sang without the accompaniment of any instruments. Then Natterjack and Draka stood up and motioned to the others to do the same. In a blink of an eye everyone formed a line, one behind another, serpentine fashion and began singing. Ian was the tail end. It was wonderful to watch.

Later a group of Dwarves living east of the Mac Mountains displayed some fancy footwork, performing round dances. Afterwards they mimed legends, stories told to them by their ancestors who learned them from their ancestors living in Northern Europe before the Great Migration. Most everyone left fairly early. Ian was having a hard time keeping awake. It has been a long tiring day for everyone. All will sleep in tomorrow.

Work usually done during the festival of Grata by the members of the Alderwild Wood and Puncum communities is being put on hold for a few days. Everyone is exhausted. The last two days of Grata begins the day after tomorrow. These two days are the most serious and important of the festival and time is needed to recuperate and get one's thoughts together and into a more solemn state of mind.

April 10

Today a good many of the folk in the Bay, including us, relaxed. Some surveyed the completed work on the docks and summer homes of the Alderlings. Others checked on those who were injured and sick.

Ian and I wandered through the Wood and chatted with Natterjack, Bracken, Draka, and Hatch. Before we left the Wood we took a moment to check on the Skunk Cabbage in the Alderwild Brook. It is not directly in the water but the mud along side it. There was an elf sitting, hunched up on top of the flower head inside the green and burgundy speckled hood. The leaves were barely visible. By the end of May the leaves are very large and have a feted odour when bruised which draws insects which will pollinate it. Until such time elves will climb inside under the hood where it is very warm.

We then walked down the hill to the river. When we reached the shore we saw that the sandbar was no longer there. The water level was up, even higher than other years. There was a great deal of snow and rain this past winter, both of which were needed. Last summer and fall had been quite dry.

No matter, Ian untied the canoe and dragged it from its winter moorings, turned it over, and lowered it into the water. The river was calm and clear. We could see to the bottom. The Zebra Mussels have been mainly responsible for the clean water. Many thousands of them! They are Nature's natural filtration system and we have some as well as

several mussels in a
large fish tank. They
are very interesting to
watch.

  There were no other
boats on the river yet.
Spring and Autumn
are my most favourite
times of the year to
be on the island and
water. It is so peaceful.
With five strokes of
the paddle we were at
the island.

  I felt such a sense

of well being and completeness. The island and water
together create a rhythm and mood for the soul to float into
and move about. Tension subsides. Anger and frustrations
concerning Trolls and their destructive powers temporarily
recede from the mind and leaves a space for Na, something
more wondrous and healing. The line between reality and
dream blurs.

  There seemed to be no noticeable animal life as yet, except
for some male Red- wings. Robins are not usually seen
on the island. The soil is not very deep, and it dries very
quickly. It does not accommodate earthworms, the food
most liked by Robins.

  The Great Blue Heron is back and standing on the
western point of the island. A couple of male Mallard Ducks
were swimming near the stand of Cattails and the mouth of
the Alderwild Brook and Willow.

April 11

This morning the two most serious days of Grata commenced. Ian and I awoke early, the sky was blue, the air warm. It seemed to summon a beautiful day. We saw several Wood Sprites and Leaflings fly past our window in the direction of the Great Hall. They were so small it was hard to follow them with our eyes. To the West we could just see a group of Gnomes, with swords and shields in their hands climbing over Hemlock Ridge.

By the time Ian and I arrived most everyone was there. All of the tables and chairs, benches, and stools had been taken from the Great Hall and set out under the trees.

Counting Wood Sprites and Nymphs, Leaflings, Rocklings, Alderlings, Puncum, Gnomes, and Dwarves, it had to be 150 to 200 inhabitants there. Even those who were infirm and still recuperating were carried out and set on chairs with coverlets over their shoulders and legs. It was exciting to behold. Wondrous! Many animals were there too. I also saw the Suund speaking with S. Oakenbaum.

A bell rang and everyone found themselves seats, on a tree branch, a bench, or a chair.

Ian and The Pancake Incident

A large breakfast was about to be spread before us. Each dish, bowl of food or pitcher of drink brought to the tables was labeled. Slugs and their eggs, Sow Bugs, and dried Fairy Shrimp were delicious to some but not to all. Ian and I had pancakes made from Cattail flour mixed with regular flour. Wild Ginger syrup was poured over them. Ian has just finished his fourth pancake and was pouring more syrup over the next two pancakes when several young male Wood Sprites began flying around our table. They were pestering everyone, especially Ian. They pulled on his hair and tweaked his nose. Ian is not in the best of moods first thing in the morning, a bit short of patience.

Forgetting for a moment that these annoying creatures were Wood Sprites and not mosquitoes, he gave one a swat. It fell into the Ginger syrup on his pancakes. Its feet and one wing got stuck.

Sprites are very small and very fragile, especially when it comes to landing in something sticky. It was a near calamity. Ian overreacted and the Sprite's other wing got stuck. The Sprite became frantic and began to thrash around. The situation became perilous. His wings could be torn off. The Sprite now laid spread eagle in the syrup on top of the pancakes. The Suund was called for.

The Suund was there sitting at a table with Silvas and several of the elders. She came quickly. As soon as She saw the child, She called for Natterjack to fetch a jar labeled mandrake root from Her apothecary. While She waited She spoke soothingly to the boy to keep him from moving any further. Time was of the essence.

When Natterjack returned the Suund took a minute piece of Mandrake root and gave it to the Sprite to chew. He was asleep in a minute. Mandrake root, although very poisonous, can be used as an anaesthetic if given just a small amount. Great caution must prevail.

Natterjack carried the Sprite still lying in the syrup on top of the pancakes into the Great Hall where the Suund and Draka looked after the boy. Warm water was slowly dripped onto his wings and legs until the sugary syrup was completely dissolved and washed away. The two women gently lifted him onto a flat dry Oak leaf and carried him into the warm sunny air. The Sprite was still unconscious. His pulse was good. The procedure took only a few minutes. He was fine in no time.

The Suund and Draka stayed with the child until its wings were dry and in working order. In an hour he was as fit as a fiddle, nothing broken and no tears in the wings. It was a sobering experience for the lad.

Ian was terribly distressed by the accident. He blamed himself totally, even though all who witnessed it told him that it was not his fault. The children had gotten too out of control. The mother of the one child was inexperienced. He was her first child. It was an accident. It was understandable. They did sound like giant mosquitoes. Ian and I will both have to be more careful of what we swat at in the future.

There were still Gnomes and Dwarves eating. The mock battle between the friends and foes of Na had not yet begun. This gave those who were involved or affected by the young Sprite's accident time to finish eating.

Ian had another four pancakes. It is always that last big toe that needs filling up. Most of the tables were folded and carried into the Great Hall. The chairs and benches were arranged for the spectators along the outer edge of the area to be used as the battleground.

Ian and I found good seats in the back row. Many of the Wood Sprites and Leaflings chose to sit on the lower branches of the Pines, Maple, and Oak trees. Others like the Alderlings and Puncum preferred to sit on the ground. Soon everyone was seated and the battle was about to commence.

Once again, just as we had seen them at Bracken's workshop, Ian and I saw the Troll masks and shields. They are to be worn by the Dwarves in the mock battle between the Trolls, Traugs, and Norgs and the Gnomes acting the part of the Defenders of Na.

In today's battle the Dwarves, Natterjack, Bracken, Azulla, and Perch are in front of a group of ten other Dwarves, fourteen strong. They were truly fearsome in appearance. There were Norgs, Traugs, Marsh Trolls, Troloxica, Atrolpia, and Trolconitum, the most deadly of Trolls.

Trolls in the wild do not use shields or swords, but take to their shovels, saws, axes, steam shovels, and bulldozers. They have no respect or concern for the environment or people about them.

The Dwarves, however, even though they are acting out a mock battle, use the shields for protection.

The bludgeons, swords, masks, and shields, for the Defenders and Warriors are made using paper-mâché and Basswood. The Defenders Lich, Caddis, Newt, and Salus in the lead, wear no masks, only their own faces, which are of gentle countenance. They carry shields with nature motifs painted on them. Their swords were finely crafted from Basswood, and beautifully painted. They all wear costumes.

We heard a loud knock of hardwood against hardwood. Then another knock from a different direction was heard, and then another and another resounded loudly. Each came from somewhere else. The Defenders and Warriors took their places. There was a moment of silence. Suddenly, in unison the knocking grew very loud and fast. The Alderwild Wood resonated in its sound. Every twig, branch, and trunk of tree, every rock, and boulder echoed its beat.

Each Defender and Warrior had a certain role to play. Every movement taken by each actor had been choreographed as in a modern dance. There was nothing haphazard about their movements.

The tempo of the knocking increased or decreased, made louder or softer with each phase of the battle. The high pitched twangs of a stringed instrument were heard intermittently.

Until five years ago the battle was not choreographed. It was Dwarves pretending to fight Gnomes with wooden sticks for bludgeons, hitting one another at random. Their movements had been clumsy. Red dye was dabbed on their clothes and skin to look like wounds.

Choreographing the battle turned it into an art form. Each movement made by an actor is tied into the movements of the others. A constantly moving and changing design of bodies intermingled; forming negative and positive shapes is created.

The battle becomes a visual tale of horror and pain, truth and love. The effect is something very beautiful and prophetic.

Ian and I were deeply moved. It was not a performance such as stage play or opera, where the audience stands up and shouts "Bravo!" and encourages more bows from the actors. It was not something one just looked at or saw but felt wholly a part of. We wanted to do more. We felt enraged. What else, what more could be done? It promoted self-examination.

Gnomes, Dwarves, Alderlings, and the other inhabitants of the Bay speak from their hearts and souls. They hold Na very dear to them. They are passionate and keep their concern in the forefront of their minds. Natterjack and Hatch endeavour to raise the level of consciousness of all humans to the plight of the Wood and Water Fairies, Alderlings and Puncum, Gnomes and Dwarves, and animals, the destruction of Na, and the pollution of their habitat. There are not enough Defenders, not enough Humans involved.

When the mock battle is concluded, there is a period of needed rest, a time for the high emotions of the battle to settle.

There is a light lunch. It had been decided earlier on that there was really no need for the adults to fast as in the past years. The past week had been an exhausting one for everyone.

Some folks took naps while others took a stroll through the Wood. We found one Gnome sitting by the brook playing his harp while another played a flute.

At 2:00 P.M. everyone was called together to hear Silvas Oakenbaum tell the story of the Creation as his ancestors were told it by the Puncum. Most everyone knows the story, for it is told annually by Silvas. It will be a part of his legacy. No one would miss it, young and old alike. It is the high point of the festival for the children especially.

In The Beginning When All Was Made

The story tells us that Er's daughter Na was born in the Land Beyond the Horizon in the East. She brought shape and form to the Land. She formed the Mountains of granite and limestone. Glaciers of ice were sent down from the top of the World, and scooped out the Valleys. The ice cut out the Gorges and Rivers, the Streams and Ponds. It was She who covered the Mountains and filled the Valleys with Trees.

When all of this was completed there was the need for water or nothing would grow. Su, the Sun, shone down on the glaciers and caused them to melt. The Rivers, Lakes,

Brooks, and Ponds were soon filled with water.

The Day was broken in two, Light and Dark, Day and Night. In the dark blue-black space of Night, Na placed an opaline Moon. The Moon was pulled across the Sky each night from East to West by the Great Tortoise. The Puncum called the Great Tortoise Anwa, which means "Slow One". Then Na embellished the Night Sky with a profusion of twinkling Stars.

Then the Rivers, Streams, Lakes, and Ponds were filled with living creatures.

With the greening of the land, leaves burst forth on the tree branches. Needles sprung forth on the evergreens. Flowers bloomed in the Woods and the Meadows.

Insects came too and helped the Trees and Flowers reproduce. Birds alighted on the branches of the trees, built their nests, and raised their young. Animals came and took their place in the scheme of life.

Su held dominion over Da (Day). Like the Moon, Su slowly crossed the Sky from East to West. It was carried on the back of the Toad that the Puncum called "Too Fast".

It was at about this time, the Time between Night and Day, before Na added Twilight, that the Puncum came to be. Na moulded a male and a female from the elements of the Earth (Er). She named them Pollis and Pellandra. It was they and their children, and their children's children who later caused Na to add Twilight to the Day, Dawn, and Evening before Night.

The Ancients wished Daylight to stay, not to disappear. Na realized her children were very much afraid of Darkness, so She gave the Early Ones Twilight, which was the Dawn before Day and Evening before the Night.

The Ancients also saw that when the Sun reached the uppermost place in the Sky, it seemed to split the day into two equal halves. The early portion of Day became known as Morning and the latter half of Day was called the Afternoon. Thus the day was divided into Dawn, Morning, Afternoon, Evening, and Night.

Soon the Ancients ascribed Hours to each of the five segments of the day. Duties and rituals were allocated to each hour. Time was set aside for eating, sleeping, hunting, fishing, and story telling.

Up until now, the first few generations ate whenever they wished. They hunted and fished by themselves. No one shared their food nor did they help one another catch or find it. No real family unit, society, clan, tribe, or community had yet evolved.

Some individuals were not as strong, tall, or as capable as others. They were not able to find enough nourishing food for themselves. Some of the young, disabled, and elderly grew weak and died.

There was no order to the lives of these early beings. In time the Early Ones realized and learned that by working together, forming a community, much more could be accomplished. The labours of hunting, fishing, and the gathering of roots, tubers, and seeds were assigned to different groups. Some males fished while others hunted. The women collected the roots, tubers, berries, seeds, and greens.

Some members of the community baked the bread. Some cooked the food. Others became potters and weavers.

All members of the settlement did a share of the chores. The food was divided equally and all were healthier and stronger for it.

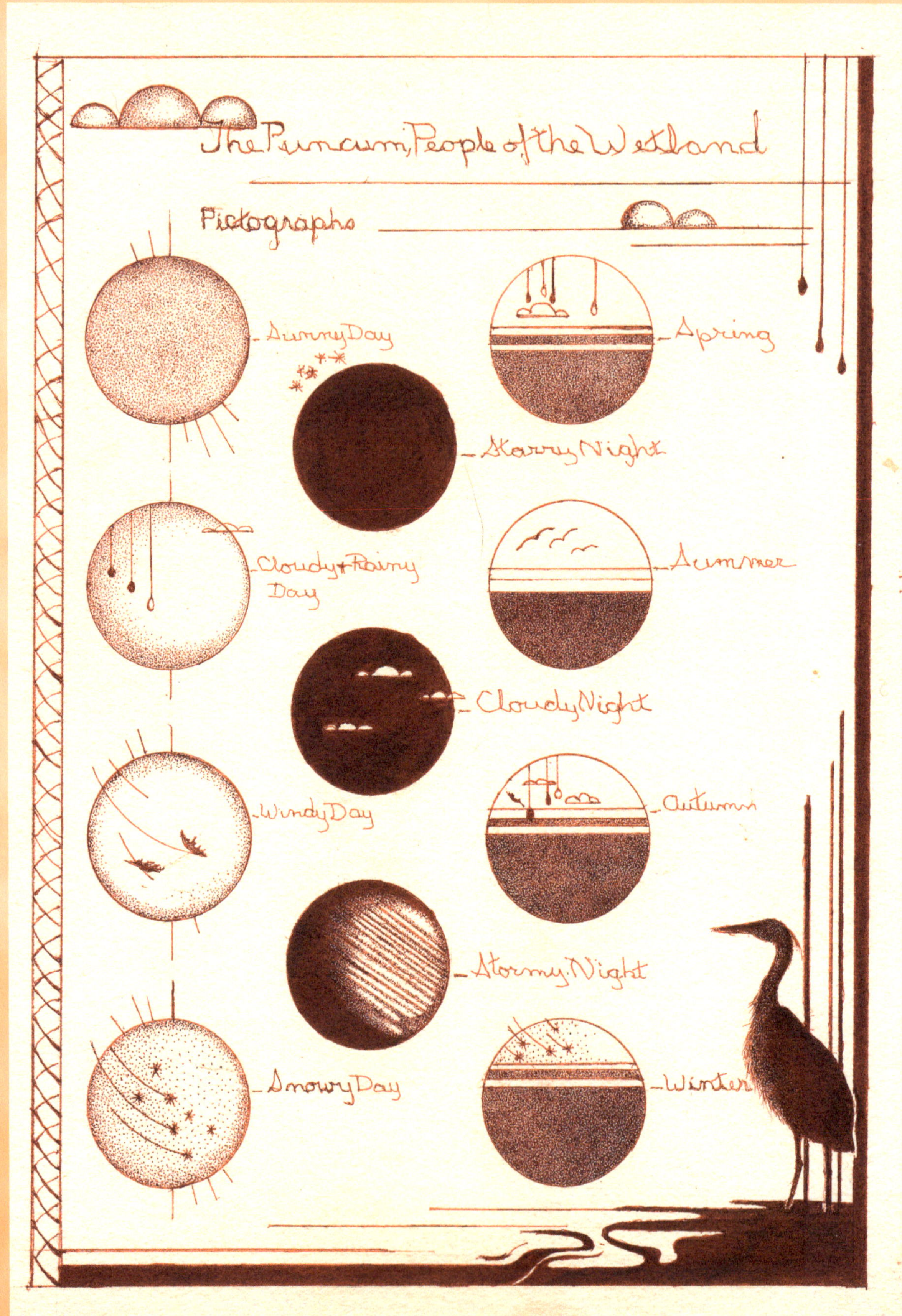
The Puncum, People of the Wetland
Pictographs
Sunny Day
Starry Night
Cloudy + Rainy Day
Windy Day
Snowy Day
Spring
Summer
Cloudy Night
Autumn
Stormy Night
Winter

Time was set aside for shared meals: early morning, mid-day, and evening. Many generations later they became known as Breakfast, Lunch, and Dinner.

The Early Ones also learned that by drying the fish they caught, the fish would not spoil so easily. They would be able to have food for the long winter months when food was scarce. They found that the same could be done with tubers, roots, seeds, and greens, which were dried and pounded into a meal or flour, then stored in clay vessels.

In time settlements of Puncum could be found in the wetlands along the banks of the St. Lawrence in the region of the Thousand Islands and Horse Thief Bay. They even built boats and crossed wide stretches of the river to some of the islands. To this day the Puncum may be found in the quiet places of the river where the strong current of the main channel cannot reach them: the coves, passages, and back waters around Hill and Club Islands, Turtlehead, and Beardstongue, Huckleberry, and our island here in the Bay.

The name Puncum does not come into use until the fifth generation. Before now they were known as the Pu .By the fifth generation the language of the Puncum became more complex. It was at this time they became known as the Puncum. They began to use symbols and groups of pictographs to describe their thoughts, ideas, and things they saw.

Those things they saw and wanted to convey to others were written on clay tablets, birch bark, and bones. The Puncum had not learned the art of paper making yet. Language gave the Puncum a better understanding of what they saw and felt. What we call Cattails or reed mace, they called Puncs, meaning Brown Heads and the word Puncum meant "People of the Brown Heads". The seed heads of the Cattails turn brown by mid- summer. The word Puncs is still in use today by the original Fairies, Gnomes, Dwarves, and Humans who have learned the wisdom of the Puncum.

The young are allowed to ask questions. Silvas readily obliges. He is in his element as storyteller and teacher. Questions stimulate the mind. He encourages discussion. Inquiring minds promote thinking.

The Puncum originally told the story of the first inhabitants of Horse Thief Bay. The Alderling were next in line to learn it. They made only a few changes to it. When the Gnomes arrived, followed by the Dwarves, both groups took the story to be a part of their history.

By late afternoon when the "Story of the Beginning" was over and all questions ceased, a group of Gnomes and Dwarves brought forth their musical instruments. They played some light music and sang several lieder.

Soon we heard a sweet, gentle sound, which seemed to surround us. We could not place from where it came. Draka, who was sitting next to us, pointed to the trees. It was the Wood Sprites, Leaflings, and some Alderlings. They were sitting in the branches, singing in a tongue we did not know. The sound was ethereal, like Zephyr winds blowing through the slender grasses in mid-summer, like the tinkling of coral-bells upon a slender stalk in early June. It was lovely.

The air became cooler and we all carried our chairs and benches into the Great Hall, where a supper was waiting for us.

By 7:00 P.M. people were leaving and heading home. Ian offered to help with the clean up but Draka said that everything was under control. Tomorrow everyone will gather for breakfast and then sit down to watch the Nada, which will take up the greater part of the day. The Festival will conclude with a great feast.

April 12 The Nada

The weather did not look very promising when we awoke this morning. All activities were to be held indoors. Breakfast with our friends was held in the Great Hall. A good fire was going in the two fireplaces, one at each end of the room. The meal was kept simple.

The Nada is a serious play. The very young were kept in an adjacent room and calmed with stories read by a teenage baby sitter and a few helpers.

Soon after eating, the tables were folded again and the chairs placed in rows before a stage. Everyone took a seat. A middle aged Dwarf, whom I did not know, came forth and seated himself to the front and right side of the stage. He was the narrator. The players were to act in mime. Silence fell over the audience.

The Nada is a play concerning the environment. The play concerns the destruction of Na, the demise of Her trees, the assault of Her wetlands, the fouling of Her water, the plight of the Fairies, and even the Gnomes and Dwarves. Now there is also the refugee problem. Where are the homeless, sick, and starving Fairies of every kind, young and old to go? The Nada addresses the problems of the animals that are on the move looking for food, clean water, and shelter. Their habitats are being laid waste.

Besides the narrator's voice, the only other sound heard is the knocking of wood against wood, only the tempo changing with the action of the play. Sometimes there is a cry, a shout from the players. As the story depicted by the players increases or changes in emotional tone, its anger, its heartbreak and sorrow, so too the emotions of those watching the performance. They begin to call out and shout. They work themselves into a state of great excitation. Others nearby stand up to support and hold tightly those who are shouting. They do not stop them but are there just to keep them from falling and hurting themselves.

The narrator tells of the plague, which has befallen Na over the past two hundred years and its ever-quickening pace. The Nada depicts how the Trolls and apathetic humans have abused Na and Her creation. The land, water, air, and even the animals and fishes have been assaulted and laid desolate.

Saws and axes have felled the trees. Machines have torn open the Land. Chemicals have polluted the air and waters of many of the great rivers and lakes, even some of the streams and ponds. Climates all over the world have changed because of this. Now the ebb and flow of Na is no longer in balance. Many animals have been over hunted or killed for the sake of killing. Some animals have become extinct and others are facing extinction.

Here in the Thousand Islands of the St. Lawrence, the Red Fox, the Mink, Beaver, River Otter, and Muskellunge are seldom seen. The Sturgeon is gone.

Too much rain rots the plants. They die! Too wet! Too much sun dries the soil. The plants wither and die. Too dry! Plants cannot grow to give shade, shelter, food, and nourishment.

When the water level drops because of too little rain or snow, the fish move to deeper water where it is cooler. The

inhabitants of the Bay have a more difficult time catching
the fish. They must depend more on collecting snails, which
have become stranded on the sandbar between the island
and mainland shore.

The marshes and wetlands too are being destroyed. They
have been excavated or filled in with rocks and soil. The birds
and animals that inhabit these areas no longer can stay. It
has been the demise of the Water Sprites.

The Puncum too have lost many of their homes in the
wetland, and many have died. The lives of all of the Fairies,
Gnomes, and Dwarves who live among the islands and
Horse Thief Bay are in peril, and are threatened by sickness,
starvation, and death. This is not just a problem for those
inhabitants of the river and our Bay but all over the world.

The shouts and expostulations of the audience cease. Their
eyes now filled with tears. They weep openly. The narrator
does not stop his telling of the story. The players do not stop
acting. The truth of Na's injuries and pain must be heard
and faced.

Horse Thief Bay still has its Wetlands and Marsh, and
its Cattails; but it is slowly being filled in. The Alder and
Black Willow trees growing at the water's edge have already
been cut down. Our Alder trees and Marsh Marigold,
Sensitive Ferns, Royal Ferns, and Skunk Cabbage in our
Alderwild Wood are still alive and well. However, the Trolls
throw their junk into the river. It floats into the Bay and
pollutes the water. The glass and cans cut the feet. The plastic
rims from six-packs get caught on some of the bills and
necks of the gulls, ducks, Herons, and turtles. They can
no longer eat and so starve to death. Spilled gasoline from
outboard motors floats on the surface of the water.

Young fish have no clean water without oil on the surface in which to swim. They are forced out of the protection of the Bay into the deeper water where they are preyed upon by larger fish. Thus there are fewer young to grow and mature. There will be fewer adults to lay eggs, fewer eggs to hatch and become the next generation of fish. The animals that drink this water become sick, Fairies too. Water Nymphs, Water Sprites and Puncum grow weak with there being fewer minnows to catch for themselves and for trading with the Alderling.

At this point the narrator stops and the actors rest. They take time out for a light meal of bread, cheese, and Elderberry wine. Some begin to play their harps and flutes. Some close their eyes and sit back and listen. Others get up to stretch their legs. They leisurely walk through the Alderwild Wood, listening to the leaves crackle and crunch under their feet. The air smells sweet. It is a time for hearts to ease, tears to dry, and anger turned to what is positive.

Talk Among Themselves

Dwarves, Gnomes, Alderling, Puncum, and Humans must focus and be thankful for whatever they still have in Horse Thief Bay that is wonderful and good. We must pledge to protect it with our lives.

These five groups must reclaim where possible, that which has been taken from them in other areas of the river. This does not necessarily mean these areas should be reacquired by force. No, it must be achieved by the enactment of laws and by enforcing those laws, which already exist to protect the environment, even though they are too often unheeded by both Trolls and Humans.

Laws alone will not stop the polluting of rivers and lakes, and the filling in or dredging of wetlands. Educating both young and old is needed. Explain the consequences, what happens when the Wetlands are destroyed. We must make them understand that the Wetlands help to cleanse and purify the water. The Wetlands are home to the Mallard Ducks, Loons, Least Bittern, Great Blue Heron, Little Green Heron, Marsh Wren, Muskrat, Turtle, Mud Puppy, and young fish.

Encourage those humans who have not yet become Trolls to take up the fight. Lastly, reach out and try to catch those people who are slipping into and on the verge of becoming Trolls. There may yet be hope for them.

Another issue is that of the refugees. How do we care for so many individuals, the sick, the injured, and the homeless? Where do we find permanent homes for them all?

A Bell Is Rung

All gather and take their seats for the final act of the Nada. There is apprehension and fear among the seated. What will the last act of the play hold for them? It will tell of the future. Is there hope? All is quiet.

The performers take their places. The narrator begins. The story continues. It tells the audience that the Puncum can no longer depend on fish as their main source of food. They must now diversify their diet in order to survive. Adapt to the changing environment or die. Find other sources of food unspoiled by pollution.

The Gnomes and Dwarves are warned that the fish they catch must be eaten no more than once a week. Mercury and PCB's have collected in their flesh.

Catch only the smaller of these big fish. Their bodies have collected fewer chemicals than older, larger fish.

Once again it is instilled in the hearts and minds of the Dwarves, Gnomes, Alderlings, and Puncum the importance of taking care of and protecting Na. The inhabitants of Horse Thief Bay must tend to Na's needs, Her resources, air, land, and water. All life springs from Na. Her needs are not many, only a few in number but very important.

Through story telling, plays, rituals, and children's games the need for conservation and preservation of Na must be promoted. One member of the audience stood up and said," The inhabitants of the Bay are already adhering to the code of laws Na gave to the Puncum in the Beginning when the Earth was Young. The inhabitants are already counting the number of fish we catch and from which species. We are already protecting the trees in the Bay and the Alderwild Wood."

"We have already planted young White Pines on Dark Point to replace those cut down by the Trolls.

"At river's edge we have encouraged Alder and Willow trees to grow to prevent soil erosion. We have spread the seeds of several species of Rush and Sedges, the Tubers of Scented and Yellow Water Lilies, Arrowhead, Frogbit, Aquatic Smartweed, Sweet Flag, Great Burr

Reed, and both Yellow and Blue Flags. All of this we have done, and the shallow water between the mainland and island was better for it. Great Blue Heron and the Little Green Heron come and visit the Bay. Mallard Ducks and Canada Geese bring their young to swim and feed here. The Raccoon visits and eats fresh water clams and Crayfish. The Muskrat dwells with her family under our dock. The Great Northern Pike, Black Bass, Bullheads, and Yellow Perch all make their nests and spawn here. White- tailed Deer and Mink walk along the shore and, from time to time, take a drink. On very rare occasions the American Bittern and Least Bittern pay their respect."

"However the lives of all of these creature are threatened by the carelessness and willful destruction of the Woods and Wetlands, in the polluting of the water caused by Humans. We have pulled from the water and mud adjacent to the stand of Cattails some plastic and glass bottles, a few plastic rings from a six pack of beer or soda, more automobile tires, and more refuge. Non-caring people have discarded all of this garbage into our river. There is only so much we can do. What more can we do?"

With this question others in the audience stood up and repeated, "What can we do? What more? What more? Others must help! The Humans! The Humans! They must help us to turn the tide and save Na"

Soon the entire audience was on their feet and chanting, "Save Na! Save Na!" There was a call to order. The narrator motioned for all to sit down. Soon the assembly of inhabitants settled and was quiet again. With order, people can think with their intellect and not with their emotions. The narrator suggested to the group since it was so late and the evening feast was just about ready to bring to the table, that further discussion of the environmental problems should be tabled until 10:00 A.M. tomorrow. Also there was still the refugee problem to be deliberated. A motion was put forth by a Gnome to have the meeting adjourned. It was seconded. Everyone helped with setting up the tables.

Soon food of every description was brought to the table. Nothing was forgotten, enough for everybody to have seconds if they wished. I was in awe of the quantity of food, which had been stored over winter. Some of the food had been dried and kept in clay jars. Others were pickled. Duck Potatoes and other tuberous roots were kept in underground cellars. Dandelion greens and soup, Milkweed buds, and other wild greens were boiled and then packaged in special containers which would not leak or crack when hung in the river to freeze.

Ian and I left by 8:00 P M. We assured Natterjack we would return for the 10:00 A. M. meeting.

April 13

At 10:00 a.m. Natterjack called the meeting together. There were fifty in attendance besides us, mostly adult men. The women had the children and some of the elderly to tend to.

The first question was - which are the most important issues to deal with first. What are the problems exactly? What should be done etc.? The meeting lasted well past the noon hour. It ended at 1:30 P.M., resulting in the formation of five committees, one for each problem:

Committee # 1 The Land: Protection of Trees,
              Wildflowers, and Wildlife
Committee # 2 The Water: The Pollution and Protection
              of Fish and Water Fowl
Committee # 3 Noise: The Effect Noise is having on
              Fairies, Gnomes, Dwarves, And Wildlife
Committee # 4 The Refugees: Loss of Habitat, Search,
              and Rescue
Committee # 5 Public Relations: Organizing,
              Campaigning and Strategy.

There are members from the Alderwild Wood, the Puncum from the stand of Cattails, and Gnomes from High Pines Point for each committee except for Committee # 5., which has only six members. The objective of each group is to:

1. Investigate and collect all of the facts and figures to the problem.
2. Specific causes
3. Other contributing factors which are not so obvious.
4. What is needed to rectify the problem?
5. Is it possible to change and solve it?
6. Find solutions for said problems.
   Once all of the material has been collected and sorted out, the specific causes should be listed. A list of what is needed to change and improve the situation, hopefully in some cases to eradicate the problem all together.

Where does one start? How does one accomplish the task of righting the wrongs and saving the woodland sanctuaries and pure waters, which still remain?

All of this information is to be written up and presented to the Public Relations Committee, which will organize all of the information collected from each committee. The members will decide how best to present it to the humans and enlist their help. This may be accomplished by means of:

For Adults
    Seminars
    Workshops
    Field Trips
    Newspapers and
    News Letters

For Children
    Songs
    Stories
    Plays
    Field Trips

The Care and Protection of Na by the humans will help save many lives, those of the Fairies, Gnomes, Dwarves, Sprites, and Wildlife, the fishes which reside in the water, the animals living in the woodlands and fields, and the insects that pollinate the flowers. Some very rare Fairies may yet be saved from extinction.

The humans will also benefit from the cleaning up of the river water, the saving of trees, wildflowers, and fauna. They will benefit from the lessening of noise emitted by the racing boats. They will feel less stressed, with nerves calmed, and perhaps hear one another when having a conversation. With their tensions eased, they will become more fully human.

The Humans may be able to be more in touch with the tender, gentler side of their nature. They may be able to see more clearly the World of Na and hear Her songs. The waves lapping against the shore. The Red-Winged Blackbird calling to its mate. The solitary call of the Loon, the Whip-Poor-Will, and the Pileated Woodpecker drilling. The humans may even take time in the quiet of the evening to watch a spider repairing its web and cutting out the pine needles, which have gotten caught in it.

Hearing one Chipmunk scolding another, that too is part of Na's music. The croaking of a Bull Frog may not be heard otherwise. We no longer have a Bull Frog in our Bay. They seem to be slowing disappearing. There is still the chatter of the King Fisher, Nuthatch, and Chickadee as well as the song of the Song Sparrow.

Ian was asked to be on the Public Relations Committee. Natterjack felt that his artistic abilities would lend themselves to designing brochures, flyers, posters, ads for

newspapers, charts, etc. Ian was quite agreeable and pleased to be asked. He felt that taking on this new responsibility would not interfere with his own artwork, that of making paper-mâché masks and dragons.

I was asked to continue working with Silvas, writing up the histories, habits, and culture along with sketches of the inhabitants of the Bay. My journal does already in large part discuss the Troll problem past and present and what effect it is having on the residents of Horse Thief Bay.

I most assuredly agreed. This was right up my alley so to speak, "My thing". Now that spring is slowly returning, I shall soon be meeting more of the Fairies up close as they come out of hibernation. We both are also on the committee with the refugees. They are in need of immediate attention.

April 14

The Skunk Cabbage at the foot of the bridge crossing the Alderwild Brook is just beginning to show its green and burgundy coloured flower head. Its leaves are barely visible through the mud. By June the leaves will be very large and if bruised, the odour will be offensively strong. There are six Skunk Cabbage heads right now They multiply very slowly.

April 16

Early yesterday morning Natterjack came to tell us that he had just received word about a group of Wood Sprites stranded on a rocky point of land just a mile west of here. The land there has been torn and stripped, blasted and bulldozed of its trees and natural beauty.

A mother and her three children, one male with a broken leg, another male lying on the ground with a torn wing, and the last member of the group, a female, was shaken but otherwise uninjured. However, all of them were suffering from lack of food and water.

The group was separated from the Fairies and fleeing Gnomes when several large boulders were pushed in front of them. This caused many smaller rocks and stones to roll, one landing on the one Sprite's leg and the other on the second Sprite's wing, tearing it. They were pinned down, unable to move.

This accident occurred in the late afternoon, two days ago. None of the fleeing inhabitants noticed they were missing until yesterday when several Wood Sprites returned to the site to look for them. It was nightfall by the time they reached them. They found them huddled together to keep warm.

The search party saw that they would need more help to move some of the stones and larger rocks. Also it was too dark to lift the injured. They built a fire to keep the Trolls at bay and keep warm.

When Natterjack heard about the accident, he went to fetch the Suund. She brought along splints, bandaging material, ointments, and herbs. Natterjack also brought with him a basket lined with Milkweed down to carry the Sprites. The four of us got into our canoe and, with motor attached, went directly to the scene.

It was an ugly sight to behold when we arrived. The damage done to the land is irreversible. Where there were once so many trees such as Junipers, Pine, Maple, and Oak, only a sparse few trees remained. The beautiful outcroppings of rock had been blasted away. The beauty of that place is now history.

We had to find the lost ones. They were soon found. Ian helped Natterjack to remove the rocks pinning the group in. The Suund was then able to reach the injured. The mother and her three children were lifted out by Ian and gently placed in the down-lined basket. The mother and one child, the one not injured, were put in the basket lined with Milkweed down. The other two were moved over to a flat rock where the Suund could examine them and tend to their injuries.

The woman's husband had been killed four days ago. Ian went to look for the body to take it back to the Bay with us. He also checked to see if there were any other Fairies dead or alive, injured or lost in the rubble. Perhaps some were hiding around the perimeter of the construction site.

While Ian was doing this, Natterjack, the Suund, and I tended to the injured.

Nat held a magnifying glass over the Sprite's broken leg in order for the Suund to see the injury more closely. Sprites on the average are only 4 inches tall. She cleaned the wound very carefully and set the bone, which had been broken in three places. Using thread from a spider's web, she sewed closed the opening. She then splinted the leg with pieces of the strong central vein of the Oak leaf.

I had taken a look at the Sprite's leg through the magnifier just before the Suund had begun to work on it. There were three or four breaks that I did not think could be repaired. It looked gruesome. However, after the Suund set the bones, she sprinkled a very fine powder over the leg and the bones seemed to be healing themselves right before my eyes. When she finished sewing the wound closed, there was barely a scar. The splints were only a precautionary measure. She was amazing.

The Suund was most concerned with the amount of blood lost by the Sprite and was anxious to return to the Alderwild Wood. The other Sprite's torn wing was much easier to mend. It just needed a little sewing up.

There was another patient found: a Gnome. His physical injuries were few and minor, some scratches and bruises, but his wounds were of the heart, soul, and spirit. He was quite elderly, and suffering from the destruction of his home; his family missing, perhaps dead; and his friends, other Gnomes, Dwarves, Sprites, the trees, chipmunks, squirrels, deer, and many other animals and birds all gone.

The Gnome was in a state of shock, babbling and talking to himself. He was incoherent. There was a far away look in his eyes. He had been walking dazedly among the boulders when the two Sprites came upon him before they themselves were injured. His spirit was in great need of the Suund's restorative powers. It would take time.

The mother's spirits were good, which helped her children stay calm.

It was not long before Ian returned, followed by five Gnome children, one Dwarf child, three elderly Wood Sprites, and a Leafling girl child, and a half dozen "Somethings." They were a human type like all Fairies but neither Natterjack nor I had ever seen this race before. Ian looked like the Pied Piper of Hamelin. Some walked while others flew. The six "Somethings" walked. We wondered where we were going to fit them all.

When Nat and I recovered from the shock of it all we became more level headed. Nat realized he had brought along an extra basket. The mother and her three children, the elderly Sprites, and the Leafling child, could travel in the second basket. Thus, it was decided that the Suund, one Dwarf child, the two baskets carrying the Sprites, one female Leafling, the one elderly Gnome, Natterjack, and myself would return to the Bay immediately. The Suund would need Nat's help with the old Gnome. It would not be safe to take any more. We only had three life jackets. Ian would remain behind to look after the five Gnome children and six "Somethings".

The return trip to the Bay did not take long. I left everyone on the mainland dock and waited until Bracken, Azulla, and Hatch came to help Natterjack with the elderly Gnome and the Suund carrying the Sprites. Azulla tied a second canoe to the back of mine. He then threw in extra life jackets and handed me a flashlight. I told him to expect eleven more besides Ian. I left immediately and reached Ian just as dusk was setting in. There was little light left in the sky to see by. We had to get life jackets on all of them and then move them into the two canoes. Some had never been in a boat before. All we had to see by was one very small light. Fortunately, the river was very calm. There were no rocks or shoals to worry about. The water was deep. The sky was now thick with stars. Each boat had a heavy load. I told the children how important it was to sit still and to never stand.

The trip home was uneventful. The children were great. As soon as we turned the point, where our neighbours the Burns, Crosses, and the Bethels live, Gnomes, Dwarves, Alderling, Puncum, and Sprites lined the shore with torches in hand, lighting the way. It was a beautiful sight and so welcoming. The health of the Wood Sprite who had lost so much blood was improving quickly.

April 20

Life along the Alderwild is almost back to normal. The Alderlings have moved back into their rebuilt summer homes along its bank. The Puncum have returned to their residencies in the stand of Cattails. Gnomes are sweeping out and airing their dwellings. The Dwarves are doing similar work on their abodes. However what is uppermost in the minds of all is the refugee crisis.

An infirmary has been set up on one side of the Great Hall. On the other side of the Hall, beds, an area for dining, and a play area have been set for the displaced children and adults who are in need of food and shelter. There is also the need for those folks found to be reunited with their lost family members, if possible.

The Dwarves, Azulla and Perch, the Gnomes Lich and Newt, and Hatch of the Alderling have made long treks through the woods west of the Bay, looking for the parents of the Dwarf and Gnome children. They were also looking for either the wife or any member of the old Gnome's family. He is still in a state of shock. His mind is not well. He calls out for his wife, Dicentra, and then just sits staring into space.

The Suund has asked a Gnome family to take the elderly Gnome into their home for the present time until a family or his wife can be found. It is critical that he be in a family setting now where he can sit by a window and see the wildflowers and small animals again. He would be able to have tea and meals with the family. The Suund feels that, given time, he will recover.

The Great Hall is a wonderful place to mend the injured and care for the sick, and house the homeless temporarily. It lacks windows and sunlight, sky, and clouds. The Hall is also a fine place to hold parties, festivals, and plays when the weather is poor.

However, when one is not well and the recuperation period might be long, a home environment is much better. The sick can hear the birds chirping and the Spring Peepers trilling.

The sights and sounds of Na are more healing and more of a restorative to good health than any pill or unguent in many situations.

April 22

The Dutchman's breeches are in full bloom now. Their greyish green leaves and white flowers are very delicate. Five or six bloomer shaped flowers hang from a nodding stem. They like the rich soil of the Alderwild Wood and the crevices along Hemlock Ridge. The blooms do not last long and their leaves will be gone in about a month.

Spring Beauty and both Blunt-lobed and Sharp-lobed Hepatica are in bloom and growing here in the region of Hemlock Ridge. The flowers of the Blunt-lobed come in several colors: pink, blue, and deep lavender. The Sharp-lobed flowers can only be found in white.

Both species close their petals as evening approaches and will open again with the morning light. I had thought that the closing of the Hepatica flowers was due entirely to the lessening of the sun. I was wrong.

I saw something quite wonderful this evening. As the lower rim of the sun touched the horizon, winged Fairies appeared. They were smaller than the Wood Sprites but definitely related. Their wings were pastel in color, more the color of the flowers, not the greens and browns of the Wood Sprites. These gentle creatures flew from flower to flower and with a light touch of the hand, they closed each bloom. Their skin was fair and their wings were different in shape and structure. There was not the bony skeleton as seen in the wings of dragonflies and butterflies. Their wings were free flowing and irregular in shape. I wondered about their ability to fly, to control their direction and lift, and landing. As I watched them for a while, I saw that they did not flap their wings like the Wood Sprites do. They glided, using the warm air currents now rising from the now heated earth. They were beautiful. They just seemed to float effortlessly.

On my return here to the island I met with Natterjack. He said that they were Flower Sprites. They tend to the flowers all spring and summer long. The Flower Sprites fly from the flowers that have gone to sleep to the ones that are in bloom.

April 23

Within the Alderwild Wood there is a small area, which receives much sunlight before the leaves on the trees appear. Many Spring Beauties grow there in mass, a carpet of very small pinkish flowers. Up close the flower petals are really white with pink veins.

This morning the Wood Sprites and Alderlings were out digging up a few of the very small tubers of the Spring Beauty plants, taking only from here and there, making sure not to deplete the area of one of their main sources of food.

After breakfast I decided to take a walk on our wooden path, which winds its way down into the Valley of the Horsetails and Fern Marsh and across the bridge over the Alderwild Brook. I built it a number of years ago, when I was in my prime. It was becoming more and more difficult for me to visit this part of the Wood without tripping over the roots and getting my feet tangled in the tall grasses. I have seen older Gnomes and Dwarves and even some Alderlings use it.

The fiddleheads of the Sensitive Fern are just beginning to push their way through the soil and leaves. The Marsh Marigolds remain in small, tight clumps. Some of the Alder trees have fallen and lie crisscrossed over the brook. I love this place. It is teaming with life.

The centipede and the millipede, the sow bugs, and the daddy-long-legs; the spider, and the beetle, as well as their larvae and nymphs live here. The Garter and Ribbon snakes live among the wild flowers and dead leaves.

In the still waters of Fern Marsh, in among the

tussocks of ferns and Marsh Marigolds, toad, frog, and salamander eggs have been laid encased in long strands of protective jelly, soon to become tadpoles and salamander larvae. They will become the next generation.

The Black, Grey, and Red Squirrels are out and about. Their young when weaned will soon join them.

Wild Columbine is found in the crags of the rocks and outcroppings in areas where the sunlight reaches. When the Columbine blooms, it is also time for the return of the Ruby-Throated Hummingbird. The flowers are red and yellow, nodding with nearly straight spurs.

Just a little further along in the shady areas, where the trees are closer together is found the Blue Cohosh. The leaves are similar to those of the Early Meadow Rue but have a burgundy cast to them. The flowers to come are burgundy in colour as well.

On my return I walked along the foot of Hemlock Ridge. My eyes suddenly focused on a deep hollow underneath one of the large roots of the Maple tree. There kneeling among a few Early Saxifrage, Dog Tooth Violets, and Pink Hepatica was a Gnome child. There was a tear in his eye. It rolled down his cheek.

A Junco lay dead before him, a friend. The child was garbed in an Oak leaf. His attention was so centered on the bird that he was not aware of my presence. I said nothing, only watched.

The child was very young but his response to the death of the Junco was mature, well beyond his years. I walked away quietly. I made a mental image of the child and bird. When I return to my studio this afternoon I will begin to work on a full color drawing and study of the two.

April 27: The Island

We arose to a beautiful day yesterday and decided to move to the island. It is a very different world here being surrounded by water.

The water level is higher this year so we needed to use the canoe. Ian made several trips back and forth carrying our food, books, art supplies, microscope, and cat Stripe as well as our dog Floristane.

The mice have left evidence of their winter visit. However, it was not as much or as bad as last year. When we closed the island last autumn, I had placed mothballs in all of the closets, the drawers, and on the beds. We immediately collected all of the balls and left all of the closet doors and drawers open and opened wide all of the windows and doors. The smell was gone in a few hours.

We shall return to the mainland each day to see how everyone is faring. Also Ian has his work on the Public Relations Committee and I have the refugee problem to work on, as well as my work with Silvas.

We do not vacation on the island, but it is a beautiful place to do our artwork. It is a change of scenery and living on the island surrounded by water is a totally different environment than living in the Alderwild Wood, which is only one hundred and fifty feet away.

The island is a good vantage point to see and study the Puncum and Water Sprites. From here I am able to watch all of the animals and Fairies as they live their lives among the Cattails, sedges, and rushes growing in the shallow water between the island and mainland.

April 28

Life on the river begins much later than in the woods and fields further inland. This is because the river water is still very cold and so all of the lands near it take longer to warm up. There is even a difference in plant growth between the island and the Alderwild Wood only a short distance away.

This evening Ian and I sat on the front steps. We were serenaded by a chorus of Spring Peepers interrupted by the very loud croak of the Bull Frog. The Leopard and Green Frogs joined in too.

The ground was damp. A sweet smell rose and floated over last autumn's leaves. The Whip-Poor-Will was singing

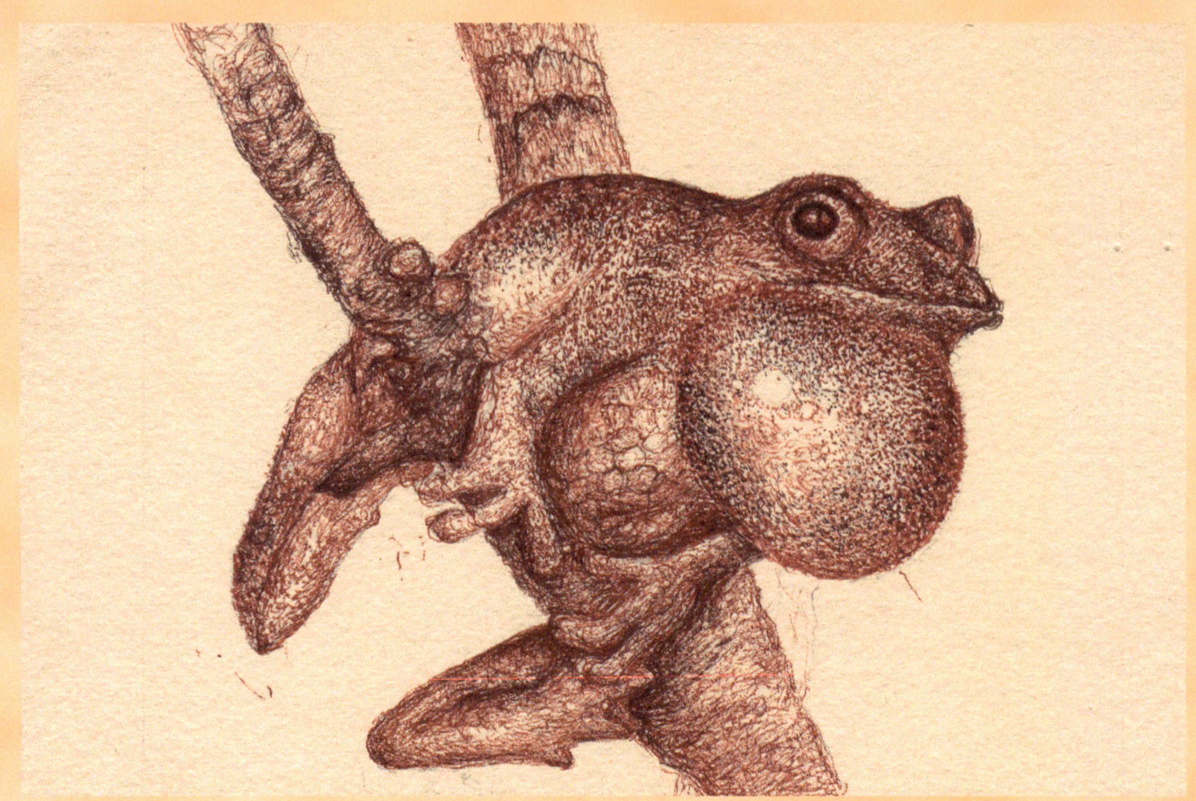

close by. The night is clear and the stars twinkle. We have settled in, and everything is in its place.

April 29

This morning I saw the Puncum. They have moved into their spring- summer dwellings located among the front one third of the stand of Cattails. Their boats are docked a short way up from the mouth of the Willow. It was difficult to see either their homes or boats from the island, even with binoculars.

Since I had met a number of the Puncum during the Festival of Grata, I did not feel as though I would be imposing on them if I paddled our canoe over to their community. This I did! They remembered me.

There were not only Puncum there but also Water Sprites sitting about. However, there was one thing I had totally forgotten about. I had forgotten how tiny their voices were.

Their mouths were too small for me to see, thus I was not able to read their lips. They also did not speak English. I should have asked Nat to come along. No matter! Next time.

We communicated with hand gestures. The Puncum were very warm and asked me to come again. Next time I should come with Nat. They said that they would tell me more about themselves. I am delighted with the prospect of further meetings and talks.

May 5 - The Month of May

I thought that spring was supposed to be here. It seems not! It has been very cold and rainy these past few days. The day is too cold to visit the Puncum. They have had to remain in their dwellings.

There were no committee meetings for us to attend today. We had no real reason to go up to the Wood, but although it was cold, the sun was out, so we decided to go across anyway.

The river was calm, its surface was smooth as glass. We could see clear to the bottom. Nothing seemed to be stirring, not even a minnow. When we reached the shore, we saw no Sprite nor Alderling about. It was too cold for them as well.

Nearer the top of the hill, there were still Hepatica blooming. I wondered if the Flower Sprites would come out to close the petals in the evening when it is so cold. As we walked into the Alderwild Wood we did

find some Dog-Tooth Violets in bloom. There were even some Blue Violets and Bloodroot out. The Bloodroot was nearly finished.

The Blue Cohosh, Jack-in-the-Pulpit, and Mandrake were just poking their heads through the fallen leaves. The Red Trillium with their nodding heads were still blooming, while the White Trillium, with their heads looking up, had just begun to open.

We came upon Natterjack collecting Bracket Fungus from the White Birch. The Wood Sprites and Alderlings were in need of it for their fires to keep warm. The weather is unseasonably cold.

We asked Nat how the refugee situation was and if he could use more help. He said that more homeless, more refugees had been found, both fairies as well as animals. He told us of a Wood Knar who had been watching over six orphaned raccoon babies. Their eyes were still closed. They were helpless and in need of both warmth and food. The Wood Knar, being a Spirit, is unable to lift and carry any injured or lost creature, whether it would be a Fairy, Gnome, Dwarf, or animal.

Wood Knars are at times visibly whole, at other times translucent. They are like shepherds keeping watch over their flock, the good inhabitants of the wood. The Knars do not fight nor do they carry weapons of any sort. They are ghostlike spirits originating from that part of the tree where the branch joins the trunk. When a tree has died naturally, in time the Knar will separate itself from the branch and trunk. It is embodied with the wisdom the tree has gained over its lifetime, whether it is a hundred years or just thirty years old. However, if a tree has been cut down with an axe or saw, or uprooted by Man, the Knar will have been killed and the knowledge, the history the tree has been witness to and stored, and the natural life and death cycle of Na will be gone. There will be no Wood Knar to tell its own story and pass on its wisdom.

    Perch, one of the younger Dwarves, and Salus, a young Gnome, had been searching a small area of the woods west of the Bay when they came upon the Wood Knar. It was standing over the Raccoon babies. It had only found them just a half hour before. He did not want to leave them for evening was approaching.

The Norgs and Traugs, relatives of the Trolls, roam the woods during the twilight hours, before nightfall and again in the early light of Dawn just before sunrise. They can be dangerous. Also the night will bring Trolls. They are deadly.

The Knar had been hoping for a deer or other passing animal whose help it could enlist to get word to the Gnomes and Dwarves to tell them about the orphaned raccoons. It was fortunate that Perch and Salus came by when they did. They placed the six babies on a layer of leaves and soft grasses in a basket, which Perch had been carrying. Then they added more grasses to cover them. It had become quite cool. The Wood Knar was very relieved. When the two friends turned to wave good-bye, the Knar was already becoming translucent again.

The Nursery

Perch and Salus hurried in the direction of the Twin Maples, the dwelling of the Suund. Darkness pursued them as if they were the quarry. Running at times, roots and vines grasped at their legs and feet. Salus fell and rose again, only to be ensnared by more roots and branches further on.

Thoughts of the Norgs, Traugs, and Trolls raced through their minds. Fear gripped them. Their hearts pounded loudly in their ears. At first they thought the thumping was the footfall of Trolls advancing behind them. They were nearly in a state of panic. They stopped and could go no further. The pounding slowed. They realized the thumping was emanating from within their chests.

Perch realized they were beginning to run blindly. He remembered what his father had taught him. Control your fears! Do not allow fear to control your thinking and actions. In times of stress keep calm. One is able to think more wisely.

They not only had themselves to consider but also they were carrying six baby raccoons. Their lives were dependent upon Perch and Salus to make intelligent decisions.

The stars were out in great number but shed little light on the two through the dense foliage of White Pine and Cedar. They carried no lamp to see with, only a few matches. However they did not light one. The ground was covered with dry leaves, twigs, and pine needles. If one spark got away they would not be able to contain the blaze. It would not only burn above ground but underground as well. The soil is primarily decayed pine needles.

Perch and Salus were also worried and concerned that their families would be in great distress. Perhaps their parents and others in the Bay might organize a search party, which would put them in danger. The Trolls would be out wandering the woods for food or carrion.

The two fellows heard a soft low voice. They turned and saw that it was the Wood Knar, the same one they had left earlier. The Knar, when it saw how quickly the dark was swallowing up the twilight and knowing how far Perch and Salus had still to travel, turned to find them. It was good that he did. The Wood Knar took on the light of the stars and moon, its body becoming the light to guide their way.

The Knar took the hand of each. The six raccoons were cradled in the basket. Although its feet looked as though they were touching the ground, no roots nor vines, no branch or brush hindered its passage or that of Perch and Salus. The three glided effortlessly and swiftly through the woods. As they were descending the rocky escarpment of High Pines Point they saw the lighted lanterns of a search party just crossing Fern Marsh. A great relief for all!

Perch and Salus were exhausted more from their fear than their journey home. Once the Knar had taken the hand of each, they were without any physical wear and tear. The Suund was there to take over the care of the baby raccoons and, with the help of Natterjack, took them back to Her dwelling.

May 6

The next day we awoke early. It was going to be a beautiful day. The sun was out in full measure. The air was already warming.

I spoke to Natterjack and I asked him if he would accompany me when I went to visit the Puncum this afternoon. I asked him to be my translator. He agreed. While I was at the mainland house I stopped by the Twin Maples under which was the Suund's dwelling. I came to see the young raccoons.

The Suund had the basket they arrived in set on the floor near Her wood stove. She had one of the kits on Her lap while She fed it.

Last night when the kits arrived, the Suund asked Bracken to look for a nursing doe from which he could draw milk. He found a female who was producing a sufficient amount of milk for her fawn and was more than willing to help out.

The kits have to be fed every two hours, night and day. They are only a few days old and will remain on a diet of milk for two months. Their eyes will open in three weeks. When their teeth come in, the Suund will begin to feed them snails, slugs, and larvae which Gnome and Dwarf children will be very happy to collect. Sow bugs and Earthworms She raises in a dark and cool room. Under normal conditions the babies stay with their mother until they are eight or nine months old. By then they will be able to eat crayfish, frogs, and fish as well. Since they no longer have a mother they will be brought up by the Suund with the help of the moms and children of the Alderwild Wood. The Suund asked Draka to organize a group of women to take turns feeding these adorable babies. She also had the health and welfare of the entire community to look after. I immediately asked that Ian's and my name be added to the list.

I met Natterjack as was planned. We paddled over to the Puncum settlement. Juncus was there holding onto one of last year's Cattail stalks. This year's Cattail growth had not yet begun to show itself. We pulled the canoe a short way up from the mouth of the Willow and tied the boat to a branch of a Black Willow. We remained in the canoe and invited Juncus to join us. We had brought a very soft pillow with us for our friend to sit on.

Juncus knew the purpose of our mission and so was well prepared to talk to us at length. I too was prepared with pen, paper, and sketch pad.

May 19

Over the last twelve days, I have been meeting with Juncus for several hours each day. Natterjack had to leave. There was still the refugee issue to tend to, thus I proceeded on my own. He has given me a great deal of information concerning the Puncum. I have organized it in outline form as I did with that of the Alderlings, Gnomes, and Dwarves

The Puncum: A Settlement of Fairies Living in the Marsh and Wetlands of Horse Thief Bay

I. Physical Attributes
   a. Average height: 6 inches
   b. Colour-complexion: medium to dark brown skin
   c. Build: slight, no wings, very lanky, muscular, and strong.
   d. Fingers and toes: toes webbed with each toe ending in a disc, excellent for walking on lily pads and where water weeds are quite dense. These features are very helpful when climbing Reed Mace (Cattails) and Loosestrife.
   e. Hair: thick, very dark brown or black
   f. Face: nose is broad, lips wide, eyes dark brown.
   g. Temperament: easy going and relaxed.
       - they are more able to endure the heat and humidity than the Alderling.
       - they take afternoon naps when the temperature and humidity is high

II. Clothing
   a. scant in summer, men wear short pants woven from Stinging Nettle fibres, sometimes shirts made from the skin shed by a snake or toad. In cooler weather shirts are made from Stinging Nettle as well as long pants of the same material. Women also wear clothing made from the Stinging Nettle fibres.
   b. shoes usually none, in cooler weather, shoes made from Softened Bullhead skins.

III. Jewelry

    a. Both males and females wear necklaces. Women wear more.

        Materials used: the shells of Horny Pea cockle, Mussels, and baby Zebra mussels. Also bones and vertebrae of Yellow Perch, Minnow, Rock Bass, and Blue Gill. These bones and shells are found on the sandy bottom of the Bay, especially between the island and mainland. There the sand is not buffeted by the waves.

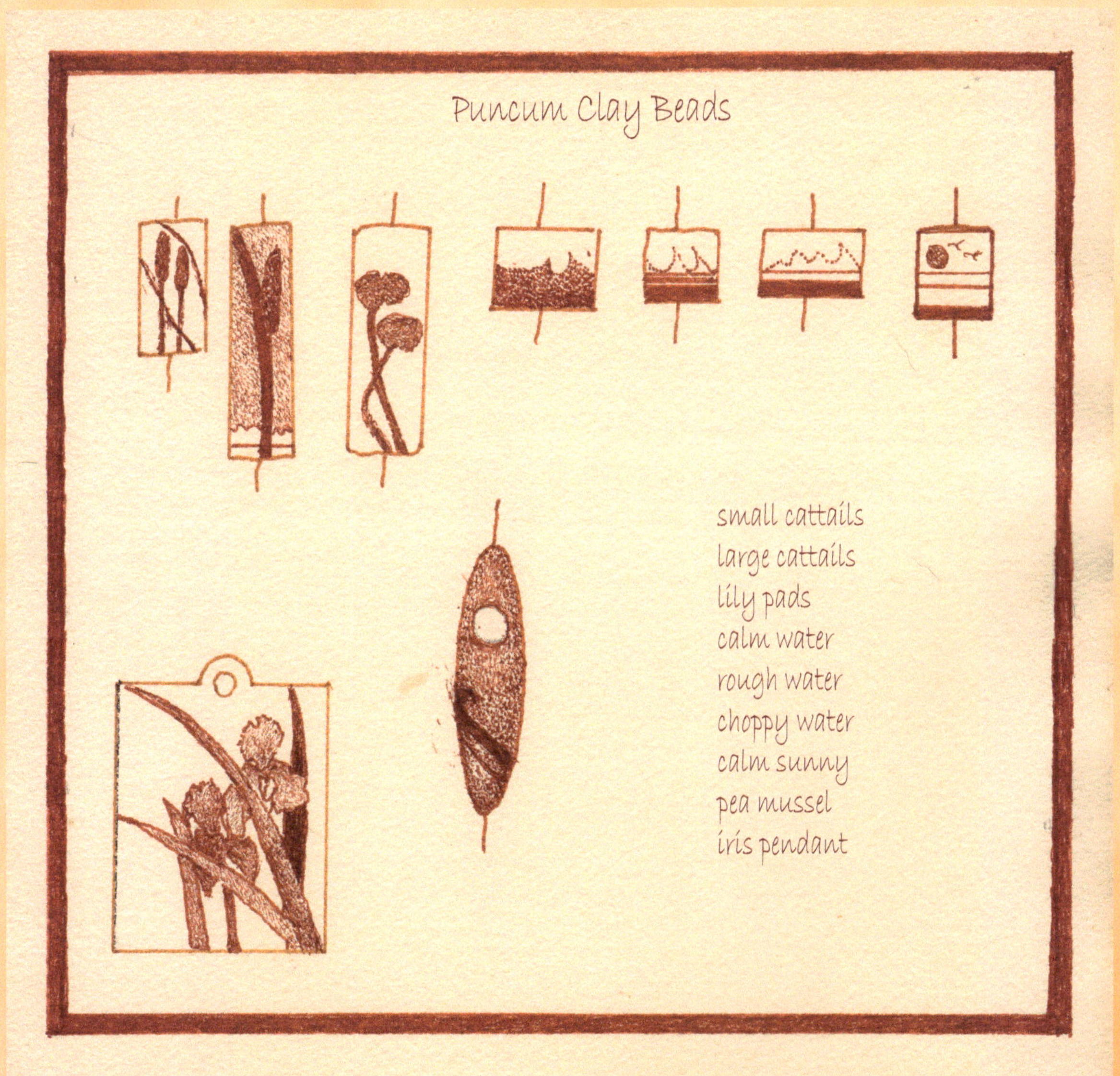

b. Puncum craft only six different shaped beads in clay with painted symbolic designs from nature on them.

i.   small cattails
ii.   large cattails
iii. lily pads
iv.   calm water
v.   rough water
vi.   choppy water
vii. calm sunny day
viii. pea mussel
ix.   iris pendant

The clay is coloured green using green algae.
To color the clay yellow or orange, they add orange lichen found on rocks. For burgundy they use Ink Berries. There are other natural colors made from plants, which the Puncum use.

IV. Pottery
a. There is no clay to be found in Horse Thief Bay. The Puncum must use the Catmarn, a type of boat, to sail across the river to the Meander Channel between Hill Island and Turtlehead Island. The channel is very shallow, there are many water lilies, both yellow and white growing at its entrance. The lilies make entering the channel difficult, which is a good thing. It prevents larger boats from motoring through. It is somewhat camouflaged by the large stand of Cattails, so that it is not noticeable from the main channel. Also the wildlife and Puncum living there are not disturbed.

b. The Puncum sail their boat to the entrance, then drop their sail and paddle the rest of the way. When they reach an area of shoreline where the Forget-

Puncum Pottery
beads & weights
vases
planters
oil lamps
pitchers

Me-Nots grow, they are able to pull close to the land and tie their boat to some small saplings.

c. The clay is loaded into reed baskets. Four Puncum usually work together when on a journey to collect clay. Wind can come up very quickly on the river, causing great waves to lash against the boat, making for a perilous voyage home.

d. The clay is used for making bowls, jars, beads, weights and measures, and clay tablets, which are inscribed with their laws for everyday living.

    i. For example, a tablet may show how many fish a Puncum may catch in a week: 1 Green Sunfish, 1 Yellow Perch, 6 Cut-Lip Minnows.

    ii. The same method is used for counting and collecting Snails, Crayfish, insect larvae, and plants gathered to use as vegetables and large fish.

    iii. Protecting wildlife and plants is very important. The Puncum are only allowed to catch fish or pick enough plants to fulfill only what is needed for the community and no more

    iv. Puncum may not take plants in the same area more than once a month, sometimes longer, depending on the species.

    v. There are instructions for planting and harvesting Na's bounty. These tablets also show how deep a seed should be planted. What time of the year Duck Potatoes should be harvested. When should Cattail pollen be picked to use as flour. Also when Cattail heads may be cut and boiled as a vegetable. Which plants are

Puncum Cattail / Fish Pictographs

Plants and Creatures from Horse Thief Bay

Single Cattail
Mayfly
Water Iris
White Footed Mouse
Arrow Head
Damselfly
Ground Nut
Caddis Fly
Great Blue Heron
Caddis Fly Larva
Canada Goose
Giant Water Bug
Mallard Duck
Giant Water Beetle

poisonous or what part of it may be eaten or used. What time of day and what month is best for fishing. What type of bait should be used for catching the fish.

    vi. These rules are taught to each generation, father to the son. The laws give the community a code of ethics, a structure, which promotes a balance between Nature and the Puncum for all time.

V. Diet

    a. They have a large and varied assortment of meats and vegetables.

    b. Plant matter gathered:

Chufa	Elderberry
Arrowhead	Duckweed
Wild Ginger	Spring Beauty
Rock Tripe	Early Saxifrage
Crisp Pondweed	Hemlock
Jack-In-The-Pulpit	Wintergreen
Duck Potato	Fiddleheads
Groundnut	Cattails

    c. Meat:

Snake	Dobsonfly Nymph
Papershell Clams	Wandering Snail
Fresh Water Clams	Green Sunfish
Dragonfly Nymph	Damsel Fly Nymph
Great Pond Snail	Great Ram's Horn Snail
Yellow Perch	Minnows

VI. Hunting and Fishing (see drawing on page 49)

    a. The Puncum have several methods of hunting and trapping snakes, Dragonfly larvae, Dobsonfly

larvae, and Caddis Fly larvae. A trap is used
for catching small and medium sized snakes,
Common Water Snake. A rectangular basket
woven from Black Willow branches and cattail
fronds with a funnel entrance are used. A small
Yellow Perch is placed inside the cage as bait.
The fish is unable to swim free because of the
narrowness of the funnel and the barbs protruding
from it. It is a one-way trap. Small fish, Frogs,
and rodents are the major foods for the Water
Snake. After the snake has entered the trap to eat
the bait and is unable to return to the surface for
air, it will drown. At that time the trap is raised
and opened to collect the snake.

b. Snakes, fish, and snails are the Puncum's main
source of protein. Since the above three animals

hibernate or move to deeper water in winter, some of the fish and snakes are dried on a long rack.

c. Plant matter is also dried.

d. All food, whether it is meat or plant, is shared by the whole community.

e. Another method of fishing used by some Puncum is the use of the Giant Water Bug or the Giant Water Beetle. These insects are used for capturing the larvae of the Caddis Fly, Dragonfly, Dobson Fly, and Damselfly. Minnows are sometimes Caught in this same manner.

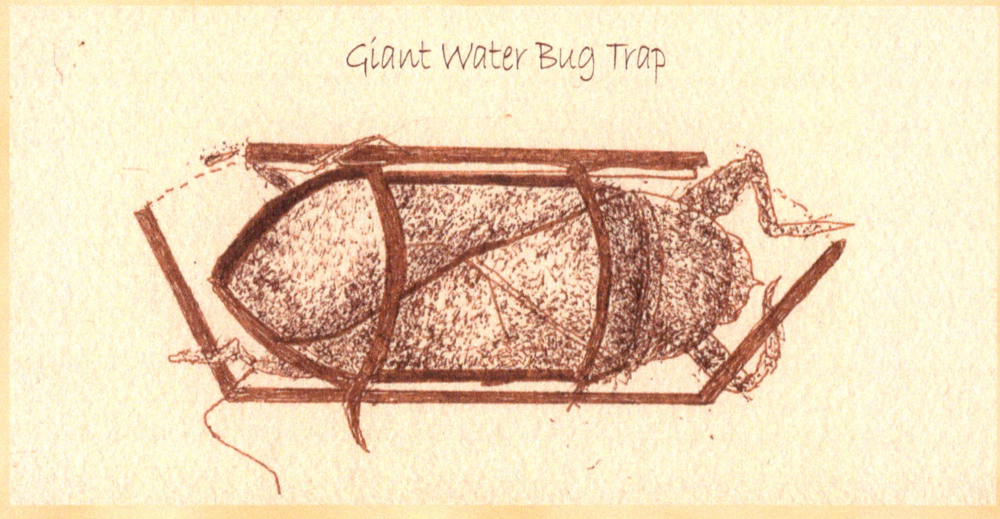

f. These two insects are quite capable of killing a Puncum adult, and even more so their children. Every now and then a child does fall victim to one of these creatures but that is Nature.

g. Only the most proficient of the Puncum adults use these insects.

h. These insects are very large, length two to three inches long, sometimes larger. They have very strong forelegs as well as powerful middle and hind legs for swimming. The Giant Water Bug has a short piercing beak it uses to grasp and suck out the bodily juices of its victims. The Giant Water Beetle uses its front legs and mandibles to crush its prey.

i. The Puncum adults work as a team, often needing eight men. Using a frame constructed of six Black Willow branchlets, two running lengthwise to the insect and four across. The two branches across the bull work of the body are tied permanently to the frame. The front and back branch rods are only tied to the frame at just one end. The other end is left free. Thus once the frame is placed over the insect and held down very tightly, the two men in the rear take the hinged stick and bring it around and across both hind legs and tie it down. The same is done to the front legs.

j. With this done, a string is attached to one leg. The bug is let loose to return to the water to catch its prey. After each catch the Water Bug is pulled in

and the prey is removed before the bug has a chance to eat or suck out the juices. The same is done to the Giant Water Beetle. One leg is tied and the beetle is released in the water to catch more prey. As soon as the beetle has caught a creature, the Puncum bring up the beetle and take its prey before it eats it.

VII. Tools and Utensils

    a. Tools are mostly made from bone. Every now and then a common Sucker or Carp will float into the Bay having been injured or killed by human fishermen. The waves will push the fish into the shallow water near the island where it will sink and decompose. Snails, Minnows, and insect larvae will eat the flesh. The bones then lay on the bottom in the sand, altogether cleaned. Only an inch or two of water covers them. The vertebrae are sometimes worn by the Puncum men as headdresses, necklaces, and other ornaments during festivals.

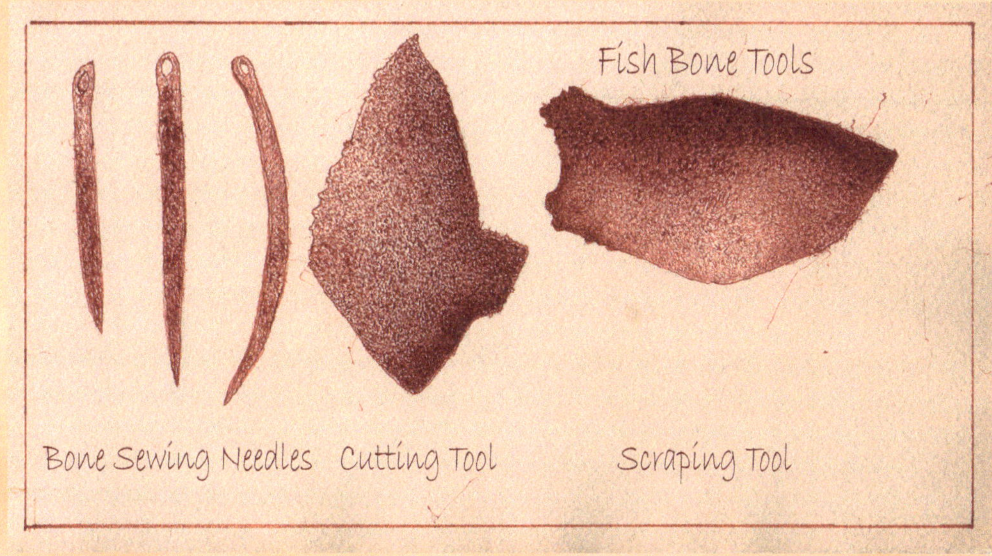

    b. They also use the larger vertebrae found for the making of pipes.

    c. The larger gill plates from dead Carp are used in the making of spearheads, combs, sewing needles, shuttles for weaving, and scrapers for cutting meat and scrapping scales off fish as well as slicing vegetables.

Puncum Water Craft
The Noe
The Ish
White Bark Canoe
Paddles
The Catmarn
The Pau

d. Also they can be made into fishing hooks, tools for digging Cattail roots and dislodging Duck Potatoes from the mud to float to the top of the water, which are then scooped up with a wooden strainer.

e. An Adze head is made from bone and tied onto a stick.

VIII. Water Craft.

There are five types of boats: the Ish, Catmarn, Noe, White Bark and the Pau.

1. The Ish is used for fishing. Black Willow branchlets are used to build the skeleton of the boat. The spine is laid to which the ribs are fastened and bent upwards. They are held in place by the rim or gunwale, which is constructed of two large branchlets tied at each end, forming an oval. Aged Cattail fronds are stretched across the ribs using pine sap to seal each one to the other. Several layers are done in this manner. Each frond is attached to the bow and stern. When all fronds are laid and stretched, the entire boat is given many thinned coats of resin and left to dry for several weeks. There is a bracket or oarlock at the stern to keep the paddle in place. At the bow a rod is mounted with a ring attached. In this manner the Quad net may be lowered or raised.

2. The White Bark is used for transporting passengers from one community to another along the main land shore. It is built by stripping a wide piece of bark from the White Birch tree. The strip is small in our measurements, and not thick so it does not hurt the tree. It is folded lengthwise but not creased. The ends are cut in a curve and the seam is glued with pine and sewed very

tightly. Two long willow branchlets are laced to the gunwale. The seats are made from small pieces of bark glued together to make a double thickness. The boat can hold twelve passengers.

3. The Catmarn is used for sailing to the islands to fish, collect clay, and trade with other Puncum communities. The deck of the Catamaran is made from Basswood saplings lashed together using the twine made from Stinging Nettle fibres. The deck is then laid upon two strong parallel Basswood saplings which have been curved upward at each end and strapped to the saplings. A mast is then erected near the front of the platform. The Catmarn is very similar to the Catamaran of the humans. The humans no doubt copied the Puncum design.

4. The Noe is used on the waters of the Willow and Alderwild Brooks. It is very strong for traveling over and near rocks and white water. It is sometimes used on the river. The Paddles: A triangular paddle blade is used in getting between rocks and a round paddle blade is used in the open water of the Bay. The boat is made from the trunk of a Basswood tree. It is dug out with an Adze.

5. The Pau (Punt) is made from Cattail stalks, Common Rush, or Basswood saplings. The stalks are lashed together with twine made from the Stinging Nettle fibres. It is a raft, which has a pointed bow which allows the Pau to access the many channels between the stalks of Cattail. The raft's point pushes aside the stalks as it moves forward. The Pau is used when the Puncum wish to catch Crayfish, Fairy Shrimp, Snails, and Zebra

Mussels and when the Cattail heads are ripe and full
of pollen ready to be collected. The Pau is primarily
used in the calm water of the Bay. It uses a paddle (1.
and 2.) as a rudder for steering or for poling. Paddle
3. Is used with the Catamaran when crossing the river
against a strong wind and current. Paddles 4 and 5.
Are used with the Noe and the Pau for getting between
Cattails and negotiating around rocks.

May 20

Both Gnomes and Dwarves have taken the art of bowing
boards to new levels of creativity and uses. Besides arcing
boards for building the hull of their boats, boards with
double arcs are used in building their homes. They bow short
boards for chairs, slightly longer ones for wheels and wider
ones for staves.

Boards are taken from oak trees, which are already very
old and standing erect. These trees have diameters of great size.
They are felled with axes, which are forged by the Dwarves.

Wooden wedges are hammered into one end of the tree
trunk to split the wood lengthwise. The split follows the grain

of the wood. The boards, once stripped from the trunk, are bowed using the following method: building a large fire and putting great pots of water to boil and using the steam created by the boiling water to warp the boards, giving the boards any size curves needed; and in some cases, double curves can be had.

No nails are used for the kegs that hold a fermented drink. Wooden pegs only. Wooden barrels were also made to hold the cooled charcoal from their wood fires, and later used in making soft soap.

They make wheels of different sizes, for large carts and small wagons.

Stones both large and small, round and flat, smooth and rough, were used for smoothing the surface of the wood.

May 21

Buds swell on the tree branches and leaves burst forth. Flowers bloom, and animals grow. There is a great flurry of activity in the Alderwild Wood, the Valley of the Horsetails, Fern Marsh, and the Wetland. The Puncum call it the Time of the Babas meaning "The Time of the Babies." The Alderling call it the Time of the Linglings. Gnomes and Dwarves refer to it as the Time of the Little Littles.

The Spring Peepers are still singing, but they have been joined now by the Common Tree Frogs. Other frogs and toads let their voices be heard. It is a chorus of male frogs all hoping to woo mates to join them in the small pools of water found in the Alderwild Brook. Here the females lay their eggs in a jelly-like substance.

The adult toads leave the water to spend their lives in the damp places of the Alderwild Wood. Frogs are more aquatic and live in and near the water. During dry spells, when all of the moisture has left the soil, the toad often returns to the water of the Alderwild to spend a little time absorbing water through its skin. It is a process known as osmosis. Toads and frogs do not drink the water.

May 23

Another beautiful day! A slight breeze blew, causing the newly emerging leaves of the Maple and Oak to flutter and dance.

Ian was working on a mask of a Flower Fairy, but I felt the need to explore the Alderwild Wood and visit the Alderlings in their summer homes.

As we crossed to the mainland in the canoe, we saw Crispus and Potamogelen. They were kneeling on their

Pau with Tria nets in their hands. They were gathering Caddis fly and Damselfly larvae. We waved to them and continued on with our own affairs.

We climbed the hill and walked the path along the hem of the Alderwild Wood on our left. To our right were the Berns. We then headed to Hemlock Ridge, meeting many Gnomes and Alderlings along the way. When we reached the ancient stone stairway built several hundred years ago by the Dwarves, we descended.

Many species of wildflowers grow along the sides of the steps. The Blue Cohosh is now a foot and a half high. Its leaves resemble closely the leaves of the Early Meadow Rue and Wild Columbine. The main difference being, the leaves of the Cohosh are much larger and of a deeper green, tinged with burgundy. The flowers are very small and Burgundy in color. The Blue Cohosh is the species of plant from which the Suund used the dried root powder to make a tea for the pregnant Gnome. It relieves the pain of birthing. The plant grows best in the shade.

The leaves of the Mandrake too are almost fully open. In a few days the white flower hidden under the large leaves will open. Mandrakes grow in mass and so provide a solid canopy of overlapping leaves. Small animals and the Alderling can find cover and protection here.

By August the Gnomes and Dwarves will be picking the Mandrake's ripe yellow fruit. A delicious jam will be made from them.

Further down the stairway, the Wild Ginger have opened their heart shaped leaves which in time will become quite large, providing more shelter to both Fairy and animal. Under one of these plants we came across a toad and mouse playing checkers. It was one of the strangest sights we have ever seen.

Silvas spoke to us about some animals being anthropomorphic, animals capable of speaking to one another. It is amazing, not something you can put into words. Wild Ginger is another plant the Suund uses in Her healing remedies.

The land on all sides of the Valley of Horsetail has become a patchwork quilt of varying shapes and shades of green. When we reached the bottom of the stairway we entered a sea of Green Common Horsetail. I could barely see the rooftops of the Alderling summer homes. We had to be very careful where we stepped.

We decided to go no further than the wooden bridge Ian and I built crossing the Alderwild Brook. We sat ourselves on the bridge. We knew that Pody and Hatch would probably see us and come to visit us there. We feared the possibility of stepping on someone's home.

Within minutes Hatch and Pody saw us and our worried look. They came and sat themselves on a large rock in the brook next to the bridge. We talked for quite a while. I have now learned the spoken language of the Alderling and have become quite fluent in it.

Hatch introduced us to many of the inhabitants living

along the banks of the brook. Many of them I had seen in the Great Hall during the Festival of Grata but had not met.

While we were talking, Hatch interrupted the conversation and pointed to a Toad and two Alderling Fairies just a few feet from us. While they stood together, the three of them seemed to be in conversation. The cadence of the words was slow and lilting. The words seemed to run into one another and overlapped as if there was more than one voice at a time. We realized the two Alderlings and the toad were in fact singing, not in conversation at all. Soon other animals, Fairies, and Hatch and Pody picked up the notes and joined in. It was a sound of supreme beauty, the likes of which I have never heard.

Before the three of them began singing, the Alderlings had been helping the Toad to shed its skin. This occurs about four times a year, as the Toad grows larger and outgrows his older skin. The outer skin loosens from the under skin and splits in half from the top of its head down the length of its back to its rear. The skin also splits at the mid-line of its lips, down its throat, and across its chest to its arms. The split continues to its fingers. The skin splits again down its belly to its hind legs and toes.

Most often, as the skin is splitting, the Toad is drawing the skin into its mouth and swallowing it. However when the Alderlings and the Suund need the skin for use in making new wings for the Elves and skin grafts, the Toad does not swallow its skin but allows the Suund to

help him to remove it so that they may have use of it.

When the toad skin is removed, the Alderlings stretch it out on a wooden frame to dry. I have often seen a toad split its skin and drawing it into its mouth to eat it. It is a slow process. Afterwards the toad soaks in a shallow puddle.

An Emergency

On our return to the island we met up with Natterjack. He has called for an emergency meeting of the Refugee Committee for tomorrow morning at 9 o'clock. There is more bad news coming from the west. More Refugees! "We need outside help! Ian, we need you to quickly design a flyer and posters to get the word around. Humans are needed. Zena, will you make copies on your printer?"

May 24

We all arrived at Nat and Draka's home promptly at 9 o'clock. Nat had been up a good part of the night worrying. He could not get to sleep thinking about the problems that lay before us all. He had made some notations as to what might be done and how we should organize ourselves.

What humans could we contact now for help? There is the need for scouting parties to investigate the feasibility of other lands:

The Forest to the North

The Plain of Wal

The lands to the east of the Mac Mountains

The Provincial Park on Hill Island

The Marshes behind Batterman's Point

The Woodland of our dear friend Rog and Margery living a few miles west of here.

Investigating all of these places would take time and man power, neither of which we have now. We asked ourselves if any one of us knew anyone, Gnome, Dwarf, Sprite, animal, or Human in any of these areas that we could ask for help. Finding permanent, safe housing for the refugees now would be next to impossible. The refugees needed shelter, food, and medical attention now, today, this morning in fact.

The Great Blue Heron living in our Bay is one that can speak in Gnome and Dwarf tongues. Late yesterday afternoon, a short while before we spoke with Natterjack, the Great Blue Heron, while flying overhead stopped here at the island to speak with Nat. The Heron had been flying over the great construction Site to the west; the same Site from which we had already rescued a number of Gnome children, Dwarves, Sprites, and other Fairies and animals.

The Site was being extended another several acres to the east. Dynamite was being used to blast away more rock. Rock fell everywhere and there was more to come. Gnomes, Dwarves, and Fairies were being killed, injured, and left homeless. More plundering of that area came very suddenly. It was not expected. Panic reigned among the inhabitants. People were running, screaming, and falling. They could not leave fast enough, and some could not move at all. They were the elderly, the very young, and the infirm. Some had broken legs, arms, or both. Some had cuts and were bleeding profusely.

The Great Blue saw this taking place. It swooped down, landing near several Gnomes who were hiding in the brush nearby. He told them to gather all of the fleeing inhabitants into one area, if possible. They would have a better chance of surviving the night and the Trolls. They were told to cover themselves with some boughs of Hemlock.

There was no way they could reach a safe haven and shelter before nightfall. The Suund had told the Heron to tell some able Gnome or Dwarf to rip some strips of clothing to use as tourniquets to staunch the bleeding of any leg or arm wounds. Also keep all who are injured from moving. Cover them with any bits of clothing or leaves. They must be kept warm so as not to go into shock. Keep the children as quiet as possible so as not to attract any unwanted attention. There is safety in numbers.

They must not light any fires. The woodland is too dry. It has not rained in three weeks. The Great Blue told them help would come in the morning.

We needed to act quickly. There was no time to waste. Having realized that Great Blue was no ordinary Heron, I asked Nat if there were any more such birds or animals who could help us. Could Great Blue carry a basket with injured Sprites or Nymphs in it? They were very light in weight. Would that be a possibility? Are there any deer we could ask?

Nat looked at me, nodding his head yes. The idea struck him as being possible. He asked Bracken to go and take the matter up with Great Blue and Nuphar, a White-tailed Deer.

The next thing was to organize a team made up of Dwarves, Gnomes, and Alderlings to set up a clinic or station at the construction site. Here the injured would be sorted out into groups with the most critically injured, either physically or emotionally needing immediate attention in one group.

Then there was the need for a member or two of the team to match the mode of transportation with the seriousness of the injury. The Dwarf, Thapsus and his son Perch volunteered for that duty.

We next needed volunteers to man the canoes. There were only four which had trolling motors attached. These would provide the quickest and smoothest mode of transportation of the critically injured and elderly.

I raised my hand for that duty. I also suggested that I take a very lightweight canoe of mine and tow it behind my motorized canoe. The Dwarves Bursa and Fraxim and the Gnome Larix would man the other canoes.

Draka was asked to organize the inhabitants to help set up more cots in the Great Hall. If there were not enough cots, then whatever else they had would suffice. Also they needed to set up a few tables to lay the patients on for setting bones for surgery.

An infirmary would also need to be set up in the Alderling Common Room. The Alderling, Alisma would be in charge of it.

Draka was also to get a group of both men and women together to care for the sick and wounded so that the Suund would be free to set the bones, stitch the wounds, and provide any other types of needed surgery.

Older children were to be asked to look after the young who were not injured but traumatized. They will need to be calmed and fed.

A search party must be organized to check the woods east of the site. All of us on the committee felt it best to bring all of the homeless, injured, sick, old, and infirm here to the Alderwild Wood. We will be able to assess their needs more effectively and intelligently. Their health needs come first. Finding a suitable homeland for all will be secondary.

The meeting just ended when Bracken returned with very good news. Great Blue with his heron friend Spargan, and Nuphar with his young friends will join us. They were standing just outside the door. The help from these four could make the difference between life and death of those critically injured.

Nat, Bracken, and Azulla hurried to put something together which would serve to carry Gnomes or Dwarves on the backs of the deer safely. The herons would each carry a basket to hold Sprites, Nymphs, and perhaps even babies.

We loaded the five canoes with blankets, bandaging material, canes, staffs, crutches, and splints. The Suund gave us Mandrake root, dried Bee balm leaves, and powdered Blue Cohosh root.

Bursa, Fraxim, and Larix were to take Thapsus, Perch, and Natterjack with them. Ian and I are to take our canoe and tow a fifth canoe. Great Blue and Spargan led the way with Nuphar and Scirpus just behind them. The four of them would arrive there before us. Ian and I brought up the rear.

Help is on its Way

We were at the construction site within ten minutes. It is difficult for me to comprehend how Trolls, who were once humans at birth, can inflict such an outrage on the land of Na. Such pain! Such hurt! More trees have been uprooted, and rocks were blasted since we were here last.

The devastation is higher up the rock face and more difficult to access. There was no protected shoreline for us to moor our canoes. We looked further, paddling around a point of land where the boats would not be battered by the wake of the speedboats. It was a safer place for the boats but it was further from where the injured lay and there were many.

We found a small patch of land where we could set up a first aid station with water, food, blankets, and medical supplies. Ian and Natterjack began clearing a path to the summit. Thapsus and Perch went ahead to assess the situation.

It was a most sorrowful sight. The animals, Fairies, Gnomes, and Dwarves were huddled together under the branches of several Hemlocks. Nearer the trunks of the trees were the injured. It was terrible to witness. Some of the injured were so badly hurt they moaned with pain, and some were dead. Mothers and children were beside them weeping.

Thapsus wondered if Great Blue and Spargan

Mycena Galericulata

together could each take an end of a small blanket and carry the injured one by one to where I was standing at the first aid station. It was not a great distance for the two herons to cover. It would also be the quickest way with the least amount of jostling to the patients. Great Blue and Spargan agreed to try it.

Thapsus laid out a blanket, and then tied two corners together. He did the same to the other end. A hammock was formed. He and Perch lifted a Gnome with a badly broken leg onto the hammock. The herons each took an end and lifted the Gnome with apparent ease and brought him to me. Great Blue said that it was not at all difficult and they could probably bring two the next time.

Seeing who we were, friend, not foe, Dwarves, Gnomes, Sprites, and other Fairies began to appear from under trees, on top of trees, and from behind rocks. Thapsus said that it was incredible. So many! He was stunned. When they arrived at the first station, I felt overwhelmed at first, but realized I could not allow myself to panic. This was a job that had to be done. People, Fairies, and animals were depending on us for help.

I mustered my courage, and with Bursa's help we forged on. We worked side by side for most of the day. We had a small fire going next to us on the rocks far from any dried leaves or grasses. We used it to boil water for cleaning wounds with a wash of Self-heal, it does not sting. It is also good for burns and bruises. We used dried Sphagnum Moss for dressing many of the wounds. The Suund gave it to me just before we left the Bay.

Some of the displaced Fairies and Gnomes were able to come under their own power using sticks and crutches.

Others needed assistance with someone on either side of them to hold them up. Still others arrived on someone's shoulders. The herons brought them in blankets and hammocks. The deer carried the Gnomes and Dwarves who were not critically injured. There were some whom Thapsus thought might have spinal or neck injuries and were laid on boards and carried to our station to be assessed. These individuals, Great Blue and Spargan carried to the Bay immediately.

There were many who were not injured physically but were in a poor mental state. They were delirious and extremely nervous. The Suund told me to give them tea using dried Motherwort leaves. For others the great trauma to their nervous systems caused them to be nauseous and vomiting. I gave them a drink of Bee Balm tea.

Children were leading other children by the hand, forming chains of five or six. Some were in tears while others were blank faced.

While checking around for more inhabitants, Perch came across an elderly female Gnome sitting by a Juniper bush. Tears were streaming down her face. Her husband was missing and the world as she knew it and lived in had been obliterated. She had lived there since birth and her parents, grandparents, and great grandparents had lived there for many generations.

Perch asked the woman her name. She said, "Dicentra." He told her that her husband had been found and was in good hands. She would see him soon. She could not speak but her facial expression told all.

Ian made many trips carrying Gnomes and Dwarves on his back to the station. He also carried babies and those adults too sick to make it on their own. The stream of homeless and injured seemed endless. I lost count.

Another Blue Heron joined us. His name was Actias. While Great Blue began carrying baskets of Sprites and Nymphs back to the Bay, Scirpus and Nuphar carried those Gnomes and Dwarves who were not seriously ill or injured on their backs to the Bay. Some were spared any physical trauma but were suffering from fatigue and lack of food and water. Others were emotionally drained. A third deer named Sagiteria was able to carry one adult Gnome and several children of lesser weight.

Natterjack and Ian laid several folded blankets in each of the five canoes. The canoes carried those who were in most serious condition but were too heavy to be carried by the herons. Two Gnomes or two Dwarves could be laid side by side on the floor of each canoe and one less injured patient could be seated in the bow while Larix and Perch took charge of the motors.

When the fellows returned with the canoes from the Bay, they brought with them more help: Lich and Caddis to man the other two canoes. Celestra, daughter of Thapsus, came to help Bursa and myself.

I asked Celestra about how they were holding up at the other end. She said, "They are managing but just. They have put out a call for more volunteers. They need one more volunteer to help the Suund and several to help the nursing staff both in the Great Hall and the Common Room". I also asked Celestra about how many refugees have been moved to the Bay thus far. She said, "The number is at least fifty, if not more. Refugees are arriving on foot. They just suddenly appear. There are the animals, most are not hurt but have nowhere to go."

She said, "The Suund is working miracles. The skin, which you had seen being removed from the toad by the two Alderlings, the Suund is now using to make new wings for some of the Wood Sprites and Nymphs. Some have so much damage to their wings that they cannot be repaired, but the Suund is making new wings from the toad skin. The Suund is also using toad skin on the wings of some of the other Sprites where the injuries are so large she cannot stitch the edges of the opening together. Thus she is using the skin as a graft which would heal and become one with the Sprite's wing skin, which will take time to heal. There is a great need for more toad skin. The Suund does have some skin remaining but it will not last very long. Toads do not shed their skins frequently. The Suund has put out a call for any toad ready to lose its skin to please come forward.

The afternoon was beginning to slip away. Shadows lengthened, the air was cooling, and still more Gnomes, Dwarves, Sprites, and Nymphs were still being found. Some were injured, and some were not. Natterjack asked Perch before he left for the Bay to bring several large yurts with him when he returned. Also more food and water was needed.

Perch returned with the yurts and extra food, which were piled high in an extra canoe he was towing. Nat, Bursa, Larix, and Hatch were assigned to set up the yurts in the rock clearing, where a fire could be built safely without worry.

Ian and I each manned a canoe, taking with us as many refugees as the two boats would hold back to the Bay.

Great Blue, Nuphar, and Spargan are to remain at the sight keeping watch for any Trolls, Traugs, or Norgs.

Great Blue has keen eyesight and hearing and can make a great raucous at the slightest disturbance. Natterjack and Bracken are staying there as well. A number of the injured can huddle against Nuphar's warm body when he lay down.

It was just about dark when we reached the Bay. Many came to the dock to help lift and carry the wounded. Ian and I were exhausted. We did not even stop by the Great Hall to speak with the Suund but came directly home. We had a light supper and then went right to bed.

May 28

Ian and I have been to the sight every day and again this morning. Today we returned by noon, which was early.

Natterjack, and crew, and both Ian and I have been working there from morning until dusk. Every tree and crag, every cave and hollow, from the Site to the Bay, A distance of a mile has been searched for any Gnome, Dwarf, Fairy, or animal too frightened to come out of hiding or too injured to move.

Yesterday and the day before, twenty were found, three of whom were dead. Their bodies, along with all of those who were killed at the Site, were brought home to the Bay.

Most of the animal population survived the devastation. They were able to leave the Site more quickly than the Gnomes, Dwarves, and Fairies. They lost their homes but there were not many killed.

Each time Great Blue and Spargan flew over the land between the Bay and the Site, they kept a look out for any animals on the run or hiding in fear. The heron's eyes are keen. The word was out that the herons would help any in need. Ian had also returned to this Site and came across a nursing White-footed mouse with eight babies. He carried them home in his hat.

Common and Star-nosed Moles, Long and Short-tailed Shrew, Meadow Voles, Wood Rats, Flying Squirrels, and Chipmunks, all the animals, young and old were carried to the Bay in large rectangular baskets mounted on the backs of Nuphar, Scirpus, and Sagiteria. Some of the stronger Fairies were able to fly back. The Black and Grey squirrels and other larger animals were able to walk the distance in stages.

Early this morning Natterjack, Bracken, and Azulla and the three deer returned to the Site, walking the entire distance to get there. They made a final search, covering every inch of ground and found five young Gnomes who were not hurt but exhausted. On their return to the Bay they repeatedly called out for anyone injured or very frightened to reveal themselves so that they could be helped and taken back to the safety of the Bay.

The Great Hall and Common Room is filled to capacity with those needing medical help of one sort or another. The overflow of those who were injured have been taken into the homes of the residents of the Alderwild Wood.

Perch, Larix, and Fraxim returned from the Site with the Yurts, blankets, and medical supplies. The Yurts were set up immediately along the eastern edge of the Wood. There are already two Yurts set up near the northwestern border of the Wood. This has made a total of five large Yurts.

The idea of Yurts came with the Great Migration while the Gnomes were staying in Iceland.

All of the now homeless refugees had been neighbours, good friends, relatives, and members of a thriving

community. It seemed to me that it would be a sad thing if this community of friends had to be broken up, parcelled out, sending twenty here, five there, and ten somewhere else. They have suffered so much already. Their emotional wounds are deep and penetrating to the marrow of their existence. To heal well, both mentally and physically, they need the comfort of their friends and family, their community. Natterjack and the others feel the same.

I phoned our dear friend Rog. He and his wife Margery have several acres of untouched woodland. I told him of the situation here. I also spoke to him about our feelings not to split this close community of friends and family up. Rog felt the same. It would be a cruel thing to do so. He had room in his woodland to take the whole community. There were already some Dwarves, Gnomes, Wood Sprites, Nymphs, and Fairies living there, but there would still be plenty of room for the whole community to settle. He was also willing to help in the construction of new homes and whatever else the new community would need.

Counting the Gnomes and Dwarves who arrived in the Alderwild Wood under their own power and those found this morning, there are approximately ninety-five to one hundred new refugees. This would amount to perhaps thirty-five families.

The Wood Sprites, Nymphs, and Leaflings are quite small and do not take up much room at all. There are a number of animals too, but their needs are not great, a little bit of turf and peace and quiet mainly.

There is still some room in the Alderwild Wood without it becoming overcrowded. Don and Lise have offered their small woods, which would hold a small group of Gnomes to be permanent residents. Also, at Joy's woods, Don said that they could take a number of the injured who needed time to heal now. Don's neighbour, Joy, too would be able to take a number of the different races of Sprites, Gnomes, and Dwarves.

However, before any type of activity takes place in preparation for a move to new woodland, there needs to be a period of rest for the refugees as well as the inhabitants of the Alderwild Wood. Everyone is exhausted and needs to get their strength back. The Suund too needs rest. She has been working night and day, always thinking of the patients and not herself. The move to a new homeland will be no easy task.

May 29

I have done very little work today. I just sat and watched.

There is a large group of Canada Geese enjoying themselves in the quiet shallow water between the island and mainland. There they can stand on their heads, eating the young, tender water weeds on the bottom.

Great Blue is standing on our neighbour's dock, considering which fish to catch. He too needs a period of rest.

He and the other two herons have been working very hard. There is nothing to disturb him there except the Red-wing on occasion who feels that the heron is too close to his territory.

A week ago, a Red-wing was quite upset with Great Blue and kept flying and diving, hitting him six or eight times before Great Blue flew off. The Red wing knows of the refugee problem and Great Blue's help in it and so pesters Blue just a little.

Natterjack stopped by at the island for a minute. We learned that the Suund was able to stop and rest. I apologized for not walking up to the Wood to help today. He said that there were no more emergencies and the women had everything under control. The Patients were being tended to. Some of the refugees are well enough to help out with the preparation of food for all. They are even helping the other patients by walking with them or feeding those whose injuries were so great they couldn't feed themselves.

Draka has done and is doing a great job getting everyone organized with the caring of the patients. She has a team collecting wild edibles and a team for preparing the food for over one hundred. Everyone has been given a specific job, which cuts down on the confusion.

May 30

Our muskrat friend is back again. He has been swimming back and forth between the stand of Cattails where the Puncum live and our neighbour's dock. It is building a nest for her babies to come. On each trip from the Cattails, it carries a mouthful of plants.

May 31

Now that the cold weather has nearly left us and the earth has been warmed, more and more Fairies are beginning to appear.

I did not realize how many different races there are. I thought there were only Wood Sprites, Wood Nymphs, Water Sprites, and Water Nymphs in the area around the water but now I see that there are a great variety of Fairies living along the edge of the Bay and in the water. Each Fairy has his or her own task to carry out in Na's plan. Some close the flowers as evening approaches. Then there are other flowers, which bloom at night and are closed by day.

It has been a cold spring up until now. This has delayed the appearance of a number of Fairies. I saw several Sprites yesterday and again this morning. They were at the edge of the Alderwild Wood, where there are fewer trees and the sun is able to shine through the branches, warming the earth.

There is a group of last year's Goldenrod Galls. They have weathered over winter and some of them have turned a silvery grey. In the summer, as the plants are growing, the female Gall Fly inserts her ovipositor into the fresh stem of the Goldenrod and through which she lays her eggs. About

Goldenrod Gall: a, b, cross-section; c, flower;
Certain insects lay their eggs in the plant tissues upon which
the larvae feed. The mechanical irritations or the secretions
produced by the larvae while feeding cause the abnormal
growth of the stem forming a gall.

ten days later the eggs will hatch into larvae, which begin to eat the inside of the stem. The irritation and saliva of the Gall Fly larva causes the stem to grow abnormally, eventually becoming a round gall. The larva remains within the gall for a full year. By autumn the gall has turned several shades of brown and hardens. The larva will chew a tunnel for its escape but does not leave the gall until the following spring. When the larva becomes an adult and leaves the gall, the gall does not shrivel or rot but remains hard. Thus the Gall Fly never uses the old galls again. However in the spring, the adult female fly will lay her eggs in a new fresh stem.

A new race of Fairies, Wood Sprites, will take over the abandoned hardened galls and ream out the interior of the gall so that it will be ready for the young pregnant Wood Sprite to give birth to three or four young. The young are not weaned until mid-July. By the end of August the young are fully grown. By mid-September the Wood Sprite has taken up residence in each of the vacated galls. It prepares for winter hibernation. The shell of the gall is very hard and keeps out the snow and rain. These empty galls can be used over again for several years before they become uninhabitable.

The Sprite's wings are varied in color. In the spring they tend to be in shades of green. In early autumn the wings turn to yellow ochre predominately.

I am looking forward to that day in mid-July when I hopefully shall see the young Sprites as they exit the gall and make their entrance into their new world. To watch their new wings open, spread out, and take their first flight would be thrilling. The young Sprites will be taking their first flight about six weeks from now.

I have forgotten to mention that the very old Gnome who had lost his wife, Dicentra has been reunited. His mental state has very much improved. She is much better too.

Much has happened since our last trip to the excavation site in May. A young Gnome died yesterday from injuries suffered as a result of a large rock falling on his chest at the Site. The Suund tried her best to save him but the damage was too great.

Out of the hundred and two refugees found, fifteen had been killed at the Site. Three were discovered dead in the woodland between the Site and the Bay. Counting the young Gnome who died yesterday, the death count is nineteen.

Many more would have died if it had not been for the healing powers of the Suund and the care by the nursing staff. Also great credit should be given to the herons Great Blue, Spargan, and Actias, as well as the five deer, Nat and company, Ian, and the many other volunteers of the Alderwild Wood community. They must all be congratulated for their quick response, organization, and bravery.

Of the sixty-two patients who were hospitalized and taken to the Alderling Common Room, The Great Hall, several homes, and one yurt, twenty-five have been released and are fully recovered.

Fourteen others have been permitted by the Suund to

take relaxing walks through the Alderwild Wood and visit
with the permanent residents. It is important for them to
remain under the Suund's care for a short while longer.
Several Wood Sprites, two Dwarves, and two Gnomes have
suffered some nerve damage. Three of the Sprites have
muscle weakness in their arms. One Dwarf's right arm
and hand muscles have seized and become quite useless.
Another Dwarf has a problem with his right leg. One of
the Gnomes has some neurological problems with his arm
and leg movements. Hopefully with specific exercises, the
strength and movement of his limbs will return, if not
completely then nearly so.

The remaining patients have suffered little physical
injury. It is their emotions which have been dealt a blow.
These patients have difficulty sleeping. They are haunted

by recurring nightmares. On hearing the slightest noise, they jump with fear, thinking that the big machines and blasting have started again. Each time this happens, they think they will lose their friends and family again. The trauma to both body and soul caused by such wanton disregard for those who live in harmony with Na is unconscionable.

Homes and other buildings will always be built; that is inevitable. However they need to build and design their homes in accordance with the environment and nature. Humans will be happier if they learn to live with Nature and Her inhabitants.

For those refugees whose emotions have suffered great insult, only time will heal. Those Fairies who have needed skin grafts will also need time for these grafts to mesh and become one with their own skin. There are five such Fairies. They will need to lie quietly in bed. Three elderly Dwarves have pneumonia. Six Wood Sprites and two Nymphs needed wing replacements. Four Gnome children have bad colds. One Gnome child had a ruptured appendix. Another Gnome child has become blind. The Suund can see no physical damage to the eyes but feels it is as a result of the traumatic experience suffered at the sight. He witnessed the death of his Sprite friend. If this is the case, he should in time regain his sight.

The Suund would like to keep the elderly Gnome couple, Dicentra and her husband under observation. Since he has been reunited with Dicentra, his mental state has improved. However he has nights when he awakens calling for Dicentra, even though she is right there, lying by his side. He is not eating as well as when they were first reunited.

The Suund has given this problem much thought and has spoken with Natterjack, Draka, Bracken, and Lich about her concerns. She asked them for their thoughts on the matter. Her idea was to build a house for them attached to the Twin Maples with a deck about three feet off the ground. Having the house so close to Her, She could look after them without having them in a hospital setting. Also having a deck, they would have a good view of the Alderwild Wood. They would be in close contact with the other Gnome inhabitants of the Wood. Everyone thought it to be a good idea. It would be convenient and practical for long-term care. The three fellows would get to work on the house right away.

Any patients who were still left in the Common Room were transferred to the Great Hall. The same was done with those patients still remaining in the yurt. However the patients left with the residents of the Wood were to remain with them. These homes are more pleasant places to recuperate in.

June 2

The Cypress Spurge is out in full regalia on the island.

Two Great Northern Pike swam into the shallow waters between the island and the mainland. The water there is warm and calm and only about three feet deep. They swam together, side by side, male and female, the one laying eggs, and the other fertilizing them. A great number of eggs are laid. The eggs are not sticky; thus they fall to the bottom singly. The Pike left soon after. Neither the male nor female remained to guard the eggs and young. The eggs will hatch in two to three weeks. Since there is no adult to guard the

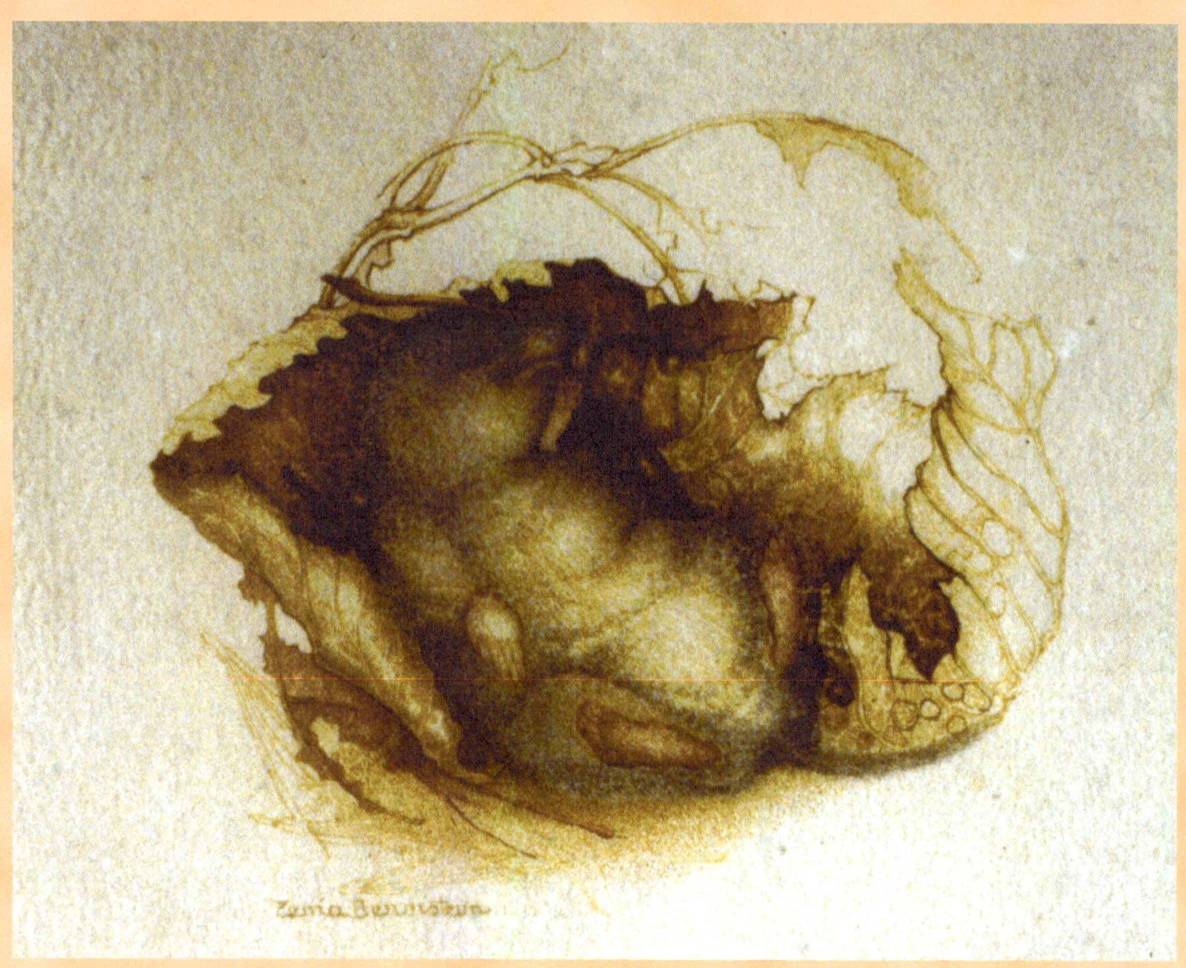

many eggs, the Carp, along with other fish, will eat many of the eggs as well as the young. The Carp swim into the Bay soon afterward in a group of eight or ten. They are bottom feeders and mainly eat the eggs. They remain only a few hours before swimming off.

The Dragonfly Larvae, the Giant Water Bug, and Giant Water Beetle also feast on the fish eggs as well as the young. Of the hundred thousand eggs laid only a few survive the Gestation period to hatch, only a few reach maturity.

Unlike the Great Northern Pike, the Small-mouthed Bass male clears a nest on the river bottom by fanning the silt away with his tail. An indentation is made for the female to lay her eggs. She leaves the nest and the male moves in to guard the eggs and young. He takes his job seriously, becoming a fierce protector of the eggs and young. He chases all other fish away. There are presently two male Small-mouthed Bass, one at each end of our dock guarding their young. Further out in the Bay, several Rock Bass have also made nests.

There is another female Muskrat who swims between the stand of Cattails where the Puncum live to the foot of Troll Hill. I do feel for her. The Troll Witch lives in that area, at the base of Dark Point. The Muskrat must be a new and inexperienced mom, not originally from our Bay. Otherwise she would have known about the Troll Witch and built her nest elsewhere. Ian thought that perhaps she might be a refugee from the construction site up river. I would think that a mile would be too great a distance for her to swim.

The Vole, sometimes called a Meadow Mouse, is also here on the island. It has made tunnels just below the surface of the soil going in all directions. Some people think of it as a pest. We think of it as just another friend. We also have bats again. They live under the Cedar shingles covering the outside wall of the studio. I think they are Little Brown Bats. They do not come out in the daylight, but as evening approaches they begin to fly out. I see them as they become active an hour or so after sunset. Their bodies and quick movements are silhouetted against the azure blue night sky when they leave to hunt for insects.

June 3

It took only a few days for the fellows to build a home for the two elderly Gnomes. It is lovely. It faces southwest so that Dicentra and her husband will be able to see the sunsets in late autumn, winter, and early spring when the trees are bare of leaves. The deck surrounds the girth of the tree. I am sure the couple will thoroughly enjoy it. They will take up residence tomorrow. Some chairs, tables, and a bedstead have been built for them. Two Gnome women are just about finished stuffing a mattress casing with Milkweed down. Pillows and cushions are already finished. There is food in the pantry and any other things needed to begin life in the Alderwild Wood.

June 4

Nat and company, along with eight strong male refugees, have gone to our friend, Roger's woods. They will clear shrubs and a few young trees to bring a little more sunlight into the woods. They have taken a good many weathered board and beams from our woodpile. They hope to get started today with the building of tree houses for both Gnomes and Dwarves. Rog said he would help the boys.

The residents from the construction Site for the most part lived in tree houses. The reason being the land there was very irregular and rocky. The Alderwild Wood has more level ground, as does our friend's woodland. No matter, they have lived in tree houses for centuries and wish to continue that way of life. I am looking forward to seeing a community of tree houses.

June 5

Many of the Spring wildflowers have come and gone. The Early Saxifrage with its clusters of white flowers on a single stem dot the island, poking out of crevices in the rocks where a small amount of soil has collected.

In late May the Alderwild and the flood plain of Fern Marsh was spangled with bright yellow flowers of the Marsh Marigold. Spotted Hounds Tongue with its spotted green leaves and pink and blue flowers bloomed at the same time as the Bellwort with their yellow bell shaped flowers.

The Rue Anemone is a most delicate flower. A single white flower tops a very thin stem, which is six to eight inches tall. They are very rare but we are very fortunate to have several blooming at the edge of the clearing in the Wood.

When the Wild Columbine blooms the Ruby-Throated Hummingbird arrives. The flowers are bright red with yellow centres. They seem to need little soil for they are found in the crags of rock outcroppings.

June 7

A young Pileated Woodpecker visited us on the island this afternoon. It could be the son of the of the pair which visits us in the Alderwild Wood. He seems to be checking out our White Pine and Pitch Pine, looking for some juicy morsels. He came without a partner, which is unusual. Perhaps he is not old enough to have a mate. I have never seen one on the island before.

Great Blue was here this morning doing a little fishing. He caught a large fish and had a difficult time getting it into the right position to swallow. Eventually he managed to get it down.

June 8

Ian and I set out for a day of sketching. We left at 9:00 A.M. We attached the trolling motor to the canoe and headed towards Hill Island. The river was calm like a mirror. No other

boats were out yet. We found an area just before reaching the Meander Channel between Hill and Turtlehead Islands. There were several old Black Willow trees with branches reaching into the water. It was so peaceful and serene. The only sounds we heard were those of the House Wren and Redwing. In the distance a Spring Peeper or a Tree Frog was peeping. Ian climbed onto the shore for a few minutes to look about and found the head and tail of a Great Northern Pike.

What was more impressive was the head and tail of a Muskellunge lying next to it. When alive and whole, the fish must have weighed at least thirty pounds. We brought it back to the island, hooked it to a stringer, and tied it to the dock so the flesh would soak off. It had a very strong odour to it. We also have two drawings each to show for our work. The water plants were hardly up yet. It has been quite cold.

June 9

Silvas came this morning. Hatch brought him to the island on a Pua. We have not seen him for an age. It was a bit of a surprise. The sun was out. It was warm with no wind. An ideal day for a hundred and thirty-five year old Gnome to be out.

He brought us up to date on all his doings. Anything

new happening in the Alderwild Wood. News of the Patients. The progress of the new community and other tidbits of news I may have missed.

First of all, the seven patients needing physical therapy for weakened muscles caused by nerve damage have improved so much that they could return to their homes, if they still had homes. However since they did not have homes, they will remain in the Great Hall until new homes are built, which we all hope will be soon.

Natterjack and company are working very hard building the new community of homes that are being constructed.

Three of the five who were suffering emotional difficulties are stable enough now to face life in a new community. They may have brief dips now and then until they have settled into their new lives. The Suund has no doubts about their ability to cope long term.

The elderly patients who had pneumonia are doing very well. They are allowed to sit in the sun and go for short walks if the weather is warm.

The four children who had colds are well again and the Gnome child with the ruptured appendix is as good as new. The child who lost his sight has not yet regained it.

Those fairies that had need of skin grafts and wing replacements are doing very well. However the Suund would like them to remain quiet for a few more days.

As for the old Gnome couple living in the new house just above the Suund's home, the one with the veranda on it, Silvas visits them every day and plays chess with Dicentra's husband, Bruno. He is one hundred and ten years old. Silvas has gotten Bruno interested in his collection of ancient relics from Europe and the early

Gnome and Dwarf settlements on the St. Lawrence. The Suund is pleased. Silvas seems to be slowly pulling Bruno out of himself. He is talking more and there is even a smile on his face from time to time.

Eight houses have been completed in the new woodland, and the brush in that area has been cleared. It is best not to have a lot of dry flammable material too close to the new homes. Eight refugee families totalling twenty-nine individuals will move in tomorrow. Another three homes will be finished by the day after tomorrow. These will be for young couples with only one child or none at all yet.

Slowly the yurts are becoming empty and folded for use in another emergency.

Caddis and Newt are two who are helping to build the tree houses in the new community. When they saw the finished homes, they were so impressed with the idea of living high off the ground they wanted to build tree houses for themselves in the Alderwild Wood. They also liked the panoramic view that a tree house offers. Both Gnomes are courting and are soon to be married in September. With the consent of their future mates they will build two tree houses for their new homes.

Silvas left at noon.

June 10

Bursa's wife, Capsula and daughter, Nitella were in the Wood cutting Bracken fronds. Its rhizome is an astringent and the fronds contain starch, which may be used as a food. The fronds are cooked and used as a vegetable.

The rhizome may also be burnt and the ashes contain enough potash to be used in the making of soft soap. It can also be formed into balls of firm soap depending on the amount of water mixed with the ashes. The best time for burning the Bracken is from June to October. The ashes must be kept dry until ready to use.

They had collected quite a few of the rhizomes and were about to burn them for their ashes. They planned to make as many balls of soap as they could to give to the refugee families.

Different members of the Alderwild Wood were making baskets, furniture, mattresses, pillows, and clothes for the families to have when they moved into their new homes.

Petra, wife to Lich, Colona, wife of Larix, and their daughter Acura were weaving yards and yards of material from the thread spun last summer from the Stinging Nettle plants. The thread when woven makes a strong durable material. It is used for making sails for their boats, as well as blankets, bedspreads, and curtains.

The Puncum Juncus, Crispus, and Potamogelen, along with Salus, and Osmunda are creating bowls, plates, mugs, jars with covers, and pitchers, all made from clay.

The Gnomes, Thamias and Sciurus, the Dwarves, Marmota and Gama, and the Alderlings Dryscopus and Selasphorus are building furniture for every conceivable use. Each team is building furniture for those people of their own stature. They know best the needs and measurements for their own kind.

The woods of the new land are more dense than the trees of the Alderwild Wood. They are actually very similar to those which once graced the Site. Thus the housing requirements and styles are a little different from what is seen in the Alderwild Wood.

Up until now it has always been thought that all Dwarves, no matter where they lived, looked alike. The same thinking was applied to the Gnomes, and the Sprites living along the mainland and islands of the St. Lawrence River. Their languages and beliefs were thought to be the same as well as their cultures. However, that is not the case. Having now met, cared for, and spoken to the refugees, Nat, Hatch, and I see that our assumption has been incorrect. They are different, both physically and culturally.

The legs, arms and fingers of both Gnome and Dwarf refugees are longer than those of the Gnomes and Dwarves living in the Alderwild Wood. The Gnomes still have their characteristic pot bellies but the Dwarves have flattened stomachs. They speak the same language but a different dialect.

I am curious as to whether the Gnomes and Dwarves living in our friend's woodland have the same differences as the refugees since both woodlands are very similar, very dense. Nat said that they were not the same. Both Gnomes and Dwarves already living in our friend's woodland were shorter in stature.

I wondered why this was so. I also wondered why none of us knew this until now, especially Nat and company. I thought for a moment why and realized that the inhabitants of the Bay travel very little outside their own community. There is enough diversification of food and habitat to satisfy the needs of all.

June 11

I have been puzzled all spring as to where the Wood Sprites and Nymphs dwellings are. I have looked everywhere but have found none. I asked Natterjack how the housing for the Sprites, Nymphs, and other Fairies was coming along at the new woodland. When will they be finished? Ian has said nothing about them, even though he has been helping with the building of the new homes. Nat smiled and said that they do not have homes.

Sprites, Nymphs, and Fairies of most races do not have homes, specific dwellings with furniture and such as do the Dwarves, Gnomes, and Alderlings. From the time the Sprites and their kind emerge from hibernation in mid to late May, they roam the Bay and Alderwild Wood as free spirits. They may be found sleeping in the crotch of a tree, sitting under a group of Mandrake leaves, or hiding under a fallen Oak leaf. Sometimes they play tricks and sit in a bird's nest with the chicks; and when the mother bird returns to feed her young, the Sprite is also fed, unbeknownst to the mother.

The Fairies eat what they find each day, a few slug eggs, berries, the sweet nectar from different flowers, and perhaps a grub or two. Since Sprites, Nymphs, and Fairies are so small, they do not require a great amount of food at one time. Their main need for survival in hard times would be some source of water found in berries or other plant material. Of course a stream or frog pond would do nicely.

June 14 - Water Nymphs

Very early this morning in the pale light of dawn I heard a beautiful sound. Whether it was a voice or an instrument, I did not know. I stepped out of bed and went to the window but still could not place its origin. I put on a T-shirt over my nightgown and went outdoors to locate the sound. I saw ahead of me the silhouette of a Gnome seated on a rock on the edge of the island. It was Silvas. He was playing his flute. The sound was so beautiful, as though angels were singing.

It was in those still hours of dreaming time when reality and fantasy blend. Water Nymphs were singing as Silvas was playing his flute. Some Nymphs danced on the skin of the water while others sat on last year's dried Oak and Maple leaves floating on the water wherever a slight breeze took them.

I sat down quietly before I ever reached Silvas. It was likened to a religious experience, I believe. The exquisite beauty and harmony between Na and her creatures is something I saw and experienced but there are no words that can describe it.

I spoke to Silvas later this morning. I wanted to know more about the beautiful creatures I had witnessed singing earlier.

We sat at the edge of the island. I had a pen and pad in hand ready to write down every word he spoke. He gave the following description of the Water Nymphs.

Of all of the inhabitants living in Horse Thief Bay, the Water Nymphs have been living here the longest. They arrived here some six to seven million years ago, shortly before the appearance of the Water Sprites. They have changed little since then. They have been able to adapt to any change in diet and environment.

However, over the past fifty years, there has been a slow decrease in the population which is strange because for the last six or seven million years up until this time, the Water Nymph population was growing by leaps and bounds.

They had managed to survive great climate changes, extreme cold, floods, and droughts. They had not only done well here in the St. Lawrence River area but also all over the world as well.

Here in the Bay their health could not have been better.

It will be fifty years since the first unexplained death of a
Water Nymph occurred. It was a female, aged twenty-four
who was found floating face up halfway between the island
and the stand of Cattails. A young Puncum, out fishing
on his Pua, found her and pulled her out of the water onto
his raft.

The Suund was called for immediately. She examined
the child and found no cause for her death. It was a complete
mystery to Her. There were no marks of foul play, no signs
that the Troll Witch had killed her. No signs of disease or
injury were found, thus her death was written in the Death
Journal, a book, which keeps account of all deaths in the
Bay, as death by natural causes. The only other remark
that was written said she did have a look of pain on her face.

Her death was considered strange because at age 24
years, she was a mere child. Water Nymphs normally live
to age two hundred, sometimes longer.

Over the following years, one or two other Water
Nymphs were found dead under similar circumstances,
floating in the Bay. With a careful examination by the
Suund, no cause of death could be found.

Different members of the community at such times
would ask the Suund if a Dragonfly larva could have
bitten the Fairy. Another question was asked about the
Giant Water Beetle or Giant Water Bug. Both are killers.
The Dragonfly larva and Giant Water Beetle were scratched
off the list of possible causes. If they had been attacked by
either of them, the bodies would have been badly mangled.
There was only the Giant Water Bug left as a possibility.

The Giant Water Bug has a sharp beak, which it uses
to pierce the body of its victim to suck the vital fluids

out. Here too not the slightest sign of any puncture mark was found. Also, if the Fairy had been attacked by such a sucking insect, the body would have become semi-transparent.

However, over the last twenty years the number of Water Nymph deaths has increased at an alarming rate. With the more recent deaths, some of the victims found had blood seeping from their ears. With further investigation by the Suund, she realized that the deaths of these Fairies were not due to natural causes but in fact were due to the increase of the racing boats on the river. Their powerful engines make a powerful noise; their loudness is extreme. The noise produced by these boats has affected the hearing, equilibrium, and pressure on the eardrums of the Nymphs, causing the eardrums to burst in some cases. It has caused extreme vertigo, loss of direction when swimming, and disorientation. Some of the Nymphs would swim deeper rather than up to the surface as they intended. Some Nymphs were swimming in circles. Often the noise would be constantly ringing in their ears and in some cases; it would overload the Nymph's nervous system, short-circuiting their lives.

Before the onslaught of racing boats on the river, Water Sprites were seen any time during the day, singing and frolicking among the sedges and rush. Now they are seen only during the twilight hours of Dawn and Evening. They spend most of the day in caves under the island where there are pools of water. There they may sit and swim. They no longer feel pain in their ears. There have been fewer deaths, but this has come at a great price. They have become an endangered species. We hear the Fairies only occasionally now. Their voices are like that of the loon that is slowly fading away.

I asked Silvas if he would mind if I joined him when the weather was right to see and hear the Fairies sing. He said he would be pleased. I also asked him if it would be all right to record their voices.

The songs seemed to have no words, or at least none that I could understand. It sounded like a series of tones sung in rounds to fill the hearts of Na's inhabitants with joy and a measure of peace and happiness.

Water Nymphs have no written or oral language. They leave no piece of pottery, sculpture, or painting behind as evidence of their existence. They leave only their music, which has never ceased. Their music has survived through war and pestilence. Their music is remembered . The beauty of their songs has been told in legends and tales from ancient times and even before. The notes may be different in each country, in each pond, lake, or river, but their reason for being is the same. Where there is discord, the songs of the Water Nymphs and Sprites bring harmony. They are a vital part of our existence.

June 16

While Ian and I paddled the canoe from the mainland to the island, we saw hundreds of carcasses floating on the water among the rushes. At first I thought they were minnows that had died. On closer inspection I saw that they were the skeletons cast off by the emerging Mayflies from their nymph stage.

Wildlife of every kind is suddenly emerging from their long winter's hibernation. Even the Water Striders are up

and about. They live under rocks or logs at the bottom of the
Bay, between the island and mainland during the winter.
When the water warms, the Striders move to shallow water
near shore. Here they find new shelters among last year's
dried Cattail stumps and Loosestrife stalks. The Striders
tend to stay in large groups. They are very difficult to
catch. There was quite a mass of newborns by our dock. They
jump and glide across the surface of the water effortlessly.

June 17 A Pleasant Trip

We went for a ride in the canoe with the trolling motor
attached. We decided to go to the Beaver lodge in the channel
behind Batterman's Point. The Channel wends its way
through a large stand of Cattails, Rushes, and Sedges. All
along the way large clumps of Yellow Flags dot the edges
of the channel. The deeper into the Cattails we pushed, the
narrower the channel became. We had to use our paddles
to push the canoe through a pathway to the end. We were
engulfed in a sea of Cattails several acres deep.

The Beaver lodge looked to be abandoned. However the carp

were there all along the way. In places their bodies would hit the boat as they scurried to get out of the way. At times it seemed as though one would surely land in the boat without the assistance of a net.

On leaving the channel I collected several handfuls of Frogbit and a couple of water lily roots that had floated to the surface of the water. We brought them home and planted them here.

There were so many Yellow Flags in bloom that I picked some. I tried to pick a few stalks with the most buds on them. The flowers only last a day. The Yellow Flags in the Bay have hardly come into bud yet. The water here is colder, being so close to the main channel, which is deep and very cold.

June 20 - The Wood Sprite

I arose early this morning. The voices of the night had faded away. The birds of the daylight were just waking. The quietness of the hour was deep and penetrating. I wondered if all the world could hear its silence. Any sound heard during such quiet moments is so clear and singular. It does not need to repeat itself to be identified. Silence is such a frail thing; it like the rest of Na needs to be protected.

Morning declared itself with a bright warm sun and blue sky. When Ian awoke we breakfasted and went about our work. Ian went back to his paper-mâché masks and I went to the mainland to study the Sprites.

The pink flowers of the Spotted Cranesbill were gone and the seeds had ripened. It was time now to spread the seeds. This plant has an amazing way of casting its seeds, which makes it great fun for the attending Wood Sprites.

The Sprites have the job of collecting and spreading the seeds of this wildflower. Where once a flower bloomed five seeds rest, ready to be launched. Each seed has its own spring-loaded catapult, which propels it some ten feet or more. Although the Cranesbill does quite well on its own, the sprites like to help in carrying them even further. They carry the seeds to the sunny areas of the Wood to mix with the white flowers of the Round-leafed Anemone and the Mandrake.

The Sprites like to make a game of catching the seeds in midair. A few male Sprites like the game of "Dare". They like to challenge one another. Who is able to let the seed drop the farthest and make the steepest and fastest dive to catch the

seed without crashing into the ground?

I was watching the Sprites playing this game. They were having a great time, but I found it too nerve wracking and stayed only a few minutes. I have heard there have been some serious accidents.

Most of the Sprites enjoy catching the seeds without any fan fare while helping Na to do her work.

The wings of this particular race of Wood Sprite are in shades of olive green with some brown. They also have structure to them, which gives the Sprites the ability to flap their wings to fly. These Sprites do not have to depend on warm air currents to keep them aloft.

Just before returning to the island, I saw Natterjack. We sat and talked for a short while. The refugees have all been relocated. Those who had required skin grafts and

new wings will be remaining with their families in the Alderwild Wood.

The yurts have all been taken down. The last one was being folded while we sat. All of the relocated refugees seemed to be adjusting very well to their new life. They had been accepted by the permanent residents and made to feel welcome. Making new friends will take time.

Nat felt that it was best for all of us to put our environment projects on hold for the moment. The rescue effort had been a major undertaking. Gruelling work! There were days with only a few hours sleep. All of those inhabitants who had been working with the refugees, the nursing care, and the relocation of all have been pressed to their limits. They are stressed out. They need some R and R, and I agree.

June 21 Summer Solstice

The Bladder Campion and Hairy Beards Tongue are out in full bloom and the Pink Corydalis is just finishing.

June 22

This evening as I was sitting in the living room, I saw a large spider on the outside of the window. It was repairing its web. As I watched it worked very quickly. When it came upon several pine needles, which had gotten stuck in its web, it stopped at one pine needle and within a split second it cut the thread at each end of the needle and let it fall. The spider did the same to the remaining pine needles. I have never seen this happen before. The same spider comes out from its hiding place each evening. I shall watch for it again.

June 23

The female Mallard Duck swam with her six ducklings into the protective sedges and rush growing in the shallow water near the island. Here they are out of harm's way, the boats, and Great Northern Pike. When they wish to rest, they climb up onto the island and sit on the warm rock. They come nearly every day.

June 24 - A Nasty Encounter

It has been some time since a Troll, Norg, or Traug has entered the nearby woods just west of the High Pines Point, the Alderwild Wood, and the rocky plateau east of the Mac Mountains.

The residents of the Alderwild Wood with all their involvement with the refugee crisis have been negligent in keeping a watchful eye out for predators. Little did any of us realize that saving the Dwarves, Gnomes, Sprites, and animals from the horrific destruction of the land to the west would create another problem. We did such a fine job in clearing the entire area at and around the site of its

inhabitants that there were no more Dwarves, Gnomes, and Fairies of all races or animals for the Trolls, Norgs, and Traugs to eat.

We in the Bay were just about to settle into a week or two of doing our own "thing". However, last night we heard in the distance, the most awful of sounds, screams mixed with a thunderous noise. None of us had any idea of what it was. We were all frightened, but none of us dared to leave our homes. All we could do was to sit it out until morning. Then we could climb the steep rock face of high pines point and investigate the source of the noise on the narrow strip of land west of it.

The night seemed ever lasting. The screams never ceased. None of us slept a wink. Our hearts were pounding, and our mouths were dry. Dawn's early light appeared, but no sounds were heard. No chirping from those birds who sing at first light. Something was wrong! No sounds of Trolls and the other fiends were heard. The silence was deafening.

We waited a short while in case any Trolls and the fiends of twilight were still around. There was tightness in our stomachs and the feeling of nausea in our throats. Nat asked the Suund if she wished to come with us. It would be a difficult and tiring journey for Her. Her legs are short. It was decided that Nat and Bracken would carry her in a lightweight folding chair between them. She was not heavy.

By 8:00 A.M. we were on our way. The grasses and Common Horsetail of Fern Marsh were quite high. The deeper into the marsh we trod, the muddier it became. The grasses wrapped themselves around our legs and in places we sunk ankle deep in mud. There were no high grasses or mud once we crossed the marsh.

The next difficulty was climbing the rocks up to High Pines Point. This was even more difficult having to carry the Suund. It was important that She come. No telling what would be needed. We persevered and made it to the top. We stopped and rested a short while and had a drink of water.

Water was also sprinkled on the moss partially covering the Suund. This was done so that She would not become dehydrated. We were soon on our way for we wished to be back in the Alderwild Wood before twilight.

We followed a narrow path running along the top of the bluff. After several hundred feet the path led us first down a steep slope into what was once a lovely dell filled with a variety of wildflowers. Then we hiked up to the top of another bluff. The air changed and began to smell rank. The further along we walked the more sickening the odour became. Then suddenly there lay before us the dismembered bodies of Traugs and Norgs. There were even the bodies of a Troloxica and an Atrolpia, two of the three deadly races of Trolls. This meant that the most deadly and fiercest of the Trolls, the Trolconitum were out in force. There has not been a sighting or encounter with one of them in years.

Fear was out there ready and waiting to grapple with our emotions. We steeled our nerves against all that we saw and what was to come. The sight of all this carnage was horrifying. They were our enemy; all of them, but such mutilation of the bodies, arms half eaten and torn from their sockets. The abdomens and chests opened and the organs pulled out lying here and there on the ground. Such brutality, we would not wish to fall upon any enemy.

There were many Troloxica and Atrolpia who feasted with the Trolconitum on the Norgs and Traugs. They ate until their appetites were sated. There must have been at least twenty bodies, perhaps more. It was difficult to tell.

Natterjack, Bracken, and Ian gathered the bodies and body parts and heaped them in a pile. The woodland was too dry to burn them. The Suund said to let the bodies rot so that those remaining Trolls and fiends would smell and see the decaying bodies.

The Suund cast a spell on the bodies so that they would never cease rotting. Their odour would fill the nostrils of those remaining Trolls and engulf them. The heap of putrefied flesh would be a constant reminder. Then the Suund untied a little bag from her waist, which contained a green powder. She threw the powder into the air on the eastern side of the pile to keep the foul odour from spreading down river.

There now remained the problem of the Trolconitum. How should we deal with them? They have become a formidable enemy. No matter how grizzly and abhorrent their acts are, it is not for us to kill them. They were humans at one time.

We decided not to go any farther. We moved away from the bodies to a place where we could not see or smell them. We sat for a while and rested. The Suund took from Her waistband another small bag of powder. The powder was the same color as the one She used when the Alderling child was killed. It was used to purify the land around the pile of bodies so that, once again, the flowers, ferns, and soft mosses would grow there.

The Suund, after thinking for a short while devised a plan, which would not totally eliminate the Trolls and other nasties but cause them a great set back and would keep them at bay for some time. Evil is never eliminated but may be confronted and dealt a serious blow.

The area where the carnage took place is high on the narrow strip of the bluff. At the foot of this bluff are many sharp and dangerous rocks and boulders. The Suund conjured up an apparition, true to life of all those killed at the "Site" and those who died afterward. Then there were all of those who were injured, the animals killed and injured, and all of those who were left homeless. They were all standing there in a massive group among phantom images of trees to give the scene a look of authenticity. It was like a great mural suspended in midair about four feet out from the edge of the cliff. It was awesome.

The Suund knows that the Trolls, especially the Trolconitum are bloodthirsty. They will rush to reach and grab for all of the creatures in the apparition, not taking the time to see what they really were. Thus they would fall to their deaths on the rocks below and, with the morning light, they would turn to stone. The Norgs and Traugs, if any were to fall, would dry and become dust.

Evil never entirely disappears, but can be delivered a set back. Those Trolls and fiends remaining will have been delivered a great set back and sent into disarray. In time they will gather together and grow in number, increasing in greed and selfishness, for they have a voracious appetite to create mayhem and the death of Na and Her inhabitants. But, as there is evil there is also good.

The Suund, the Dwarves, the Gnomes, Alderlings, Puncum, Sprites, and many of the humans are here to counter the Trolls and fiends. However, there are not enough humans helping out. More humans with conviction and steadfastness are needed to do more than just talk.

It was mid-afternoon when we turned to head back. The Alderwild Wood and Bay never looked so good.

We have done all that we can to save High Pines Point and Horse Thief Bay and its environs. Now we just have to wait. It is 6:30 P.M. We had a light supper. The Suund took a nap when She returned to her home under the Twin Maples.

I would think it would take a great inner strength and concentration for the Suund to conjure up such a mural of woodland inhabitants and even trees. As for Ian and myself, we were both physically and emotionally drained and exhausted.

Ian stopped by my room just now to say that Nat, Bracken, and he are going up to the top of the bluff. They will be in a place where they can see the mural but no one can see them. They are wondering whether the Trolls, having seen the front row of fiends fall off the cliff, will bypass the carnage and continue on towards the Bay. The fellows took lanterns with them. They did not know when they would be back.

Draka and Bracken's wife have come to the house. We will all wait together.

It is 9:30 P.M. A thunderous noise and screams just commenced about five minutes ago. They are becoming louder as I write. I hope the fellows will be all right.

1:00 A.M.: No sign of Ian, Natterjack, and Bracken. The screams and moans continue but not as loud or as frequent as before. Perhaps the cries are from some of the Trolls who have fallen off the cliff but were not killed on impact and still linger. My mind is racing through many different scenarios. What if? Will they? Are they? When? Draka has laid her head down for a few minutes sleep. She could not keep her eyes open. I told her I would wake her if there is any news or they have returned.

6:00 A.M. The three have returned. We are all too tired to hear what has taken place.

We slept late this morning, nearly to 12:00 noon. We slept without worry. When we awoke it was a bright sunny day. The Redwing and Chickadee, the House Wren and Song Sparrow, all were singing and chirping. It seemed to me they were all rejoicing. Perhaps that is what I am reading into it.

The Trolls had a bad night. Many of them fell off the bluff to their deaths on the rocks below. Some Trolls, when they reached the edge of the cliff, realized what was happening. They turned to warn the others. However, the others behind them refused to believe them, thinking they were lying, not wanting them to share in the feasting. Thus, those Trolls behind pushed forward those who were thought to be liars.

Before they realized it, they were on the brink of death. They tried to hold onto some rocks and tufts of grass. They called to the other Trolls. There were Trolls standing there in a position to help but instead chose to give them a little extra push. However as fate would have it some of those tufts were not grass but Troll hair. Thus, many more died. Trolls are not very bright. Trolls, especially Trolconitum, think that with brute force they can do as they please. Not so.

Ian, Nat, and Bracken did not have to kill any Troll, Norg, or Traug. The Trolls themselves, driven by avarice, greed, and a lust for blood and destruction fell victim to their own brutality. Those Trolls who survived went skulking back to their lairs. They have been defeated, losing many, only a skeleton of their troupe remains. They have been deprived of their sting and venom. The inhabitants of Horse Thief Bay and the Alderwild Wood are safe for a while.

A Night of Thinking

Last night, during those long hours of waiting I found myself thinking about the Suund and the Trolls. The Suund is endowed with great powers. Her wisdom is without flaw. Her kindness and generosity, her caring and patience are boundless. She is the embodiment of all that is good in the world. She is a mentor and counsellor to all of the inhabitants of Na who will accept and believe in Her.

I wondered if the Suund had a counterpart, someone or something who is endowed wholly with evil. The Trolls, even the worst kind, the Trolconitum are evil but theirs is a force, not a power. They do not seem to be capable of reason and logic. Perhaps once long ago they were.

June 29 - The Woodcock

We have a Woodcock living in the Valley of the Horsetails. Yesterday evening, while I was visiting some of the Alderling families one flew straight up vertically, not horizontally like most birds. It did not sing or chirp but whistled by rubbing the three outer feathers of each wing together. It is a stubby looking bird. Its body is short, and its bill is long. They are quite rare, at least around here.

June 30

The Snapping Turtle was up on the island early this afternoon. She dug a hole with her front legs. They have sharp nails on them. Then slowly one by one she dropped the large, round eggs, about twenty-five of them into the hole. It took quite some time to lay them. She closed the nest with dirt pushed in with her hind feet.

There seems to be a great many Common Water Snakes on the island this year. They enjoy lying on the rocks while basking in the sun. We have even found one lying asleep in the canoe , which made me wonder how did it get into the canoe when the sides are so smooth. They are quite harmless and slither off as soon as we approach them. Kiri chased a four foot one the other day. Kiri is our new dog, mostly German shepherd. We had to put Floristane to sleep. She had a tumour on her spleen. She was twelve and a half years old. Both dogs came to us from the S.P.C.A. Mongrels, or dogs of mixed breeds, make good pets. They are healthier and also the dog's life is being saved.

July 1

I saw a strange thing occur this evening. I was writing at my drawing table when I happened to look up. I saw Spargan and Nuphar standing together on the mainland shore at the foot of Dark Point. Walking towards them was a Red Fox. Both Spargan and Nuphar noticed the Fox, but they did not move away. I thought this was odd.

As I watched, the Fox stopped only a foot or so away from them. From the movement of their bodies and heads, it looked as if they were having a friendly conversation. I reached for a stool so that I might sit by the window and

watch them better with my
binoculars.

Yes, they truly were
talking. I saw the bill of
Spargan and the Mouth of
Nuphar and the Fox moving
and their heads nodding
in response to each other. I
wondered what they were
speaking about. Was there
a way I could understand
them and even speak to them?

I saw Natterjack and several other Dwarves speaking to
Great Blue during the rescue effort. I wonder if I could learn
to speak to them as well. I shall speak to Silvas about it.

The more I become acquainted with all of the inhabitants
of the Bay and the deeper I delve into their lives, the more
mysteries are revealed. However, the mysteries are not
necessarily understood. Perhaps all things in Nature, in
life for that matter, need not be scientifically dissected to
revel in their beauty and content. Like a piece of music, I
need not know its structure to enjoy it. Thus, I do not need
to know how they are capable of speaking but only what
it is they have to say. Nuphar, Spargan, and the Fox are
dependent on one another to help keep a balance between the
inhabitants of the Bay and Na's resources.

All life, whether it be the same species or race, is
dependent on one another. It is like a spider's web; each
thread must be attached to another to make the web strong.
If a thread is broken or a hole appears in the web, the spider
spins another thread of like material to mend it.

It is the same with Na. The flowers depend on the birds and Sprites to spread the pollen of one flower to another so that a fertilized seed will develop. When the seeds are mature the birds and Sprite are called upon to carry those seeds near and far. For the seeds to ripen and grow, water and rich soil are needed.

Wood Sprites must have the nectar from certain flowers to survive. All of Na's creatures from Human to Dwarf, Gnome, and Sprite to the Mole need trees for shade and shelter. Animals need trees, their branches, trunks, and roots to live in and under.

Trees need soil and water to grow. Wood Sprites, Nymphs, and other Fairies have no permanent dwellings. They depend upon fallen tree leaves and the leaves of the Mandrake to provide shelter from the rain and hot sun.

The soil needs the debris of fallen leaves, twigs, and branches to die and give nourishment to all the plants and trees that grow on it and in it. All kind of insects lay their eggs in the soil. The eggs hatch and larvae develop, which in time become fully grown insects again. The cycle begins anew.

Air needs trees to cleanse and purify it. All life needs clean air to keep it healthy for friend or foe alike.

The Dwarves, Gnomes, Alderling, Puncum, and animals are keenly aware of this interdependence between

one another and with Na. They have, over thousands of years, learned that one thing depends on another. They realize that there must be a balance between Na and Her inhabitants.

If too many trees are cut in one area, the habitat for many animals, Fairies, Gnomes, and Dwarves will be destroyed. There will be soil erosion. Selective cutting and the replanting of new trees must be undertaken.

There is just one very large group of beings, the Humans and their kind, who do not take seriously the need for conservation, the need to keep a balance of Na's resources. Na's original inhabitants, the Sprites, Puncum, and Alderling have cared for and protected Her for many thousands of years. These creatures tended Her with loving care and have enjoyed the fruits of Her labour.

July 5

Last night we had our usual July 4th treat: Toasted marsh mellows and chocolate between two graham crackers. We lighted two giant sparklers and then watched the fireworks display across the river.

This morning I was in the

Alderwild Wood. I went to visit Silvas. Just before I reached his dwelling I heard a very faint crying in the distance. I looked around and realized that it was coming from high in one of the Twin Maples. All I could see was a Grey Squirrel's nest. However it was not the sound of a baby squirrel. Squirrel babies were born some time ago, in March I believe. This crying sounded like more of a human baby or several babies but not quite like that either.

Petra, Lich's wife, saw me and came to see what I was looking at. I pointed to the nest. She knew immediately what it was all about. Five Leafling babies were born yesterday. I wished somehow I could see them.

Leaflings

Leaflings are born helpless, nearly hairless, and blind. Within a week their bodies are covered with a soft, beige down to match the interior of the nest, which has been lined with the fluff of several Cattail heads. When a squirrel abandons its nest there is almost always someone to take residence in it.

Leafling babies' wings are just nubbies. They will suckle for two months. In mid-September they will live with their mother and go into semi-hibernation. Then they are nursed occasionally until the following May when they awaken. At that time they will lose all of their down, except the hair on their heads, which will be very curly and fuzzy.

They do not reach their full height and wingspan until they are five years old. By then their wings are strong enough to fly long distances. Up until that time they are only capable of flying short distances between branches.

The Leaflings' skin and wings change to become the same colour and shape as the leaves from the tree they are born in, to blend and appear as some of the actual leaves. Thus, the wing colour allows them a protective measure so that birds will not see them, thinking they are insects to be eaten.

Some leaflings on occasion have been mistaken for insects and met their deaths in this manner. Their clothing is scant. It is made from toad skin, which has the same properties as their wings. It can change colors. Their colors will also change in the fall when the leaves on the tree turn to autumn colors.

When the female Leafling and her young emerge from hibernation in May, the male returns from his hibernation with other males. He takes up his duty as parent again, feeding the five babies and relieving the female so that she may find food for herself and the babies. Their main food source are mosquitoes.

By the end of the summer the young are flitting about on those branches closest to the nest and catching some mosquitoes on their own. The first two years of a Leafling child's life is fraught with many dangers. They may be eaten because their wings are not strong enough yet to fly or hide from predators, or they could get stuck in pine sap from the White Pine.

In an effort to reduce the number of deaths from falls, Natterjack and Bracken have secured nets made from the finest Stinging Nettle threads, to tree trunks or branches where Leaflings have their nests.

The wings of the Leaflings become the shape of the leaves of the tree in which they were born. For example, if they were born in a Maple tree, their wings will be the shape of a Maple leaf. If they were born in an Oak tree, their wings will look like Oak leaves. If there are six or seven different species of trees, as there are in the Alderwild Wood, there will be that many types of Leaflings. They will all socialize with one another, their children will play together, but the adults will only mate with their own species.

Leaflings are only one step up the evolutionary ladder from plants. Like plants, they are only able to propagate with like species.

July 7 - Animal Life in the Bay

Now that we are living on the island, we are seeing different species of birds and animals than in the Alderwild Wood. A King Fisher just flew across the Bay, landing on a branch of a Willow. He was chattering all the way. His visit was brief, gone in seconds, only to return later.

Not long after, a female Mallard Duck swam into the Bay, followed by seven half-grown ducklings. They began to feed on the water plants in the shallow water. While in the water, the ducklings tipped their heads down and their tails up but because of their smallness, they were completely covered by the water. They stayed for quite a while, climbing

on to a sunny rock on the island to rest. Every now and
again, the mother with her young climb onto a rock on the
western side of the island to bask in the sun.

Before long a flock of twelve grown Canada Geese
entered the Bay but remained in the deeper water.

July 8

This afternoon I saw something black and rather large
on our mainland dock. At first I thought it was two crows
huddled together pecking at some carrion. Then suddenly
one jumped, then another and another. They turned out to be
half grown black minks. They began to play, chasing one
another, tumbling, and then off again on a chase.

One of them accidentally met the female muskrat and
her young who have a nest there. The muskrat mother charged
after the mink. They had a bit of a set to. It lasted only a few
seconds. Neither the Muskrat nor the Mink were hurt.

July 9

The Purple Loosestrife are up but will not bloom for
another week or two.

The water weeds are slowly making their way to the surface of the water. The Cut Lip Minnows are two and a half inches long, almost full grown.

On the undersides of the fallen Oak leaves lying on the bottom of the river, snails have laid their eggs in small jelly like strips or small round masses.

The Frogbit plants that I collected in June near the Beaver Mound and then threw into the water near our mainland dock are doing well. I find their shape and size very beautiful. They look like miniature water lilies. The Aquatic Smartweed floating on the surface of the water near the Frogbit is multiplying. Its flower is not yet in bloom.

The Redwing young are out of their nests and capable of flying but are insistent on still wanting to be fed. They are continually squawking.

The Water Strider's young have just hatched. There are hundreds of them gliding effortlessly across the smooth surface of the water.

July 10

The Flowering Rush is just beginning to open. The cold weather lasted so long into the spring that the water plants are slow in growing this year. It has however made it easier getting around with a trolling motor attached to the canoe. The water weeds do not become entangled around the propeller.

July 11: A Close Encounter

Earlier this evening just after supper Ian and I motored up river. We thought that we would see if there was any sign of life in the area around or near the Site. Half way to the Site, there is a large smooth rock, which gently slopes into the river. Many years ago mom and I used to take a picnic lunch with us to that small cove and sit on this smooth rock, enjoying the river from there. It was such a beautiful and peaceful place.

As Ian and I approached the rock, two Traugs were sitting there. I quickly shut off the motor. The river was calm and there was not a strong current to carry us away. They saw us but stayed where they were. They stared at us and we did the same to them. I had my camera. I moved slowly to unpack it and raised it to my eye. Snap, snap. I was able to take five pictures and still they did not move.

I could not believe what was happening. What luck! Why did they not run and hide? Why did they not try and chase us away? They had a small fire going and seemed to be roasting meat of some sort. I thought they only ate carrion raw. I guess they sometimes roast it too. I wondered if they were the only two nasties left? I am still wondering.

I wonder if they were feeling unafraid because most or all of the Trolls had killed one another or fallen off the cliff? Were the Trolls their greatest enemy? All sorts of questions raced through my mind and there were no answers. Perhaps I shall never know.

We moved the canoe a little closer. I held my breath. I wanted to know if they had sharp pointed teeth as I was told. As we paddled a slight bit closer, I gave them a wide grin. I hoped they would respond the same way. The Traug closest to us did put on a great show of teeth. It was great but gruesome. Flesh hung from the sides of his mouth and from between his very sharp pointed teeth. His teeth were stained yellow with areas of green, which looked like mold or fungus.

He had long thick black hair, which was tied in a knot on top of his head. It looked very greasy too. Long strands of slime hung from his nostrils. He also smelled bad. I felt sure I was about to lose the contents of my stomach right then and there. I took several deep breaths through my nose and collected myself.

I suddenly realized that we had drifted very close to shore and were about to hit it. Ian had become so fascinated by the Traug's display of teeth that he had forgotten to drop the anchor. He quickly back paddled just in time. Evening was drawing to a close and the first stars of early night glinted in the heavens. I had not realized how late it was. We turned around and headed for home.

I wish to go back and see them again. We shall try again tomorrow, weather permitting. I feel quite sure that they will come to that same rock again. They were repulsive and fascinating at the same time, a great mystery.

July 12

We arose with the early awakening of a few chirping birds. It took us a few minutes to shake the sleep from our eyes. We are not used to getting up so early. However the morning twilight does not last very long. The Traugs will go back into hiding as soon as the upper rim of the sun slowly rises from behind the horizon.

We had a bit of cereal and milk and were off. I packed my camera, sketchpad, notebook, and recording machine. The river was calm and the air cool. We reached the rock in minutes. They were there with a third creature. Its features were quite different. We thought that it might be a Norg. I wonder if they stayed there through out the night. All three of them grinned. We did the same.

I learned from Silvas and Natterjack, that Traugs supposedly only eat carrion and not Gnomes and Dwarves, but looking at their wide grins, I was not so sure. Could their grins be a deception? Had the fiends entertained any other ideas about us? Could we be on their menu, the entrée? We must be careful. I stopped the motor rather close to shore and Ian dropped the anchor. I wanted to encourage some kind of dialogue, something up close and personal. They looked different today. One had twigs sticking out of his hair, clamshells hanging from his ears, and a necklace of fish bones. The second Traug had a bird's nest perched precariously on his head. There were squirrel leg bones piercing his earlobes and the poor animal's skull hanging as a pendent from his neck. The third creature, the Norg, had old fishing lures, and red and white plastic bobbers hanging from his hair, ears, neck, and waist. There were also coloured bottles tied around his waist. All three creatures were a sight to behold.

I said "Hello," smiled, and waited for a response. They were sitting on their haunches and still grinning broadly. I was a little nervous. I heard much grunting amongst themselves. I was bound to take more photos. They did not seem to be afraid of us but were glancing from one to another and then to us. Their grins began to look menacing. I had a feeling  they were up to something. I asked Ian to begin pulling up the anchor slowly. Just as the anchor reached the surface of the water, the larger of the Traugs lunged forward to take hold of the boat. I put the motor in reverse. He missed us by a few inches and fell into the river.

The Traug quickly pulled himself out of the water and onto the rocks. He headed towards the other two nasties that were heading into the dark recesses of the woods. The sun was just beginning to show its head above the horizon. It was a close call for them as well as for us.

I should have known better and stayed further out from shore. I was too curious but I think that I was able to take some good photos of the creatures. I cannot wait to have them developed. We were a bit out of breath and shaken when we returned to the island and were also very excited. We could hardly wait to tell Nat and Silvas about our experience.

10:00 A.M. we crossed to the mainland and walked up the hill. We did not see Natterjack but did see Silvas sitting on a large rock. He motioned to us to come and sit by him. We described every nuance of expression, every detail of their garb and decoration, right down to the minutia of each of the three creatures.

Silvas was shocked to learn how close we had anchored our canoe to the Traugs and Norg. What were we thinking? He told us that we were living dangerously by getting so close to such fiends. He was, however, anxious to see the photos.

I asked Silvas if these creatures were born as humans like the Trolls. He felt that they were to a degree. He has always known about Trolls. There have been stories, both oral and written since the beginning of time. The Puncum knew about Trolls. However, Traugs and Norgs are relative newcomers to the scene. Silvas feels they have only been in the area of the St. Lawrence for the last fifty years. He had never seen any up close, only in the distance for a fleeting moment.

Silvas thought that both the Traugs as well as the Norgs could be teenagers or young adults in their early twenties who used Trolls as their role models, thus becoming more and more trollish in appearance and deed. However he did not feel that they would inevitably become full-fledged Trolls. There was the chance that when they matured and in the right environment, they could change for the better.

I am an ardent optimist but it is difficult for me to believe that these creatures which we saw before us could ever change into beings who could show care and concern for others.

The sky is bright with stars. I have learned much today. The Wood Knars will keep watch over the Alderwild Wood.

July 14

As I looked out the studio window this afternoon, there were two male Mallards perched on one of the old pilings where there was once a bridge to the island. They were basking in the sun and preening themselves. A third Mallard was swimming among the Cattails, and a male Red winged Blackbird chased, pecked, and dived at the Duck. Its nest was nearby.

July 15

The sun rose high in a sky of cloudless blue. The river was calm. No other boats were out and about. There was nothing to stir the water.

I decided to take my yellow canoe out. It is much lighter in weight than the larger aluminum canoe and easier for me to handle when I am alone. I paddled slowly around the Bay. I allowed the canoe to float freely while I knelt on the floor with my head over the side, viewing the life below.

There were schools of newly hatched minnows and other young fish, which were larger. There were young Yellow Perch and Small-Mouthed Bass. Nearer the mainland shore, amongst the Cattail stalk was a large nest of Bullhead young. The river bottom in this area of the Bay is sandy with a scattering of rocks. As I moved to where the water was only a foot deep, I could see more clearly the creatures who spend all or part of their lives on the bottom, among the

small rocks. There was a Johnny Darter resting on the sand. It is a small fish, only an inch and a quarter long. When I disturbed the water it darted off to another spot and rested only a few inches away. They are very quick and do not swim.

There were also Caddis Fly larvae crawling along the bottom in their protective cases made of bits of wood, pine needles, and very tiny shells as well as granules of sand. The larvae remain in these cases until they are ready to climb up on a rush and take flight as full-fledged adults. I reached down and moved a couple of small rocks. A Dragonfly larva crawled out from under one of these rocks and a Damselfly emerged from under another.

As I drifted close to shore where Purple Loosestrife grows, Juncus, Crispus, and Potamogelen were standing on a Pau, a raft constructed from Cattail stalks lashed together. The stalks are coated with oil rendered from boiling Bullheads or Eel. The oil will float to the surface to be used to waterproof the boat.

Juncus and Crispus were collecting snails, Cyclops, Daphnia, Clam Shrimp, and Fairy Shrimp with the smallest of the Puncum Tria Nets. Potamogelen was catching two inch sized Yellow Perch with the largest of the Tria Nets.

Along the hard packed sandy soil, surrounding the back section of the Island nearest the mainland, several Puncum women were drying the fish, which Potamogelen was catching. The women sang while they worked. I rested the canoe on a patch of raised sand and listened.

Puncum families live in a tight communal society. Their homes are situated about two feet up the Cattail stalks.

They are low enough to be protected from the wind and high enough to escape from being swamped by the waves.

Some of the homes look like modern day condominiums. Extended families live in these dwellings. Grandparents, parents, and married children with their children live in these elongated homes. Each of the three generations has their own set of rooms, which can be made private when desired by a reed mat, which may be rolled up or down. Each set of condominiums and single-family dwellings are connected to another by suspended reed walkways and bridges.

After all family members have returned home from fishing or other chores and have eaten supper the elders finish the evening with the telling of stories.

The stories are told of the Ancient Ones and ancient times when life began and from whence the Puncum came. The stories give their lives meaning, an explanation, and what purpose their lives serve. The elders speak of death and the Land Beyond the Horizon. Such stories give their lives continuity from one generation to the next. They make the unknown, the events of Na which the Puncum have no control over less fearsome. Each act of nature is given a meaning, a reason for its occurrence. Thus the lives of the Puncum may flow in harmony with Na.

<h1 style="text-align:center">July 18</h1>

For the last two days, the weather has been poor. The sun was out for a short while this morning. This afternoon, shortly after lunch, a strong unceasing wind began to blow. The river became angry and violent. The waves were topped with white caps, which sent sheets of spray over the water. The gulls and terns had great difficulty keeping on course. The sky turned dark and threatening. I could hear the heavy rumbling of thunder in the distance. It was not long before a great down pouring of rain arrived. I was glad Ian had turned the canoes over and tied them securely to the dock yesterday.

This evening both wind and rain have ceased. I do wonder how the Puncum have fared. We must check with them in the morning. I am sure that Natterjack and Bracken made their way through the marsh as soon as both wind and rain subsided.

The Alderwild Brook has no doubt overflowed its banks as it entered the Valley of the Horsetails and flooded the

fairly level ground of the valley and Fern Marsh. When the summer homes and docks of the Alderwild were destroyed during the flood last April, those needing repairs also had their pilings made stronger.

The Puncum have contingency plans for such emergencies. They usually move to their winter quarters in the rear of the Cattail stand bordering on Fern Marsh. I hope they had time enough to do this.

July 19

This morning we checked with the Puncum. All is well. No one has been injured. They did move to their winter quarters. Their homes sustained little damage. One bridge was blown loose at one end. A minor and relatively easy repair.

The inhabitants living along the Alderwild Brook and in the Alderwild Wood also fared well. A great relief!

The river was choppy most of the morning and early afternoon, calming down by 2:30 so Ian and I decided to attach the trolling motor to the canoe again and see how the landscape stood up to the storm. Tree branches and pieces torn from old docks floated past us.

As we approached the cliff where the apparition of Gnomes, Dwarves, Fairies, and all took place, I looked up. This place holds frightening memories for me. It was not that long ago that Gnomes, Dwarves, Sprites, Fairies, and animals were fleeing for their lives. Some ran, others hobbled and dragged themselves, and still others were carried along the narrow strip of woodland across the tops of the cliffs. Trolls, the Troloxica, Atrolpia, and the most deadly of Trolls, the Trolconitum, were pursuing them.

It is here not long afterwards where the Trolconitum and the other nasties, along with the Traugs and Norgs, came upon the apparition conjured up by the Suund and fell to their deaths. We saw all these twisted bodies of the Trolls turned to stone lying broken in heaps on the rocks below. The bleached bones and dried shrivelled skin of the Traugs and

Norgs lay draped over the rocks and the shore as well.

We soon arrived at the Site where once there was a thriving community of Gnomes, Dwarves, and Fairies living in harmony with Na. A building of great size was being erected. The hill of red granite and White Pines lay in rubble. Some of the remaining White Pines were black and without needles. There was no sign of life. We passed by the place quickly and turned the canoe around to head home.

July 21 - The Trolconitum

Who or what are the Trolconitum? I have had a number of conversations with Silvas concerning these creatures. The following description is taken from my notes during our conversations.

The Trolconitum are deceitful and malicious beings. They are more terrible and deadly than any of the other Trolls. They are bad-tempered, dirty, and foul smelling. They stand erect. Like the Troloxica and the Atrolpia, their hair is dark, usually black, long, and oily. It is never washed. Lice find their hair a nice place to dwell and multiply. Each female adult louse lays approximately three hundred eggs a month. They love their environment.

The Trolconitum exude a poison through their skin. This contaminates everything the Troll comes in contact with. Even the sputum of this particular race of Troll when spat out upon the ground will cause the plants in that spot to turn black and die. Gnomes, having come in contact with it unknowingly will become very sick. Smaller and less robust individuals such as Alderlings and Sprites have died from it. Thus the reason and the need for the Suund to come to that place and purify it.

Some Trolconitum live under trees. The tree or trees, which were living above that Troll, die and turn black for their roots have absorbed their poison.

Other Trolls of this race live in rock caves, which they have excavated by digging out and splitting rocks. They push these rocks and let them roll down hills, killing and maiming all living things in their paths.

These Trolls like the other Trolls are nocturnal. They wander the wooded hills and flatlands at night, ravaging trees and tearing out Poly Pody Ferns, Columbine, Hepatica, and the lovely and lush green pillows of moss, which have all taken up residence in the niches of rock outcroppings.

The Trolconitum snatch up mothers and their chicks from their birds' nests. The birds have just had their second brood. Sleeping squirrels and chipmunks are wrenched from their resting places. They become a nice snack. They also like fresh Alderling, Gnome, and Dwarf. Much meat is found on the last two. Fortunately, this does not happen very often. Gnomes and Dwarves keep a watchful eye for such dangers.

All Trolls, no matter which race they belong to, must return to their lairs before the twilight of Dawn. Otherwise, they will turn to stone, remaining where they were caught by the sunlight for all eternity.

Only the Trolconitum have the ability to take on the appearance in both shape and voice of humans. By some manner, they are capable of concealing their ugliness of body and mind in the presence of people they so desire to impress. They may be recognized by another Trolconitum, whether it may be in a similar guise or in its natural state.

How this change is possible Silvas does not know. The physical chemistry of the body must change. The Troll is a wolf in sheep's clothing. I find this amazing.

July 22

Walking up from the dock this morning we passed a large group of Mandrake plants. Their fruit has turned yellow. It is ready to be picked now, If the fruit was still green, it would be very poisonous. The ripe Mandrake apples are ready to eat as a dessert. Some women like to serve them with wild ginger syrup drizzled over the apples.

During the summer months, the large leaves provide the Alderlings and other Elves some shelter from the rain and gives shade from the hot sun. The Alderlings and friends hold summer time festivities under them.

A flock of eight Canada Geese swam into the cove early

this evening. They floated in the shallow water between the island and mainland feeding on the young water plants. They stayed just a short while. They will be back again.

As I sat on the dock, the evening twilight deepened around me and one by one the lanterns hanging at the bow of each Pua were lit. No Puncum were fishing, but were relaxing with their families, drifting, and singing softly. The air was warm but not hot, a whiff of it now and then gave the boats motion. I thought that I was dreaming. It was something ethereal.

July 23 - A New Friend, Bufo Americanus

Late this afternoon I met an elderly male American Toad. I could tell its gender by the width of the whitish irregular stripe running down the centre of its back. If the stripe on its back is wide, the toad is a female, if narrow it is a male.

The toad has no external ears, only two flat round discs, one on either side of its head just behind the eyes. They are called tympanic membranes. When I picked the toad up, it struggled until he was firmly in the palm of my hand.

Toads do not cause warts on the hand, even if they urinate from nervousness. They become quite tame within a short period of time.

This toad looks very much like the Suund but is smaller. He is also not capable of standing on two feet, nor is it able to speak. He is not anthropomorphic.

I put the toad down again and turned over a damp piece of bark lying on the ground. There were many Sow bugs huddled together, one was pregnant. Her white egg case was attached to her underside. All of the bugs began to run in all directions, having just been disturbed. With several quick flicks of the tongue, the toad ate them all.

Toads also like to eat earthworms. I found a few worms under some moist debris. One was very large, a night crawler, the other two were much smaller. I gave him the large one first. With each gulp he pulled his eyes down into

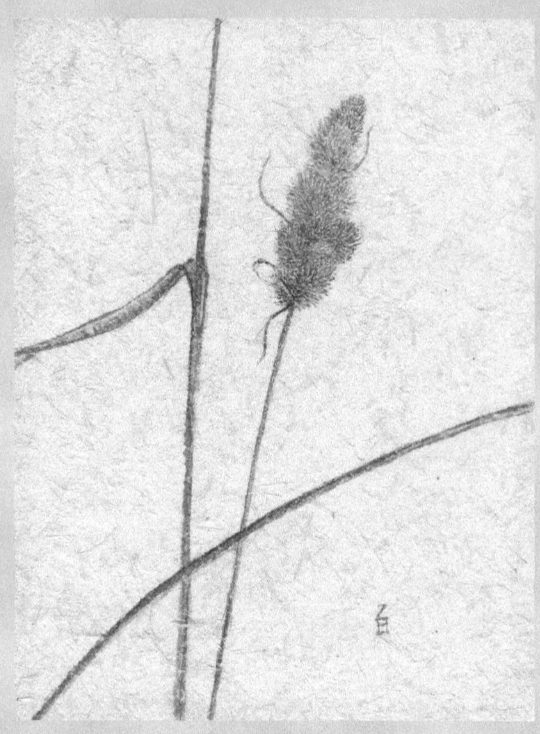

the roof of his mouth. This aids him in swallowing food.

I had one large male toad and one half his size when I was younger. I threw them a couple of worms. The smaller toad snatched the larger worm. It was really too big for it but he persisted in trying to swallow it. The worm was bigger and stronger than he was. The larger toad could not resist catching the other end of the worm. A tug of war ensued. During a momentary rest taken by the smaller toad, the larger one took advantage of the situation and gave a great pull and won the meal.

July 24,

The days are becoming quite hot and the shallow soil here on the island very dry. It is mainly composed of decayed pine needles.

The Spotted Knapweed is in front of the cottage and holds many blooms, even though some heads have already gone to seed. The tall grasses have turned to yellow ochre. The Bittersweet and Rose Hips are maturing.

In our small cove Water Sprites are ready and waiting to catch the black seeds of the Vetch. The vines creep along the water's edge, their tendrils clinging to rock and root. The seedpods are ripe and ready to burst. The Sprite gives the pod a tap and the two halves spiral like a corkscrew, and the seeds are expelled in all directions. The Sprites carry these to sunny areas on the mainland to plant where none now grow. The Cottontail Rabbit and the Muskrat, like to feed on it while it is still green.

A Ribbon Snake glided smoothly and silently over the leaves and between the slender shafts of grass growing along the upper ridge of the cove. Its head was erect; eyes glistened and tongue out sensing the air for some scent of insect, toadlet, or Sprite to dine on.

July 25

We woke early this morning and already the Alderling women, Alisma and Gramina among them, were in the midst of the Groundnut vines at water's edge along the mainland shore. The vine grows profusely near our dock, its tendrils stretching out and clutching every twig and blade of grass it encounters. I have often come across Green Frogs sitting underneath.

The flowers of this plant are pinkish brown. They look like the flowers of the Sweet Pea vine. As the ripening pods mature and dry, the Alderling and Puncum collect the seeds to be eaten raw or cooked.

The roots of the Groundnut have runners just below the surface of the ground. Attached to the runners are small tubers, roundish nuts growing a few inches apart. They too may be eaten raw or cooked like potatoes. Lich and Caddis were digging for these. They only take some, and not all from the same patch to insure the continued growth in these areas.

The Alderlings, Gnomes, and Dwarves also dry the tubers, ourselves. With a little salt and butter, they taste very good.

July 26

The inhabitants of the Bay are already preparing for winter.

In the month of June, the roots of a few of the Round Leafed Anemone were gathered up and given to the Suund. She hung them to dry. They were ready today to be ground into a powder. She will use it to treat diarrhea, gastric problems, and headaches. The Dwarves Berga and daughter Celestra helped Her prepare and store the powder into covered jars made by the Puncum.

The Dwarf Thapsus and the Gnome Tamias collected Bracken fronds to use presently to keep mosquitoes and other bothersome insects away. Each household receives a moderate sized bundle to cut up and burn in a small bowl, an incense burner. The smoke from the fronds is what keeps the insects at bay.

The bracken is also gathered in quantity to make soap. The children of both the Gnomes and Dwarves carefully cut each frond at its base and bring it to the clearing by the water. The ground there is hard and any fire set there will not travel underground. The fronds are set ablaze. The cooled ashes contain a large quantity of potash. Then the cooled ashes are put into a large bowl and water is added to be mixed with the ash. Balls of soap are formed. Some of the ashes are saved and stored. This same process was used for making soap for the refugees this past Spring. The balls of soap are small items but refugees are so glad to receive them.

The stems are also used as thatch for constructing the roofs of the Alderling summer homes and Gnome and Dwarf homes. When Natterjack and friends built our home,

it was used in some areas.
It is most noticeable on our
porch roof.

Natterjack told us that
the Bracken also makes a
very good mulch to protect our
plants in winter.

The Puncum have been
fishing in the Bay all
morning. The fish they catch
will be hung up to dry, along
with the minnows and perch
they caught yesterday. There
are already racks of minnows

and perch drying in the sun. All of the fish which are
drying now will be eaten during the Winter months when
fresh food is hard to come by.

Earlier in the summer the Puncum, along with the
Alderling and Gnomes, harvested the pollen of the Broad
Leafed Cattail heads. The Cattail head develops into two
sections. The top section is the staminate which provides the
pollen. The Staminate, as it matures, becomes very yellow
with the pollen. When it is at this stage, it is ready to be cut
and dried.

The Puncum and Alderling work together to stretch a
net, just a few inches below the brown heads, to catch the
pollen laden top section when it is cut off. It is a tricky
business for the Puncum and the Alderlings. The Redwing
Blackbirds nests are in the lower portion of the Cattail
stalks and leaves. Thus, they must be very careful for the
Redwing is very protective of its territory and dives at

anyone or anything it perceives to be a threat to its nest with young.

Two Gnomes sit in a flat bottom duck boat. One Gnome paddles and steers while the other Gnome catches each net filled with pollen and ties each end of the net so that none of the pollen spills out.

The Pollen heads are laid out on a board to dry for a week. Later, the young Dwarf children strip the pollen from the stems. Then three or four elderly Dwarf women sit and pick out any insect that may have been living in it. The pollen is then put into an oven and baked to sterilize it and kill any critters, which may have been missed. It must be bone dry for storage in the clay jars. Then when each family of the Alderwild Wood and the Bay wish to prepare pancakes, bread, or muffins, they will mix the dried pollen flour with regular flour, half of each kind for baking.

The bottom section , the Pistillate, matures and, at the end of the Summer, will be soft enough and ready for the female Water Sprite Mother and her two daughters to take up residency for the Winter.

July 29

The Yellow and Blue Flags have finished blooming and the seed heads are already forming .

The Aquatic Smartweed will soon flower. There are two kinds. One grows in the shallow calm water at the rear of the island. It has stems and leaves reaching some two feet above the water. It will bloom in late August. The second species has two opposing leaves, which float on the surface of the water and each has a small delicate pink flower. It grows by the mainland dock.

Earlier this morning before any speedboat had violated the serenity of the river and our Bay, the Water Sprites, Nymphs, and Puncum children were playing hide and seek among the Cattail stalks.

The Water Nymphs, so frail and delicate, were dancing on the skin of the water. It was like a dream. The water was so still and clear. It was as if Humankind on the river suddenly awakened to the fact there is more to life than noise and commotion, speedboats, and jet skis. What happened at that moment? Was the silence just an accident? Did some humans finally take notice? Did they see? Did they suddenly become aware of life around them, of Na?

July 30

Another hot day but the air is clear.

This morning Natterjack, Bracken, and Larix came to the island to help Ian build a compost heap. Many water weeds cut by motorboat propellers and pulled from their moorings on the river bottom by wind and wave have washed up on the rocks in our small cove. The four men with long wooden forks carried the weeds to the farthest

point of land on the island. They layered the grasses, adding to each layer rotting Carp, other dead fish, soybean meal, shredded newspaper, and soil. Ian will wet it every few days. As the water weeds and dead fish float into the cove and Bay, they will be added to the pile. Water weeds break down very quickly.

By summer's end, a rich pile of compost will be had. Ian and our friends will carry it up to the Alderwild Wood. This will make new fertile soil, which will be spread out over the community herb garden and turned under in readiness for next year's garden.

August 1 - A Committee Meeting

We attended an important meeting for all the inhabitants of the Alderwild Wood today. The gathering was held in the open Wood. It was a beautiful day, not too warm, a slight breeze, and not too many mosquitoes.

Over the last two and a half months, small groups of us have gotten together to discuss what we have done on our own, concerning the environmental problems facing us which were brought up at the April meeting.

It has been difficult to bring together a full meeting of the community before now. Having to deal with the construction site disaster, the burial of the dead, caring for the injured, and the relocation of all the survivors was a monumental undertaking. This was followed by the Traug, Norg, and Troll problem

And then in June more bad news had reached us. The problems never seem to cease, and more of the woodland to the west has been destroyed. The land of the Gnomes, Dwarves, Sprites, and fairies is disappearing by leaps and bounds. There is no end to it, more construction. More refugees. No stopping them, the Trolls.

High Pines Point is the only remaining bastion of land to our west untouched by Trolls. The Point is all that stands between the Bay and the Dark Point.

The Trolls are devouring the woodlands as they advance. Those bright lights of twinkling stars of hope have fled from our hearts. A great darkness of spirit has fallen upon us.

Is Horse Thief Bay entering its twilight?

For so many millions of years Na reigned supreme. She gave Er trees to grow and protect her wildlife, water to quench their thirst, plants, insects and small animals to satisfy their hunger, and sun to give them warmth.

The Water Nymphs and Sprites and the Wood Nymphs and Sprites, the Puncum and the Alderling came, the Gnomes and Dwarves followed and all lived in harmony with Na. Then came the humans, who were indigenous to the lands. They too understood the importance of caring and protecting Na. They had great respect for Her.

Even the early pioneers who felled many trees in the

area, clearing land to graze their cows and plant their gardens, even they did not wreak such havoc on the land as has occurred these last fifty years.

Upon hearing such woeful news, a young Gnome named Acura asked if there had been progress at all since the April meeting? Is all the news so bleak? Is there no room for optimism and hope?

Natterjack stood up and addressed Acura in a fatherly manner. He realized that our emotions were over-charged concerning the expansion of the two construction sites.

He told her that yes there was some positive news, but also there was still more negative issues to deal with. He suggested that we all listen to the news from each Committee:

The news from Committee # 1 The Land: Protection of Trees, Wildflowers, Wildlife.

Bursa, the leader of the committee, then reported on the work, he, his wife, Capsula, and daughter Nitella had accomplished.

Upon hearing from a Deer and a Red Fox who frequented our woods that the Woodland just Northeast of here was being measured and marked off with stakes, and orange plastic ribbons, preparations to sell lots for new homes, Bursa realized that action had to be taken immediately.

However, at the same time, the residents of the Alderwild Wood were very much occupied with the refugee crisis. The whole community, of sick, injured, and homeless inhabitants needed to be cared for and relocated. There were only a handful of Gnomes and Dwarves living in our woods who could help out, just not at that moment.

Captain Bursa and his family were on their own to

investigate the situation and take charge of any and all problems connected to it. It was a very big responsibility on Bursa's shoulders, but he felt sure that he could handle the job which lay before him. He would have the help of both Nuphar and Scirpus, two anthropomorphic deer, and the Red Fox, Philaenus, who could also speak.

At the end of April, Bursa, Capsula, with their daughter Phaedra left the Alderwild Wood on Scirpus back. Bursa and family were very nervous. They had never left the Alderwild Wood and their home in Horse Thief Bay before. The group crossed the main road without incident, no cars. Nuphar lead the way, taking them along an old path long forgotten by humans. He lead them across the Plain of Wal, then north through a narrow band of woodland to a dirt road. There are some houses on this road owned by humans. No trolls, as yet, lived in that area.

Nuphar and Scirpus walked along the road at a nice even pace, so as not to jar their passengers. It was not long before they reached the woodland in need of attention. They saw the long strips of orange plastic ribbons tied to the trees and posts. The tracts of a bulldozer were evident and a large boulder and some soil had been removed.

The two Deer knelt down so that Bursa and his family could slide off their backs to the ground. They were all concerned at seeing the tracks. Nuphar said that they were not there two days before. Bursa, Capsula, and Phaedra sat down. Bursa pulled a note book and pencil from his pocket.

Some of the inhabitants of this woodland began to gather around. Squirrels, rabbits, chipmunks, raccoons, Wood Sprites, Gnomes, and countless other Fairies or creatures of one kind or another advanced slowly. Even birds of different species sat on branches above, seeming to listen.

This was a situation of great importance that could not be put on the back burner so to speak. Action had to be taken now, immediately. Fortunately it was a Saturday. No one would be operating the bulldozer until Monday. They had two days in which to relocate all the inhabitants and wildflowers from that place, before anyone was injured or plants killed.

There was one thing in favour of the rescuers and those to be rescued. Since the woodland was still pretty much intact, no one had been injured yet. Some wildflowers had already been killed in that area, where the bulldozers had been, most of the inhabitants would be able to help in the relocation process.

The Gnomes could help pull the sledges carrying their household belongings, chairs, tables, beds, etc. Those Sprites who were winged, once they were shown the directions for getting to the AlderWild Woods, could fly there. Wingless Sprites could ride on the backs of the deer, even Philaenus the Red Fox. More deer could be rallied to the cause. Animals too could follow in short stages.

Even most of the wild flowers could be saved, taken and transplanted in the AlderWild Wood. Many of the plants are needed for medicinal properties. The Suund uses them to heal the ill and injured. Some are used for the birthing pains of pregnant mothers.

No less important is the beauty and good cheer they bring to those who behold them. They are food for the soul.

Bursa, as he looked at the woodland noted that there was no need to blast any rock face as there were very few rocks.

This being the case, there would be less trauma to the land and hopefully more trees would be left standing. Then, when the new homes had been constructed and all is finished, there may still be a few niches left wild or semi wild where birds and small animals could live.

Eight sledges were sent for. Nuphar carried a note from Bursa to NatterJack asking for more sledges and small baskets in which to place the plants. NatterJack could only spare five sledges, for many were still in use carrying construction site victims. Baskets, yes he had many. Tapsus would be returning with Spargan. Thapsus sat on Nuphar's back while the five sledges were dragged, tied one behind the other.

While Nuphar was gone, Bursa and the inhabitants of the wood split up into two teams. One group of Gnome women would label each piece of furniture with the owner's name. Several of the men carried each piece of furniture to the area of ground where the bulldozer had begun to clear.

By the end of the day, with the aide of a third deer by the name of Dryocopus, most of the wingless Sprites and small animals, plus furniture had arrived at the AlderWild Wood.

The Sprites and animals were exhausted. There were plenty of Mandrake, Wild Ginger and Sarsaparilla leaves in which they could sleep and rest before moving to the

Puncum Language
= 1   = 5   = 10   = 50   = 100
Green Darner
Wetland
Calm Water
Alderwild
Choppy Water
Willow
Rough Water
Frog Pond
a. b. c. a. f. g. h.
i. j. k.
l. m. n.
a. Palisdes
b. Hill
c. Coland
d. Cslands
e. White Pine
f. Hemlock
g. Oak
h. Maple
i. Pitch Pine
j. Birch
k. Basswood
l. Black Willow
m. Cronwood
n. Alder
= Yellow Perch
= Bullhead
= Green Sunfish
= Northern Pike
= Eel
Grassy Arrowhead
= Common Cattail

large wooded land just east of the Mac Mountains which our good neighbour Joy donated.

On the following day some of the winged Sprites flew to the old AlderWild Woods. However the journey was long and arduous for them. The Sprites who followed found that riding on the back of a rabbit, squirrel or crow, was faster and less tiresome. The animals were more then willing to assist in transporting them.

The very young and elderly Sprites, Fairies and animals were placed on the sledges carrying the remainder of the furniture, stored foods in clay jars, and wildflower plants.

The Gnomes, both men and women searched for those animals and fairies who had been too frightened to come forward and be counted with the inhabitants, preparing for their evacuation and resettlement. There were some who could not bear leaving their homes. They had lived in that woodland for their entire lives.

Those animals living underground such as the Star-Nosed Mole, the Common Mole, the Short and Long Tail shrews, the White Footed Mouse, the Chipmunk, and Toad, were awakened and encouraged to come up from their dens. Soon all of the inhabitants, Gnomes, fairies and animals of that community were accounted for.

The birds too were preparing to leave.

Perhaps some day when all the construction is over and some trees are left and the quietness returns to that place, perhaps then some of the birds and small animals will go back.

The Plants Saved

Blue Cohash	Red Baneberry
White Trillium	Jack-in-the-pulpit
Interrupted Fern	Smoothest Yellow Violet
Red Trillium	Maiden Hair Fern
Mandrake	Dog-Toothed Violet
Lady Fern	Virginia Waterleaf
Wild Ginger	Sensitive fern
Ostrich Fern	Blood Root
White Baneberry	Carrion Berry Vine

Trees

American Linden	Oak and Maple
Witch hazel	Basswood

The inhabitants of these woods have lived together side by side for generations upon generations, centuries upon centuries. They have been the caretakers, the guardians of the woods.

The following day the bulldozer laid waste that land in a matter of hours.

In concluding his report, Bursa told everyone at the meeting that all inhabitants of that community were successfully relocated to the Woodland East of the Mac Mountains, even the mother White footed mouse and her six babies. With Bursa's last remark the audience gave him a enthusiastic burst of applause.

NatterJack thanked Bursa for the report. He said, the relocation of the entire community without bodily injury to any of the refugees and no lasting psychological trauma to the elderly was a great accomplishment.

When all was quiet, Natterjack called on the Dwarf
Marmota, the spokesperson from Committee #3 Noise: The
Effect Noise is having on the Fairies, Gnomes, and Dwarves
of Horse Thief Bay, to give his report.

Marmota stood up and told the group that he had some
positive news to share with them. Humans working in
concert with Gnomes and Dwarves have managed to have
the owner of an air boat take his boat elsewhere. The noise
was ear shattering. It was even worse than some of the
speed boats. This shows what can be done when people work
together, take a stand, and make their voices heard to protect
Na.

There has been an increase in the number of large
speedboats over the last five years, and thus the noise has
become greater.

However, because there has been so many complaints
lodged against the owners of these boats by humans,
Gnomes, and dwarves living along the river, the level of
noise during the day and mid morning hours has been on
a decline. Too many people had been awakened from their
sleep. Even some Trolls have complained about the noise.
Perhaps the willingness of the boat owners to comply with
the outcry of the complainants was not out of respect for
them but for fear of them. It was done to placate them,
hoping that no one would press further for more regulations
for owners to obey. The speed limits for such boats to truly be
enforced in certain inhabited areas might be banned. People
wishing to travel at great speeds to take their machines to
the wide open waters of Lake Ontario or down river where it
is less dangerous to wildlife, and Gnomes, Puncum, Sprites,
Nymphs, Dwarves, Fairies, and humans.

For whatever the reason, the decrease in the level of noise during the morning hours has been helpful. The Puncun, Water Sprites and especially the Water Nymphs have suffered greatly due to the noise. Some of them have even died from it, placing them on the Endangered Species List. A reprieve. How long the reprieve will last is uncertain, that is up to the humans.

When Marmota finished his talk there was another great round of applause.

NatterJack thanked Marmota and added that it is an excellent beginning, but we must keep the issues of speed and noise control on the front burner. Keep a dogged watch. It is and will be an ongoing problem and we must fight.

We must also demand that boats using the river be built with quieter motors to cut down on the noise emitted.

Committee #4: The Refugees: Loss of Habitat, Search and Rescue. The Gnome, Lich was in charge of this committee and was next to be called upon to give his report. Lich stood up and hesitated, saying it is difficult to know where to begin.

"Our group has been overwhelmed by the number of refugees needing our help almost from day one, the day of our first meeting in April, when we formed the committees.

"We have been under constant pressure to find new woodlands. It is becoming more difficult to find large tracks of land to relocate whole communities, housing all of its inhabitants - the Gnomes, Dwarves, Sprites, Fairies and all the wildlife.

"Overcrowding of the woodlands here on the mainland area will soon be an issue to be reckoned with. Both woodland and open fields are being gobbled up for the construction of new homes. It is all happening faster than we are able to keep up with.

"Thus far we have done very well caring for and relocating all the refugees. Fortunately two friends, Joy and Don, living close by had woodland large enough for two whole communities."

"The refugee situation is not only the relocation of one group of woodland inhabitants from one place to another. Many of the refugees were seriously injured, having broken legs, arms, or broken ribs. Some had open wounds that became infected. Others had broken wings, some Sprites and Nymphs have had to have their wings replaced with wings made from toad skin. These individuals need long term care.

"There is also the sociological assault to the minds of these individuals. An indelible mark has been made on their memories. The Trolls have done their work well.

"The Suund, with the help of Berthas, Draka, Berga, Petra, and Osmunda, have looked after, cared for, and treated all of the inhabitants of the wood and water of Horse

Thief Bay. She and the women helping her have attended to all those refugees needing medical treatment. It is arduous work. The Suund and those helping her should not be expected to shoulder such an enormous job and responsibility alone. They need help and we humans must do it.

"In the medical community of the humans, doctors, when they are able, practice preventative medicine. The idea being to catch a possible problem and treat it before it becomes a serious problem.

"We must approach the refugee and relocation problem in the same manner. Thus far we have been reacting to these problems at the time the plundering of the land has just taken place, or is about to. So was the case with the second relocation operation.

"Bursa, with the help of Nuphar, got to the construction site the day after the bulldozer had moved a very large boulder and nothing more. Having responded to the problem so quickly all the inhabitants of that community were saved from possible injury or death. No family members were separated or lost. Panic had little time to set in. Everyone kept a cool head. They did not let fear take charge.

"What if we took some time out now to explore the lands to the North and North West of the Bay? Check them out. Take notes as to what species of plants, shrubs, and trees

may be found there? Who or what dwells in that land? Does it have a source of drinking water? Is there a marsh? Who or what is the land most suited for: Dwarves, Gnomes, Fairies, Sprites and animals? How many of each group can the land support comfortably? How large in size is the Woodland? Could it support and sustain a whole community? Is the land already inhabited, and if so, by whom or what? How many dwell there? Are they hostile or friendly? Are there Trolls, Norgs, or Traugs living there or nearby? If any refugees did settle there would it be a temporary matter, only lasting a couple of years before they would have to move again because Humans or Trolls are settling in there? Does the area look promising for long term settlements?

"There is also the land on Hill Island, just behind Batterman's Point. It is owned by the Province, thus no homes can be built there. The land is unspoiled. It does not have its original trees, for they had been cut down for lumber many years ago, but the new growth of trees has become old, judging by the largeness of the some of the wood. It is deciduous in nature with a sprinkling of White Pine.

"On Hill Island, just behind Batterman's Point is a Great Wetland covering a large area. There are also large areas of Woodland. All of this information was given to me by Zena and Ian. They have seen this place while visiting the beaver lodge in their canoe. However they have not walked in this woodland so do not know much about its inhabitants. They have only seen Deer and their tracks along the shore.

"This is a land which must be investigated. It will take two, possibly three groups, made up of Dwarves, Gnomes,

Alderling, Puncum, and Wood Sprites. We will also need the help of the crows, Selasphorus and Photolinus. Spargan the Great Blue Heron and other friends will most likely be called upon as well.

"Each team must include one person of each race. That way the representative of each race will know what to look for to sustain that group for long term settlement. Dwarves, you will be needed for your size to push through the thickets for those to follow.

"Gnomes, you work well with animals. You know their language if they speak or their body language if they do not. The animals may know where to find wild flowers which are edible. They may be able to show us where there is good land for homes and gardens.

"Juncus, we will probably need more than one Puncum for each group. There is a vast area of wetland and marsh to explore. Besides looking into the many types of sedges, rush, and of course cattails, you will need to study the wildlife in the water, fish, insects, and mollusks.

"And you Wood Sprites have a sharp eye, and are capable of seeing extraordinary distances from the top of trees.

"Hatch, the Alderling, have sharp eyes to see the slightest movement in the trees and leaves, in the tall grasses, and brush that others are not always able to observe."

Natterjack gave a little cough. He motioned to Lich and mentioned it was getting late in the day. No one had eaten anything since early morning. He asked if the remainder of the report could be concluded tomorrow morning. Everyone was in agreement. The meeting ended.

August 2

When we awoke this morning the air was sultry. Our environment is changing so fast this summer. There is a New owner of High Pines Point. Many trees have already been cut down over the last few days. However I do not think a bulldozer will be used. There is already a house and a guest cabin there.

I took my tape recorder to the meeting again today. It really helped me to transcribe all that was important from yesterday's meeting. It is a difficult job for me to write down notes fast enough of everything that is important. Because I do not hear well, I must read lips to know everything that is being said. Thus the recording machine picks up all that I have missed.

Today's meeting was shorter. It was decided that the reports from Committee #2 and #5 should be shelved for the moment. Our attention must focus on the Hill Island Park land.

We decided to have three groups leave early in the morning of August 5th just as dawn was awakening. All is quiet and still with the inhabitants of the river at that time.

Animals and Gnomes are just shaking the drowse from their eyes while others are preparing for sleep. It is a good time to learn the lay of the land.

August 3

We had a near tragedy in the woods this morning, A Gnome child ate a berry from a Baneberry plant. The berries are bright red now and are very attractive. All parts of the plant, root , leaves and berries are very poisonous.

This child has only recently come to the Alderwild Wood. He and his family were one of the hundreds of refugees that were displaced by the Trolls who laid waste the land West of here, at Construction Site# 1. Everyone has been so busy trying to find places for the victims of the flood of new immigrants that no one has warned the family or child about how poisonous the white and red Baneberries are. I think that everyone assumed that the Baneberry plant is common in all woods, and the family would be knowledgeable about the poison the beautiful berries carry. The

berries of the White Baneberries have not yet changed to white. They will not change until later this month, lasting through October to the time of the frost.

The child became nauseous and was vomiting, dizziness overcame him, and in a matter of minutes, he became delirious. His pulse had quickened. The Suund came quickly and inserted a fresh Horsetail Stem through his mouth and into his stomach.

The Horsetail is hallow and worked as a tube in which the Suund poured a liquid that caused more vomiting. She then removed the tube and gave him warm milk to drink to coat the lining of his stomach, hopefully to prevent any further damage.

The Suund stayed with the boy all day. She is still there and it is 7:00 P.M.

NatterJack just stopped by a few minutes ago. He gave us the latest news on the boy's condition. The child is slow to recover, but the Suund feels that the child will pull through it. She will stay the night with him.

August 4

Good news this morning. The child's health is improving. Draka and Petra are staying with the boy while the Suund sleeps.

August 5

When we awoke this morning the stars had not yet shed their glow from the dawns early light. The birds had not awakened and the silence of the night had not broken.

We ate quickly. Ian packed my camera, tape recorder, note pad and pencil. He took a can of insect repellent in case the horseflies were bad. By the time we finished eating, with dawn's light, we made our way to the canoes. We paddled across to the main land dock.

Spargan and two other Great Blue Herons, the two crows
Phatlimus and Selasphorus, were already standing near
the dock.

A large group of inhabitants from the Alderwild Woods
were just making their way down the hill with NatterJack
in the lead. From the stand of cattails to the west came
eight Puncum carrying several sizes of Tria Nets. They
were followed by an entourage of Puncum and Alderling
carrying two Catmarns and two Pau on their shoulders.
A moment later a half dozen Wood Sprites, having put on
special wings for the occasion, flew into the trees above us.

The Three Groups

D Dwarves, G Gnomes, A Alderling,
P Puncum, and S Sprites,

NatterJack- D	Larix- G	Fern- A
Lich- G	Hatch- A	Tamia- A
Pode- A	Papilo- A	Mustela- P
Danus- A	Crispus- P	Nesta- S
Juncus- P	Tipula- P	Hyalo- S
Plantago- P	Chrysopa- S	Plathemis- S
Laxaulus- S	Azulla- D	Actias- Heron
Bracken- D	Salus- G	

There were three other canoes at the dock beside our two.
The Puncum boats were lifted onto our yellow canoe. Their
boats are like children's toys to us.

Each of the three groups loaded their Tria Nets, to be used
to catch small fish, minnows, and Yellow Perch, etc. Pads
of paper were brought to write down any notes concerning
the types of fish which inhabit the water. Smaller nets
were brought along as well, to check for different species

of snails, larvae, and any other creature, which might be living on the surface of the mud.

Plastic containers were also taken. They would be used for holding samples of water plants and algae. Among the plants and algae, there live Cyclops, Daphnia, Clam Shrimp, Horny Pea Cockles, Rotifers, and Fairy Shrimp as well. The health and condition of the water can be determined by the number and type of creatures living among them.

Notebooks, pens, camera, sun hats, life vests, insect repellent and drinking water and picnic baskets were all placed in each canoe. Small first aide kits were taken as well.

canoe #1	canoe #2	canoe #3
Natterjack	Bracken	Azulla
Lich	Larix	Salus
Pode	Hatch	Fern

Each canoe was fitted out with a trolling motor.

The Alderlings Danus, Papilo, and Tamia climbed onto the backs of Spargen and the other two Blue Herons. The Puncum, Juncus, Plantago, Crispus, Tipula, Mustela, and Philaenus, came with us.

Three other Wood Sprites, Laxaulus, Chrysopa, and Nesta, also joined us. Plathemis and Hyalo hoisted themselves onto the backs of the crows

Phatlimus and Selasphorus. It would be too tiring for the Sprites to fly to the Island on their own.

Nuphar was not coming with us. There was no way for him to get there. However he did speak to Lich, Larix, and Salus and showed them the signs and spoken words to use so that we all could communicate to any Deer we met up with. With these passwords and signs the Deer will know that we explorers are friends. Also that the animals have come to their land not to hurt them but to live with them and Na in harmony. Knowing this, the Deer will help them in any way possible. They would most likely carry any member of the groups on their backs.

It was 7:00 am before we all set out. The two Herons, and the two crows took the lead. They knew the way. We followed and caught up with them a little later.

The river was calm and its surface as smooth as glass.
There were no boats, or jet skis in sight. We crossed the main
channel and reached Batterman's Point in no time. Just past
the Point the water weeds, Hornwort, and Tape Grass had
reached the surface of the water. The weeds on the surface were
very dense, making it difficult for the canoes to get through.

Duck Weed and Blanket Weed, Water Lily's and
Frogbit, were all biding for a place on the water's surface.
There was a very narrow channel which skirted the weeds
and allowed us to continue on for a short while more with
our motors. Soon the channel widened again into a vast
area of Cattails extending some fifty feet or more out
from the shore. In front of the Cattails was a sea of rushes
and sedges, Compact Rush, Hard Rush, Flowering Rush,

Common Sedge and False
Fox Sedge. Juncus and the
other Puncum could hardly
believe their eyes. They were
in awe of the vastness of
this wetland. They wished
to explore the area right then
and there.

I turned the motor off so
that they might debark and
launch their own boats. Ian
pulled the second canoe that
we had been towing along
side ours and lifted the
Catmarn and Pua out and
placed them onto the water.
He handed the Tria Nets and

plastic containers to Juncus and Crispus. They all climbed onto the boats and took their places. The sails were hoisted and with a breeze behind them they were off. It looked magical, a place of enchantment.

I decided to pull the motor out of the water. We paddled the rest of the way. Just before the channel narrowed again, large clumps of Yellow Flags rose up in the calm water in front of the Cattails. They had mostly finished blooming.

The water was becoming more shallow and muddy and the channel narrower. Very large Carp began to bang against our boat. We pressed through the Cattails as far as we could. By now the Cattails and Sedges surrounded us. We were closed in, and were still twenty to twenty-five feet from shore.

Natterjack and his crew left our group of boats earlier. Upon seeing another passage through the Cattails on his right, he decided to take it. Just a short distance ahead of him was a woodland. It was less dense than the woods we were about to explore.

Bracken and his group took a channel to the left where the high rock face of red granite lay before them. It was well treed.

Azulla followed us. He and Salus would help Ian to forge a path through the Cattails and underbrush once on land.

Actias was standing on a branch high in a White Pine tree near the waters edge. He had a keen eye and saw all 4 groups making their way to the different areas of woodland. He saw both Azulla and us stranded in the Cattails. He flew down to us and stood in the water by Azulla's canoe to hold it steady while Laxaulus, Chrysopa, and Nesta climbed onto Ian's back. He carried them to an open area near the shore.

Then Azulla, Salus, and a somewhat wet and muddy Ian, bent cattails and laid them flat on the mud for a path

they were constructing. This would keep us from sinking into the mud when going back and forth to the canoes, and also for possible use in the future. The area looked to be inhabited.

Walking is very difficult for me especially through tall grasses and over roots and fallen branches. Thus I did not venture inland with them. I stayed on the shore, and sat on a low stool I had remembered to bring along. I focused my attention sketching the surrounding environment and some of its creatures including a couple of Gnome children playing near the water. They were not afraid of me. By the end of the day I had finished a great many drawings and studies of some of the wild life.

Since I was not able to explore the woodland on my own and see first hand the lay of the land and its creatures, I

gave to each member of the four groups a list of questions
for them to take notes on.

By mid-afternoon, all the members of Azulla's and
Salus's groups and Laxaulus, Chrysopa, and Nesta
returned tired but very pleased. They had a good day of
gathering information. Tomorrow we will study the notes of
each group that I shall type up later. All were anxious to tell
me about their findings.

I glanced at the notes as they were handed to me. It
looked as though they had gained a wealth of information,
as well as having some adventures. It was time to find
the others and open the picnic
baskets.

We met up with the other 2
groups when we reached the open
area of water and when we saw the
Puncum we were surprised and
amazed. Juncus, Crispus and the
others were just lolling about on
their boats. Some were dozing
while others were swimming and
fishing in relaxation in the full
sun of the day.

It is rare to see Puncum
on their Catmarns and Puas
enjoying themselves during the
brightest hours of the day in
Horse Thief Bay. Such pleasures
only occur in the Spring and
early September. During the
summer when the air and river

water are at the warmest the Puncum have only the early hours to fish, collect snails and insect larvae. It is also the only time for them to bath.

By 10 a.m. each day, the waves from many of the big boats owned by humans make their way to the back of the Bay churning up the silt and mud from the bottom. Early morning and evening are the only time the Puncum have to enjoy the river without threat to their health and lives.

Within minutes all the Puncum had their nets, notes, and containers of water weeds, algae, and creatures collected from the surface of the mud, packed. Ian helped them into our canoe. Their boats were lifted into the canoe we were towing.

I spoke to Natterjack and since everyone was so excited about their findings, we decided to listen to each group while we floated gently in the open water entrance to this magical Wetland and Woodland.

I had given each member of the four groups a list of questions for them to take notes on. The list is as follows:

Questions asked of the members from each of the Groups.

1. I. Trees
   a) Species
   b) Approximate size of area each species covers, large medium or small.
   c) The girth, circumference of some of the largest Trees.
   d) Approximate age of the Trees
   e) The health of the Trees
   f) Are there any Trees growing from the ancient forest of long ago?
   g) Has there been any logging over the last 50 yrs or very recently?

2. Animals
   a) Species
   b) Approximate Size and number of each species
3. Population
   a) Are there any Dwarves and or Gnomes inhabiting
       the area?
   b) If Dwarves and Gnomes do inhabit the land would
       they be likely to be friend or foe?
   c) If there are Dwarves and Gnomes, are they as
       advanced as the Dwarves and Gnomes of the
       Alderwild Wood?
   d) Are their lives simpler?
   e) Are they able to live closer to Na?
   f) Are their lives less stressful and unencumbered
       by the trials and tribulations suffered by the
       inhabitants of the Bay and Alderwild Wood, at the
       hands of the Trolls, Norgs, and Traugs?
4. Dwarves and Gnomes
   a) If Dwarves and Gnomes do live on Hill Island do
       they have the same concerns and fears as those
       living in Horse Thief Bay?
   b) Are the Dwarves and Gnomes of the parkland
       different in anyway physically, language, habits,
       clothing, or culture/
   c) Is there a noise Problem? If so what is the cause?
   d) Are they aware of the fact that there are Dwarves
       and Gnomes living on the mainland?
   e) Do they know there are big environmental problems
       on the mainland not far from them?
   f) Is there enough area of woodland and wetland to
       sustain a whole community of displaced persons

and wildlife? Would the present inhabitants
of that woodland and wetland accept a new
community to settle in their land?
5. Food
   a) Are there many wild edible plants?
   b) Are there many plants that may be used
      medicinally?
   c) Are there large numbers of such plants or only a few?
6. Fish
   a) Number of species?
   b) Are there many fish or only a few?
   c) Do the fish carry PCBs or Mercury in their flesh?
   d) Do they seem in good health? Some time ago many
      of the Yellow Perch in our Bay had a white slime
      cluster attached to their bodies and they died.

General Findings from Beyond Batterson's Point.

Everyone was eager to talk about what they had seen. Natterjack asked that Groups 1, 2, and 3 headed by Ian (non-dwarf), Salus, and Azulla begin.

Before reaching land our three groups passed a large marsh, sedges and herbs on both sides of our canoes. To our right lay acres of Upland Shrubs.

Upon disembarking Azulla and the Wood Sprite Nesta turned left in an easterly direction. They found a great wood of White Pine and Hemlock. It was dense with few wild flower plants, a few shrubs and many large trees in good health. A few deer were seen passing for there was little vegetation for them to feed on, but the denseness of the trees provided them a protected habitat. A quick assessment - no trees had been cut for a very long time.

Only a few animals, other than the deer were seen. Perhaps they were well hidden.

There were both Dwarves and Gnomes inhabiting the woodland, but no sign of Wood Sprites.

The Dwarves and Gnomes were physically different than those of the Alderwild Wood. The skin tones of both Dwarves and Gnomes were darker. The hair color of both was darker. The Dwarves' hair was dark brown, the Gnomes a lighter brown. The way each wore their hairstyle was quite different. It was longer and both braided their hair using different patterns.

Both groups were dressed in animal skins.

The physical build of both Dwarves and Gnomes were more muscular and they were shorter. The eyes of the Dwarves were brown and the eyes of the Gnomes were hazel.

The inhabitants of the park woodland seemed as though they would be friends, or at least friendly. Their lives are more simple and rugged. They have a great respect for Na. They are not necessarily closer to Na than those of the Alderwild Wood, but they seem to commune with Na in a different manner. Much more information is needed to give a better account of these people.

The language of both Dwarves and Gnomes is Germanic, but spoken with a different dialect.

Ian and the Wood Sprite, Laxaulus entered the northern most area of the White Pine and Hemlock woods that Azulla and the Sprite, Nesta, were investigating. However, when Ian and Laxaulus came upon a small stand of Oak, a different species than those growing in or near the Alderwild Wood, they turned Westward. Soon a large area of Pitch Pine presented itself. Neither Ian nor Laxaulus had ever seen so many Pitch Pines in one place. They are lightly scattered in Horse Thief Bay and its immediate surroundings. This species of Pine is uncommon this far north. They do not propagate very easily and seem to hang onto life by the thinnest of threads. The Sprite Laxaulus first flew to the upper branches of these trees, then to a lower branch and onto the ground. He made notes on all aspects of each tree. Having the ability to fly made the job much easier.

Some of the trees are old and past their prime but still hanging onto life. A small number are old with dead branches and on those branches, which still have life, the needles are thinning. They will die in a year or two. There is a good stand of moderately old trees in good health and with new growth. There are some younger trees but very few.

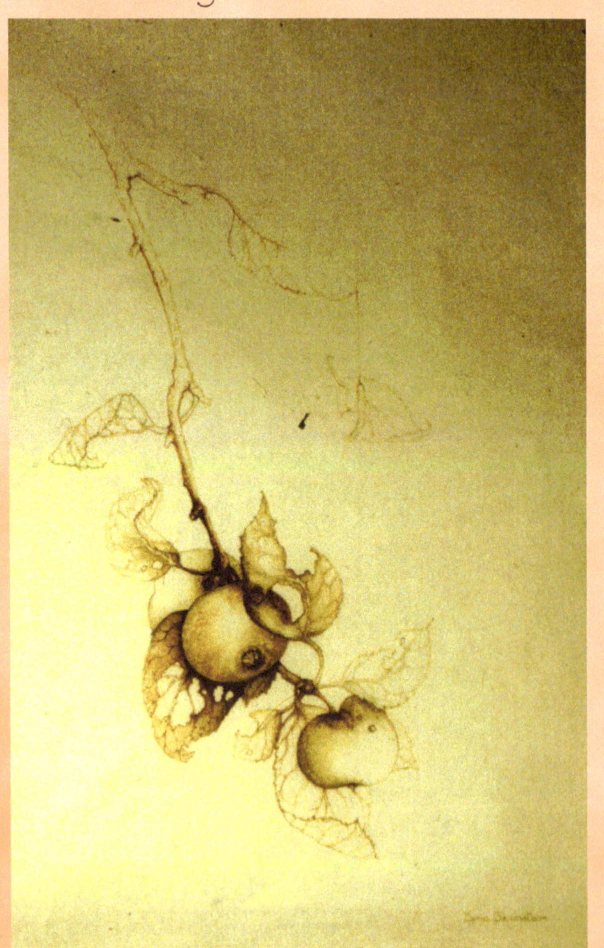

There are no seedlings. The lack of new seedlings is due to the environment, not the result of construction.

Laxaulus explored the trees and surrounding area, keeping in mind the feasibility of these woods for habitation by the Sprites, Nymphs, Leaflings, and other Fairies. He saw that the upper tree branches served as resting places for small birds, crows, and especially the Great Blue Heron. The Herons are always looking for a

tall tree, which would afford
them a good view of the river
and the islands from the
deep places within the woods.
As Laxaulus flew from
tree to tree, inspecting all
thoroughly, he soon realized
that the only life forms using
the upper branches were birds.
He had not seen any Sprites,
Nymphs, or Leaflings thus far.

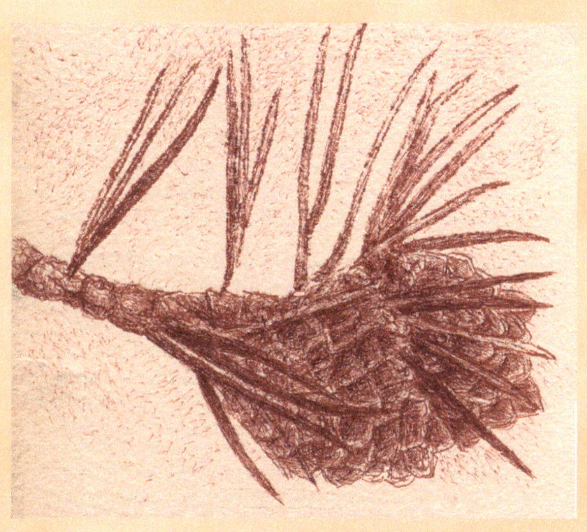

   He could understand the reason for the lack of
Leaflings for there were no trees bearing leaves. This area
of the park was mainly coniferous woodland, meaning the
majority of the trees were evergreens.

   He then searched the lower branches of these trees.
However, Pitch Pine do not begin to branch out until some
distance up from the ground.

   Laxaulus felt some disappointment at not finding
suitable habitation in these trees. He flew to the ground
where he found British Soldier Lichen, Trumpet Lichen, and
Parmelia growing in the areas with the greatest sunlight.

   There was an area of granite with a thin layer of soil
here and there on the rock. At the base of some of the more
sheltered tree trunks there were raised hillocks covered with
these lichen. These mounds had small openings where doors
are usually placed. The mounds were not all the same size,
some were larger.

   Laxaulus sat down on the ground and rested. As his
eyes adjusted to the light and texture of this woodland, he
saw Fairies. They were of small stature, even smaller than

himself. They were of the same build as the Alderlings but they had fairer skin and light coloured hair. They had no wings. They blended with the lichen and grey rock. The hillocks of lichen were their homes. As Laxaulus focused on the larger area of lichen and moss, more of these beings could be seen. He saw some of these Fairies entering and exiting their homes.

After a while, he grew tired and lay down. An hour or so later, Ian found him asleep while he was looking over the plant life in that area. He was also hoping to find signs of animal life. He did find - Early Saxifrages, Queen Anne's Lace, St. John's Wart, a Garter Snake and a Black Rat Snake. Ian too was disappointed.

A Near Catastrophe

Ian rarely looks down at his feet when walking. Therefore he often has no knowledge of where he is stepping and what or whom he may be stepping on.

As Ian woke Laxaulus, a large group of Fairies, most of them of the same Rigida species that Laxaulus had seen earlier, were gathered around them. They were shouting and

kicking at Ian's ankles. He could not hear or feel them. He had long pants on. Some of these Fairies climbed up his pants leg and began to pull the hair on his legs. These Fairies were very upset and angry.

Ian was about

to overreact to the situation, which would have made the problem even more disastrous. Fortunately, Laxaulus awoke in time to stop Ian from injuring any of them. Some had climbed up to his shoulders and were pulling his hair. He started to swat them, thinking them to be insects, not realizing they were Fairies. Laxaulus heard the Rigid and tried to calm them down.

Their language was unfamiliar to him but he was able to grasp the meaning of their excitement and anger. They led him to an area of the ground where Ian had walked. Not realizing it, Ian had flattened five of their homes. Fortunately no one was inside them at the time. Ian felt remorseful but muttered "Why did they have to build their homes so small and on the ground, where animals or people walk?" He sat down and made his apologies.

Ian and Laxaulus returned to the canoe. They were both very tired.

The Gnome Salus, the Alderling Fern, and the Puncums Tipula and Mustela headed in a westerly direction in their canoe, paddling slowly and quietly through the sedges and rushes. The edge of the island was approximately four hundred feet away.

Trees were seen in the distance. Black Willow were scattered lightly along the shoreline mixed with large areas of shrubs. On the most distant horizon White Pine and Hemlock could be seen. However that was an area for Salus and his group to check out.

Were there any Gnomes, Alderlings, or Puncum inhabiting this wetland? Yes, all three groups were living here. There were Water Sprites and Water Nymphs living in this sea of sedges and Cattails. They were very similar to all three groups living in the Bay, yet different.

The wings of these Sprites were more free form in shape and more colourful. They had no fear. They did not need to have wings of a certain color or shape to camouflage themselves.

Their spirits were free and unburdened. They knew nothing of the world beyond their wetland. There were no Trolls or humans to cause them to be fearful. They had never seen or heard of them.

They did not flee upon seeing Salus, Fern, Tipula, and Mustela. They were very curious. They flew to the canoe, not away from it. The Water Nymphs responded in the same manner.

The Water Nymphs in those rushes and sedges were extremely beautiful, even more than the Water Nymphs living in Horse Thief Bay, so they thought. But why? They soon realized the beauty was written in their faces. These Fairies expressed delight and happiness and were free of concern.

They let their hearts ring out in song.

The Water Sprites there were also very happy and free of worry and fear. They loved music. The song of both races of Fairies was their spoken language. They spoke no other tongue.

The Sprites sat on the pads of the White Scented Water Lily. The Nymphs seemed to prefer the pads of the Yellow Water Lilies. They all enjoyed swimming and weaving gracefully in and out among the lilies and sedges. The water was warmed by the sun. It was clear and there were Carp swimming lazily

with Water Sprites riding on their backs. There were no Great
Northern Pike or Black Bass to eat the Fairies. The small fish,
Yellow Perch, Sunfish, and minnows knew the Fairies well.
They let them be. There was plenty of other food for them to
eat.

They were all living in a noise-free environment away
from any boats. This wetland was vast. They could live their
lives freely in this open space from early morning until
dark under the light of the moon and stars. There were no
Trolls living in this land.

As the foursome paddled deep into the reeds, the more
closely the plants grew, crowding one another for space.
Many more species of reeds and other plants appeared. It was
soon becoming an area where Puncum dwelled or could live
if none were living there already.

Tipula and Mustela rejoiced in the wealth of plant life.
They identified:

Great Pond Sedge	Compact Rush
Common Sedge	False Fox Sedge
Spatterdock	Water Plantain
Flowering Rush	Yellow Pond Water Lily
Hard Rush	White Scented Water Lily

Situated in front of the Cattails nearest the open water
were clumps of:

Yellow Flags	Water Fern
Arrowheads	Sweet Flag
Great Burr Reeds	Duck Potato
Marsh Milkweed	

Plants Growing Under Water

Tape Grass   Slender Smart Weed

Water Starwort   Rigid Hornwort

There were also a great variety of water plants, which have edible seeds, tubers, or roots, and some can be eaten raw or cooked.

There are a vast number of edible plants to sustain an entire community, not just Puncum but Dwarves, Gnomes, Alderlings, Sprites, Nymphs, and any other Fairy that may already be living in the park Woodland, Wetland and open water.

Conservation and good management already set into law, has been rigidly adhered to and practiced over many hundreds of years. The reason why this wetland and woods is so wonderful and in such good health is the direct result of good management by the Gnomes, Dwarves, and all Elven life living there.

For this woodland and marsh to continue and flourish, good conservation practices must be maintained. Any new folks wishing to settle here in this wetland must follow these same laws. These rules must be applied to the number of fish caught and snails collected. The cutting down of any trees must be limited. It would be wise to use already fallen limbs and branches for the building of any new homes and shelters.

Conserve, Conserve, Conserve. Hopefully every one will be willing to follow these rules so no one will have to be forced to do so. Everyone will be the better for it.

The animals already living in this wetland and the woodland around it are Muskrat, Painted Turtle, Bullfrog, Deer, Chipmunk, Squirrel, Raccoon and numerous other animals.

The Puncum of the Reed Mace

Tipula and Mustela told of the Puncum already inhabiting this wetland. Their homes are scattered throughout this vast expanse of Cattails and sedges.

Their dwellings are at different levels and sizes. The houses are built using Cattail stalks and fronds. They are similar to those built in Horse Thief Bay. The floors, sides and roofs are double thickness for these homes are used all year round.

At the end of the summer the Puncum do not have to move. They are able to stay in their own homes but move to the rear of them which is deeper into the sand bank and is warmer. There are no waves or rough water to disturb their dwellings.

The Puncum of this wetland are physically different. They are taller and more muscular. Their faces are bronzed by the sun, their skin roughened by the air, which causes them to look more advanced in years. They live long beyond the span of humans. Their toes are long and broadened at the ends, helpful

when climbing Cattail stalks. Their hair is black, straight, and tied in a knot. Their eyes are dark brown.

The Puncum men wear loincloths, the women wear skirts. They weren't sure about the clothing worn in the winter, or whether they hibernate or not.

No clay is found in this area of the park, thus the Puncum trade for it with the tribe of Puncum on the western side of the island where there is clay. The area known as Eleanor's Ditch.

Dwarves and Gnomes inhabiting the White Pine and Hemlock woodland lying between the two tribes act as intermediaries. In return the Dwarves and Gnomes receive many types of woven baskets made by these Puncum.

The Puncum on the western side also receive the baskets for the clay they gather to trade with the Puncum of this wetland. Clay beads, pendants, bowls, pitchers, storage jars, and mugs are made by both Puncum tribes.

The language of these two Puncum tribes is different from that spoken by the Puncum of the Bay.

However this didn't hinder the communication today with Tipula and Mustela.

The Puncum have a written language, which they all share. It is that of pictographs on clay tablets and also on paper which all the Puncum make.

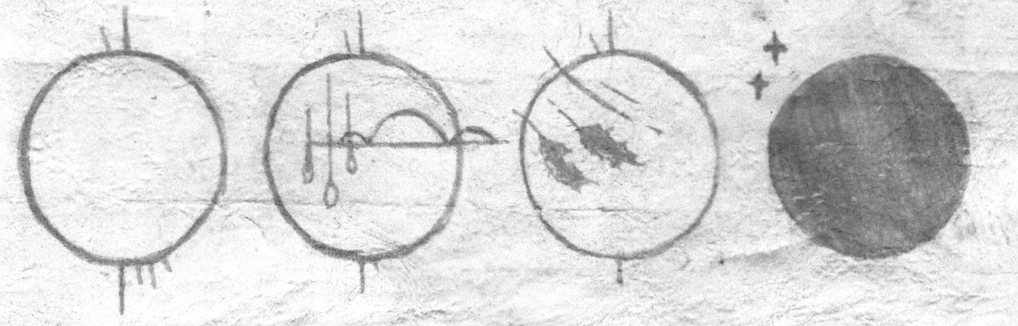

In the future these Puncum will be referred to as the Puncum of the Reed Mace. Like the Puncum of Horse Thief Bay, the Puncum of the Reed Mace and those of Eleanor's Ditch hold the wisdom of Na close to their hearts. They live simple lives. They too have disciplined their minds in the tradition of their forefathers to conserve and protect the land and its bounty. Further information on the Puncum of the Reed Mace will have to wait for another day.

When Salus and Fern reached the shore, there was a cleared area of sand beach, dotted with a few rocks. There were also several little docks with Gnome-type boats tied to them. Salus was overjoyed.

There was no room at any of the docks for him to tie up, so he pulled the canoe up on the sandy shore.

There were Gnome dwellings just ahead tucked in among the shrubs. An old Gnome was sitting in front of his cottage, smoking his pipe. He did not change position or expression at the sight of Salus and Fern. He followed them with his eyes.

A young male Gnome who was cleaning a few Yellow Perch a short distance away motioned to them to come to him. A young female, perhaps his daughter sat near him weaving a basket. Other finished baskets were on the ground beside her.

Salus walked quickly up to them, almost running. He was filled with excitement. The Gnome looked bewildered but not fearful. From where did Salus and Fern come? They seemed to appear out of nowhere. It was quite obvious to see that Salus was a foreigner and not a member of his tribe.

Salus was shorter with lighter coloured hair and had a paunch. Gnomes of the Reed Mace do not have paunches.

They are darker skinned and have brown hair, which is braided. The Gnome's eyes were dark brown. He had a short cropped beard but no moustache and he was quite muscular.

Upon reaching the young Gnome, Salus gave him a customary bear hug, which all Gnomes of the Bay give each other when meeting instead of simply shaking hands. It was quite obvious that it was not the custom here. However, the Gnome did not recoil from that embrace but did have a quizzical smile on his face.

Salus spoke to the Gnome and realized that the Gnome did not have the slightest idea what he was saying, nor did Salus understand the Gnome. By using hand and body language, plus pictographs like those used by the Puncum, they were able to communicate with each other. Salus was able to learn from where the Gnome's ancestors came from long ago. They came from Spain in the second migration of Gnomes from northern and western Europe.

Fern and Salus did not walk about exploring the area but were drawn up in a meeting of minds with the young Gnome. Each plied the other with many questions. Salus learned that the Gnome's name was Rhus.

Salus also felt that the language Rhus spoke now was Spanish in origin. However, over the centuries, the Gnomes of the Reed Mace, not having lived in Spain and not having any contact with any Spanish speaking people, have developed a new language, but retaining the flavour and bouquet of the original language.

Fern and Salus did not obtain any statistics as to Gnome, Dwarf, Puncum, or Sprite populations. Nor did they learn of the species of the number of animals or any information pertaining to the flora and fauna of the area.

However, they did come away with some knowledge and insight into the character of these people through Rhus.

Rhus spoke of the simple grace and curve of the Hard Rush. The delicacy of the Blue Damsel Fly. The beauty of the Flowering Rush. The ripple on the water and of the Water Striders as they glide upon its surface. He noted the different attitudes of the weather and its effect upon the reeds and water. The circles which increased in number as they spread out across the water with each drop of rain.

He spoke of the wavelets which hit against the sedges, reeds, and cattails which all curve deeply with the wind. The Sprites and Puncum take shelter deep within the cattails.

The Gnomes hunker down in their homes and batten down their window shutters. The wind rushing through the cattails, makes strange whistling sounds. Lightning splinters across the sky and the roar of thunder can be heard.

Rhus is so much a part of Na. He feels that he is of equal standing with the deer and other animals. He feels that he is no more important or better in the realm of Na. It is up to him and the other inhabitants and humans to keep Na in its natural state.

He pointed to the Great Blue Heron standing high in a dead White Pine. A King Fisher flew by chattering. He spoke of the Red-Winged Black Birds calling and proclaiming their arrival to the marsh in early Spring and the song of the Whip-Poor-Will in the late evening.

Rhus is a story teller. Each story he told gave meaning and purpose to all of the elements belonging to the world of Na. It makes those things in Nature which are frightening less so and gives to all elements of Na a greater appreciation and respect.

The excited conversation returned to Natterjack. It was obvious that not all of today's findings and adventures could be told while we floated here. It was very late in the afternoon and time to return to those waiting for us in Horse Thief Bay.

Answers to all of our questions at this time can only be general in nature. Many more visits to Hill Island will have to be made and the specific areas which we have just visited will need further exploration. A true picture and assessment of the inhabitants, flora, and fauna cannot be made without them.

I suggested to the groups that an aerial map of the area might be of real help and I would attempt to get one quickly.

We turned our canoes and headed for home.

Our Return to the Bay

There was much excitement and joy upon our arrival. Everyone wished to talk to everyone else about everything wonderful that had been seen. Everyone was speaking at the same time. Even the Water Sprites and Water Nymphs were there, gathered around the boats as we paddled in.

The boats were all pulled up on shore and turned over.

Everyone was ready for a hot bath or shower, but it was not to be just yet.

A bell was heard and a feast was laid before us. There was food of every kind, for every race, for the Dwarves, Gnomes, the Alderling and Puncum, Water Sprites and Nymphs. The food was carried down to the river bank where a large group was already gathered.

A green table cloth was spread out and clay bowls

of Slug eggs, Great Rams Horn Snail bodies, already removed from their shells, and newly born minnows just at their peak of sweetness. For a special beverage, the Puncum drank the liquefied jelly from frog spawn.

Everyone wanted to eat quickly, for they wished to talk with those folks who were members of the exploratory teams investigating "The Great Wetland" also referred to as "The Reed Mace" behind Batterman's Point. They could not eat fast enough because of their excitement.

Upon hearing snatches of conversations about the new wetland, about Its vastness, its quiet waters, the whispering of the reeds, it sounded incredible, like a Paradise, too wonderful to believe.

For those of us who were there, it was. The Silence found there was incredible. The Silence allowed one to hear Na's voices; the Wind blowing through the reeds, the frogs croaking, the chirping of the crickets rubbing their wings together, and even the whine of the mosquitoes.

The Puncum and the Sprites would have liked to leave fairly soon for The Great Wetland, but realized there were many things that had to be done in preparation for moving. There were many questions for everyone to consider.

Natterjack was asked to lead the discussion. The first question

asked of him was "Should every member of each race leave Horse Thief Bay for the new wetland?"

"Wait a minute. Hold your horses! Are we not getting carried away here? Would that not be a hasty decision? Why must everyone of each race leave now?

"Does no one enjoy living here in the Bay and the Alderwild Wood, where all of your friends and neighbours live? Our relatives too? These are questions we need to think about very seriously or there will be big problems down the road. Believe me! Let's not get into a Panic. Everything will work out. It has before.

"We have faced worse problems before. Remember the flood in April this past year? What about the refugee problem from the construction Site? All of those who were hurt and those who lost family members? We had to return twice to the Site. The second time we went, there were many more refugees hurt, both physically and psychologically. Those were very stressful times. Their wounds, their cuts, their broken bones have all been healed. The emotional problems we are still tending to will take more time. There is great Improvement in that respect. So long as we keep our heads.

"I realize I am losing my grip here too. I'm sorry. Let's call it a day and return to the subject of The Reed Mace tomorrow. Everyone will be told of what has been found there. Lots of discussion will be required among all our peoples. Thank you to everyone who participated today, and thanks for the wonderful supper. Goodnight everyone."

August 9

A great gathering of Sprites from many races has been assembling here in Horse Thief Bay and the Alderwild Wood these past few days. Even Sprites who have no wings have been coming with Dwarves and Gnomes bringing up the rear. This is looking more like a convention than a casual gathering.

Some of the Sprites arrived in the wood early, not knowing that there were going to be others, besides themselves . When they met other winged Sprites, they all took to flying, chasing the leaves and milkweed seeds. They were surprised to see that they were the only ones in their birthday suits. They had a wonderful time playing and meeting new Sprites from other races.

Word has gone around that there needs to be a meeting of minds to discuss the over population of our lands. The Woodland is quickly disappearing and being turned into manicured lawns. Something must be done now!

This was not a planned meeting. It all began as a simple conversation between Larix and Natterjack, who were very concerned about the disappearing woodland. When the two men departed for what everyone now is calling The Reed Mace, they did not know that they had started a tsunami. There has been an upwelling of minds having similar fears and concerns throughout the Alderwild Wood and the Bay. Other folks of the Bay continued the talk, and thus it spread from a small meeting to something much larger. This talk was about their concerns too.

Gnomes and Dwarves from other communities over heard snatches of the conversations. They picked up this talk while walking in the woods with other friends, or when they

· 386 ·

were fishing, or swimming in the Bay. So many different people, Dwarves, Gnomes, Alderlings, Puncum, and Wood Sprites, even the communities of Gnomes, Dwarves, and all elven folk from other communities living east of the Mac Mountains and those living west of the Alderwild Wood.

Even some of the anthropomorphic deer and other animals that live here, such as the Great Blue Heron, have taken an interest in this problem. Everyone decided to get together for a "Gathering" in The Alderwild Woods.

August 10 - The Gathering

Natterjack and Larix heard the talk in the Wood and the Bay but did not realize that their concerns were shared by so many. No flyers were needed. Everyone from the Wood and the Bay just showed up and asked Natterjack and Larix to lead the gathering. They knew that Natterjack was a good leader and organizer. One of the best.

Natterjack in Command

"We cannot approach this problem haphazardly. There must be some organizing, planning, a strategy as to how we should go about solving this problem of over population, if it can be solved."

Many were in attendance, three times as many more than had ever come to a meeting previously. Tables and chairs were set out, along with many cushions for the multitude to sit on the ground. Even with all the cushions handed out, many of the Sprites had to sit on the lower branches of the Hemlock.

A great feast was being prepared. After having seen so many folks in attendance, more of the women chipped in to help prepare the various dishes and collect more of the food ingredients, for they were running low and even out of some foods. This was not a great concern to the women. They knew that it would take time just to set out the food they had already prepared.

Each group of Gnomes, Dwarves, Alderlings, Wood Sprites, Leaflings and many other Elves were present. From where did they all come? I do not know!

"There were fewer of you in our community before we left for "The Great Reed Mace. Now there are three times as many of you. How is that possible?"

All was revealed. Gnomes, Dwarves, and Sprites from Don's community had spoken to the elven community living in Joy's woods. The Water Sprites and Nymphs living there heard the excitement and chatter over ''The Great Reed Mace' going around in Don's woods. They became very interested for they had great difficulty getting down to the river for bathing and fishing.

Joy's property was situated on a high bluff. It was a long walk down to the river's edge. Up until now, they only had rain water which they collected in large basins to bath in. They felt most grateful for Joy's help in a time of great need. Not many people would be willing to take on a whole community of Gnomes, Dwarves, Puncum, Alderling and Sprites of every race, but Joy did it without any hesitation.

She had no warning, no idea of how serious the problem had become. In the confusion and sorting out of the refugees I had forgotten the special needs of the Water Sprites and Water Nymphs! She was most gracious and kind. Before the relocation of the refugees the Water Sprites, Nymphs and Puncum had been living in a wetland mainly of Cattails and other rushes with some areas for swimming and fishing. Joy's property had none.

The food was laid out on a very long table and served buffet style. There were platters of Northern Pike, Small Mouthed Bass, Yellow Perch, and Minnows for the Sprites. For vegetable dishes the flower buds of Milkweed were steamed. Dandelion greens, along with Dock leaves, were boiled twice, throwing away the first water and boiled again in a second pot of water because the leaves of both plants are bitter.

The ripe Mandrake apples are ready to eat for dessert. Some women like to serve wild ginger syrup drizzled over the Mandrake apples.

For bread, Cattail muffins were served. There were also some dainties for those who like to explore new tastes.

All of the folks who were attending the meeting, decided to hold the discussions concerning "The Great Wetland," "The Reed Mace" until after the meal. The meal should be enjoyed and savoured. It was not necessary to make such important decisions right now, on an empty stomach. First! A little wine please!

Later, after everyone had eaten their fill and the excited buzzing of hundreds of voices had quieted a little, Natterjack rose to his feet.

"Our decisions during the next several weeks will greatly affect our future and that of Horse Thief Bay. It is wonderful to have discovered "The Reed Mace" and the large woodland around it, but lets be reasonable, be sensible.

"I agree with all of you. The Alderwild Wood is becoming over crowded not just with Gnomes and Dwarves and Elves but animals as well. We are almost splitting at the seams.

"There needs to be a basic plan to work by, as our ancestors had when they left northern Europe for here. It does not have to be quite so elaborate or complex. We are already quite knowledgeable about the climate conditions at "The Reed Mace". They are basically like ours but not so windy, the water, not so rough, and not so deep and not so cold but warmer in the summer.

"Life would be less stressful for the Water Sprites, Water Nymphs, and Puncum. The Puncum could fish any time of day they wished to. Noise would be nearly gone or altogether eliminated. Waves from motor boats, tour boats, and especially the racing boats would be gone.

"Water Sprites and Nymphs would find that they could sit on the lily pads and ride on the backs of the many Carp that live there, any time of day, singing joyously.

"Their songs in early morning and again at twilight here would be sorely missed if they all were to leave. Their Bell Canto voices give our Bay a beauty no other indented cove has. I know that they must be the ones to make that decision. I hope we can persuade some of the Water Sprites and Nymphs to remain here."

"An aerial view of this area is a great idea put forth by Zena. It would show us where there are just a few trees and where there are many, a forest, a woodland, a field, or a meadow. We would then be able to draw a fairly accurate map to give us some idea of how close or how far away we must journey in order to be safe.

"An aerial view will show where there are indents, coves, bays, places along the mainland shore and perimeters of some of the nearby islands. There must be other areas, quiet, shallow places where cattails, sedges and water lilies grow, where Puncum can fish and Water Sprites and Nymphs can swim and frolic without fear."

September 1

The wind picked up and rain clouds began to roll in. Chairs, tables, and pillows were hurriedly moved into the Great Hall and then the tables were set up again - two tables wide and three tables long.

This was done so that all could take a look at the aerial map which we now have. We also have water color sketches of the Great Reed Mace Wetland. They are just to give us an idea of the vastness of that area.

Over the past several weeks, small groups of Gnomes, Dwarves, Alderling, Puncum, Water Sprites and Nymphs, Wood Sprites and Leaflings got together with other members

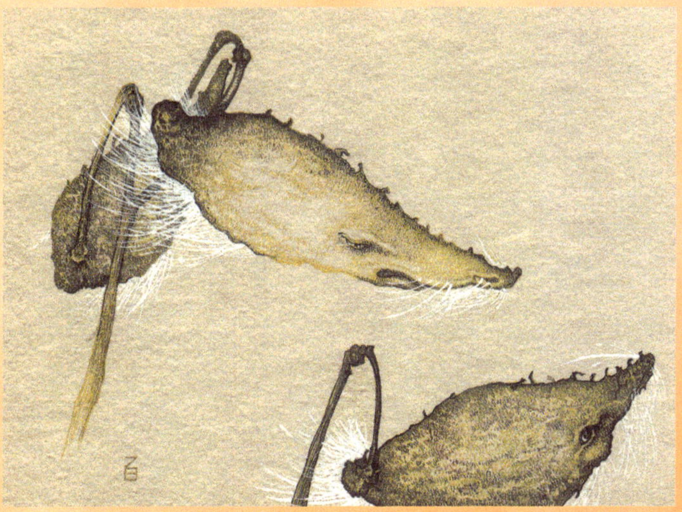

of their own race to discuss issues pertinent to themselves, their needs. These groups included many of the refugees for whom the The Great Reed Mace and the surrounding woodland would be ideal.

Most of the original inhabitants, those living in the Alderwild Wood and the Bay before the refugee crisis, wish to remain here.

Many of the Puncum, Alderling, Water Sprites and Nymphs living here wish to go to The Great Reed Mace. A small group would like to stay here.

Ian and I, as well as many of the older Gnomes and Dwarves understand their desire to move. They would be free from the noise and large waves of the motor boats. The silence found there would be most welcomed by the refugees.

Time was needed for thinking, to mull over the pros and cons of moving. A number of trips were made back and forth to the Reed Mace.

Natterjack took small groups of refugees there to see both the woodland and the wetland. When each of the groups of refugees returned, the younger folks thought it would be a wonderful place to live. However, some of the older refugees wish to remain in the Alderwild Wood. They are welcome to live with us, to become an integral part of our community.

Some of the young and middle aged Gnomes and Dwarves from our Bay and the Alderwild Wood wish to leave with the refugees and folks from other communities.

They have decided to leave in the Spring.

The homes left empty here in the Bay and Alderwild Wood will be given to those refugees from other communities who are feeling the extreme pressures from the human population.

Natterjack and Salus have decided to stay for several months at the Great Reed Mace. They will help organize, find safe areas in the woodland to suit the needs of each race. Some communities will need enough arable land to grow vegetables for themselves and, if possible, for trading with other newly formed settlements. For now Natterjack and I felt that the different races should remain separate according to their culture, language, and habits.

Many of the refugees who wish to settle in the woodland surrounding the Reed Mace and Wetland are from different races, different communities. When they arrive at the Mace they will join other members of their race, but yet they will be strangers to them. The need now is to form new small settlements of like kind. Having neighbours with similar language, customs and for some, specific needs, such as those of the Water Sprites.

Friendships will form more easily. The strangeness of their new Homeland will become less so.

The Suund is very busy, more so now upon hearing of the great move by many from Horse Thief Bay to the Mace in the Spring. She will have help. During the last evacuation and rescue, while caring for the sick and injured, she found a young Gnome girl who seemed to be a natural healer with whom She shared her knowledge and skills. She did not realize at the time that She was actually preparing her for the migration to the Great Reed Mace in the Spring.

The Wood Sprite refugees who lost their homes when the human population was growing, upon hearing about the finding of the new Promised Land, hoped to move there and make their new homes in the woodland surrounding The Reed Mace.

The Suund and the Wood Knars will remain in the Alderwild Wood. Those refugees, Puncum, and Water Sprites who have already moved to the Great Reed Mace and Woodland will discover Wood Knars there. I expect the Knars will be many centuries older than those living here in the Alderwild Wood.

A figure like the Suund will make him or herself known to the inhabitants of those woods. There will be an Ancient One, who will take the place of the Suund, to be found in the Great Reed Mace. The new Ancient One may not appear immediately to the new inhabitants of the Mace but in time.

There are very old Carp living there. I think that one of those ancient Carp might come forth as the Healer and the Wise One, knowing all. Carp have been here since the beginning of time. They are ordinary looking, humble.

In Europe, Carp were the basic food, the mainstay for the poor and middle class people. When folk from the Alderwild Wood and Bay were looking for new lands which could be settled, they met up with Rhus. At that time, there were Water Sprites and Nymphs riding on the backs of some of the Carp.

November 1

After almost two months Natterjack and Salus came home to the Bay. It was a joyous occasion. Natterjack and Salus were pleased with how quickly the new settlers were organizing themselves. They had even formed a council, with an elected member from each community, to discuss several pertinent problems to their settlements that needed a consensus of opinion. The whole of the Great Reed Mace, both the woodland and wetland have a bright future.

Life has had its ups and downs, its triumphs and tragedies, its births and deaths, so much measure to the soil, a time when great friendships were forged and wisdom gained.

However, our environment, the woodland around us, is becoming less and less. More trees have been cut down and replaced by manicured lawns. There must be more attention, more care given, to saving our wildlife and wild flowers. Where will the Dwarves, Gnomes, Alderling, and

all of the Elven folk live? They too need a woodland where they will be able to live and wander freely. They need clean water too. We all need clean water!

I do Hope and Wish that more humans and especially young children will join us, the inhabitants of the Alderwild Wood and Horse Thief Bay, in caring for Nature, especially when Nature can't care for herself.

What joy, what fun, the children would have if an area of their parents property was set aside to grow wild. The many new species of insects they would find, the toad or salamander living there. There is so much to be learned about the wonders of Nature. Soul food! The happiness to be found. Immeasurable!

We must teach the children about Na and Er. Tell them about Anwa the tortoise, who carries the moon on his back across the sky from East to West and why he was called the Slow One. Then there is Tapol, the Toad who carries the Sun from Dawn until Twilight. He was named Too Fast because the inhabitants of Er at that time were afraid of the dark and wanted the sunlight to brighten the sky all of the time.

Listen! Listen to the rain drops as they fall and hit the ground or your living room window.

In the morning, when first waking up, listen to the birds when they begin to lose their drowse as the sky brightens.

Remember what Natterjack and Larix have taught us. Remember the Alderwild Wood. Do not forget what we have learned. Do not put it on the back burner of your minds, thinking we can do it tomorrow. No! Nothing will be accomplished. Good intentions become just words. Believe! There is still much that can be accomplished, saved.

Tomorrow is another day. You may see Natterjack and friends when you go on your next walk.

Good bye. Perhaps we shall meet again.

p. 1	Great Blue Heron	pigma pen
p. 2	Carrion Flower berries	pigma pen
p. 3	Chickadee/milkweed stalks	watercolour
p. 4	Animal Footprints	pigma pen
p. 6	Natterjack's Floor Plan	pigma pen
p. 9	Elf Footprints	pigma pen
p. 11	Linden Leaves	pigma pen
p. 12	Great Burr Reed	pigma pen
p. 15	Portrait of Natterjack	pigma pen
p. 16	Amanita Mushroom	pigma pen
p. 17	Birth of A Fairy	watercolour & pen
p. 18	Gathering Acorns	watercolour & pen
p. 19	Linden Leaves	watercolour & pen
p. 22	Troll Carnage & Crows	pigma pen
p. 25	Single Milkweed pod	watercolour
p. 27	Ground Cherry pods	pigma pen
p. 30	Chickadee/Carrion Berries	watercolour
p. 31	Autumn Oak & Bass Leaves	pigma pen
p. 35	Iris pods in the Fall	watercolour & pen
p. 36	Deer with Three Gnomes	pigma pen
p. 38	Milkweed & Stinging Nettle	pigma pen
p. 40	Handmade Toys	pigma pen
p. 42	Foods from Horse Thief Bay	pigma pen
p. 49	Food Collecting Tools	pigma pen
p. 53	Alderling House Floor Plan	watercolour & pen
p. 55	Water Filtration System	pigma pen
p. 56	Facades of Six Dwellings	pigma pen
p. 57	Home Heating System	pigma pen
p. 59	Carved Burial Paddles	watercolour
p. 61	Trolls Trapped in Tree Roots	watercolour
p. 69	Wild Turkey Feather	watercolour
p. 75	Wintergreen Berries	watercolour
p. 78	Squirting Cucumber Pod	watercolour
p. 80	Bittersweet Berries (winter)	watercolour
p. 81	The Alderling Alphabet	pigma pen
p. 82	Page Written in Alderling	pigma pen
p. 84	Christmas Tree with Toys	pigma pen
p. 85	Christmas Invitation	pigma pen
p. 88	Pondscape in Winter	pigma pen
p. 91	Oak Galls With Snow	watercolour
p. 94	Gnome Winter Scene	watercolour & pen
p. 101	Chickadee in Winter	watercolour
p. 102	Winter Snowfall	watercolour
p. 106	Portrait of Silvas Oakenbalm	pigma pen
p. 113	Tree Bending (Method #1)	pigma pen
p. 114	Tree Bending (Method #2)	pigma pen
p. 115	Tree Bending (Method #3)	pigma pen
p. 119	Ships Used by the Gnomes	pigma pen
p. 128	Mushrooms in the Woods	watercolour & pen
p. 130	Migration Route Map	pigma pen
p. 131	Bittersweet Berry Branch	watercolour & pen
p. 132	Scarlet Woodland Berries	watercolour
p. 134	Rose Hips in Autumn	watercolour
p. 136	Cricket	pigma pen
p. 137	Linden Leaves in Autumn	watercolour
p. 138	Buckthorn Berries	pigma pen
p. 141	Animals of the Woodlands	pigma pen
p. 142	Fall Sumac Leaves with Galls	watercolour
p. 145	Amanita mushrooms & Leaves	watercolour & pen
p. 146	Map of Moe Island & Bay	pigma pen
p. i, 148	Moe Island 800 years ago	pigma pen
p. 162	Musical Instruments	pigma pen
p. 170	Snowdrop Flowers	watercolour
p. 178	Bloodroot Plants	watercolour & pen
p. 180	The Suund (Herbalist)	watercolour
p. 183	Dragonflies in Flight	watercolour
p. 185	The Suund on Zena's Hand	pigma pen
p. 189	Skunk Cabbage Plants	watercolour
p. 198	Puncum People (pictograph)	pigma pen
p. 206	Sweet Flag plants	watercolour
p. 210	Chickadee on Pussy Willow	watercolour
p. 218	Dutchmen's Breeches Flowers	watercolour
p. 220	Blue Hepatica Fairies	watercolour & pen
p. 222	Pink Hepatica blooms	watercolour
p. 223	Red Trillium Flowers	watercolour
p. 224	Friends	watercolour
p. 226	Bullfrog on Reed Stalk	pigma pen
p. 227	Cluster of Bloodroot Plants	watercolour
p. 228	Bloodroot Plant Study	watercolour
p. 229	The Wood Knar	pigma pen
p. 235	Puncum Ceramic Clay Beads	pigma pen
p. 237	Types of Puncum Pottery	pigma pen
p. 239	Puncum Fishing Pictograph	pigma pen
p. 240	Water Plants and Creatures	pigma pen
p. 242	Water Dwellers of the Bay	pigma pen
p. 243	Water Beetle Trap (top view)	pigma pen
p. 244	Puncum Chieftain Headdress	pigma pen
p. 245	Fish Bone Tools	pigma pen
p. 246	Types of Puncum Watercraft	pigma pen
p. 249	Wood Bending Method-single	pigma pen
p. 250	Wood Bending Method-double	pigma pen
p. 250	Handmade Wooden Products	pigma pen
p. 252	Wild Ginger Plants	watercolour
p. 253	The Alderwild Wood & Brook	pigma pen
p. 254	Checkers	watercolour
p. 255	Mandrake Leaves	watercolour & pen
p. 257	Journey to High Pines	watercolour
p. 261	Mycena Mushrooms	watercolour
p. 268	Monarch Fairy Birth Stages	gouache & pen
p. 288	Goldenrod Gall Studies	watercolour
p. 271	Beech Leaves & Catkins	watercolour
p. 274	Bellwort Flowers	watercolour
p. 276	The Troll Witch	watercolour
p. 278	Vole or Meadow mouse	watercolour
p. 279	Denizens of the Marsh	watercolour
p. 280	Hummingbird at Columbine	watercolour
p. 282	The Bittern of the Marsh	pigma pen
p. 283	Wrens on a Pine Branch	watercolour

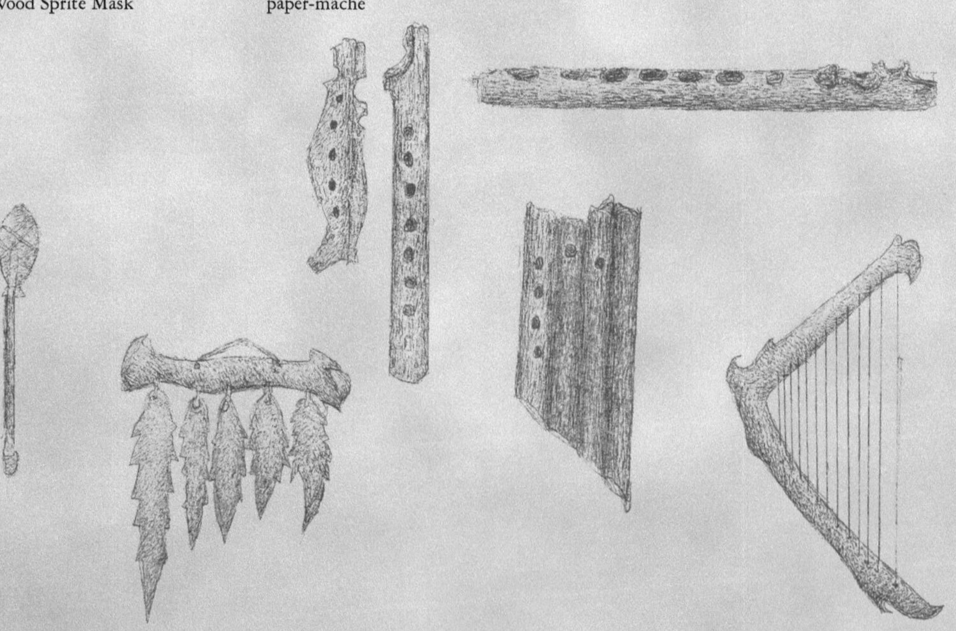

The Suund or Herbalist:
Known as the healer. She is an ancient toad.

The Dwarves:
Natterjack - the lead designer and builder of our house.
Draka - the wife of Natterjack and a great chef.
Bracken - The eldest son of Natterjack and Draka.
Cymbella - The wife of Bracken.
Azulla - Bracken's younger brother.
Bursa - a very good musician and singer.
Capsella - The wife of Bursa. She is also a singer.
Nitella - The only daughter of Capsella and Bursa.
Fraxim - The only son of Capsella and Bursa. He is an artist.
Thapsa - an older male dwarf.
Berga - the wife of Thapsa. Also an older dwarf.
Celesta - the older daughter of Thapsa and Berga.
Onoclea - the younger daughter of Thapsa and Berga.
Perch - the young son of Thapsa and Berga.
Marmota - a young male who helps build furniture.
Gama - another young male who helps build furniture.

The Gnomes:
Larix - also a designer and builder of our house.
Colona - the wife of Larix.
Lich - son of Larix and Colona, and a builder of our house.
Petra - the wife of Lich.
Caddis - the son of Lich and Petra. A young gnome boy.
Salus - the second son of Lich and Petra. A young gnome boy.
Newt - the second son of Larix and Colona, and a builder of our house.
Osmunda - the wife of Newt.
Awra - the only daughter of Larix and Colona.
Silvas Oakenbalm - a very old gnome. The community historian.
Dicentra - and elderly female who gets separated from her husband.
Bruno - and elderly male married to Dicentra.
Acura - a young gnome girl at the August 1st committee meeting
Thamias - a carpenter who helps build furniture for the Alderling.
Sciurus - another carpenter helping to build replacement furniture.
Berthas - a female who helps the Suund care for the refugees.
Rhus - a male gnome who lives in the Reed Mace. A storyteller.

The Alderlings: elves (fairies) about 12" in height. They do not fly.
Hatch - a young adult male.
Pody - a young adult male and close friend to Hatch.
Alisma - a young adult female. A good nurse.
Gramina - a young female gathering Ground nut seeds and tubers.
Dryscopus - a young male who helps build furniture for the refugees.
Selasphorus - a young male who also helps build furniture.
Danus - a young male who travels to the Reed Mace.
Fern - a young male who also helps explore the Reed Mace.
Tania - a young female who travels to the Reed Mace.
Papilo - another young male who travels with Hatch to explore.

The Puncum: elves (fairies) of the Wetland. They don't have wings.
Juncus - a young male fairy of the Wetland.
Crispus - a young male who makes pottery with the Gnomes.
Potamogelen - a third male who is also a potter.
Mustela - a young female who helps explore the Reed Mace.
Plantago - a male who helps explore the Reed Mace.
Tipula - another male who travels to the Reed Mace.

The Leaflings: are winged fairies with wings shaped like leaves. They fly.

Wood Sprites: small fairies with wings looking like insects. They fly.
Laxulus - a male who also travels to explore the Reed Mace.
Chrysopa - a female who travels to the Reed Mace.
Nesta - a young female who travels to explore the Reed Mace.
Hyalo - a young male who travels to explore the Reed Mace.
Plathemis - another male who travels to the Reed Mace.

Water Nymphs: small winged fairies, the oldest inhabitants of The Bay.

Wood Nymphs: small winged fairies, the oldest inhabitants of the Wood.

The Wood Knar: a tree spirit and protector of the Trees.

The Anthropomorphic Characters:
Great Blue - a Great Blue Heron who helps transport the injured.
Spargon - another Blue Heron and friend of Great Blue.
Actias - a third Blue Heron who helps carry baskets of sprites.
Nuphar - a deer who helps transport the injured.
Scirpus - a second deer who helps the fairy folk. Friend of Nuphar.
Sagiteria - a third deer who helps carry the gnomes to safety.
Dryocopus - another deer who helps the wingless sprites.
Philaenus - a red fox. Helps the deer carry the wingless sprites.
Phatlimus - a black crow that accompany everyone to the Reed Mace.
Selaphorus - another black crow that goes to the Reed Mace.

The Trolls: There are three main groups of Trolls
Trolconitum - are the most terrible and deadly of the Trolls.
Troloxica - trolls with poisonous skin. Their poison can kill.
Altrolpia - hideously ugly and no respect for Na(°).
Enough has been said of these malicious, destructive beings!

Norgs and Traugs
Troll-like creatures that also destroy Na, but they still have an opportunity to return to their humanity.

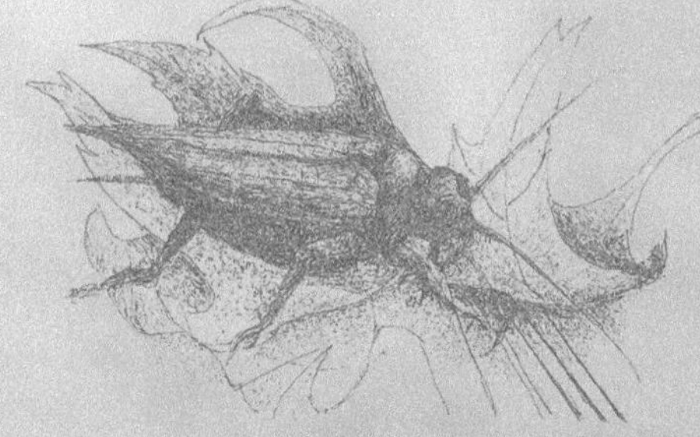